PRAISE FOR *THE COWBOYS* SERIES

BUCK

"*Buck* is a wonder American romance! Leigh Greenwood remains one of the forces to be reckoned with in the American romance sub-genre."

—*Affaire de Coeur*

"A rip-roaring good time. Leigh Greenwood pens the finest stories in romance Fiction."

—*The Literary Times*

"One more keeper for the booksheves. There are very few authors who maintain Greenwood's standard of excellence."

—*Heartland Critiques*

WARD

"*Ward* has all the tension and excitement of *Jake,* the first book in this series...The author plays with the readers' emotions and surrounds them in a maze of conflict. *Ward* is joining *Jake* on my shelf of classics."

—*Rendezvous*

"Few authors write with the fervor of Leigh Greenwood. Once again [Greenwood] has created a tale well worth opening again and again!"

—*Heartland Critiques*

JAKE

"*Jake* is an exciting, fast-paced Reconstruction Era romance....Readers will definitely want more from this great writer and will want it soon. Leigh Greenwood has another winning series in the works."

—*Affaire de Coeur*

"Filled with laughter, tenderness, and wonderful family loyalty...Jake is so beautifully rendered that readers will be left feeling as if they have been held in his arms."

—*Romantic Times*

DREAM COME TRUE

"I'm confused."

"What about?"

"Everything. I didn't like men. I didn't like you. I planned to learn all there was to know about ranching and then get rid of you. Now I don't like cows, I hate roundup, and I don't want to think of you ever leaving."

"Then don't think about it," Buck said. He turned her face up to his so he could kiss her. "Just think about me holding you, kissing you."

"I can't think when you do that."

"Then don't."

He kissed her gently. She was so trusting. She might say she'd never trusted him, but they'd both trusted each other from the beginning. It must have come from something they'd learned about each other six years ago, something he couldn't see then for the anger and the hate.

He didn't hate her. He never had. He'd probably been in love with her from the beginning. He was just picking up where he'd left off in his dreams.

The Cowboys

BUCK

LEIGH GREENWOOD

LEISURE BOOKS NEW YORK CITY

To my editor, Alicia Condon.
Without her confidence in me,
there wouldn't have been any Brides or Cowboys.

A LEISURE BOOK®

March 1998

Published by

Dorchester Publishing Co., Inc.
276 Fifth Avenue
New York, NY 10001

ISBN 0-8439-4360-2

The Cowboys

BUCK

Prologue

"Let go, you damned brat. You're going with Mr. DesWaldo. All this crying and screaming won't make a bit of difference."

Buck Hobson's grip on his sister tightened. Maybe if he cried loudly enough, Mr. DesWaldo wouldn't want him.

"You sure he's worth five hundred dollars?" DesWaldo asked. "He looks awfully puny."

"He's just ten. He'll grow," Buck's pa said.

"Why don't you give me the girl instead?"

"Are you kidding? In four or five years she'll draw in more pigeons than I'll have time to pluck."

"Just like her mother used to do."

"Don't mention that bitch to me. If she hadn't run off with that shyster lawyer, I wouldn't be living in this dump."

9

The hotel room that had been home to Buck, his father, and his older sister for the last five weeks was small and dingy. The muggy, salty air of Galveston Bay had caused the cheap wallpaper to pull away from the wall in spots. A portion of discolored ceiling threatened to fall any day. Buck could remember when they had had a suite in a grand hotel where the furniture was covered in red velvet, and servants cleaned their rooms each day. There hadn't been many of those times since his mother ran off.

His pa had never had such a prolonged run of bad cards. It had been weeks since they'd had enough to eat. And now his pa was selling him to pay a gambling debt.

"Give me a hand here," Buck's pa said to Des-Waldo. "Take hold of the boy."

Mr. DesWaldo gripped Buck by his arms. Buck's father took hold of his sister, Melissa. They were brutally torn apart.

"Don't take him away!" Melissa cried, reaching out for her brother, her ivory cheeks streaked with tears.

"Take him and get out," his father yelled at Mr. DesWaldo.

"Melissa! Melissa!" Buck cried, his young soul ravaged at being torn from his sister, the one person in the world who truly loved him.

"Please, Papa, don't make him go," she pleaded.

"Shut up," their father said. "He never was any good to me. Maybe he'll make a decent slave boy."

"What'll I do with him when he grows up?" Mr. DesWaldo asked.

"I don't know," his father replied. "If you don't want him, sell him to somebody else. Don't bring him back here. He'd just be an extra mouth to feed."

Buck

Buck struggled with all his might, but his strength was no match for the man who now owned him. He was dragged inexorably across the room toward the door.

"I'll come back, Melissa," Buck cried. "I promise, no matter what happens, I'll find you again."

Chapter One

Texas Hill Country, April 1872

"That's all the eggs I can spare today," Hannah Grossek told the Rafter D cook. "I'm saving up to set some hens."

"Mr. Gillett won't be pleased to hear that," the cook said. "He can eat eggs three times a day."

They stood in front of the Grossek home, a neat, rectangular house with a cedar-shake roof and real glass windows. To keep her chickens safe from foxes, Hannah confined them to a coop and large pen. Nearby a combination garden and orchard covered several fenced acres. A large barn, a smaller cow barn, and a pig house stood in the distance. A stranger would have been forgiven for mistaking the ranch for a farm.

Hannah took a large chunk of butter wrapped in oiled paper out of a jar she kept in the stone well.

"With all the butter he eats, he ought to be bursting his seams."

"He looks like he hasn't eaten in a week," the cook said. He frowned. "Sometimes he acts like it, too."

She handed him a carefully wrapped package. "This apple cobbler ought to improve his disposition. Remember not to cook it too long."

"He'd like it a lot better if you'd come cook it for him."

"I've told Mr. Gillett a hundred times I don't intend to get married. When is he going to believe me?"

Lyman Gillett had started courting Hannah a year ago. He had come by at least once a week until she asked him to stop. Now he sent his entreaties via his cook.

"Mr. Gillett is used to getting what he wants, and he wants you."

"He'd change his mind quick enough if he had me."

"But—"

"Tell him I like my ranch, and I don't mean to give it up to get married." She didn't add that she'd never marry Lyman Gillett, despite his handsome face. She had the feeling there was a streak of cruelty in him. She'd seen too much of that in her father.

The cook settled his purchases in the buckboard. "If you change your mind—"

"I won't."

The Rafter D cook left, and Hannah's mother emerged from among the cabbages.

"Why do you disappear whenever anybody comes?" Hannah asked.

Hannah had hoped her mother would recover from the abuse she'd suffered at her husband's hands. Nathaniel Grossek had been dead for eight months now, but her mother still avoided men.

"I don't trust Gillett."

"Neither do I, but his cook is harmless. You can't hide once we hire someone to work for us. He'll be here all the time."

Mrs. Grossek placed her cabbages in a basket. "Nobody's going to work for us, not when we don't have any money to pay them. Like Joseph Merrick said, you can either get married, or we can sell."

Hannah refused to consider marriage. She'd seen what had happened to her mother and had sworn it would never happen to her. If she could, she wouldn't let any man set foot on the ranch.

"Merrick is like every other banker," Hannah said, "thinking only of his money. He doesn't care what happens to us."

Her mother's gaze held resignation and some apprehension.

"I don't want you to marry if you're against it, but we can't run this place by ourselves. Even your father couldn't do it. And if we sell the way things are now, we won't get enough money to last a year."

"We don't have to run cows," Hannah said. "We can make all we need from the garden and the livestock."

"More than a dozen men tried to farm this county. They all failed. Can you do better than they could?"

Hannah's rebelliousness cooled in the face of stark reality. "Maybe not, but I won't ignore advice like Papa did."

Sarah Grossek picked up a hoe and began the task of breaking up the ground for planting. "A man is coming today," she said, avoiding her daughter's gaze. "Mr. Merrick says he's willing to work in exchange for a share of the ranch."

"Why didn't you tell me?" Hannah asked.

"Because I knew you'd be angry."

"Of course I'm angry. You're giving up without even trying."

"I've tried until I'm tired of trying. It's time I let someone else do the trying for me."

"I'll do it."

"I'm sure you will. You'll work yourself to the bone, end up looking older than me in five years, and still have to sell out."

"Mother—"

"My mind's made up."

When her mother said that, she wouldn't listen any more. And Hannah couldn't blame her. Without help, they couldn't run the ranch.

Hannah had expected their hands to stay on after her father's death, but he'd never paid decent wages, never found reliable workers. Maybe that was why they'd drifted away, why the ranch was failing. No, her father hadn't known anything about ranches or cows. She and her mother knew less. Maybe the man coming this afternoon knew more.

Hannah opened the chute on her irrigation canal and let the water run into the rows of cabbage, kale, and early peas. Her garden was several acres in size. It included a young orchard as well as two grapevines. As long as water ran in the creek, they would have plenty to eat.

But the creek had run dry last summer. And the summer before.

She looked at her mother struggling to prepare the thin, rocky soil for planting. They both worked hard in the garden and taking care of the livestock. Jars of pickled beef and pork, canned fruit and vegetables, along with butter and eggs, had provided the money that kept them alive these past months.

But their stock was getting low. Because of her father's death, there'd been no roundup last fall, no sale of cattle. If they couldn't sell this year, they'd have to work very hard to have enough food to survive the winter. If the creek ran dry, they might not.

She knew someone was coming when her mother stopped work. Looking up, Hannah saw two men approaching on horseback. When they were still a hundred yards away, her mother left the garden and went into the house. Hannah's throat tightened with emotion. Would her mother ever be comfortable around men again?

After working in the garden all morning, Hannah had dirt on her apron and perspiration on her forehead. She wasn't a vain woman, but she didn't want the men to see her with a dirty face. None of the women in town would be seen in public looking like this.

Nathaniel Grossek had been the only farmer among the original settlers not to give up his land and move to the tiny settlement of Utopia. In ten years it had grown into a successful community of merchants and craftsmen along with a bank that served the ranches in the area. The women worked hard, but they wore clean dresses and lived in neat houses on streets with stone sidewalks.

Nathaniel Grossek had kept Hannah and her mother isolated on the ranch, had forced them to tend the garden and look after the chickens, pigs, and milk cows. For the most part, Hannah hadn't minded. She'd never been anxious to seek the admiration of men, but her pride wouldn't let her appear before anybody looking like a grubby urchin. She ran into the house.

In the kitchen she discarded her apron and washed her face with cold water. She looked at herself in her father's small shaving mirror, the only one he had allowed in the house. What she saw didn't please her. Her skin was brown from the sun, her blond hair coming loose from its pins. She hurriedly removed the pins, gave her hair a few quick brushstrokes to remove the tangles, and pinned it in a knot on top of her head.

"Are you sure you don't want to come outside?" she asked her mother.

Her mother shook her head. "You're the one who vowed to run this ranch by yourself. I'm leaving it in your hands."

From being ignored and left in ignorance of all the business of the ranch, Hannah had been thrust into the role of trying to save it from ruin. She knew nothing about the job, but she was determined to learn. She was never going to be ignorant again.

She opened the door and stepped outside. A belt of mature trees along the creek provided a cool retreat even in the hottest weather. She walked over to a chair her mother had placed there and sat down to wait for the men to arrive.

The nights were still cool, the days comfortable, but the scattered cactus, plentiful mesquite, rocky ground, and stunted oaks provided plenty of evidence that summers in Gillespie County could be brutally hot and dry.

A cold winter and a wet spring had produced an abundance of wildflowers. Meadows were calf-deep in bluebonnets, their blanket of blue punctured by the red and yellow of Indian blanket, Indian paintbrush, and coreopsis. Hannah had to look harder for the less widespread yellow primroses and white prickly poppies her mother favored. Hannah preferred the dense clusters of blue flowers of the mescal bean, but that evergreen grew on steep slopes far from the house.

As the men neared the house, she realized the president of the bank hadn't come. Both were strangers. She tried to quell the fear rising in her. Mr. Merrick wouldn't have sent two men he didn't trust. Still, she and her mother were alone, and Hannah's experience said men might respect other men, but they used women.

Now that Nathaniel Grossek was dead, Buck hadn't expected to feel anything when he returned to the ranch.

He was wrong.

Riding by abandoned fields where he'd worked until he'd collapsed from exhaustion, barnyards where he'd been ankle-deep in muck, the barn where he'd been beaten and locked up like an animal—often too weak to escape even if the door had been left open—he relived a past that had never really left him.

Despite the passage of six years, the emotion was so raw he could almost taste it. If he hadn't been coming back to take the ranch for himself, he would have burned it down. His hatred for the man who'd tortured him had grown until it encompassed the farm and everybody on it. He would have this place if it cost him his life. Only then could he feel he'd gotten revenge for what had happened to him.

"I don't like the looks of the place," Zeke said.

"It doesn't have to be pretty to make money," Buck replied.

"I wasn't talking about that. I haven't seen any cows to speak of the whole way in. This is supposed to be a ranch. A ranch is supposed to have cows. How're we going to make a go of it without any stock?"

"There's stock here. We just have to find it."

"Where?"

"In the draws, canyons, thickets."

"On another rancher's land."

"That, too, I expect. You thinking about backing out?"

"Hell, no, I just want you to know you're in for a fight."

"I expected that."

"Then why didn't you stay with Jake? He'd have given you a ranch. Hell, he wanted to give me one, too."

"Why didn't you take it?"

"I ain't taking nothing from white people."

"Other people might care about your color, but Jake and Isabelle wouldn't have adopted all of us if they cared about things like that."

"If they're so wonderful, why didn't you take the ranch he was trying so hard to give you?"

"Because I want *this* ranch," Buck said. "More than anything else in the world."

Zeke pulled up. "Why this place?"

"You know."

"Tell me. I want to hear you say it."

"Because this is where that bastard treated me like a slave."

"Beating a dead man doesn't seem like much of a victory to me."

It wasn't for Buck, either, but this was something he had to do. From the moment he read that advertisement, he hadn't been able to think of anything else. It had become more important even than finding his sister.

"I mean to stand in the doorway of that house I was never good enough to enter and look out over this land knowing it's mine. I want to be able to say that I finally got the better of that black-hearted son-of-a-bitch. Old man Grossek bought all the land of the farmers who drove Jake out. I'll be getting back his range as well as a place of my own."

"And what am I supposed to do?"

"You'll stay here with me, of course."

"You going to put half the place in my name?"

Buck had never considered that. The whole point of getting the ranch was to own the land of the man he'd hated for so long. Sharing it with someone else, even Zeke, wouldn't be the same.

"I didn't think so," Zeke said.

"It's not that—"

"I know what it is," Zeke said. "I'll stay as long as you need me, but I'm making no promises after that. Now you'd better stop daydreaming about what you'd do to Grossek if he were alive and decide what you're going to say to that woman sitting under those trees. She doesn't look like the type to just hand over this place."

Buck looked up. Hannah Grossek. He remembered her well. Once he'd stopped the old bastard from beating her. His reward had been one of the worst beatings of his life. She never spoke to him after that, just looked right through him. Probably thought he was lusting after her. He had been, but after she started giving him the cold shoulder, his dislike grew a little more each time he saw her.

"You think we can pull this place out of debt in six months?" Zeke asked.

"I don't know. All we've got to lose is our labor."

"And our necks trying to rustle back rustled cows."

21

"We don't know that yet."

"Then where are they?"

Buck had wondered that, too. Maybe Hannah could tell him.

He had fortified himself against her loveliness by concentrating on her selfishness, but he experienced a jolt when she walked from the shade into the sunshine. He'd last seen her when she'd been a young woman of fourteen, just coming into the promise of her womanhood. That promise had been more than kept.

She wore a tight-fitting faded gray dress with long sleeves and a high collar that did little to disguise the smallness of her waist or the enticing curve of her bosom. She had pinned her golden hair atop her head, but her loveliness reminded him of why he'd dreamed about her so often six years ago. Big round eyes of startling blue, high forehead, prominent cheekbones, a dainty nose, and stubborn jaw. She stood waiting for them, quiet and composed, small and slim. Everything considered, Hannah Grossek was lovely enough to make any man forget the past.

Any man except Buck Hobson.

Hannah watched the two men ride toward her, several questions in her mind. Had they come together? If not, which one was coming to take the job? Neither one of them looked happy about the situation. The tall white man looked absolutely furious; the other looked fierce.

Something about the angry man struck a chord in her memory. Maybe she had seen him one of the few times her father had allowed her to go to town. He dismounted and started toward her. No, she hadn't met him before. She would have remembered this man.

Hannah's father had never let her forget that she was unfashionably petite. This man was more than a foot taller than she was. His powerfully muscled shoulders tapered down to a slim waist. He had that slightly rolling walk of a man who spent most of his time in the saddle; his legs were long, his thighs powerful.

But his most striking feature was his eyes. They were as old and weary as his body was young and vigorous. Anger smoldered there, ready to flare up.

Hannah felt unaccountably drawn to him. Not in a friendly way, but rather like a moth to a flame, drawn irresistibly toward its own destruction. Never having been attracted to a man, Hannah was unprepared for the effect he had on her. She felt incapable of moving, of wanting to move. She couldn't imagine a more inappropriate response to a man she'd never seen before. More than that, she was a fool to be attracted to a man who frightened her.

"Are you Hannah Grossek?"

The voice startled her. She was certain she'd heard it before. Or a voice very much like it.

"Yes, I am. And you are?"

"Where's your mother?"

If he was aware that it was rude to ignore her question, he didn't show it.

"In the house. She's not feeling well." Hannah was glad her mother had gone inside. These two men would have terrified her.

"Can you speak for her?"

"Of course."

"You're awfully young."

"I'm twenty, old enough to be considered a spinster by some." Her age didn't appear to impress him.

That inexplicable flutter was still there. She started to tell him to go away, but something held her back. Possibly her acute awareness of his size, his shoulders, his long legs. His eyes. She felt hypnotized by the contradictory currents she sensed in this man.

Hannah was shocked she could be so foolish. She couldn't allow herself to be overwhelmed by a man. She was too old, too sensible, too aware of the danger.

"We can't pay you," Hannah said, hoping that would discourage him. "We won't have any money until the cows are rounded up and sold."

"I'm not looking for money," the man said. "I'm looking to do all the work in exchange for a half interest in the ranch."

"Half!" Hannah hadn't accepted the necessity of giving up any part of her ranch. Half was out of the question.

"You'll get two of us. Zeke can do as much work as I can."

"More," Zeke said.

"I prefer someone willing to wait for his pay until we can sell a herd," Hannah said, finally regaining command of her tongue. She could try a bluff. It might work.

"You have no herd," Zeke said. "We didn't see a dozen cows coming in here."

"They're out there, hundreds of them."

"You won't get anybody to work for wages you can't pay until next year," the man said. "Not even if you offer double the normal pay."

"I'm offering thirty-five dollars."

She'd planned to offer twenty-five, thirty at the

most, but she was desperate. She didn't want a partner, but she needed cowhands.

"The banker said your cowhands took your horses, saddles, ropes," the man said.

Hannah felt a sinking feeling in her stomach. She knew the horses were gone. She hadn't thought about the equipment.

"I'm bringing four hundred acres to the deal," the man said, "all of it along the river."

"Where would you get land around here?" Hannah asked.

"From Jake Maxwell. You ought to remember him. Your father and his friends burned him out several years back. Tried to kill him."

Hannah knew there had been a ranch in the area when they arrived, but it had looked deserted the one time she'd seen it. She didn't know anything about burning anybody out. Her father had been a cruel man, but she didn't believe he would try to kill anybody.

"I know nothing about Mr. Maxwell, and I don't want your four hundred acres."

"You will when I settle on it and start stealing your cattle."

"I'll have you arrested."

"I won't be stealing them from you," the man said. "I'll be stealing them from the men who've already stolen them from you."

This man looked angry enough to do anything, even rustle her cattle. Moreover, he seemed to be angry at her, and she didn't understand that. She didn't know him. She hadn't done anything to make him hate her.

"Who are you?" she asked.

"I'm Buck Hobson," the man said, "the boy your father bought seven years ago, and almost beat to death."

Chapter Two

The shock was so great that Hannah nearly sat down right where she stood. She hadn't forgotten Buck Hobson, but she remembered him as a dirty, silent, skinny boy who avoided her, even seemed to hate her. He'd run away. She'd been glad her father didn't find him. For weeks she'd dreaded hearing that he'd died of starvation, that animals had scattered his remains.

When several months had passed, she started to believe he had escaped. After a while she had taken it for granted. After that she hadn't thought of him much, then almost never. She had been certain, no matter what happened, he would never return.

Yet now he was standing before her, huge and handsome enough to cause strange and unfamiliar feelings to disturb her sense of calm.

"I can't believe you've come back," she said. "How did you know I needed help so badly?"

"I haven't come back to help you," Buck stated. "I'm a grown man. I want a man's place. I'm willing to work until I drop to get it."

The coldness of his tone chilled Hannah's enthusiasm faster than spring frost could kill sprouting corn. He didn't like her, and he didn't bother to hide it.

"You misread the advertisement," Hannah said, still hoping to escape giving up part of her land.

"I didn't misread anything," Buck said. "I know what you need, and nobody's going to do it but Zeke and me. You take this deal, or you and your ma get thrown off the place."

Cold panic nearly overset Hannah's control. If she lost the ranch, she'd have to marry any man who proposed just to survive. But was taking Buck's offer any better? He saw her as a wolf sees a wounded deer, fair and easy game. He was determined to take cruel advantage of her helplessness, but she was just as determined not to let him. Somehow she would survive. And she would do it without getting married.

"Your terms are unacceptable."

"You haven't even heard them," Buck said.

"I don't need to."

"No sensible man refuses an offer before he's heard it. No sensible woman, either."

He didn't fool her. He didn't think she was sensible. She doubted he thought a woman could be.

"Okay, Mr. Hobson, state your terms."

"I want a half interest in the ranch, everything from the stock to the buildings."

She opened her mouth to tell him to stop right there, but he ignored her.

"I'll throw in the four hundred acres I own. Zeke and I will do the riding work. You and your ma will take care of the livestock and the garden. You'll also cook and wash for us. We'll need the use of a room in the house."

"You can stop right there, Mr. Hobson. I don't know what made you think I would listen to an offer like that, but I have no intention—"

"This." He took a letter out of his vest pocket and held it out to her. "It's from your banker. He said I was to give it to you if it looked like you were turning stubborn."

Hannah opened the letter. It was signed by Joseph Merrick, addressed to her mother.

Dear Sarah Grossek,

This young man has agreed to take on the ranch. He's discussed his terms with me. I realize it's not what you want, but he has my approval. Your husband's creditors are pressing for payment.

I urge you to accept his terms. They're the best you're going to receive. If he returns to me with this letter, I'll have no choice but to arrange the immediate sale of the ranch and its assets to satisfy your creditors.

I would remind you of a more agreeable arrangement. My son, Amos, is most anxious to marry your daughter. Could this be arranged, I'd be more than happy to settle your debts and welcome you both into my home.

Prickles of fear raced up and down Hannah's spine. The people who'd sworn to protect her and her mother from the outside world were now threatening to strip them of their possessions.

She also felt guilt. Her mother was tired and frightened. She would welcome a secure home. But Hannah had already refused to marry Amos in order to keep this ranch. She wasn't about to hand half of it over to this brash cowboy. Desperation gave her courage to turn him down.

"You've wasted your time, Mr. Hobson. I couldn't possibly consider your offer."

"Hannah."

Hannah spun around. Her mother stood in the doorway.

"Come here."

"Excuse me," she said and started toward the house.

"Invite him to get down," her mother said.

"He wants half the ranch. He—"

"I heard what he wants. Now invite him to get down and come in."

"Mama, you can't give him half of the ranch."

"I don't want my half. He can have that."

"I won't let you do it."

"I'm tired of this place. I don't want to be worried with it anymore. If you won't ask him to get down, I will." Her mother went back inside and closed the door.

Hannah was tempted to ignore her mother's wishes, but she couldn't. Her mother owned the whole ranch. If she decided to sell, Hannah would virtually be forced to marry one of her suitors.

Hannah would rather have married the bull that gored her father to death. Amos was taller and younger than Lyman Gillett—possibly more manageable—but he already showed a strong tendency to be like her father. Buck might hate her for what her father had done to him, but he wouldn't beat her. She would also have six months in which to figure out how to keep the ranch *and* escape the prison of marriage.

"Please come in, Mr. Hobson. It seems I have no choice but to consider your offer."

He didn't look pleased that he'd won this first tussle. "You can show me where Zeke and I can sleep."

"I'm not sleeping in a white woman's house," Zeke said. "You shouldn't, either."

"Where do you think we should sleep?" Buck asked.

"Where'd your father's hands sleep?" Zeke asked Hannah.

"In the barn. He turned a feed room into a bunkhouse."

"We can sleep there," Zeke said.

"I'm not sleeping in that barn," Buck said, his face set hard. "That's where Grossek beat me and fed me slops. I'm sleeping in his house, in his bed."

"My mother sleeps in that bed," Hannah said, "but there is another bedroom, one my father built for his sons."

Hannah hated that room. It symbolized a position in her father's affections she had never had. She wondered if he would have acted differently if he had had sons.

"I want to see it."

She hesitated. His presence disturbed her, and she was certain it would be worse in the close confines of the house.

"My mother isn't feeling well. It would be better—"

"I won't disturb your mother."

"Your very presence will disturb her."

"Then I suppose it can't be helped."

"I won't allow you to upset my mother."

Buck's look was unrelenting. "If she accepts my offer, half of that house will be mine. I'll enter it whenever I please."

Hannah's mouth opened to tell him he was mistaken, but she closed it again. "You can see the room tomorrow."

"Now."

He started toward the house.

"Show him the room," Zeke said, his expression even harder to decipher than Buck's. "We got work to be doing."

Badly shaken at the rapidity with which things had moved out of her control, Hannah hurried to catch Buck before he could burst in on her mother. "Wait a minute," she said as she reached out and took hold of his arm to stop him before he could open the door. He recoiled as though she'd struck him.

"Don't ever touch me again!" he hissed, fire blazing in his eyes. "Your father has already left the Grossek stamp on me."

Hannah fell back from the heat of the fury blazing in his eyes.

"I need to go in first," she said, forcing herself to look away from his eyes, to forget the raw emotion that flamed there. "I need to be with Mother when you come in so she won't be frightened."

"What's wrong with her? I'm just going to look at a room."

How did she explain the effect of years of abuse to a man who'd been abused himself? He'd probably think nothing that had happened to them could compare with what had happened to him.

Maybe it couldn't. Hannah couldn't judge. She only knew what it had done to her mother, and she had no intention of allowing Buck's unfeeling behavior to make her condition worse.

"She's nervous around strangers," Hannah explained, "men in particular."

"I'm surprised she married such a cold-blooded bastard as your father."

"She didn't have any choice," Hannah spat at him. "Her parents forced her. Now stay here until I call you. I won't be long."

She went inside, closed and bolted the door. She didn't trust him not to come in anyway. She wondered at her own courage to defy him. Yet though he seemed to hate her, she didn't fear him. She wondered at that, too.

As she expected, her mother had retreated to the kitchen.

"He wants to sleep in the boys' room."

"Why can't he sleep in the barn?"

"He's Buck Hobson, the boy Papa had working here several years ago, the one who stopped him from beating me." Hannah sat down next her to mother. "He's still mad. He wants to sleep in the house to get back at us. I can still tell him to go away."

"No," her mother said. "Bring him in. I'll stay here while you show him the room."

Certain he would have many sons, her father had made the room twice the size of Hannah's. He never forgave his wife for being able to produce only one daughter.

"We'll have to cook his meals and wash his clothes," Hannah continued. "The other man, too— Zeke. He's going to stay in the barn."

Her mother didn't respond.

"It'll be a lot of work. You won't like him being here."

"Show him the room."

Hannah gave up and went to open the door.

"You locked it," Buck said. He looked more forbidding than ever.

"I didn't trust you to wait. You're not used to it. Now try to smile. If you can't do that, at least look pleasant."

Buck's expression didn't lighten when he entered the house. A hallway ran the length of the building and was lined with pegs for coats and racks for shoes. On the left was the parlor, on the right her mother's bedroom. Farther down the hall, the empty bedroom was on the right, her bedroom on the left. Behind that the kitchen opened onto a porch that ended in a room that doubled as pantry and storage.

When they entered the kitchen, her mother sat almost out of sight behind the big iron stove, shelling some early peas. At the sight of Buck, her hands stopped. Even her breathing seemed arrested.

Only then did Hannah realize how much room Buck took up. It wasn't his actual size but the animosity that radiated from him. The room wasn't big enough for her to get away from the feel of it on her skin. It was like heat from a fire.

"Mama, this is Buck Hobson. You remember him, the boy who ran away."

The information had no visible effect on her mother. She continued to stare at Buck.

"I'm going to show him the room now," Hannah said.

"Is she wrong in the head?" Buck asked as they stepped out onto the porch.

"No," Hannah replied angrily. "She's just not comfortable around strangers."

"That's more than being uncomfortable. She's scared out of her mind."

"She's uncomfortable around men," Hannah said, starting toward the bedroom.

"Why?"

The single word was uncompromising, but Hannah had no intention of explaining that her father had beaten her mother for years.

"She's shy."

"You're not."

"What makes you say that?"

He looked at her as though she was a simpleton. "You're not hiding in a corner or trembling in fear. If you could figure out a way, you'd throw me out."

His view of her startled her. She wasn't nearly that courageous. "I'm not entirely comfortable around you, either. But even though you hate me, I know you won't hurt me."

He stared at her a moment, his eyes seeming to bore right through her. "What makes you so sure?"

"You were only a boy, tired and hungry, but you threatened my father with a pitchfork. I don't know what's happened to you since, but that boy is still inside you somewhere."

She was surprised at her own words. Did she believe that boy still existed? She wasn't sure.

If she had expected her faith in his better nature to soften his attitude toward her, she quickly discovered her error. The fury blazed in his eyes again.

"All the thanks I got was to be ignored. I wasn't good enough for you to speak to, even look at. Not even one tiny smile of thanks. What was wrong? Did you think your poor little slave boy might start to think he was human, might even presume to think he had a right to speak to you?"

The anger directed at her was so scorching, Hannah could only stare. She'd never considered that he might interpret her actions that way. He'd be stunned if he knew how many nights she had gone to bed thinking of him.

"If I'd spoken to you, my father would have beaten you. If I'd tried to be friendly, he'd have beaten you worse. The only way I could thank you was to pretend you didn't exist."

He didn't believe that either. She could see it in his eyes, in his stance. His fists were balled, his jaw clamped hard. Oh, well, she wasn't going to waste her time trying to convince him.

"The room probably hasn't been dusted for some time," she said.

She turned and walked through the door from the porch into the hallway. For a moment, the only sound that broke the silence was the soft tread of her own footsteps. Just as she was about to turn, she heard the sharp click of his boot heels on the bare floorboards.

Hannah opened the door to the room her father had built for sons he never fathered. After a slight hesitation, she stepped inside. An odd sensation flooded through her, as though she had broken some taboo. An enormous four-poster bed dominated the room. Two wardrobes stood facing each other on opposite walls. There were curtains at the window, three rag rugs that covered most of the wood floor, as well as three chairs, two tables, and a desk.

All empty. All never used.

Compared to her own room, it was luxuriously furnished, further proof of how much more her father valued sons he never had over the daughter he did. Hannah told herself she was foolish to let that continue to hurt her, but she couldn't stop it. Being in this room was like opening a fresh wound.

"It's plenty big for Zeke and me both," Buck said.

The sound of his voice startled Hannah. For a few seconds, she'd forgotten he was behind her.

"Did you choose the furniture?"

She looked him square in the eye. "I was never allowed in this room."

Surprise drove some of the scowling anger from his face. He grew more handsome. She was right. Despite his size and power, something of his boyish innocence still lingered.

He didn't have a heavy beard like her father or the other men of her sect. She could see the shadow of his beard, along his jaw, on his chin and upper lip, but his cheeks were smooth. His eyebrows, strong and dark, didn't come together across his nose. His skin had tanned to a golden honey, not the leathery brown she was used to. His hair had been cut short and neat.

But his eyes stopped her in her tracks. There was nothing young or innocent about them, nothing friendly or warm. His body betrayed nothing; his eyes shouted his rage.

"Didn't you even go in here to clean?"

"No." Obviously her father wasn't the only man who figured women were good for little else. "You probably ought to open the window. It's been closed up for years."

"Don't worry about it," Buck said. "After sleeping in that barn of yours, a little dust isn't going to bother me."

"You haven't slept in that barn for years."

"I remember it well."

She was sure he did. He looked like a man who never forgot anything.

"Mama and I will clean it tomorrow," she said. "If you'll just—"

"I don't want anybody in my room." He wasn't trying to lighten their workload. He was ordering her to stay away from him. "If I want anything done, I'll do it myself."

"Good." She wasn't going to fight him. "Now I have to see about dinner. When do you like to eat?"

"When I'm here, it doesn't matter. When we're working away from the ranch, whenever we get in."

"You'll have to do better than that. My mother and I can't just throw something together."

"You'll have plenty of time if we've been out on the range. It'll take a while to care for the horses and clean up."

She was surprised and glad somebody had taught him to clean up. She had the distinct feeling that Buck Hobson wasn't a man who would take suggestions easily, especially not from her.

"When do you want to eat today?"

"An hour after sundown ought to be about right. Zeke and I need to look around. Before we settle on anything, I want to be sure what needs to be done."

She looked at him suspiciously. "Why?"

"I want you to put our agreement in writing."

"You don't trust me?"

His look was penetrating. "You don't want me here. I'll bet you'd do just about anything to keep from giving me any part of this ranch."

His slight to her integrity made her furious. She might be Nathaniel Grossek's daughter, but she wasn't a liar or a cheat.

"I would never cheat on an agreement. Neither will you cheat me. I want a written agreement just as much as you."

Chapter Three

Buck bit back an angry retort. He'd never cheated anyone. He would have this ranch—he wouldn't allow anybody to stand in his way—but he'd come by it honestly.

He hadn't expected the ranch to be in such desperate shape. He had to consider the possibility that he couldn't save it, that he'd have to take what he could from the wreck and try to do better next time. But that wouldn't satisfy his lust for revenge. He had to have *this* ranch. He had to succeed where Grossek had failed.

Mrs. Grossek bothered him, too. Something was wrong with her. Hannah might say she was only uncomfortable around men, but there was more to it than that. That woman was scared to death of him.

Then there was Hannah. Once he had lusted after her, dreamed about her, lived in hopes of getting a glimpse at her. One smile from her would have enabled him to forget the misery of his existence for weeks, maybe even months. But she had been too good for a slave like him, and she'd made certain he knew it. When he was tempted to forget, the welts on his back reminded him.

Neither did he understand Hannah's reluctance to give up any part of the ranch. He couldn't see her as a rancher's wife. It surprised him she hadn't married. That would have been the obvious solution to her problem.

Buck told himself to stop wasting time in idle speculation. He didn't need to understand anybody here. Or they him.

He left the room and closed the door behind him. He'd bring his stuff in later. He found Zeke making himself at home in the barn.

It wasn't easy to go through that door again. Damp and foul-smelling after a rain, dark and cold in winter, the place had made him feel alone in the world. Every night he'd cursed his father for selling him, imagined what he'd do if he ever found him. He'd dreamed of Hannah to make the hours of darkness bearable, to forget the feeling of being totally alone.

Jake and Isabelle had saved him from that. He'd tried to think of them as his parents, but he couldn't. He guessed there came a time when you were too old to pretend your real parents weren't your parents at all.

Buck wished he could have loved Jake and Isabelle the way the younger boys did, but he couldn't. He'd tried to feel the orphans were his brothers, Drew and baby Eden his sisters, but he'd failed. That was why he couldn't quit looking for his sister, even though he hadn't heard anything in six years of searching. When he found her, he'd have his *real* family.

He pushed aside memories and hopes that hadn't materialized. He had a chance to grab onto something concrete now. He wouldn't let it slip through his fingers.

"You get everything settled?" Zeke asked when Buck entered the converted feed room.

"Won't know until we have a good look around," Buck replied. "Then I'm putting everything in writing."

"I don't trust writing," Zeke said. "It kept me a slave."

"Jake said it's time Texans learned to use the laws to help themselves. He said too many ranchers think they own the land just because they live on it."

"Don't start quoting Jake. I got enough of that back at the Broken Circle."

"No point in ignoring something just because you don't like where it comes from," Buck said. "Those weasels in Utopia stole what other people thought belonged to them. I don't intend for that to happen to me."

"I don't know nothing about the law," Zeke said, "and I don't want to. But I do know something about beef, and I say we're in trouble unless we find more cows out there than we saw."

That worried Buck, too. "Saddle up. I'm not signing any agreement until I know we've got something to work with."

"There used to be cows here," Zeke said to Buck. "I see their droppings. But they ain't here now."

Buck could see the signs of far more cattle than they'd counted in the five hours they'd ridden over the ranch. If he'd still been living with Jake, he might have taken time to admire the silver ribbon of the Pedernales River as it wound through low hills, or watch a white-tailed deer fawn learn to stand up. But he was on his own now. He had to be the one to anticipate problems and have an answer ready before they became disasters.

The new spring grass was mostly hidden by wildflowers, but he could tell last year's grass had been grazed down to the roots. Paths used by cattle as they walked through the areas of cactus and mesquite to water were still clear.

The cattle had been here, but where were they now?

Zeke pointed to a rider. "Somebody's coming."

Buck hadn't met any of the ranchers in the area, but Jake had told him several who didn't belong to the sect in Utopia had moved into Gillespie County west of his old ranch. Buck intended to get to know them. He might as well start with this man.

He pulled up on the crest of a ridge to wait for him.

"I'm Walter Evans," the man said when he pulled up alongside them. "I own the Double-D Ranch east of here."

They shook hands.

"I'm Buck Hobson," Buck replied. "This is my friend, Zeke."

"I've seen you three times this afternoon. You know you're on Grossek range?"

"Yeah."

"You thinking about buying it?"

"Maybe."

Evans didn't seem put out at Buck's evasive answer. "You'd better bring your own cattle. I don't think there's many left."

"What do you mean?" Zeke demanded, suspicious.

"I didn't know much about Nathaniel Grossek's business, but I think he was running right at three-thousand head. I doubt you'll find half that many."

"Why?" Buck asked.

"How do you know?" Zeke added.

Evans studied them a few moments without answering.

"You raised a serious question," Buck said. "Are you going to answer it?"

"If you'll tell me your interest in this place."

"Will you tell me yours?" Buck asked.

Evans nodded.

"I'm thinking about signing on as a partner," Buck said. "Or at least I was until I found there aren't many cows or young stuff, just steers as wild as antelope."

"And your friend?"

"We're working together. Now what's your stake in this?"

"I want to see that Mrs. Grossek isn't cheated of what little she has left. That banker in Utopia is anxious to sell the ranch for what he can get. I saw his boy on the place a time or two. I wouldn't be surprised if Hannah married him."

Buck didn't want Hannah to marry. He didn't want to deal with a husband. Besides, if her husband decided to sell the property, Buck would lose his chance to get the ranch.

But he realized he especially didn't want Hannah to marry Amos Merrick, and that bothered him. Her selfishness should have been enough to cure him of any concern for her. But he'd seen Amos in his father's office—young, callow, conceited. Buck wouldn't wish Amos Merrick on anybody, not even Hannah.

"Her father didn't know a thing about ranching and hired cowhands just as bad," Evans said. "His cows wandered all over. There's a bunch of them on my land right now."

Buck felt his muscles tighten.

"If you decide to stay, you're welcome to look for yourself," Evans continued. "You can join me in spring roundup. But I'll warn you, you won't find any cows or young stuff on my place."

"Why?" Buck thought he knew, but he wanted Evans to confirm his suspicions. Apparently Evans wasn't willing to do that.

"We had some pretty rough weather this past winter," Evans said. "Grossek's stock could be half-way to the Pecos by now."

Buck thought he had a nearer destination in mind.

"What's west of here?"

"Five or six ranches. I guess you'll be riding that way soon. It's always a good idea to get to know your neighbors."

"When do you start roundup?"

"In about a month."

"Do you do it together?"

"Sometimes, if we think there's a lot of drifting, we send a rep to lend a hand and bring back the strays."

"Mind if we send a rep with you?"

"You're both welcome to come if you like."

"Will the other ranchers feel the same?"

"You'll have to ask," Evans said. "I make it a practice never to speak for another man. Enough trouble knowing my own mind."

"Especially if you're married," Buck said.

"Widowed with a daughter to raise by myself," Evans said, some of his cheerfulness disappearing. "My wife died of cholera a few years back."

"Sorry," Buck said.

"No worry of yours. But this place will be." Evans tightened the reins and clucked to his horse.

"What do you think he meant?" Zeke asked as Evans rode off.

"I don't know," Buck replied, "but I think he's saying one of our neighbors has something to do with the lost cattle."

Buck felt reluctant to leave his room. He told himself there was nothing special about eating his first meal with Hannah and her mother. He also told himself that in a few days mealtimes would become so familiar, he wouldn't notice who was at the table. But he didn't really believe that. No man could ignore Hannah Grossek, even if he disliked her.

He felt on edge. He'd changed his shirt. He always changed his shirt before he sat down at Isabelle's table, but he'd told himself he wasn't going to go in for such foolishness when he got a place of his own. Yet here he was with a scrubbed face and a clean shirt.

Maybe he was edgy because they still had to hammer out the written agreement. He wasn't as enthusiastic about this place as he'd been when he first read the notice, but he still meant to have it. It would just take more work. It was important to get an agreement as much in his favor as possible.

Then this would be his room in his house on his ranch.

Buck had never had his own room, but the prospect didn't give him the feeling of gratification he'd anticipated. Even the knowledge that it was the room Nathaniel Grossek had built especially for his sons failed to give him much satisfaction. If a man could curse from the grave, he was certain Grossek was cursing him at this very moment.

He opened the door and left the room.

Buck entered a big kitchen warm from the heat of the large iron stove that filled one corner. Flowered wallpaper and oak wainscoting covered the walls. A large work table dominated one part of the room, the dining table the other. Behind the stove, pots and pans arranged according to size hung from the wall in neat rows. China decorated with a blue design filled a glass-front cabinet. Rows of shelves contained dozens of boxes, sacks, and tins. Plain white curtains framed windows that faced the barn.

The aroma of coffee mingled with the smells of hot bread and baked chicken. Someone had covered the table with a white cloth, one place set neatly at each end, glasses and cups on the side. It reminded him so much of Isabelle's kitchen, he almost felt homesick.

Hannah and her mother shuttled between the stove and the work table.

"You only set two places," he said.

Hannah turned from the stove as her mother carried a closed tin into the pantry. "Mother and I will eat later."

Buck couldn't accept that. "We'll all eat together."

"We'd rather not."

Buck didn't know why Hannah didn't want to eat with him—she probably thought she was too good—but he was certain Mrs. Grossek was too frightened.

That hit him where he was most vulnerable. He'd lived with fear most of his life, fear of his mother's temper, his father's drunken fits, his owners' whips or fists. He was intimately acquainted with the sick feeling of knowing he was helpless, of never knowing whether a hand would feed him or club him. Nor had he forgotten the sense of desperation that accompanied fear. He had vowed never to cause anybody such pain. He wasn't about to begin with Mrs. Grossek.

He opened the china cabinet.

"What are you doing?" Hannah demanded.

"Getting dishes to set two more places."

"I told you Mother and I would eat later."

"We'll have to talk regularly about the ranch. We probably won't see each other except for meals."

He found what he needed and set the table. He'd had years of experience at the Broken Circle.

"It's almost time to eat," he said to Mrs. Grossek.

She watched him from the pantry doorway, her gaze moving from Buck to Hannah and back again. He wasn't sure she was afraid so much as determined to keep her distance. She didn't trust him. Just like Hannah.

"I set a place for you."

Buck was relieved to see she didn't cringe, but she didn't move. Zeke entered the kitchen but stayed by the door, watching.

"Hannah's about ready to take the bread out. Isabelle—that's the woman who adopted me and Zeke—always said you had to eat bread while it was hot. Why don't you let me take you to the table?" He held out his hand, but Mrs. Grossek didn't move.

"Isabelle grew up in a grand house in Savannah.

She says all proper ladies get escorted to the table by a gentleman. I can't claim to be a gentleman, but I'd be honored to escort you to the table."

Mrs. Grossek still didn't move.

"You're the lady of the house, ma'am. Isabelle would wring my neck if she found out I sat down at the table before you. She's very particular about things like that. Fair drives Jake into a frenzy sometimes, but she always gets her way."

Buck took hold of Mrs. Grossek's hand. It felt fragile, the skin soft. He didn't know how she had the strength to do so much work. He tugged gently. Mrs. Grossek let herself be led out of the pantry. Buck guided her to her chair and seated her. Zeke still stood by the door. Hannah moved from where she'd stood, immobile, by the stove.

"Would you like your coffee now or later, ma'am?" Buck asked Mrs. Grossek.

"Now." She spoke so softly Buck could barely hear her reply.

"I'll get it as soon as I set out the rest of the food," Hannah said as she set the breadbasket down on the table.

"I'll get it," Buck said. He took the coffee pot from the stove, brought it to the table, and poured Mrs. Grossek's coffee. "Do you want anything in it?"

"She likes two lumps of sugar," Hannah said as she set a plate of chicken down in front of Zeke's place.

"I asked your mother," Buck said. "She can answer for herself."

"Two lumps," Mrs. Grossek said, her voice stronger.

Buck dropped the sugar in the coffee. "Taste it, ma'am. See if it's okay."

Mrs. Grossek picked up her spoon, stirred, and tasted.

"Is it okay?"

She nodded.

"Good." He turned to Hannah. "Anything else I can help you bring to the table?"

She looked at him as if she thought he was joking.

"Jake adopted eleven of us," Buck explained. "Isabelle said she'd cook, but we had to do the rest. We learned to set the table, bring in the food, clear away, and wash the dishes."

"Then you can get the peas," Hannah said. "Use a cloth. The dish is hot." She set a bowl of applesauce down and looked at Zeke, who sat down to the table without offering to help. "How about him?"

"He helped Isabelle, but he won't help you."

"Why?"

"Your neighbor Rupert Reison beat him and kept him chained in the barn. I had to saw a pole in half before I could get him away. You can depend on him if you're in danger, but don't expect him to be nice about it."

Both women blanched. Buck didn't know whether it was the mention of Rupert's name or the fact that he'd chained Zeke in the barn. As far as Buck was concerned, either one was enough.

"Anything else?"

Hannah looked startled by the sound of his voice. "No. We can eat."

They ate in uncomfortable silence. Zeke spoke only when he wanted something passed to him. Mrs. Grossek didn't talk at all. Hannah limited her conversation to what was necessary for the serving of the meal.

Buck kept his attention on his plate. The less he looked at Hannah, the more comfortable he was.

He was a twenty-three-year-old male with limited experience of women. But even if he'd been too young to have reached puberty, he'd have been old enough to know Hannah was a very attractive woman, to feel the force of that attraction. But he didn't want to be attracted to her. He didn't want to feel anything at all for her. He wanted her ranch. It would be easier if he concentrated on his hatred of her father.

But that wasn't easy to do when she sat next to him, when even a slight turn of his head would bring her into his line of vision. He was fast discovering that disliking and distrusting a woman was one thing, being immune to her attraction quite another.

He realized he'd never sat down to a meal with a pretty girl, at least not a *nice* pretty girl. All of Hannah's stubbornness seemed to fade into the shadows cast by the coal-oil lamp. Her soft, gentle appearance disturbed him.

Her voice lacked Isabelle's authority or Drew's youthful exuberance. She spoke with a low voice that sounded like a purr as her tongue, weaned on German, struggled with the stubborn American vowels. It was the most exotic, sensual sound he'd ever heard, nothing like the Texas drawl.

She looked slim and innocent and lovely. She hadn't smeared her cheeks with rouge or painted her lips red. Her skin looked soft. He imagined how it would feel to touch it.

Buck pulled himself up with a silent curse. He was acting just the way he had when he was her father's slave. But everything had changed. He had to remember what he'd come here to do.

Zeke finished eating and pushed back his chair. "I'll see to the horses." He got up and left the room.

"Are you going to see about the horses, too?" Hannah asked, clearly irritated by Zeke's rude behavior.

"No. I've got to tell you what I found today. Then we have to talk about this written agreement."

Chapter Four

Hannah felt her body tense. She'd been worrying about this all afternoon, wondering what demands Buck would make. The way he'd treated her mother had so surprised her, she'd nearly forgotten. When he'd started toward the pantry, she had been poised to thrust herself between him and her mother, to shield her from his harshness. But he'd been gentle and kind. Gentlemanly.

Hannah didn't know Isabelle, but she had to respect any woman who could get a man to set a table, hold a chair, or remain standing until the women were seated. None of the men she knew would have thought of it, or done it if they had. They would have been pleased to have the table to themselves, to be waited on while they ate and discussed matters too weighty for women to understand.

But the Buck who looked at her now didn't resemble the man who'd been so kind to her mother. He was the man who'd ridden up this morning and demanded half her ranch.

"What did you find?" she asked. She was afraid of the answer, but she had to know.

"You'd better sit down."

"I can listen while I clear away. It'll be harder if I leave it." It was also easier if she didn't have to look into his eyes. Her father had beaten Buck, but his antagonism was directed at her.

"Okay. First, Mr. Merrick was right about the equipment. There's nothing in the barn—no saddles, no bridles, no harnesses. All you have is a bunk room and two of the worst mattresses I've ever seen."

"Papa said he wouldn't waste money on mattresses for men who were used to sleeping on the ground."

"You needn't tell me what your papa thought about the people who worked for him."

It mortified her to remember what her father had done to Buck, but it also angered her that Buck continually threw it in her face.

"Go on." She busied herself putting food away while her mother scraped the dishes and put them into hot water.

"The barn is in good condition, but you've got no wagon. Not even a buckboard. Of course that hardly matters when you don't have a horse to pull it or a harness to put him in."

Why would their hands have stolen the wagon, the buckboard, or the harnesses? It could only have been in retaliation for her father's treatment.

"You have no riding stock, but there might be some running loose. Zeke and I saw some horses when we were riding in, but we couldn't get close enough to read the brands."

"We had more than a dozen horses," Mrs. Grossek said. "I heard my husband say that to one of the men."

Both Hannah and Buck looked up, surprised.

"They aren't here now," Buck said. "The corrals and pigpens need some work, but the fences around your garden and the chicken yard are in excellent shape."

"Mama and I check them every day," Hannah said.

Buck didn't react. He probably didn't believe her. Most likely he didn't think women could fix a fence.

"The worst news is about the cows," Buck continued. "Your neighbor says your father ran about three thousand head. Does that sound right?"

"I guess so." She was ashamed to admit her father had never told her. He never figured it was anything a woman should know.

"Evans says I won't find half that number, and he's right. Worst of all, I don't see many cows or young stuff. There ought to have been at least seven hundred cows. I didn't see seventy, nowhere near enough to produce a decent calf crop."

Hannah tried to keep fear at bay. Even if she could pay off the debts, there'd be nothing left for her or her mother to live on. She could see her chance of freedom slipping away.

A second thought occurred to her. How did she know Buck was telling the truth? He might be planning to rustle the stock he said was missing, sell it, and pocket the money for himself. Then he could buy the ranch when she was forced to sell.

It was a perfect scheme, something almost any man would have tried to pull on two helpless women. But then she thought of the way he'd treated her mother. Those weren't the actions of a liar and a thief.

"What do you think happened?" Buck asked.

Hannah turned to face him. "Papa never talked about the ranch to me. Do you have any idea?" She could tell he did. He had the look of a man who had to make a choice and was weighing his options.

"Your hands probably did take a few steers. Maybe a lot more drifted during the winter. But that doesn't account for the absence of cows and calves. I think they've been rustled."

"By whom?"

"I don't know."

"What are you going to do?"

"Get them back."

"How?"

"With guile if possible. With guns if necessary."

She couldn't believe he was serious. The men of her sect preached against the use of guns except for hunting.

"Do you know Walter Evans?" Buck asked.

"He came in for a cup of coffee once, but it made Papa so angry, he didn't do it again."

Hannah noticed her mother stiffen. She wasn't surprised. Her father had struck her, shouted at her for days about *entertaining men*.

"Would he steal your cattle?"

"I don't think so. What do you think, Mama?"

Sarah Grossek shook her head without turning around.

"How about your neighbors to the west?"

"Lyman Gillett's cook buys butter and eggs from us. I don't know anybody else."

"Would he steal from you?"

"No. He's been trying to get me to marry him ever since Papa died."

"But that might explain why he's doing it, to wear you down."

Hannah found that hard to credit, but Buck's expression was angry and determined. She was sure he'd expected to get more out of his half ownership of the ranch. For a brief moment she wondered if he'd meant to get her. Marriage would give him the whole ranch. No, he hated her too much for that. She hadn't expected it to bother her, but it did. No one had ever hated her, not even her father. She didn't like the feeling.

Besides, she could like Buck well enough if he gave her a chance. Her father had never let her visit or make friends. All the hands had kept their distance. Except for her mother, Hannah had been virtually alone.

She'd love to have someone to talk with about the things that confused her, someone to confide in. There was so much she wanted to know, to say, to learn. She wondered if other people felt the same things she did, had the same hopes, the same doubts. Her mother had been a wonderful companion, but Hannah had always wanted a friend her own age.

She doubted Buck would ever be her friend. He hated her and wanted her ranch. He might even be planning to rustle her cows. That wasn't a good starting point for a friendship.

"We'd better start working on that agreement. You sure you want it?" she asked Buck.

"Sharing ownership is not the same as hiring someone to help you," he said. "I want to know exactly where I stand in this partnership. I'd expect you to feel the same way."

"I do."

She dried her hands, opened a drawer, and withdrew paper and a pen. She placed them on the table. "Do you want to write it or shall I?"

"You." He pushed the paper back toward her. "We need to list all the property involved in the partnership. That includes the house, all the buildings and corrals, all the cows with your father's Tumbling T brand, any riding stock we can find, and the land deeded to your father. You can also include the land deeded to Jake Maxwell."

She wondered if he could read and write. So many men couldn't. He was certainly businesslike about all the rest.

"How does Zeke figure into this?"

"As far as this agreement goes, his work is my work."

Good. It was much better to get the work of two for one.

She'd been writing in silence for some minutes when Buck said, "If we can't clear off the debt and you have to sell, we'll split any money we get. If we do pay off the loan, I want the option to buy your half."

Hannah was so surprised her pen splattered across the page. "You want to buy the ranch?"

"One of us will have to sooner or later."

Hannah was too embarrassed to admit she hadn't thought beyond paying off the ranch's debts. Neither had she thought of community reaction to Buck's staying in their house. She'd been too concerned with her own reaction.

"I want the same privilege," Hannah said.

Buck looked surprised. "Why?"

"This is my home."

"You can't run this place by yourself."

"That won't be your concern."

"Okay, but I'd insist you pay cash."

"I'll make the same stipulation."

"Can you spell that word?"

His question startled her. Then she got angry. "What makes you think I'm stupid?"

"I don't. Many of your kind don't teach their women to read."

She'd been lucky. Her mother had taught her. "I can. I can also spell stipulation. Can you?"

He shocked her by grinning. "No, but I can read and write. Isabelle made all of us learn."

She wanted to meet this Isabelle. She'd never met a woman who could make a man do anything, especially against his will.

"Our horses and gear aren't part of the partnership," Buck said. "Everything Zeke and I rode in with goes with us."

Hannah thought that was fair enough. She wrote it down.

"We also get to keep any horses or cows we find that don't carry the Tumbling T brand."

Hannah sensed a trap. "What do you mean?"

"There are wild horses in the area. Cows, too. Any we find and brand belong to Zeke and me."

"Is this how you expect to buy my half of the ranch?"

"It's one way."

"How do I know you won't spend all of your time rounding up wild cattle?"

"Because if I do that, we won't be able to pay off the debt on the ranch and there won't be any ranch to buy."

"You could be planning to buy it from the bank."

"I could."

He could brand cattle and hold them anywhere.

As long as they didn't carry the ranch brand, they wouldn't belong to her, even if they had been her cattle in the first place.

"Okay, but I have an exemption of my own."

"What?"

"Mother and I take care of the garden, chickens, and milk cows. We sell anything we don't use. That money will belong to us."

"You won't sell everything and leave nothing for Zeke and me to eat?"

"You won't put your brand on my calves?"

"You don't have any calves."

"When I do?"

"You think I'd cheat you?"

"Do you think *I'd* cheat *you*?"

He didn't like having his questions turned back on him, but it caused his scowl to lighten. He didn't look so thunderous. He actually looked thoughtful.

"I don't know."

"I don't know about you, either."

"I have another stipulation," Hannah said, "one you won't like. You don't get half of the ranch until the end of six months, and then only if you save it. Otherwise, you get your land back, and I pay you and Zeke two hundred dollars each for your work."

"No."

"I won't budge on that. Do you agree, Mother?"

Mrs. Grossek thought a moment and then nodded.

Buck studied Hannah for a long, intimidating moment. He looked more fierce, more determined, more dangerous than when he had arrived. She wanted to squirm, to look away, but she forced herself to return his look.

"Okay," he said.

Hannah forced herself not to relax visibly. She

would have given in if he had held out. "Anything else you want in the agreement?"

"You're to provide us with two meals a day and wash our clothes."

Hannah wasn't sure why that should have angered her. She'd tacitly agreed to do it. Men couldn't cook or wash. But putting it in a contract made it different.

"That makes it sound like we're slaves."

The change in him was instantaneous and frightening. He brought his fist down on the table so hard that the lamp nearly turned over. Her mother uttered a small shriek. Hannah gasped in surprise.

"You don't know a thing about being a slave."

His expression was full of rage, his eyes alive with fire. The softness of his voice made his fury all the more ominous.

"You weren't kept in a barn, made to sleep in the dirt, fed food not fit for hogs, worked until you were exhausted, beaten when you were too weak to stand up."

The look of anger—almost hatred—made her draw back from him.

"Ask Zeke what it was like to be chained to a stable wall each night. Ask Perry Halstead what it was like to be beaten to death because he couldn't work long and hard enough. You didn't know Rupert Reison killed him, did you? You don't believe me, either. You want proof? I can show you where he's buried. Reison followed me all the way to the New Mexico Territory to kill me so I couldn't tell anybody. And you know what's funny?"

Buck's smile wasn't the slightest bit humorous.

"Reison was killed by the men he hired to rustle our herd, a theft he planned to use to cover up my murder."

Shock held Hannah immobile. Not even a whimpering sound from her mother had the power to loosen her muscles. She knew Reison was dead. A letter had come from the commander of the army fort outside Santa Fe saying his body had been found by some passerby and buried.

She hadn't known any of the rest. Had Reison followed Buck to the New Mexico Territory to kill him? She hadn't known Perry Halstead, hadn't known anything about Reison beating anybody to death. She found it hard to believe so much evil could exist around her without her knowing about it. But she did remember what her father had done to Buck. If he could do that, couldn't others do the same, even worse?

"Mama and I will wash and cook for you," she said when she managed to find her voice. "It's just that putting it on paper makes it sound like we're being punished."

But Buck wasn't listening to her. He was looking at her mother. Hannah had been so upset that she hadn't realized her mother stood dazed, white as a sheet. Buck got up and took the half-washed dish from her hand.

"I'm sorry I lost my temper, Mrs. Grossek," he said. "I won't mention it again."

He led her from the sink to a seat at the table.

"Can I get you anything?"

"She'd probably like some coffee," Hannah said. "She always has a cup after we finish in the kitchen." Hannah started to get up, but Buck was faster. He remembered the two lumps of sugar. He didn't cease his attentions until her mother's color had returned.

"You can forget the part about cooking and washing," he said.

"No," Hannah said. "It ought to be here. I'll also write down that you'll keep the buildings up and make repairs to the corrals and fences."

"You said you took care of the fences."

"We'll be too busy washing and cooking to do that now."

He nodded. "Anything else?"

"No." She finished writing, signed her name.

"We need two copies," Buck said.

"Why?"

"So we each can have one."

"You don't trust me not to destroy this one?"

"If we each have a copy, that won't be a worry. I can copy it out if you like."

"No. I'll do it." She made the second copy, signed it, and passed the paper and pen to Buck. He slid it in front of her mother.

"You've got to sign it, too, Mrs. Grossek."

Hannah's mother looked at Buck as if he'd asked her to rope a steer.

"Mama's never signed anything in her life," Hannah said.

"It didn't bother you."

"I don't plan to depend on a man for anything," Hannah declared. "I intend to conduct the business of the ranch myself."

She hadn't meant to lay down the gauntlet so soon, but it was just as well Buck knew where she stood. He'd told her he meant to have her ranch. She'd told him she didn't mean to give it up.

Buck's look was noncommittal. "Why are you so against marriage? It would solve all your problems."

"You know what my father did to me and my mother. Do you think I want to marry a man like that?"

"Not all men are like your father."

"All the ones I know are."

"Zeke and I aren't. Jake isn't. None of the other orphans are either."

"I thought Jake adopted all of you."

"He did."

"Then he's your father and they're your brothers. Why don't you call them that?"

She could see she'd stumbled into awkward territory, though he looked more embarrassed than angry.

"I have no brothers, only a sister I can't find."

It irritated Hannah that he wouldn't consider these people his family. She'd have given a lot to have a family, even an adopted one.

"Sign the agreement, Mama. Mr. Hobson probably wants to talk things over with his *brother*, Zeke, before he goes to bed."

Buck's anger flared, but Hannah stared right back at him before turning to her mother.

The unsigned paper still lay before Mrs. Grossek.

"You've got to sign it," Buck said, pulling his attention from Hannah. "You husband didn't leave a will. Nothing will be legal and binding without both your signatures."

Her mother looked as though she still couldn't believe she was allowed to do this, but Buck was able to get her to do things no one else could. There was something about him that convinced her mother of his sincerity. Hannah wished he would direct some of that sincerity to her. She was tired of all the anger.

Her mother signed the two copies with painstaking slowness in a beautiful copperplate Hannah had been taught to copy.

Buck signed the first copy and passed it back to Mrs. Grossek.

"Have your daughter put this away somewhere safe."

He signed his copy, folded it, and put it in his pocket. "Zeke and I will need breakfast at five. I want to be in the saddle at dawn."

Hannah started to say she didn't get up that early but changed her mind. If she wanted to keep her ranch, she was going to have to be willing to work as hard as Buck. If that meant having breakfast ready at five o'clock, she'd do it.

"When do you want dinner?"

"Don't expect us until after dark."

When Buck left the room, he left an unfamiliar emptiness behind.

Ever since she could remember, Hannah had enjoyed her father's absence because it meant relief from tension and fear. The muscles in her body would loosen, her watchfulness ease. Her mind would open up, her thoughts roam free. Her emotions would thaw enough to feel something more than fear.

Buck's absence wasn't like that. A certain amount of tension did leave, but as it faded, she became aware of the absence of something vital, vibrant, maybe even essential. How could she feel anything about a man she didn't fully trust? Hannah didn't understand it. She felt slightly diminished, deprived by his leaving. This frightened her but excited her as well.

Despite any questions she might have about Buck's integrity, she didn't fear him. His threat to her ranch didn't conceal a threat to her. At least, not her physical well-being. Her peace of mind was something else.

"That man could be a powerful lot of trouble if he wanted."

Hannah's thoughts scattered. When she turned, her mother had gone back to the sink, where she stood washing dishes, her back rigid but her eyes unusually alive.

"How do you mean?"

"Men like him can make girls do things they regret later."

Hannah couldn't believe what she was hearing. Her mother never mentioned men in that way. In fact, she didn't talk about men at all.

"Let's leave this place and move to Utopia," Sarah Grossek said. "You need a husband."

"I don't want one."

"There must be some nice men somewhere. Maybe we could go to Boerne or New Braunfels."

"Men think women are good only for having sons and taking care of them. If we fail at either, they beat us."

"Buck doesn't act like that."

"I don't trust him."

Sarah looked up from her work. "Do you think he'd try to cheat us?"

"I don't know. He's kind to you, but he looks at me like he wants to strangle me. He's also made it plain he wants this ranch. I don't think he'll let anything stand in his way. If that means cheating us, I think he'd do it."

Sarah turned back to her work and washed two dishes in silence.

"He's angry. He intends to get back at Nathaniel through us," she said at last, "but he won't cheat us or steal from us."

"You may be right, Mama, but we can't depend

on it. We've got to make enough money to buy his half of the ranch."

"Why do you want this place? I thought you hated it."

"It's our home."

"And no man will come all the way out here to bother you."

"That, too."

"You shouldn't close yourself off. Not all men are like your father."

"Do you know any who aren't?"

"I did once, before I was forced to marry Nathaniel."

Hannah had always wondered what kind of parents could have forced their daughter to marry a man she disliked. Now she wondered if her mother had been in love with another man.

"Women need to marry," her mother said. "They need a husband to care for, children to nourish, or they aren't whole."

"I feel just fine as I am," Hannah said. "I don't say I wouldn't like having children, just not enough to put up with a man."

"We've got two of them to put up with," her mother pointed out.

"Only for six months."

"It won't do any good to buy him out. You don't know how to run this place."

"But I will," Hannah said, her determination stiffened by the written agreement in her pocket. "By the end of six months, I intend to know as much about cows as Buck Hobson."

Chapter Five

Even though the Rafter D was the biggest ranch along the Pedernales River, the two-story stone ranch house surprised Buck. Painted, neat, better kept up than houses in Utopia, it had the appearance of the home of a wealthy man.

"I still say we shouldn't have come," Zeke said. "If he's rustling our cows, you won't do nothing but put him on his guard."

"Just because we saw some of our cows on the way in doesn't mean he's been stealing them," Buck replied.

"We've seen four or five times as many here as anywhere else," Zeke insisted. "He's got to be stealing."

"We don't know that. Cattle drift all the time. Worse during the winter. This is the closest ranch. They'd naturally drift here first."

"I say we take the cows and explain later."

"Jake says do things up front, that it saves trouble in the long run."

"Why're you always quoting Jake?"

"Who else am I going to quote? My pa? Old man Grossek?"

"That's stupid advice. It'll get you shot."

"We'll see."

"I'll stay out of sight," Zeke said. "Won't nobody trust you if you show up with a black man."

Buck tried to change Zeke's mind, but as usual it was impossible.

Buck was afraid there wasn't an innocent explanation for the drift. Practically everything they'd seen was cows and young stuff. If his livestock had drifted here in the normal way, there ought to be a mix of cows, yearlings, and two- to five-year-old steers.

He recognized the cook as the man he'd seen leaving Hannah's ranch that first day. "I'm Buck Hobson. Is your boss around?"

"Over at the corral," the cook said and disappeared inside the house.

Lyman Gillett was watching a cowhand break a horse. He wasn't at all what Buck had expected. Neat, clean, slight of frame, and baby-faced, he wore a white shirt and tie under his simple black vest. A heavy gold chain and two rings made him look something of a dandy. Nothing about him said he would be the kind of man to rustle cattle.

Except his eyes. They looked as hard as steel.

Determined to be friendly, Buck dismounted. "Howdy," he said in greeting. "I'm Buck Hobson. I'm working for the Tumbling T."

"Then you're off your range."

Buck hadn't expected a warm welcome, but this was an unmistakable cold shoulder.

"I thought I'd introduce myself," Buck said, trying to keep a friendly sound in his voice.

"So?"

This man was more than unwelcoming. He was hostile. "I think it's good to know your neighbors."

Gillett barely took his eyes off the man and horse in the corral. The horse had learned to accept the bridle. The saddle came next. "It's a waste of time."

Clearly, trying to be friendly was also a waste of time.

"I found some of our cows on your range," Buck said.

Gillett jerked his head around, his full attention on Buck. "What did you say?" His eyes reminded Buck of those of a rattlesnake about to strike.

"Nobody looked after the Tumbling T this winter. We had a bad drift. I expect I'll find cows from here to the other side of the county."

"I got none of your cows here."

"I saw them."

Now Gillett looked just plain angry.

"I'm planning to ask the ranchers to go on roundup together," Buck said. "I hope you'll join us."

"Why should I? My stock hasn't drifted."

"Maybe not, but the roundup will go faster and cleaner with more hands."

"Nobody but Rafter D hands work my cows."

"Okay by me," Buck said, beginning to get angry himself. "We'll just round up any of our stock that's drifted onto your land."

"I don't have any of your stock."

"I say you do."

Buck couldn't see what this man had to gain by denying what anybody could see by looking.

"I'll talk to the boys when they come in," Gillett

71

said. "Maybe they'll know what you're talking about."

"Maybe." Buck had the feeling he was riding the edge of a very sharp blade. A wrong move and—

"We're not branding for another month yet," Lyman Gillett said. He watched Buck closely. "I like to wait until most of the cows have dropped their calves."

"You'll let us know when you start?"

Gillett's gaze was still measuring. "Yeah. I'll send one of the boys over."

"You can send the cook. He comes to buy butter and eggs."

"I'll do that." Lyman Gillett grinned unexpectedly. "Quality stuff those Grossek women turn out. Not bad themselves. Been trying to talk that young one into moving over here. I even offered to buy her place."

The wave of anger that flooded through Buck was unexpected. For all his looks and neatness, Gillett was a thief and probably a scoundrel as well. Buck meant to straighten him out about Hannah.

"You're a little late. Mrs. Grossek sold me a half interest in the ranch yesterday."

Gillett's smile vanished. "I thought you were just a hand."

"You thought wrong. You're wrong about Hannah, too. I'd be obliged if you were more careful what you said. I'd hate for people to get the wrong idea."

Gillett's eyes turned colder than ever. "And if I don't care what ideas people get?"

"I'll have to see you learn to care."

Gillett's gaze held Buck's, measuring, never wavering. "You seem to be wearing a mighty big pair of boots."

Buck grinned. "I've been thinking about getting a new pair. These pinch a mite." He mounted up. "I'll be expecting to hear from you in about a month."

Lyman Gillett didn't reply, just stood there watching with a gimlet-eyed gaze.

"You think he's gonna tell us when he starts roundup?" Zeke asked when Buck related what had happened.

"No, but he knows I'll know the minute he does." They rode for a while in silence.

"He's going to fight if you set one foot on his land," Zeke said.

"I know."

"What are you going to do?"

"Set both feet on it."

Zeke grinned. "Now you're sounding like Jake. You'll get yourself killed."

"Jake never got killed."

"He's a lucky sonofabitch. You and me, we ain't never had any luck."

"We got lucky when Isabelle found me and Jake hid you from Rupert Reison."

Zeke's silence didn't surprised Buck. Zeke hated to be told he owed anything to anybody.

They rode for a while, Buck talking about his plans for the ranch, Zeke telling him how impossible they were. Buck occasionally glanced over his shoulder. He wouldn't have been surprised if Gillett had sent someone to make sure he left the ranch, but no one followed.

"Is that smoke?" Zeke asked, pointing to a thin trail of gray showing against the distant trees.

"Looks like it, but what would anybody be doing with a fire this time of day?"

"You think someone's branding rustled cows?"

"I'll check it out."

"And I'll watch your back."

By the time Buck got close to where Zeke had seen the smoke, the gray streak had disappeared.

"I don't see it anymore, either," Zeke said as he rode up, "but I'm sure it was smoke."

Buck turned his face into the drifting afternoon breeze. "I can smell it. It's coming from those trees over there."

They found the remains of a fire.

"These coals are still hot," Buck said as he kicked sand over the fire.

"They probably saw us coming and lit out," Zeke said. "Come on. Let's see if we can find where they went."

They followed the hoofprints in the soft dirt. When the tracks disappeared, Zeke looked for broken twigs and trampled grass. It wasn't long before they found a yearling.

"Let's get a rope on him."

"I've never seen this brand," Zeke said when they had the yearling on its side.

Buck stared thoughtfully at the six-pointed star. "Neither have I, but it fits right over the Tumbling T brand. It's a perfect operation."

"Let's go back and get the bastard," Zeke said, springing to his feet.

"No. Just because it happened on Rafter D range doesn't mean Lyman Gillett is responsible. Rustlers could be hitting both of us."

"I don't believe that."

"Neither do I, but we can't do anything without proof."

Buck let the yearling up. It bawled in protest and headed toward some low hills at a run.

"Probably headed to a canyon where he spent the winter," Buck said.

The idea struck them both at the same time. If there was a Tumbling T yearling in that canyon, there might be cows there as well. They trailed the yearling only to find the other cattle had already been branded with the new brand.

"We ought to drive them back to the ranch," Zeke said.

"We'd be rustling," Buck said. "I've got to have time to think."

"You'd better do it fast."

"I will. In the meantime, let's see if we can find any more canyons."

They did. A nearly invisible fence of brush covered with morning glory vines had been constructed at the mouth of a canyon. All the cows behind it bore the Tumbling T brand. None of the calves had been branded.

"Let's take these back," Buck said as he began to tear down the barrier.

"You think we can get them back to Tumbling T range without anybody on the Rafter D knowing about it?" Zeke asked.

"Probably not," Buck replied. "They'll stir up enough dust to be seen for miles. Let's start them at a trot. I want to get off Rafter D range fast."

But it wouldn't be a quick dash. Even at a trot, it would take at least an hour to get the cows back to Tumbling T range. Buck didn't dare go too fast. The newborn calves couldn't keep up.

Buck wondered how many more of his cattle were secreted away in canyons along the river. He also wondered how he was going to find them without waging an all-out war with Lyman Gillett. Buck didn't know how many hands Gillett employed, but he imagined he and Zeke would be badly outnumbered.

He wondered if the other ranchers had been losing stock. He would have to talk to Walter Evans about it.

They had almost reached their range when Zeke called out, "Somebody's coming."

Buck looked back. A single rider was approaching at a gallop. Buck looked around. He didn't see any other riders, but he wouldn't put it past Gillett to have someone following them under cover. "I'll talk to him," he called back to Zeke. "You keep the stock moving."

Buck turned to meet the oncoming rider. A thin, sandy-haired young man came racing up.

"What the hell are you doing?" he demanded, his gun pointed directly at Buck.

"I've been talking to your boss about a joint roundup," Buck said.

Buck was relieved to see that mention of his meeting with Lyman Gillett relieved some of the cowhand's suspicions, though not enough to cause him to put his gun away.

"What are you doing with those cows?" the cowhand demanded.

"They're ours," Buck said. "We found them in a canyon back yonder. Figured we might as well drive them to our range as long as we were here. You're welcome to check the brand."

"You're damned right I'll check 'em."

He jammed his gun into its holster, drove his spurs into his mount's flanks, and galloped off after the cows. Buck followed more slowly. He looked around but didn't see anyone else. Apparently the young cowhand had come alone. Buck had to admire the courage it took to face two strangers who could be rustling his boss's cattle. This was the kind of hand Buck wanted working for him.

"Did you find any Rafter D brands?" Buck asked when the cowhand has finished checking the cows.

"No. Sorry to pull a gun on you, but I can't let strangers run off with cattle without checking."

"I understand. Been here long?"

"Does it show that much?" The cowhand relaxed and smiled. "Just signed on. Don't want to mess up my first week."

Whatever Gillett was doing, this guy knew nothing about it.

"You can tell Mr. Gillett what I've done. Make sure to tell him they were all my brand."

"I thought two women owned the Tumbling T," the cowhand said.

"They did until I bought half. I'm Buck Hobson. My friend is named Zeke."

"Tom Gladdis," the cowhand said.

"See you at roundup," Buck said and rode off.

"He going to cause trouble?" Zeke asked when Buck caught up.

"No."

"You think he'll bring Gillett down on us?"

"I doubt it." He kept looking over his shoulder, but Tom Gladdis was soon out of sight.

"How many more you think they got hidden away?" Zeke asked as they approached the limits of Rafter D range.

"Several hundred at least," Buck said. "They've had nearly a year to rustle them."

"How many do you think they've branded?"

"I can't tell. I wasn't looking for that brand until we found the fire."

"They could get nearly everything branded in a month."

Buck had realized that, but the sound of a bullet whizzing by his head and the echo of a rifle shot gave his thoughts a whole new direction.

"Somebody's shooting at us!" Zeke shouted as he leaned low in the saddle and galloped his horse toward some tall brush. "Looks like your Tom Gladdis went for help after all."

Buck galloped after the cows, which were in full flight.

"Gladdis rode in the opposite direction."

Two more shots rang out.

"Keep driving the cows toward our range," Buck shouted.

"We're on our range," Zeke shouted back.

Another shot echoed through the hills, but not before Buck felt a searing pain in his shoulder. His strength seemed to drain from his body, leaving him weak and struggling to stay in the saddle. He cursed the cowardly rifleman who had drygulched him from cover. Buck had expected Lyman Gillett to face him in the open, like a man.

"We're almost out of range," Zeke shouted. "You take the cows in. I'll go back after him."

Buck used what little strength he had left to keep from falling, but he didn't have enough. He could feel his grip on the saddle loosen. The tops of cedar bushes lashed his face. He closed his eyes, concentrated on remaining conscious.

Just when he thought he could hold on no longer, he felt a strong hand grasp his shirt and lift him back into the saddle.

"Why didn't you tell me the sonofabitch hit you?" Zeke said.

"Had . . . to . . . get . . . the cows . . . back."

"Damn the cows! They won't do you any good if you're dead."

Buck tried to grin. Zeke was so sentimental.

* * *

Hannah had had a very frustrating day. Nothing had actually gone wrong, but everything felt wrong. It began when her mother got up before dawn to fix Buck's breakfast. Sarah Grossek avoided men; she didn't cook their breakfast. The fact that she tried her best to disappear into the wall when Zeke came to the table left Hannah feeling guilty because she had failed to hold up her part of the bargain on her first morning.

"There's no need for both of us to be up so early," her mother had said once the men had left.

"I made the bargain," Hannah had replied. "It's my responsibility to stick to it."

"You have more than enough to do outside. I can tend to the cooking."

"Make sure you wake me tomorrow," Hannah had said as she headed out to do the milking.

Next Hannah had been surprised that her mother didn't run into the house when Walter Evans rode up. Ever since the day her father had hit her for offering Walter a cup of coffee, she had avoided him.

"Did you hire those two young men I spoke to yesterday?" Walter asked as he sat down to enjoy the cup of coffee Sarah brought him.

"Not exactly," Hannah said. "He was looking for a partnership, not a job."

"You sent him away?"

She thought Walter tensed. Now why should he care what she did?

"No. The bank didn't give us any choice." She hated to tell him that, but she figured he'd find out soon enough.

"Good. He seems a very determined young man."

He relaxed. She wasn't mistaken. He actually

leaned back in his chair. Now what could that be about?

"I won't care what he's like if he can help me pay off the debt on this place."

"You planning to stay here?"

"Why not?"

Walter shaded his eyes from the sun and looked up at her. "I thought your mother might prefer to live in town. It must be hard work to run a place like this."

"We'll manage."

"You like ranching?"

"Yes."

"Your mother, too?"

The faint tone of skepticism in Walter's voice stopped Hannah from saying yes. She didn't want to live in Utopia, but did she really prefer ranching to living in a town? She thought she did, but she felt certain her mother didn't.

Walter didn't wait for her answer. "Your garden's ahead of mine," he said. "What are you planting this year?"

She ended up discussing vegetables and promising to sell him any she could spare.

After Walter left, her mother went inside. Hannah finished her work in the garden and went inside to find that her mother had spent the last couple of hours cleaning Buck's room from top to bottom.

"He said he didn't want us in here," Hannah said.

"He didn't mean it," her mother said. "Men never want their things touched, but they always want them kept in order."

"Then why did he tell me to keep out?"

"It makes them feel strong, like they don't need anybody."

Hannah looked at her mother with new eyes. As long as she could remember, her mother had hardly seen any man except her husband. Yet here she was talking as if she'd studied men all her life.

"What makes you say that?" Hannah asked.

Her mother smiled faintly, and Hannah felt a warmth surge through her. She couldn't remember when her mother had smiled.

"I haven't been locked up in this house all my life. I was late marrying, like you."

"I'm not getting married."

"I was also pretty. I had lots of gentleman callers. Until we moved here, we lived in town. I talked with other women, observed their husbands and what they required. Nearly all men are the same."

"If you had so many suitors, why did you marry Papa?" Hannah's mother had never talked about her life. Hannah had never known any of this.

"Nathaniel Grossek offered my father money. Now we'd better start thinking about what to cook for dinner. I imagine those men are going to be starved when they get in."

Hannah had been too stunned by her mother's disclosure to pay much attention to her rambling conversation about the probable likes and dislikes of Buck and Zeke. She had always known her mother didn't love her father, but it shocked her to know she had been bought and sold like a slave. No wonder her father had treated his wife like a piece of property. That was exactly what she had been.

An icy fear crept through Hannah. Would her father have sold her into marriage to Lyman Gillett or Amos Merrick if he were still alive? Somehow she expected he would.

Hannah was deep in thought when she heard her mother gasp. When she looked up, her mother was staring out the kitchen window in the direction of the barn.

"What is it?" she asked.

"It's Buck," her mother said as she took a pot off the stove, wiped her hands, and hurried to the door. "He's been hurt."

Chapter Six

Hannah raced outside and across the packed earth toward the barn, her thoughts and emotions in a wild jumble. She couldn't explain why she should be so upset over an injury to a man who had arrived little more than a day before. But somehow she knew nothing would ever be right again if anything happened to Buck.

When she got close, she saw that a dark patch of blood had soaked his shirt. "What happened?" she cried.

"Some bastard on the Rafter D shot him," Zeke said.

Hannah tried to hold Buck in the saddle until Zeke could dismount. He felt warm, soft, vital. She couldn't believe he could die.

"What were you doing there?"

"Buck had the crazy idea he ought to tell Gillett

your cows had drifted onto his land before he went looking for them."

Her mother helped her support Buck's weight until Zeke could catch him.

"But why would anybody shoot him?"

She wanted to help Zeke carry Buck, but Zeke could do better without her help. She ran ahead to open the door. Her mother had already run inside.

"We found some of your cows in a canyon," Zeke explained haltingly as he labored under Buck's weight.

"What were they doing there?"

Zeke paused long enough to cast her a withering glance. "Somebody put them there. The Rafter D is rustling your cows."

Hannah might not want to marry Lyman Gillett, but he seemed too respectable and handsome to be a thief.

She ran ahead to Buck's room. Her mother had already turned down the bed. Towels and a basin of water waited on the table.

"Lay him on his stomach," Hannah said. "We'll have to cut off his shirt."

"No. Unbutton it."

Buck's voice was weak and faint, but his ability to argue encouraged Hannah to hope he wasn't seriously injured.

"Buck's the stingiest man alive," Zeke said. "No point in throwing away a perfectly good shirt when all it needs is mending."

"And a good washing," Hannah said, marveling that Buck could worry about saving money at a time like this.

Zeke turned him over and Hannah started to unbutton his shirt. Buck made a feeble attempt to push her hands away.

"Zeke," he said.

"Taking care of sick people is women's work," Zeke said. "I'm going to get the man who shot you."

"No. There's too many of them," Buck said. "They'll kill you."

"They won't see me. I don't aim to walk up and introduce myself first." He turned to Hannah. "You better not let anything happen to him."

It was a warning, even a threat. "He needs a doctor," Hannah said. "The closest one is in Utopia."

Zeke didn't hesitate. "I'll get him."

"He won't come," Buck said. "I remember him. He—"

"He'll come," Zeke promised.

Hannah thought she detected a slight quiver in his voice. If so, it was the first sign of emotion she'd seen Zeke display.

"We'll have to see to his wound," Hannah said to her mother. "He could bleed to death before the doctor gets here. Help me undress him."

But her mother backed away. It was clear that her new-found ease around men didn't extend to undressing them, even if it was only removing a shirt.

Hannah didn't feel too comfortable herself. She'd always been kept away from men. She'd never been allowed in the kitchen while the hands ate their meals. She'd never touched a man's body in her life. She'd never seen one naked, not even to the waist. She'd certainly never contemplated undressing one.

Tremors of excitement shot through her. She remembered the hard feel of Buck's body, the weight, the size. He was young and handsome and virile, and she was responding to him in a way that had never happened with Amos Merrick or Lyman Gillett. The chance to touch him was impossible to resist.

"Don't bother," Buck said.

"I have to clean the wound."

"The doctor can do it."

"He's not here."

"He will be. I can wait."

Hannah realized he wasn't saying this from a sense of modesty. He didn't want her to touch him. His dislike of her went so deep, he'd rather lie in his blood and dirt than have her touch him.

"You don't have to like me to let me help you."

His look was stony.

"I don't have to like you, either."

No change. That made her angry. He was being stupid and stubborn. She didn't think much of the male intelligence, but she'd expected more from him.

"You can't fulfill your part of the contract like this," she snapped angrily

He glared at her, but said, "Okay, go ahead."

Despite his acquiescence, his look dared her to touch him. She reached out but drew her hand back.

"I won't bite you," Buck said.

"I'm not so sure," she replied, disgusted with herself for being cowardly, angry at Buck for sensing her uncertainty.

"You must know how to undo buttons. You've got a whole row of them down the front of your dress."

She was suddenly acutely aware of the feel of her clothes against her body, the pressure they exerted on her breasts, waist, and abdomen. It was almost as though Buck himself were touching her with his eyes. She had to struggle against a compulsion to draw away from him, to cover herself.

"I know you can't stand me," he said. "Forget it."

"That's not it," Hannah protested. "It's just that I'm not used to men."

"Maybe I should have asked Zeke to stay and sent you for the doctor."

Hannah was getting madder and madder at herself and at Buck, but not quite mad enough to overcome her reluctance to touch him.

"If you'd close your eyes . . ."

"Oh, for God's sake," Buck exclaimed, but he did close his eyes.

Hannah forced herself to reach out and begin to unbutton his shirt. She made a fierce effort to think only of the buttons and the thick material of the shirt. But as the shirt opened to expose Buck's chest, it was impossible not to think of the man inside. His chest was white and smooth. A light sprinkling of fine black hair curled between well-developed muscle.

She tried to concentrate on the blood that stained the shirt, but trying to undo the buttons without looking only caused her to touch him more frequently. The last button revealed a faint dusting of hair around his navel. Hannah refused to think of the rest of his body. She could feel herself blush furiously as she pulled his shirttail out of his pants.

"Are you done yet?" Buck asked. "Much longer and I'll go to sleep."

Hannah gave the shirt one last tug. She wasn't entirely sorry when she saw Buck wince.

"You'll have to turn over," she said. "I can't get your shirt off if you don't."

"I can't."

"He could lose too much blood," Hannah said to her mother. "You have to help me. I can't do it by myself."

87

Hannah could see her mother's struggle. Buck could as well. It brought about the same transformation in him she'd seen yesterday in the kitchen.

"It's all right," Buck said in that tone he had so far reserved for Hannah's mother. "You don't have to touch me if it upsets you."

Hannah didn't understand what magic Buck possessed, but it released her mother from her indecision. Between the two of them, they rolled Buck over and positioned him in the middle of the bed. After a good deal of struggle, Hannah was able to get the shirt off his good shoulder. She pulled it to one side.

She gasped in shock when she saw his back.

A mass of scars covered his skin from neck to waist, from side to side, even along his shoulders and upper arms. Time and care had healed the flesh, but Hannah had no trouble seeing that Buck had been beaten cruelly and often.

This was what her own father had done to him.

She looked up to see her own horror reflected in her mother's face. She didn't know what she could have done to prevent the beatings, but she felt tremendous guilt that she hadn't even known about them. Her father had never hit her or her mother hard enough to leave scars. Their bruises healed without trace. She'd assumed it had been no worse for Buck. He had endured all this in silence and had still stopped her father from beating her that hot August afternoon.

She had rewarded him by ignoring him.

It didn't matter that she had done to it to keep him from getting more beatings. It didn't matter that she had been grateful to him, had worried about him, had even prayed for him. It only mattered that she had done nothing to stop this from happening to him.

Little wonder he hated her and wanted to take her ranch.

Staring at those scars brought the misery of the last years flooding back. Hannah remembered the fear in her mother's eyes as she moved about the house trying to anticipate her husband's wishes, to avoid his attention. Hannah remembered her own fear as she tried to protect her mother from rages that grew worse as the ranch sank deeper into debt.

Hannah turned away from Buck's scars and forced herself to speak. "Can you lift yourself? I want to get the shirt off without moving your arm."

"Just pull it off," Buck said.

"It'll hurt."

"Just do it."

Before her courage could desert her, Hannah took hold of the shirt and pulled. Buck groaned, but the shirt came off. Her mother moistened a cloth and handed it to Hannah. Slowly and carefully she cleaned the blood away from the small, ugly-looking hole where the bullet had entered his shoulder.

But even as she cleaned the blood from his skin, Hannah found it difficult to accept that Buck was lying there with a bullet wound in his shoulder. She had known there was violence in the world, but the men of Utopia shielded their women from seeing it. Seeing Buck's scars made Hannah feel naive and stupid.

Equally upsetting was the disturbing confusion of feelings that touching Buck created in her. Somewhere deep inside her, masked by fear, revulsion and guilt, another set of feelings stirred to life. Unnamed and unanticipated, they caused her body to act in a totally unexpected fashion—nerves seemed to twitch and flutter, her limbs took on a slight tremor, and a decidedly uneasy feeling settled in her belly.

Hannah had never experienced anything like this, but she decided it wasn't the shock of seeing so much human blood. There was something too pleasant about these feelings, which made them all that much more perplexing.

She picked up his shirt. There was a second bullet hole in the front. "The bullet went through."

"Good. At least the sawbones won't have to dig around in me to get it."

"Dr. Yant is a very fine doctor."

He was also a member of the council that ruled Utopia. She doubted he could be persuaded to come this far for a non-Utopian, particularly by a black cowboy.

"I'll let you know what I think of him," Buck said.

Hannah decided she must do what she could to make him comfortable, then leave him alone. Following her mother's whispered instructions, she folded pads over the wound and bound it up so it wouldn't bleed.

She suddenly remembered their dinner left on the stove. "Are you hungry?"

"Starved," Buck replied.

But she didn't know what to feed a wounded man. "I'd better wait until the doctor gets here."

"If you weren't going to fed me, why did you mention it?"

"I guess because I'm hungry myself. We'll wait."

"Your mother's hungry. She's got to eat."

Hannah looked up, but her mother shook her head.

"Mother says she'll wait, too."

"I hope that doctor isn't long getting here," Buck muttered.

He got there a lot quicker than Hannah expected.

"That damned black fool held a gun on me all the way here," the doctor announced the moment he stepped through the door.

"Would you have come if I hadn't?" Zeke asked.

"Hell, no. I missed my dinner."

"You can eat with us as soon as you've taken care of Buck," Hannah said.

"I never had anybody drag me out this far for a cowhand," the doctor fumed. "They usually just wrap it up and keep going."

"Buck is more than a cowhand," Hannah said, irritated and embarrassed by the doctor's attitude. "He wants to buy an interest in this ranch."

The doctor looked surprised. "Does Joseph Merrick know that?"

"He said if I didn't take Buck on, he'd sell the ranch."

"Money's tight," Dr. Yant said. "Joseph can't afford to ignore your father's loans. That money is needed elsewhere."

"That's because your people are fool enough to try to farm land that's not good for anything but running cows," Buck said.

"Our people aren't ranchers," Dr. Yant said, looking at Buck for the first time. "They're merchants and craftsmen."

"Then they ought to move to Austin or San Antonio."

"We prefer to build our own community."

"Stop gabbing and fix him up," Zeke said. "We don't care about you or your community."

The doctor looked at Zeke as if he was something he'd like to squash under his foot, and Hannah felt embarrassed all over again. That must have been how her father had felt about Buck, too.

"I cleaned the wound and tried to stop the bleeding," Hannah said, drawing Dr. Yant's attention to Buck. "I think the bullet passed through."

"Then you shouldn't have bothered me," he complained. "There's nothing I can do."

"You can make sure he doesn't get gangrene," Zeke said.

"Nobody can guarantee that," the doctor said.

"You'd better. If he dies, you die."

Hannah decided Zeke meant exactly what he said. Apparently Dr. Yant thought so, too. He gave Buck his full attention.

"There's nothing more I can do," he said about fifteen minutes later. "You did a nice job cleaning him up. Just keep the wound bandaged. Sprinkle it with bacilicum powder if you change the bandage."

"Make sure you boil those bandages before you wash them," Zeke added.

"Who told you to do that?" Dr. Yant asked, suspicious.

"We lived next to a *real* doctor where we grew up," Buck explained.

"You two grew up together?"

"We were adopted by the same family."

Dr. Yant's expression made it plain that he felt he'd wasted his time. Hannah was relieved when he decided not to stay for dinner. After the way he'd acted, she wasn't sure she could have served him. She was certain he wouldn't have agreed to eat at the same table with Zeke.

"I'll be back with your dinner soon," she said to Buck when she returned after seeing the doctor out.

"I can go to the table."

"No. You can't work unless you get well. You'll

stay in that bed until I say you're ready to get up."

"You going to change my clothes and give me a bath as well?"

She couldn't decide if he was angry, taunting her, or both. It didn't matter. For the next few days, she was in control.

"Zeke can help you undress," she said and hurried out the door before he could make a response.

Hannah knocked on Buck's bedroom door.

"Come in."

She entered and set his dinner on a table by the bed. Zeke had helped Buck out of his clothes. His pants lay across the end of the bed; his boots stood in the corner. It made her nervous to know he was naked under the sheet. She couldn't believe she was even thinking about such things, but the awareness wouldn't leave her. The sight of Buck's bare chest set her heart to beating so fast that she felt light-headed.

"Mama has your dinner on the table," she said to Zeke.

"He can eat in here with me," Buck said.

"It would make a lot of unnecessary work for Mama. He can come back later to talk about anything you haven't discussed."

"No need," Zeke said. "I know what I'm going to do." He went out without a backward glance.

Hannah pulled a chair up next to the bed. She sat down and took up a bowl and spoon from the tray.

"What are you doing?"

"I can't feed you standing up."

"I can feed myself."

"No, you can't. You're injured."

"That bushwacker shot me in the right shoulder. I eat with my left hand."

"I don't mind feeding you."

"Put it on the tray."

Hannah put the bowl and spoon back on the tray, folded her hands in her lap, and leaned back in the chair.

"I suppose this is as good a time as any to have a talk," she began.

"Dammit, woman, give me my food. I'm hungry. I don't want to talk."

"We'll talk first. Then you'll eat."

"The hell I will."

"That's something else I want to mention."

"What?"

"Profanity. You won't use it in the house. It upsets my mother."

That got him. He opened his mouth a couple of times but obviously rejected his choice of words. "Why?" he finally asked.

"Because she was taught it was the language of the Devil."

"That's the most preposterous thing I ever heard."

"Possibly, but it still upsets her."

He looked mulish. "Okay, I won't cuss when she's around."

"Not in the house. Men shout when they get angry. They forget people can hear through walls."

"I don't shout. Isabelle wouldn't allow it."

She had to meet Isabelle. This woman apparently had the power to turn men into half-human creatures.

"Now can I eat?"

"We haven't talked."

"I just promised not to cuss in the house."

"I just thought of that."

Buck's expression was one of strained patience. "What else?"

"Are you going to tell me what happened, who did this to you and why?"

"Don't worry about it. I'll take care of it."

"You're not going to tell me?"

"Why should I?"

"Because this is still my ranch."

"You take care of everything here at the house. I'll take care of the rest."

"Maybe I could help."

"You can't."

She struggled to control her frustration. "What do you propose to do about it?"

"I haven't decided yet."

"Will you tell me when you do?"

"I'll tell you anything you need to know."

He wasn't going to tell her. He was like every other man she had ever met. He didn't think women had the sense to understand a man's business, wouldn't want them meddling anyway.

She considered withholding his food until he told her, but decided that wasn't a good idea. He'd probably do himself an injury trying to reach the tray. He'd dislike her even more.

"You have anything else to complain of?" he asked.

"You don't like me," she said when she felt calm enough to speak without spitting the words at him. "I guess I can't expect you to after what my father did to you. But if we're going to work together, we've got to come to some kind of understanding."

His expression remained fixed.

"I never suspected my father beat you as badly as he did. I couldn't believe what I saw when I removed your shirt. It won't help to tell you I hated my father, that my mother and I were both afraid of him. I think you know that already."

He didn't make any sign that he understood or cared.

"I don't know what I could have done to stop him, but I'm ashamed I didn't try. I thought I was doing the right thing when I ignored you. I see now I was wrong. I was only fourteen. I didn't understand what was going on. I'm not offering that as an excuse. I'm just trying to explain the way things were."

His face might have been carved out of stone, but hostility flamed in his eyes. He might pretend to feel nothing, but she could tell rage still burned in his heart.

"I wanted to like you when you rode up yesterday. I wanted to believe you were here because you wanted to help Mama and me. I understand now how foolish that was, but that doesn't mean we can't at least be civil with each other."

"Why should you care whether I'm civil or not?"

He asked the question in a soft voice, but Hannah felt the dammed-up emotion behind it.

"I used to worry about you. Mama, too. I know you don't believe that, but we did. We knew my father worked you too hard. I worried when you ran away. I hoped you were safe."

It was obvious he didn't believe anything she said. Maybe he'd been emotionally battered for too long to believe anybody could care about him.

"I don't know why you're so nice to Mama, but I would like you for that if nothing more. She doesn't avoid you. Even though she's nervous, you can get her to do things I can't. I want her to be the sweet, smiling woman I remember. If you can do that, I'll be forever grateful."

"Your mama went through hell."

"And you think I didn't?"

His silence was her answer. It made her angry.

"I didn't get treated a badly as you and Mama, but I've seen more than enough to know I'll never let a man get control of me."

"What do you aim do to?"

"Live on this ranch."

"You don't know how to run it."

"I'll learn from you."

"You're in debt."

"You're going to get me out."

"Suppose I want this ranch, too?"

"You can't have it."

"Suppose I take it?"

"I won't let you. I want to be friends with you, but if you give me no other choice, I'll be your enemy. I'll dog your footsteps. I'll learn what I have to know, I'll keep this ranch, and I'll prosper. Know one thing, Buck Hobson—no man is ever going to do to me what my father did to my mother. I'd kill him, first."

Hannah picked up the bowl and spoon and handed them to Buck. "You'd better eat your dinner before it gets cold."

Chapter Seven

Buck watched Hannah close the door behind her with a feeling of relief. He didn't know what to think about her, and he didn't want her to see his confusion. He didn't want to believe she had ever thought or worried about him. He didn't want to believe she was sorry she hadn't tried to stop her father from beating him. He didn't want to believe she was glad he'd come to help her and her mother.

Most important of all, he didn't want to want her around. He didn't want to see her smile, see the soft curves of her body, feel her touch him, hear her soft tread as she passed his door. Neither did he want his body to swell with hunger when he thought of her sleeping just across the hall.

He hadn't put too much store in such feelings at first. Any normal male would react that way when brought into close contact with an attractive female. He was young, healthy, and sex-starved. It worried him now, though, that with a hole in his shoulder he still lusted after her.

All his life he had exercised tight control over his feelings. It was the way he kept his sanity. Now he was losing his grip, and he didn't like that. He hadn't suspected this weakness in himself. He certainly hadn't expected it to surface with Hannah. Fortunately for him, she didn't appear disposed to take advantage of it.

She wasn't a sentimental female. She wanted him well so he'd be back in the saddle as soon as possible. That was okay with him, but he didn't want her to care, or even to offer sympathy. He couldn't afford to be sidetracked by emotion, not even gratitude. That always led to liking. No telling what might happen after that.

He had to figure out how to get back every longhorn that had "wandered" onto Rafter D range without getting himself and Zeke killed. The wound in his shoulder made it clear that Lyman Gillett didn't mean to give up a single animal, not even the ones that carried the Tumbling T brand. He could only guess how many Gillett had already rebranded.

He intended to get those back as well, but he needed a plan. Jake said a smart man always had a plan. He said the earth was full of the bones of people who barreled headfirst into danger. Buck had no intention of adding his bones to that collection, but he must have those cows. They represented success for him and would provide Hannah and her mother with enough money to get settled somewhere else.

He didn't put much stock in Hannah's vow never to marry. Lots of women declared men worthless, vowed they wanted nothing to do with them, then fell in love with the first handsome, good-for-nothing who came down the road. Buck didn't think Hannah was that flighty, but he was certain she'd accept a decent proposal of marriage rather than attempt to run the ranch by herself.

But not Amos Merrick. Somebody who'd be nice to her and her mother, make them feel loved and valued. They deserved someone good just for having survived Nathaniel Grossek.

Zeke came in without knocking. "You feeling okay?"

"Better since I ate."

"How long you figure on staying in bed?"

"I'll be back in the saddle tomorrow."

"That's what I figured you'd say. You're not getting into any saddle until that arm is well."

Zeke would be appalled to know he was looking at Buck exactly the way Jake did when he was about to deliver a lecture.

"I can't wait that long," Buck said. "We've got to find those cows."

"Yeah, and get yourself killed because you aren't strong enough to fight or stay in the saddle?"

"What do you propose I do, give up and go back to Jake?"

"No. Stay here and get well."

"What are you going to do? You can't fool me into thinking you're going to help Mrs. Grossek with her garden."

"Gillett doesn't know about me," Zeke said. "I'm going to search his place tonight."

"They can still shoot you."

"They won't know I'm there. You can't see black people in the dark," he said dryly.

"If you're all that sly, how come you got captured and sold to Rupert Reison?"

"That was Indians, and I was just eleven. I'm better at it now."

"I don't like it."

"When we go after our cows, we have to know where they are and the quickest way to get them out."

"And you expect me to lie here for days doing nothing while you risk your neck?"

"If you've got to do something, talk to the other ranchers. Gillett's probably been stealing from them, too. Knowing he shot you while you were trying to round up your cows might stir them up. We're going to need help when we go up against him. But if you stay here, stay away from that girl."

"What girl?"

"Hannah."

"Hannah!" Buck couldn't believe Zeke would make such a statement.

"I've seen the way you look at her."

"What the hell are you talking about?"

"You let her feed you."

"I fed myself. I'm not helpless."

"She stayed in here while you ate."

"I didn't think it was a good idea to throw her out. It's her house."

It was absurd to think he was falling for Hannah. She was pretty, sure, and a man couldn't help but indulge in a little fantasizing now and then, but she was Nathaniel Grossek's daughter.

"A man doesn't think right when he's laid up," Zeke said. "That makes it easy for a woman to wiggle her way right where he doesn't want her. Jake didn't want to marry Isabelle until she nursed him back from death's door."

Buck made an exasperated noise. "Jake was in love with Isabelle weeks before. Even Will and Pete could see that. You ought to be damned glad he finally worked up the courage to admit it. You and I'd be dead by now if he hadn't." Not even Zeke could deny their debt to Jake and Isabelle. "Stop worrying I'm going soft over Hannah." Just thinking about her wasn't going soft.

"You're a man without a woman. Seeing her around all the time might make you forget what happened years ago."

"Go to bed, Zeke. You're so tired you're thinking crazy."

"Just as long as you don't start *acting* crazy."

"I'm not likely to forget why I came here. And no more talk about riding all over Gillett's range at night. I don't know what we're going to do, but I'll think of something."

"You take care of your business, and I'll take care of mine." Zeke closed the door behind him with a bang.

Buck frowned. Zeke ought to know Buck wasn't about to let himself get caught on any hook baited by Hannah Grossek. She could wiggle her shapely hips all she wanted. She could wear dresses so tight that his mouth watered just thinking about her breasts, so tight that his hands itched to get around her waist, but it wouldn't do her any good. Just the thought of kissing her made him feel queasy.

And if she thought saying she wanted to like him, that she'd thought about him—actually worried about him—was going to change his opinion of her, she was sadly mistaken. He might be sexually deprived enough to dream of her once in a while, but he was too smart to put his head in the mouth of that particular lion.

Correction. Lioness. There was nothing the slightest bit masculine about Hannah Grossek.

*   *   *

Hannah sank onto the down mattress on her mother's bed. "Buck says Lyman Gillett is rustling our stock. He got shot bringing back some cows he found over there."

Her mother had been sitting up in bed, brushing her hair. She laid down her brush. "How do you know?"

"I listened through the door when he was talking to Zeke. Zeke plans to go out tonight and search in the dark."

"I'm ashamed of you, Hannah Grossek. I never taught you to do that."

"I wouldn't have to if that big idiot would just tell me what's going on."

"Maybe he thinks it's not fitting for women."

"Neither is starving to death or losing our only means of support." Her mood changed abruptly. "He means to get our cows back, even if he has to fight."

"With guns?"

"Rifles, I expect. Guns don't shoot far enough."

"I can't believe you're speaking so casually of people shooting at each other. Buck could get killed."

"I know. Then we wouldn't be able to pay off the debt."

"Aren't you concerned about him?"

"Of course I am. If he's flat on his back, he can't do his job."

"Hannah, I'm surprised at you."

"I'm sorry, but I'm angry with him for not talking to me. Now I'm scared he's going to get himself killed and we'll be penniless."

"Don't you care if he gets killed?"

"I just said—"

"I mean *care?*"

Hannah stopped abruptly. "I don't know him well enough to care."

"Do you remember when he stopped your father from beating you?"

"Of course."

"Do you remember what you told me then?"

"No." She had said a great deal about her father, but she didn't remember saying anything about Buck.

"You said you couldn't help him then except by ignoring him, but if you ever got a chance, you'd lay down your life for him."

Hannah wasn't ready to go that far, but she didn't want anyone hurt. It would be a particular shame if someone as young and handsome as Buck were to be killed. A girl somewhere must be pining for him right now. Not that she thought Buck was pining in return. All he yearned for right now was her ranch.

"That was six years ago, Mama. I was too young to know what I was saying."

"You could at least be concerned for his safety."

"I guess I am, but it's hard when he treats me like I'm too stupid to understand anything about men's business."

"I don't know why you'd want to."

"So I won't ever be in this position again. I don't intend to have to marry some man just to have a roof over my head."

"Then let him do what he came here to do. If he wins, so do we. Now get your rest. There's always a lot more to do when there's a sick man in the house."

Hannah kissed her mother and went to her room, but her room seemed empty and friendless tonight, her bed cold and lonely. Odd, she'd never felt that way before. She'd looked forward to the solitude and the quiet. It had been a place of repose, refuge, release from the tensions and uncertainties of the day.

But not tonight, and it was all Buck Hobson's fault. He had upset her equilibrium and sowed seeds of doubt. Hannah didn't like that. She preferred to be absolutely certain of her course and its rightness.

She moved away from the bed toward the window. But staring into the deep shadows provided no answers. She had to be honest. She had to blame herself for her loss of equilibrium. Buck hadn't done anything to make himself attractive, hadn't even tried to be nice. Hannah had let herself be dazzled by his masculine good looks.

Hannah didn't know why she should be attracted to Buck—and she admitted now that was the embarrassing source of her problem—and not Amos Merrick. Both were big, handsome men, sure of themselves, not aggressive but confident, exactly the kind of man any woman would swoon over.

But not her.

She knew what men were like, even the best of them. Her body had never betrayed her until now. *It* made her feel cold and lonely. *It* kept her awake when her mind said it was time to rest. *It* kept reminding her there was a man in the next room, naked beneath those covers. *It* reminded her of the warmth of his skin, the hardness of his muscles.

She folded her arms and hugged them to her body to ward off the night chill. Or was it a chill of the heart? Her body cared nothing for his stony silences or pitiless glances. Instead it recalled the feel of his hard body as he tumbled from the saddle, the gentle rise and fall of his stomach under her fingers as she unbuttoned his shirt, the intense heat that flowed into her fingertips every time she touched him.

Hannah felt her nipples grow hard, her skin so sensitive that she could hardly stand the feel of her rough nightgown. The slightest movement sent tremors all through her. Nothing like this had happened before. It left her casting wildly about for some way to regain control over herself.

Reminding herself that Buck didn't like her, that he intended to take her ranch, didn't seem to be enough tonight. Every time she concentrated on that, she would remember his kindness to her mother and know he wasn't as hard and unfeeling as he pretended.

Or was he? He liked Zeke, though they seemed to have nothing in common beyond having been beaten and treated as slaves. Maybe that was the reason he was kind to her mother—he saw her as one of them. Maybe he would dislike and distrust anyone who hadn't suffered as he had.

The endless questions exhausted Hannah. She could see no point in looking for answers. She didn't want Buck to remain on the ranch one minute after his six months was up. She intended to send him off to worry somebody else out of their sleep.

She crawled into bed, turned on her side, and pounded the feather pillow with her fist. She *would* go to sleep. But the bed didn't feel any warmer or less lonely.

Buck sat at the kitchen table and stared at the food on his plate. It looked like beef, but it tasted as if it had been soaked in vinegar. "What is this?" he asked, irritable because his shoulder pained him and because Zeke hadn't come up to the house for breakfast. Buck was worried he'd gotten himself shot.

He was also irritated that his attraction to Hannah seemed to be stronger than ever. Having to stay in the house for several days would only keep his body in turmoil. He wanted to throw her down and lose himself in her softness. Maybe then his thoughts wouldn't be cloudy, his body on fire, his brain hot with lust.

"It's beef," Hannah said.

"What did you do to it?"

"It's pickled."

He pushed his plate away in disgust. "I can't eat that."

Mrs. Grossek silently offered him a plate filled with what appeared to be a white paste with large lumps in it. "What in God's name is that?"

"Dried herring," Hannah said.

It smelled like rotten herring.

"Don't you have anything normal like pork chops or bacon? How about jelly and biscuits?"

"You didn't complain yesterday," Hannah said.

"That's because you fixed sausage and those pancake things. I didn't mind them."

"They were potato fritters."

"I don't care what you call them. I can't eat this."

"What do you usually eat?" Hannah asked, annoyance in her tone of voice.

"Bacon, beef, and venison when we could get it. Vegetables, canned fruit, tomatoes, rice, beans, and potatoes."

"I mean for breakfast."

"Fried bacon or sausage, potatoes or corn cakes with biscuits and jam, though I wouldn't mind some of those eggs over yonder."

"I'm saving them to sell."

"The agreement says you can sell what we don't need here. I think you can spare three for breakfast."

Hannah looked as if she was about to refuse, but apparently she reconsidered. "I'll make biscuits."

"Isabelle makes the best biscuits you ever tasted."

That piece of information didn't appear to please Hannah. "I'm sure mine won't be as good, but I doubt you'll choke. You will have to wait while I make them."

"What are you going to do with that?" he said, pointing to the sour-tasting beef.

"I'll eat it."

Buck cringed. "I'll go see what's keeping Zeke."

"Would you like me to make coffee?"

Buck turned, surprised that Sarah Grossek had spoken to him. "Yes, please. The stronger the better."

Mrs. Grossek nodded and went on eating that terrible mess on her plate. Buck hurried out of the kitchen.

Zeke rode in just as Buck crossed to the barn.

"You shouldn't be out of bed," Zeke said when Buck reached the corral. Zeke was unsaddling his horse. The animal looked sweaty and tired. Whatever Zeke had done, he'd used his horse hard.

"I was coming to make sure you hadn't gotten yourself killed," Buck said.

"I rode all over Rafter D range, nobody any wiser. I brought a dozen or so cows back with me."

"You are crazy."

"Nothing to it. Those people are so sure of themselves, they don't post night guards."

Buck knew it was useless to tell Zeke what he was

doing was dangerous. He'd have to tie him up to stop him.

"Well, what did you find?"

"I found Tumbling T stock everywhere. Not all that's missing, but maybe half of it. Most of it's mixed in with their stock. No way to get at them without combing the entire range."

"How much of that new brand did you see?"

"Enough to account for the cows we're missing."

That was what Buck had figured. And if he was any judge, Gillett was going to set every man on the place to branding Tumbling T cattle before the roundup. If he got most of them branded, he'd probably join the roundup just to prove that only a few Tumbling T cows had drifted onto his land.

Buck had to figure some way to avoid that, but right now he couldn't think about anything except his empty stomach.

"Come on up to the house. Hannah's fixing eggs."

"I don't like eggs much."

"You'll like them a lot more than that sour beef she tried to serve me."

"Maybe we could get Isabelle to teach her how to cook."

"Hannah listen to Isabelle! She'd serve us roasted coyote first."

"You wouldn't like it," Zeke said. "Too stringy."

"You ate coyote?"

"You eat what you can find when you're on the run."

Buck decided he never would know Zeke. Every time he thought he knew all there was, Zeke would come up with something like that.

Buck settled into the chair, unable to make up his mind whether to be angry or to sit back and enjoy being taken care of. His plans for riding had come to nothing. Neither Hannah nor Zeke had to tell him he was too weak to stay in the saddle, much less climb into it. After breakfast he'd gone back to bed hoping to feel stronger by midday. He didn't. It was either go back to bed, stay in the house, or sit outside.

He chose outside, but he was restless. Every minute he stayed here he could feel his chances of getting this ranch slipping away. Every day, every hour, gave Gillett a chance to brand more cattle. It made Buck nearly wild with impatience, but if he even tried to ride, Hannah would wake Zeke to pull him out of the saddle.

She'd told him so.

Mrs. Grossek was the other part of the problem. She had fussed over him, fixed twice as much food as he could possibly eat, made certain he was comfortable, changed his bandage, brought him coffee, tried to do everything for him. Even after she started work in the garden and he dozed in a chair, she came over to make certain he wasn't hungry or thirsty.

It made him uncomfortable when people did things for him. That kind of attention wouldn't last. His parents had gotten tired of him and thrown him away; others would, too. If Mrs. Grossek hadn't been as skittish as a chipmunk, he'd have told her flat out to leave him alone. As it was, she didn't slow down until Hannah complained that she had worn a path through the garden.

He'd never had the opportunity to sit and watch women work before. He'd taken it for granted that working with cows was more difficult. More important. In addition to fixing meals and cleaning up afterward, the two women had cared for the livestock, milked, picked up eggs, and strained the milk.

After that, Hannah and her mother had worked steadily in their garden. Buck thought it ought to be referred to as the five-acre field. They couldn't possibly break it all up by hand. He'd have to ask Evans if he could borrow a mule and a plow. Zeke would hate it, but he could break up the garden in a day. It would take a month by hand.

Sensing danger, Buck opened his eyes. Hannah stood over him, staring down with a steely gaze.

"You spent the morning in bed."

He covered his eyes so he could look up at her. "So?"

"So you can't be sleepy."

"I can't ride. What do you expect me to do?"

"You could help us."

Buck looked at the perspiration on Hannah's forehead, the dirt streaked on her cheek and arms, the smudges on her dress.

"How?" All of the boys had been required to help with Isabelle's garden, but he wasn't about to let Hannah know that.

"You can plant the potatoes."

"I can't drop them into a row and carry the basket at the same time."

"I'll do that. You can cover them up."

"I can't use a hoe."

"Then use your feet to push the dirt over the potatoes."

He looked down. He was wearing lace-up boots.

"Don't tell me you're too weak to push a little dirt around. Or is working in the garden one of the things men don't do?"

He stood. He would help her plant her damned potatoes.

"Don't forget your hat," Hannah said. "I wouldn't want the sun to get in your eyes."

She turned and marched away before he could tell her he didn't appreciate uppity females. He didn't believe in mistreating women, but he believed they ought to be respectful. That was the only thing he held against Isabelle. There were times when she made it clear she didn't think there was a male on the place with the sense God gave a goose. It never bothered Jake, but it always annoyed Buck.

He picked up his hat and followed Hannah into the garden. The dirt was soft under his feet. He didn't want to think of the hours of backbreaking work that represented. He might not like Hannah Grossek, but he couldn't say she didn't carry her part of the load.

"Don't put more than an inch of dirt over them," Hannah told him as she dropped potato slices into the prepared row. "It's still cold at night. If we get a heavy rain, they'll rot before they can sprout."

"I know that." Isabelle had taught him more about gardening than he ever wanted to know. He pushed dirt over the first piece of potato. He covered it too deep. It was easier to do this with a hoe. He dragged some of the dirt off.

"If you don't speed up, I'll have to do half your work for you."

He looked up. Hannah was already a dozen feet down the row. She didn't stop or look up as she talked. She kept right on dropping potato slices at regular intervals. Every one landed in the center of the row. At this rate, she'd be finished before he got really started.

"I can do this right, or I can do it fast," he said.

This time she did stop and look up. "Mama can

113

do it fast and right. You want to change with her?"

Mrs. Grossek was staking peas, something Buck couldn't possibly do with only one arm.

"Don't worry. I'll get them covered."

"I'll be done milking first."

He hated sarcastic women. "Probably."

He worked steadily, refusing to look up, refusing to discover if Hannah continued to pull away from him. He was feeling stronger this afternoon. He'd be back in the saddle tomorrow. Then she could deal with her garden by herself.

"Are you sure this isn't going to hurt your shoulder?"

Buck was still unused to hearing Mrs. Grossek speak. He wondered if she had ceased talking to keep from offending her husband.

"He's not a baby, Mama," Hannah said. "A little pain won't hurt him."

Male pride caused Buck to square his shoulders and swagger just a tiny bit. "I'm fine, Mrs. Grossek, but thanks for asking." He kept right on covering potatoes. Now that he had the hang of it, he moved faster. He looked up. He wouldn't catch up with Hannah, but she wouldn't get any farther ahead. She paused to examine his work as she passed him going down the next row.

"You learn quickly."

He couldn't figure out whether she was merely surprised or was baiting him. Either way, he didn't like it.

"A man can do anything a woman can."

That statement wasn't a challenge, simply the consequence of his irritation at her constant needling. He could feel the heat of her gaze on his back. He turned to find her glaring at him with fire in her eyes.

"But I suppose a woman can't hope to do half the things a man can."

Buck cursed his careless tongue. He was lucky he'd never made such a remark to Isabelle.

"Look, I'm planting your damned potatoes. You don't have to keep picking at me."

"And you don't have to keep acting like you've been sent by some benevolent God to save us poor women from extinction."

"You ought to be thankful somebody sent me. It's the only way you're going to keep a roof over your head."

"I'll get down on my knees in thanks when you're out from under it."

"God, I hate sharp-tongued females."

"And I hate men who think they're everything and women only fit to serve their needs."

"Where the hell do you get off saying that? I've ridden over half this county looking for your cows, gotten shot doing it. What have I asked you to do besides feed me?"

"You didn't *ask*," Hannah reminded him. "You wanted it put in the contract."

"I said you didn't have to."

"Now you lie about all day, letting my mother wait on you hand and foot—being extremely ungracious about it, I might add—and you throw a fit when I ask you to do a little bit of work?"

"Throw a fit! If you think this is even close to a fit, you're in for a big surprise."

"Nothing would surprise me about you. You're a man."

"And damned proud of it. At least I don't go plumb crazy and attack people for no reason at all. You sure you're not having your time of the month or something?"

Mrs. Grossek turned red. Hannah picked up a clod and threw it at him. She had good aim for a woman. She hit him.

"My, my, when are you two going to announce the engagement? Or maybe I missed the wedding? You're already fighting like husband and wife."

Shocked by the sound of a male voice, Buck turned to see Walter Evans sitting astride his horse, grinning broadly at both of them.

Chapter Eight

"I found some of your steers I thought I'd bring over." Evans pointed to a group of longhorns grazing alongside the garden fence.

"Drive them away," Hannah said. "If they find out what's inside the fence, they'll push it down."

She raced across the field, shouting and flapping her apron. The steers, essentially wild animals with an instinctive distrust of humans, threw up their heads, bellowed, and thundered off into the distance.

"She even scares the hell out of wild animals," Buck muttered half under his breath. He turned to Evans. "You'd better ride out before she puts you to work in this damned garden. She poked and prodded until I got up just to prove I wasn't a useless weakling."

Evans dismounted. "I'm surprised to find you at

home. I thought you'd be out scouring the range for your cattle."

Buck turned so Evans could see his shoulder. "I found some and got this when I tried to bring them back."

All the amusement fled from Evans's eyes.

"Who did that?"

"I don't know. They shot from ambush."

"Where were you?"

"The Rafter D. I also found a yearling that had been freshly branded with a six-pointed star that just happens to fit nicely over the Tumbling T brand."

A shadow crossed Evans's face.

"You suspected rustling, didn't you?" Buck asked.

The other man nodded.

"What are you going to do?"

"Get them back."

"How?"

"I mean to go on roundup with the Rafter D."

"Will Gillett let you on his range?"

"He doesn't want to, but I'm thinking of inviting all the ranchers in the area to go together. If they agree, he'll find it hard to hold out."

Evans looked thoughtful. "Might be difficult to talk them into it."

"Not if they've been losing stock, too. Why should the Tumbling T be the only one? You short any cows?"

"I might be. Have you mentioned this to Hannah?"

"No."

"Why not?"

"Because she practically spits and claws at me every time I open my mouth."

"What's got into her?" Evans asked.

"I don't know. She's been angry as a treed cat all morning. I don't think she likes having me underfoot. She hates men, and I seem be at the top of her list."

"Her father was a cruel man. He—"

"I know about her father. I worked for him."

Evans eyes narrowed. "Is that why you're here now?"

Even though Buck had said more than he'd intended, he hadn't expected Evans to be so acute.

"That's part of it."

"Just don't let it reach to Mrs. Grossek or her daughter."

Buck stiffened. "What do you mean?"

"You said we have to look out for each other. Well, I'm looking out for Mrs. Grossek."

"You think I'd steal from them?"

"I don't know you well enough to know what you'd do."

"Look at them," Hannah said to her mother, "their heads together, discussing things too important for a female to understand."

Hannah handled the pea plant she was staking so roughly, she broke off a stem. She tossed the broken piece aside. She didn't understand why she should be so upset. She had actually shouted at Buck, hit him with a dirt clod. What was wrong with her? Even more inexplicable, why had he let her get away with it? Her father would have beaten her. Buck never made a single threat. It was hard to believe she could provoke him with impunity.

But he didn't seem provoked. Just irritated, as if

it wasn't her business, but not angry because it wasn't her right. There was a difference, and it was important.

"I can do this by myself," her mother said

"I'll help."

"I'd rather you didn't if you're going to keep breaking the plants."

Hannah looked down, dismayed to discover she'd broken another stalk. "Maybe I'd better start dinner."

"It would be better if you could get rid of your anger. Whatever Buck's doing, he's trying to help us."

"He's not interested in helping anybody but himself," Hannah said, being careful not take out her anger on the next pea bush. "If he helps us, it'll be purely coincidental."

"That'll be just as well."

"Not if he gets himself killed. He hopes to force his way onto the Rafter D during roundup. If they shot him yesterday for just riding across, you can imagine what they'll do then."

Her mother's face reflected the fear and sense of helplessness Hannah felt.

"Is there no other way?" her mother asked.

"I'm sure there is, but they'd never listen if I suggested it. They'd be sure it wouldn't work."

"They're probably right. Men usually are about these things."

"For goodness sake, Mama, they're men. Not gods. They can be wrong."

"Maybe."

"What do you mean?"

"Men aren't like women. They have no trouble doing things that women would have great difficulty making themselves do."

"Like killing each other?"

"Yes."

"I don't consider that a good thing."

"When somebody evil is willing to kill, there has to be somebody good who's also willing. If not, life for women would be even worse than it is."

Hannah wondered if she could kill someone, even if that person intended to kill her. She didn't know. She hoped she'd never have to find out.

"But the wrong people can get killed," she said.

"Like that poor boy who worked for Rupert."

"Did you know anything about that?"

"No."

She wondered what had happened to the other boys. She remembered that there had been several in the beginning.

"You must tell Buck he can't go," her mother said.

Hannah's hands stilled in the process of gathering up another pea plant for staking. "What makes you think he'll listen to me? He doesn't want us to do things for him, Mama, or know what he's up to. He intends to follow the contract to the letter and feel nothing, owe nothing."

"How do you know?"

"He's made it clear."

"I'm worried about him."

Hannah held the bush for her mother to tie up. "I can tell. You've been hovering around him all day, taking him coffee, asking him how he feels, wanting to know if he's tired."

"He's a nice man."

"You don't know that. He's been here just three days."

"He's a good man." Her mother finished tying the plant, looked up at Hannah. "He might make you a good husband."

121

Hannah didn't know why she didn't faint from shock. Or sit right down in the dirt. In the several moments it took to collect her wits, her mother had started tying up the next plant.

Even more surprising was the quickening beat of her own pulse, her lurching heart, the excitement that danced along her nerves at the thought of what her mother's words implied. It had to be purely physical, an animal response.

"After everything Papa did to us, you think I would marry anybody?" Hannah finally managed to ask.

"He's not like your father."

"How can you know?"

"By the way he treats us, even when you're rude."

It upset Hannah that her mother took Buck's side against her. "Are you going to speak to him tonight, tell him he can have me?"

Her mother didn't appear the least bit upset over Hannah's sarcastic remark. "I don't plan to speak of this matter to anyone but you. I don't imagine he'll ask you."

"Or I accept him if he did." She should have been repulsed by the idea. She wasn't.

"No. I wouldn't expect that either."

"Mama, I don't understand you. I thought you hated men."

"I would hate any man who treated me as your father did."

"But they're all like Papa."

"Not the man who adopted Buck. Neither is Mr. Evans."

Hannah gaze narrowed. "What do you know about Walter Evans?"

"Only that he wouldn't treat any woman as your father treated me."

"You don't know any such thing. Amos Merrick smiles and wheedles and pretends—"

"Amos Merrick will be like your father. Don't marry him."

"I don't intend to marry him or anybody else."

Her mother looked up. "A single woman is at a great disadvantage in this world. You need a husband."

Hannah was so angry, she pulled a pea plant up by the roots. "I don't need any man. I never will."

Hannah set the bowl of potatoes on the counter with an audible thump. On her way back to the table to remove the rest of the dinner dishes, she looked out the window. "They've still got their heads together," she said to her mother. "I've a good mind to go out there and listen. That ought to break it up."

"What's got into you today?" her mother asked. "You haven't been like yourself from the moment you got up."

"Why should I? I've never seen you act like this, either."

"How's that?"

"It started when you fussed over Buck like he was an invalid. Next you said I ought to marry him. Then you invited Mr. Evans to dinner and waited on him hand and foot." She stopped talking long enough to raise the window and listen a moment. "They're talking about the ranch. They couldn't possibly discuss it at the table. I might overhear something that would strain my limited female intelligence."

"Men don't like to discuss business in front of women. It makes them uncomfortable."

"It's my business. It makes *me* uncomfortable when they won't discuss it with me."

"Men don't see things that way."

"Well, it's high time they did." Hannah peered out the window. "Walter Evans is just as bad as Buck."

"I imagine we'll be seeing a lot more of him—if he's going to help Buck," her mother added at Hannah's sharp interest.

"How about the other ranchers?" Hannah asked, watching her mother closely.

"Them, too." Her mother seemed complacent.

"I don't understand," Hannah said, puzzled. "I thought you were afraid of men."

"I was afraid of your father's rage. Arguing with him only made him worse. I developed a habit of hiding, or becoming so small a target I might be missed, just as you developed the habit of silence. I clung to my memories of other times and other men, and that enabled me to endure. I'm just having a hard time letting go of the habit now that I don't need it. Buck's being here has helped."

Hannah gave up. Buck's coming had upended both their lives. She didn't understand any of it, particularly why everything he did suddenly seemed to irritate her so.

Watching the two men through the window, she saw Buck smile. Hannah felt something inside her clench. Buck *was* handsome. He smiled at her mother like that. No wonder she was falling over herself to spoil him.

It would be nice if he smiled at her once in a while.

She put that thought out of her mind, told herself not to be foolish. He was just like every other man she knew. Pleasing a woman wasn't important to them.

"I can't stand it anymore," Hannah said. She threw down the cloth she'd used to wipe the table and took off her apron. "This is our ranch. I have every right to know what they're saying."

Her mother said something Hannah didn't catch. It could wait until later.

The temperature had dropped nearly twenty degrees since sundown, but the nip in the air didn't cool her anger. They might have frost in the morning. Good thing her potatoes weren't up. She'd have to wait a while before planting corn, squash, and summer peas.

Buck and Walter didn't look up when she came out of the house. They probably didn't think her worth noticing. That thought made her cheeks burn. Her step became more brisk, her heels digging a little deeper into the packed earth. Coming right to the point, she asked, "What have you decided to do about the rustling?"

Her blunt question took Buck off guard but didn't startle him. He just looked at her as if he wanted to pat her on the head. Walter looked from one of them to the other. She thought she detected the slightest glimmer of a smile.

"You might as well tell me," she said, facing Buck squarely. "If you're going to come home shot up, it would be helpful if we had some bandages and medicine ready. If you're going to get yourself killed, I'll have to find somebody to replace you."

Walter grinned. She was quite positive about that. She couldn't be nearly so certain about Buck's expression.

"Zeke and I will take care of the ranch."

"So you said. I still want to know how."

"Why?"

Blockhead! Did he think she had no curiosity about what happened to her own property? Or him. She couldn't be so insensitive to him as she'd pretended to her mother. She tried, of course, but the possibility that he could be killed had preyed on her mind since he'd returned to the house wounded.

"Those are my cows," she said, sounding a bit like the witless female he thought her. She didn't mind *acting* like one, if that got her the information she wanted. "I don't want them chased over half of Texas, bullets flying over their heads, upsetting them and scaring the wits out of their babies."

Buck looked at her as though she'd lost her mind.

"I think it's cruel to burn them with a red-hot branding iron. You could tie ribbons around their necks instead. Of course, they might not stay on. Do you think painting their horns would work?"

A slow grin raised the corners of Buck's mouth. "That's a good idea. We could use a sassy red for the girl cows and a royal blue for the boy cows. That ought to help them out during breeding season, too. You know, ease the confusion for the first-timers."

"I think you'd better explain your plan to her," Walter suggested.

"Oh, all right," Buck said, exasperated. "Evans and I were just discussing how best to get the ranchers to work together."

"Do you think they will?" she asked Evans.

"It depends on whether they've been losing cattle, too."

"Why shouldn't they be?" Buck asked. "If you're going to rustle at all, no point in limiting yourself. This whole area is honeycombed with canyons and draws. You could hide hundreds of cows."

"After shooting at you the first time you set foot

on his range, you think he's just going to let you ride in and take your cows back?" Hannah asked.

"What do you suggest I do?" Buck demanded.

"I suggest you talk to the sheriff in Utopia. If Gillett has my cows, he can get them back."

"The sheriff has no jurisdiction out here," Evans said.

"There must be a marshal in Austin."

"By the time we could get a marshal out here, Gillett would have rebranded every cow he's rustled."

"Then talk to the army. There has to be somebody who upholds the law in Texas."

"There is," Buck said, "people like Evans and myself."

"So you go in there and get yourself shot."

"Not if we all go together," Buck said.

"He's right, Hannah," Evans said. "If all the ranchers band together, Gillett won't be able to stop us."

"He won't have to," Hannah said, "if he's already rebranded all my cows."

"She's right," Evans said. "What are you going to do about that?"

"I don't know, but I will get them back."

"He'll shoot you," Hannah said.

"I'll shoot back."

"He's got more men."

"Then I guess I'll have to be more accurate. Anything else you want to know?"

He was humoring her again. He acted as if he was answering her questions, but he wasn't. He was waiting for her to go away and leave him to discuss the real business with Walter.

"Yes. I would like to know what you *really* mean to do. I would also like to be included in your discussion *before* you make up your mind."

"You've got all you can handle right here," Buck said. "It makes sense for you to leave the rest to me."

"I don't intend to leave anything to anybody. I intend to know how to run a roundup, brand a calf, and when a steer is ready for market. I don't plan ever to need a man to help me run this place again."

"No woman goes on roundup," Buck said.

That got Hannah's back up. "Why not?"

"Because it's noisy and dirty and no fit place for a lady."

He wasn't going to try to forbid her. He just thought it was unsuitable. She hadn't realized he cared that much about her sensibilities.

"When did I get to be a lady?"

"Every female is a lady unless she's a . . . she's—"

"Something else," Walter Evans offered helpfully.

Hannah was amused to see Buck turn slightly pink. She didn't know he could.

"There's nothing but men around on roundup," Buck continued. "They get dirty and stay that way, sleep on the ground, and don't watch their language."

"I'll ignore everything I see or hear."

"You'd upset them too much. They wouldn't get their work done."

"Why not?"

"No man can think straight around a good-looking woman. They'd be as likely to rope their partner as a calf."

Hannah felt herself growing warm again. She hadn't known Buck thought her pretty. He'd seemed impervious to her. He might dislike her, but apparently he wasn't immune to her. Knowing that made Hannah feel a hundred times better, Watching Buck closely, Hannah said, "You've managed well enough."

"I have a reason. They don't."

He might think her pretty, but he hadn't forgiven her. She hadn't expected he would, but the unfairness of it rankled.

Several faint sounds disturbed the strained silence. Hannah would have ignored them but for the effect they had on the two men. Their eyes met; their bodies stiffened; they waited.

"What is it?" Hannah asked.

"Shhhh."

At least a minute passed. The men tried to relax, but Hannah could see the tension in them.

"What was it?" she asked again.

"It sounded like gunshots," Buck said, "but it was too faint to be sure."

"It's probably somebody hunting turkeys," she said. "There's lots of them around here."

Walter Evans looked up at the sky. "It's a little dark for that. It's best to hunt turkeys at dusk. That's when they go to roost."

"Those were pistol shots," Buck said.

"And you don't hunt turkeys with a pistol?" She didn't need an answer. She already knew.

"Where's Zeke?" she said, suddenly aware she hadn't see him since he got up from the table.

"Out there," Buck said. He pointed in the direction of the shots.

Chapter Nine

No one slept well that night. After the burst of gunshots, they had all listened, fearful of what they would hear. Being brought up against the very real possibility that Zeke was badly wounded or dead had made Hannah's glib talk of bandages and looking for Buck's replacement sound cruel. She had never taken his intention to steal back their cows lightly—she knew there could be shooting, someone could be injured—but she'd never really thought it would happen.

Now those vague worries had become reality. Zeke hadn't come back.

"I didn't see any sign of him in the barn," Buck said when he came into the kitchen for breakfast. He'd gone out to check the barn twice during the night. An early morning rain had prevented him from going out a third time.

"Did you hear any more shots?" she asked

Mrs. Grossek looked up from the stove, a troubled expression on her face.

Buck shook his head. "I'll have to go look for him as soon as I finish eating."

"You're not fit to ride," Hannah said.

"I can stay in the saddle."

"You might break open your wound."

"I can't stay here doing nothing!" Buck said, losing control of his temper. "I should have gone out looking for him last night."

"That would have been stupid," Hannah said. "If there was someone after Zeke, you'd have been easy prey."

"You don't think much of me, do you?"

"I don't think you can use a rifle with only one hand. Nor can you use a gun and hold the reins at the same time."

"I'll stay under cover."

"And what will you do if you find Zeke hurt? You can't move him or load him on his horse. You won't even be able to get back in the saddle to go for the doctor."

Buck brought his fist down on the table. The table settings jumped, but not as much as Mrs. Grossek.

"If you break your other hand, you'll be able to do even less."

Buck glared at her. "You like making fun of me, don't you? Why do you hate me so much?"

His attack shocked Hannah. She didn't hate him. If anything, she thought about him too much.

"I don't hate you," she said, trying to sound as impersonal as she could. "I was just trying to point out you're in no condition to ride. You can't use one arm and you're still weak."

He didn't seem mollified. "Nevertheless, I'm leaving after breakfast."

"I'll go with you."

"You'll do nothing of the kind."

"If we do find Zeke, I can help."

"I won't let you come."

"You can't stop me," Hannah said, handing Buck the plate her mother had prepared for him. "I can ride a horse. I can even saddle it." She'd never saddled a horse by herself, but she'd seen it done. It didn't look too complicated. She was reasonably intelligent, despite what Buck and her father thought.

"There's not an extra saddle on the place, and the only horses belong to Zeke and me."

His expression said he knew he had her cornered. It didn't tell her whether he cared.

"How does your shoulder feel this morning?" Mrs. Grossek asked.

"Much better," Buck said, turning away from Hannah's all too evident resentment.

"We ought to change the bandage."

"I will as soon as he eats," Hannah snapped.

"Wait until I get back," Buck said. "In case it gets dirty."

They talked of other things during the meal, but Hannah couldn't get his refusal to take her with him out of her mind. Nor could she forget the fact that he thought she hated him. She didn't. She never had. If he weren't forcing her to give up half of the ranch, she could like him quite well.

Actually she liked having him around. If men weren't such abominable creatures, she might even consider marrying someone like him. She'd rather remain single, but if it came down to a choice between Amos and Lyman and Buck, she'd choose Buck.

Hannah couldn't imagine why she should be letting her thoughts wander in such absurd directions. Not even a pair of rich black eyebrows could excuse that.

But if his brows attracted her attention, his dark brown eyes fascinated her. They seemed to be watching her, gauging her actions, the underlying meaning of her words. Yet they remained unchanged by all they saw, looking out on the world with no joy, no enthusiasm. Only grim determination.

He was a good-looking man, even if his short hair did refuse to conform to any pattern except when wet. The moment it dried, it spiked in all directions, as though he'd been running his hands through it. He had a long face with a cleanly formed nose. She couldn't tell if she liked his mouth. Frowns and scowls too often ruined its shape.

He hadn't shaved. The black stubble showed strongly against his skin. It gave him an almost boyish look. She hadn't thought she would like that. A man ought to look like a man—solid, dependable, experienced—but then, Buck's ancient eyes more than made up for his youthful countenance.

"That was mighty good, ma'am," Buck said to Mrs. Grossek as he pushed away from the table. "For a woman who's never cooked American, you sure catch on quick."

It irritated Hannah that her mother tried so hard to please Buck. She didn't resent her mother's renewed enjoyment in life. She resented that Buck should be its source.

But she shouldn't care that Buck was nice to her mother and mean to her. She wanted nothing from him but his help in paying off the debt. She would be delighted to wave good-bye to him any time he wanted to leave.

"I'll change your bandage now." She was aware

of the sharp edge to her voice, but she couldn't do anything about it.

"It'll wait."

"No, it won't," she said, more brusquely than she intended. "If you insist upon going off despite my objections, your shoulder needs to be bound tightly to keep the wound from pulling open."

Buck looked about to refuse.

"It'll take longer to heal. You'll be sitting around here an extra week driving me crazy."

"Think of all the potatoes I could cover."

"I'm done with the potatoes. Next I do the corn, beans, squash—"

"Stop," Buck said, with the very faintest suggestion of a smile. "You can bandage my shoulder as tightly as you want, as long as I can still breathe."

Hannah had expected to change the bandage in the kitchen, but Buck went back to his room. Even before she had collected everything she needed, she felt the tension ignite inside her. She considered asking him to come back but changed her mind. She didn't want to give Buck any reason to suspect the effect he had on her. She didn't want her mother to know, either.

He was sitting on his bed when she entered the bedroom, his shirt halfway off, tugging to get his injured shoulder free.

Hannah's legs nearly gave way under her. Mortified by her weakness, she schooled her thoughts and her undependable legs and made her way into the room. Her entire body shook. Even her hands trembled.

She'd changed his bandages before, but her mother had always been with her. Now she was alone in a room with a man naked from the waist up. Hannah wasn't prepared for the feeling of intimacy. She barely recognized it, had no idea what to do about it. It had never occurred to her that a man could affect her this way, not even a man like Buck.

Out of the chaos of her thoughts, her mother's suggestion that she marry Buck suddenly rang in her ears. The thought of having this man to herself, as her own, was exhilarating. To be able to touch him at will, to lie close to his strength at night . . . well, that was an aspect of marriage Hannah hadn't considered. It appeared to have been a serious oversight.

But he would also lie close to *her*. He would touch *her*. He would even . . . The near certainty of what would happen between them exploded in her brain. She'd never let such thoughts enter her mind before. She'd never wanted them, but now she couldn't stop them.

Hannah could hardly believe that her feelings toward Buck had changed so drastically. This was the man who was determined to take her ranch from her, but that no longer made her angry. Maybe she didn't believe it anymore. She could only state for certain that if Buck Hobson reached out for her at this very moment, she didn't know if she'd be able to stop him.

She became aware of a sensitivity in her nipples. The material of her dress seemed rough. She had to restrain an impulse to rub them, to discover what made them push out against her bodice.

Determined that Buck would not guess the turmoil in her mind and body, Hannah placed the basin and bandages on the table beside the bed. "Let me help you off with that shirt."

Buck had freed his wounded shoulder. Hannah took hold of the shirt and Buck shrugged his arm out of the sleeve. She hadn't had to touch him. She tossed the shirt aside. But when she started to remove the old bandage, she couldn't find a comfortable working position.

If she stood, she would have to bend at an awkward angle. It would also place her head uncomfortably close to his. If she sat on the bed, she'd be next to him *on the bed*. Just the thought caused her knees to go wobbly again. If she called for her mother, she would proclaim herself a coward.

She stood behind him and bent over his shoulder. He turned his head to watch her progress. Their hair practically touched. She felt his breath on her fingers.

She fumbled with the pin.

"You want me to help you?"

"I can get it. Just stop wiggling trying to see what I'm doing."

Instead of looking away, he looked straight into her eyes.

"I'm making you nervous." It was a statement, not a question. "Why?"

She wished he'd turn away. She couldn't think with him looking at her like that. Not even Amos had stared at her so intently. Amos had leered. That made her mad. Buck looked straight inside her. That left her defenseless.

"I said I'm not ner—"

"We're partners. You don't have to lie to me."

She didn't feel like a partner. She felt weak, incapable of doing her job.

"I'm not used to being around men," she finally managed to say. "This close, I mean."

He just looked at her.

"I've never touched a man before."

"Is it so strange?" he asked. His expression didn't change, but she thought his voice did.

"Yes."

"Why?"

"I don't know."

"I won't hurt you or your mother."

Her hands had come to a complete stop. She had never thought he would hurt her. So why should his saying so nearly turn her into a blob of jelly? Her hand started to shake. He took it and held it still.

"Why are you shaking?"

"I don't know," she whispered.

He released her hand. It started to tremble again.

"Can't you stop?"

"Not as long as you look at me like that."

He turned his head the other way. "Is this better?"

"Yes." It didn't feel better, not yet anyway, but she forced herself to begin to remove the bandage. She couldn't bear to have her vulnerability exposed by his questions. Not until she'd had time to study it, shore up her defenses.

His wound was healing quickly. Her mother would say it was a sign of a healthy body. Hannah didn't need the wound to tell her that.

"It's healing nicely," she told him, trying to ignore the feel of his skin under her fingertips. But it was impossible not to feel the muscles in his shoulders, notice the slow rise of his abdomen as he breathed, feel the warmth of his body.

It was equally impossible to ignore her body's response. The difficulty came in trying to understand what it meant. Neither Amos nor Lyman affected her this way. She had no girlfriends to ask, to compare notes with. Maybe this happened to every girl. Maybe it was ordinary.

Somehow she didn't think so. She was normally calm, deliberate, able to think quite clearly. She couldn't do any of those things now.

"Don't wrap it so tightly," Buck said. "I do have to be able to move my shoulder."

Her nerves had become so taut, she had pulled the bandage strips too tight.

"Sorry. I haven't done this very often."

That wasn't the reason, but she didn't want him to know. It took her entire concentration to keep her breathing normal.

"Why don't you ask Mr. Evans to go with you?"

Maybe if she concentrated on the danger, she could forget this strange feeling in her abdomen, the weakness in her lower limbs.

"If I can't handle the job, I need to find that out now."

"What will you do if you find Zeke—" She couldn't finish her question.

Everything about Buck changed. She felt the muscles harden under his skin. His eyes had always seemed too cold to show emotion, but now they were filled with fire. He clenched his fist until the knuckles turned white.

"I'll find out who's responsible," Buck said. "Then I'll kill him."

Shock riveted Hannah to the spot. Her sect preached love and peace. Though she knew they didn't always live up to those high ideals, she'd never known a man to speak so openly of killing. It stunned her that Buck should do so.

"How can you say that?"

"What would you do if someone killed your best friend?"

She didn't know. She didn't have a best friend.

"There must be another way."

"Some men only understand killing."

"Well, we don't know anything has happened to Zeke. He seems like a very clever man, one who's not likely to get caught. He might be riding in this very minute."

The tension in Buck's body eased. "Zeke is like a shadow. You don't hear him. You don't see him often either."

"You love Zeke a lot, don't you?"

Buck started to say something but then changed his mind. "We went though the same thing. Nobody else understands."

"That isn't the same thing as love. Are you afraid to admit your feelings? He's your brother. You shouldn't mind—"

"I don't have a brother," Buck said.

"You said you had nine, that your parents adopted—"

"Jake and Isabelle aren't my parents. The boys aren't my brothers."

Hannah knew he thought the world of Jake and Isabelle. He quoted them, talked about his brothers all the time. She felt as if she knew Drew and Will. She couldn't understand why Buck didn't think of them as his family.

"They're your legal parents, whether you accept it or not," Hannah said. "Your legal brothers, too."

"I have a real mother and a father. A sister, too."

"Then I don't under—"

"My mother ran off, and my father sold me. I won't have a family until I find my sister. I intend to pay Jake back for everything he did for me."

"You can't pay him back for giving you a family," Hannah said. She could tell Buck's mind was closed, that he was pulling away from her, but she couldn't stop. "From everything you've said, they loved you and did as much for you as real parents. You can't repay that kind of debt with money—only with respect, loyalty, and love."

Buck didn't answer or meet her gaze.

"Being a parent is more than physically creating a baby," she continued, refusing to give up. "I'd have traded my father for Jake any day and been proud to say I loved him."

"If you're not going to finish that bandage, I will. I've got to find Zeke."

For a brief moment, she had felt that he had reached out to her, that he could talk to her as an ordinary person. Now she felt a coldness close around her. He was pushing her away. Any inclination he'd had to share a part of himself was gone.

Hannah felt terribly sorry for Buck. The cruelty of his mother and father had left him unable to accept the love his adoptive parents wanted to give.

She wondered if he could truly love anybody, if he would always attempt to equate people's feelings with money. That seemed a greater tragedy than the beatings.

"I hope you find him," she said, tying the last bandage strip in place. "Even if you don't call him brother, I think you love him like one."

Buck still didn't speak, but his gaze grew more intense than ever. He started to put his shirt on.

"Let me help," she said.

"I can do it."

Hannah refused to let him push her away. She picked up his shirt. He didn't move. For a moment she thought they would have a contest of wills, but he shrugged and eased his wounded shoulder into it. He pushed the other arm in.

"Would you button it up for me?"

She hadn't expected that. He had dressed himself

this morning. She saw challenge in his eyes. Maybe he was testing her. Whatever he was trying to do, Hannah was determined he wouldn't find her wanting.

"I'll help you with the saddle," she said as she reached for the first button. If she could talk about something else, she wouldn't have to think so much about what she was doing. "You can't lift it with that shoulder."

"You going to help me into the saddle as well?"

"Probably. You can't help me pay off the debt if you can't get up on your horse."

"The debt's the only thing you care about it, is it?"

She paused at the last button, at his navel, just above his belt. She couldn't do it. He'd have to do that one up himself. "Would you be concerned about anything else?" She wasn't so rattled that he was going to catch on her that question.

He looked down at the remaining button, then up at her. "It depends." He did the button.

"On what?"

He looked at her once more. "I don't know yet."

Hannah heard someone ride up to the house. Buck's manner changed abruptly. He left the room and headed toward the front of the house without tucking in his shirt. When he opened the front door, Hannah saw Walter Evans dismounting.

"Have you found your friend?" Evans asked when they stepped out on the porch.

"No," Buck replied. "I'm just getting ready to go look for him.

"Mind if I go with you?"

Hannah didn't know why Evans should take an interest in their affairs, but she was grateful he wanted to go with Buck. In the meantime, she made up her mind to buy herself a horse at the earliest opportunity. She refused to be left at the ranch again.

"Won't you come inside for a cup of coffee?"

Hannah turned, surprised to see that her mother had also come out on the porch.

Walter Evans smiled at her mother. "How did you know I rode all this way hoping you'd offer? I still remember that first cup."

Hannah turned to her mother, worried that the reference to the time her father had hit her for "entertaining men" would upset her. She did grow a little pale, but neither her expression nor her posture changed.

"You're welcome to stop in any time," she said. "We keep the pot on most of the day."

"I'll remember that."

"It won't take me long to saddle up," Buck said. "I'll be back in—"

He broke off. Hannah looked up at him, but he was looking at something to the west. She looked but couldn't see anything.

"It looks like we're going to have company," Buck said.

"I don't see anybody," Hannah said.

"I see dust," Buck said. "It's either riders, or the longhorns are running."

"Riders," Evans said.

"That's what I figure," Buck replied.

Hannah's mother retreated inside. Apparently her new-found confidence didn't extend beyond Buck and Mr. Evans.

The two men talked about the condition of the range, the spring rains, the best time to start roundup and how it should be organized. Hannah got the feeling Buck was giving only part of his attention to their conversation. He kept looking west. She could finally see the riders, but she couldn't tell who they were.

"It's Lyman Gillett," Buck said.

"How can you tell?" she asked. "I can't make out anybody."

"Who's with him?" Evans asked.

"Tom Gladdis, the guy Zeke and I met the day we found our cattle in that canyon, and somebody I don't know."

"I don't know how you can tell anything from this distance."

"Good eyes," Buck said. "I never read anything I don't have to."

Hannah wasn't sure anybody could see that well, regardless of how little they read. However, Buck was soon proved right.

The expression on Evans's face suddenly changed.

"What's wrong?" Hannah asked.

"That man with Gillett," Evans said. "I know him."

"Is he a gunfighter?" Buck asked.

"Yes."

Hannah had never seen a gunfighter, not even heard one mentioned by name, yet one was about to ride up to her door. He could even be the man who'd shot Buck.

"Who is he?" Buck asked.

"Sid Barraclough," Evans replied. "He hires out to anyone who'll pay his price. He's been working for Gillett over a year now."

"Why is he coming here?" Hannah asked.

"We'll know soon enough. We might as well sit down and wait."

Buck and Evans settled themselves into chairs on

the porch. Hannah didn't know how they could possibly act so calm. A gunfighter was coming. He must intend to shoot somebody.

"I'll get your guns," she said and turned toward the house.

"Leave them," Buck said.

"But he's got a gunman with him."

"He's going to tell us something. The gunman is to give weight to what he says. He won't use him until later."

"How do you know?"

"I've faced gunmen before."

For the first time, Hannah remembered there was a great deal about Buck she didn't know. He could be a gunfighter himself.

Too nervous to sit around doing nothing, she walked to her garden. But she couldn't concentrate on the new growth or her planting schedule. She couldn't think of anything but Gillett and the gunfighter with him. She told herself she ought to pick the peas before it got hot. She should check the potatoes, see if the carrots had sprouted, decide whether to irrigate. She should try to figure out how much extra food she would need for Buck and Zeke.

She still hadn't done any of this when Gillett and his men rode up. She didn't like the look on Lyman's face. He was furious. And his anger was directed at Buck.

Quite suddenly, and totally unexpectedly, Hannah got mad. This man had no right to be here, intimidating her and causing her mother to hide inside. He had even less right to be angry at Buck. But above all, he had no business bringing a gunfighter onto her ranch. She didn't like it, and she wouldn't have it. She marched out of the garden and up to Gillett before he could dismount.

"Good morning," she said. "Have you come courting again?"

Chapter Ten

Gillett's gaze jerked away from Buck and Evans. He looked irritated, impatient. "Not today." He didn't dismount.

Hannah had always had the feeling there might be a streak of ruthlessness in Gillett, but his polished manners had kept it out of sight. Today it was present for all to see. Still, Hannah wasn't about to let him get away with being rude and abrupt. "That's probably for the best," she replied. "It's about time to feed the pigs."

Hannah didn't know what had come over her. She had turned into a woman she didn't know. She did know her attraction to Buck had triggered her present uncharacteristic behavior. She might be mad at Gillett for taking her cows and resent his rudeness, but she also was determined to protect Buck. No one was going to shoot him while he was unable to defend himself.

147

"Don't let me stop you," Gillett said. "Now I—"

Planting herself directly between Gillett and Buck, she said, "I don't believe I've met your friends."

Thoroughly put out, Gillett dismounted.

"I'm Tom Gladdis, ma'am," the young man said. He dismounted and doffed his hat. "Pleased to meet you."

"I'm Sid Barraclough," the other man said. He was slow to follow Gladdis's example, but he, too, dismounted and tipped his hat.

"You expecting trouble?" Hannah asked, indicating the gun he wore at his side.

Barraclough's grin was slow and lazy. "A man sorta feels naked without it."

"One of my men was shot last night," Gillett said, his anger pushing aside polite conversation. "I came to see if you knew anything about it." He directed the last sentence at Buck.

Without answering the question, Buck asked, "What happened?"

"I don't know," Gillett said. "He can't tell me. He's dead."

Fear knotted inside Hannah. She'd never expected that trying to get her ranch out of debt would get somebody killed.

"You think I had something to do with his death?" Buck asked. He hadn't moved, didn't seem the least bit afraid.

"You were nosing around my place a few days ago," Gillett said. "Gladdis said you ran off some cows."

"They was Tumbling T cows, boss," young Gladdis said. "I checked every one of them."

"I don't like strangers wandering around my range," Gillett said, his angry gaze still on Buck.

"So he hired me to make sure it doesn't happen more than once," Barraclough said. Menace shadowed his words.

"What makes you so nervous about a man riding across your range?" Buck asked.

Hannah wished Buck wouldn't try to provoke Gillett. He was already angry enough. She kept glancing back at the gunfighter. Instinct told her he was the real danger.

"They might not always be so careful to read the brands first."

"You're welcome to check any animal you find on my range," Buck said. "Though you won't find many cows or young stuff. For some reason they wandered off while the steers stayed behind. Can you explain that?"

"I don't know anything about your cattle," Gillett said. "I'm looking for the hombre who killed my cowhand. What's to tell me you didn't do it, that he didn't get a bullet into you before you shot him?" He pointed to Buck's wounded shoulder. "When did you get that?"

"Two days ago," Buck said, "just after I ran into Gladdis. Somebody shot me from ambush."

"How do I know that?" Gillett was clearly trying to push Buck into something. Hannah was afraid he'd brought the gunfighter along for just that purpose.

"I can vouch for the day and time of Mr. Hobson's injury," Hannah said. "So can my mother and Dr. Yant. If you wish to come back this evening when I change the bandages, you can see for yourself it's not a fresh wound."

Even though stymied by evidence he didn't expect, Gillett didn't give up. "Who's to say you didn't go out last night and try to get even?"

149

"I can," Walter Evans said, speaking up. "I came by yesterday with some steers that had drifted onto my range. Mrs. Grossek invited me to stay for supper. We were all standing in the yard when we heard pistol shots. It was sometime after nine o'clock."

"That's the time," Gladdis said. "It was me found Simpson."

"I haven't been any farther than the barn since then," Buck said.

"Go look," Gillett ordered Gladdis.

"Look at what?" Hannah demanded when the embarrassed boy started toward the barn.

"It rained last night," Gillett said. "If anybody's ridden in or out of here, there'll be hoofprints."

Evans started forward, but Buck motioned him back. Hannah was horrified to see Barraclough's gun appear, almost like magic, in his hand. Barraclough had drawn his gun and pointed it at Buck.

Instant rage filled her. Without thinking, she struck Barraclough's arm, knocking the gun from his hand. She stepped forward and placed her foot on the weapon. "Don't you ever draw a gun in my presence," she ordered.

"If you'd bothered to look," Buck stated as calmly as if nothing had happened, "you'd see Evans and I aren't wearing guns."

"Get your foot off my gun," Barraclough shouted.

Hannah stepped back, and he picked up his gun.

"It's got dirt in it," Barraclough said, angrier still.

"A good cleaning ought to set it to rights," Buck said. "You do know how to clean a gun, don't you?"

Barraclough was too angry to answer.

Gladdis's return broke the tension. "There's no hoofprints anywhere. No black horses, either. Just a paint, a dun, and the finest looking Appaloosa I ever set eyes on."

"Why a black horse?" Buck asked.

"Couldn't have been anything else," Gladdis said. "I heard him ride off, but I couldn't see a thing."

"You could have saved yourself the trouble of checking," Buck said. "As long as my shoulder is like this, I can't cinch a saddle or mount up." His expression had been rather flat up until this point, but now it turned stern. "When I can, I'm coming over to see who put this hole in my arm."

"None of my men did that," Gillett said.

"It was on your range."

"You haven't been here long. You probably don't know where one man's range stops and another begins."

"I know," Buck said.

"Well, it wasn't one of my men."

"I'll let the sheriff in Utopia decide that, but I will be over to see you come roundup time."

"There's none of your cows on my place."

"There were two days ago."

"I told my boys to chase off anything they saw."

"You'd better do like Mr. Gillett says and stay off," Sid Barraclough said.

"If what you say is true," Walter Evans said to Gillett, "I don't see why you should object to us sending a rep along with you. He'll be able to back up what you've said."

"I don't need anybody to back up my words."

"Nevertheless, I think it would be better if we all did roundup together," Buck said. "That way you can make a clean sweep of the range."

"I don't give a damn about your range," Gillett said.

"Your choice," Buck said. "I'll see you in about a month."

"I'll see you first," Sid Barraclough said.

"If that's the way you want it," Buck said.

Hannah couldn't understand Buck. He'd remained seated the whole time, looking at Gillett as if they weren't talking about anything more important than the weather. The gunfighter had just said he was going to stop him. Hannah's heart was in her throat, but Buck didn't look the least bit upset. Didn't he understand what that man was talking about?

Gillett mounted and turned his horse.

Barraclough tipped his hat and mounted up.

"Glad to meet you, ma'am," Gladdis said, his troubled expression momentarily gone. "It's always nice to know there's a pretty girl in the neighborhood."

"Unless you're meaning to pull your time, you'd better come on!" Gillett shouted over his shoulder

"Gotta be going." Gladdis tipped his hat, threw himself into the saddle, and kicked his horse into a canter to catch up with his boss.

"What do you make of that?" Evans asked as they rode off.

"He's going to have that horrible man kill you if you set foot on his ranch," Hannah said.

"That was pretty much the impression I got, too," Buck said.

He *knew* what Gillett was talking about, and he didn't seem the least upset.

"What are you going to do?" Hannah demanded.

"Right now I'm going to look for Zeke," Buck said, getting to his feet. "But I feel a whole lot better knowing the other man is dead."

"How can you say that?"

"Because if he was alive, it would probably mean Zeke was dead."

"But a man is dead," Hannah said. "How can you talk about him as if he were of no more importance than one of my cows?"

"That man tried to kill Zeke just like someone tried to kill me."

Hannah realized she was in over her head. She'd seen cruelty, even violence, but this was more like war. Someone had probably tried to kill Zeke. Gillett had made it clear he'd hired Barraclough to shoot anybody who got in his way. None of this was an accident. It was planned.

A sudden outburst from the chicken house startled Hannah. She turned to see hens scattering in all directions across the yard, wings flapping, their raucous squawks shattering the morning quiet.

"There must be a coyote in there," Evans said. He got up, walked down the steps to his horse, and pulled his rifle out of its scabbard.

"Why hasn't he upset the hens before now?" Buck asked.

To their collective surprise, the door to the chicken house opened, and Zeke came out, massaging his back.

"You people make so much noise a man can't get a wink of sleep. Did you leave me any breakfast?"

They'd been worried sick all night about him, had faced a fight with Gillett over him, and he'd been safe in the chicken house all along!

"I expected to find your hide full of holes," Buck said.

"I told you nobody was going to see me."

"Then what was the shooting about?"

"There's a lot of branding going on over there. I came across three places where they'd built fires."

153

"Forget the branding," Buck said. "What about the shooting?"

"I was checking out the last place," Zeke said. "I'd just uncovered the coals when someone shot at me out of the dark. I dived for cover and put two shots into the bushes where the shots came from. I heard somebody grunt and then crash through the brush. I worked my way over until I saw this man sprawled on the ground."

"You don't know who he was or why he was shooting at you?" Evans asked.

"I didn't get a chance to ask. He was dead."

"Where have you been all night?" Hannah asked. "Buck has been worried sick about you."

Brief as it was, Zeke flashed the first smile Hannah had ever seen. "That young fella we met the other day came nosing around, so I cut out fast. I left my horse in a little draw about a mile from here. Went to sleep in the chicken house. I figured nobody'd look for me in there."

"I wouldn't be surprised if the hens refuse to lay for a week," Hannah said. She felt shaky. That surprised her. But then, she'd never had a morning like this.

"Go on inside," she told Zeke. "Mama will fix you something to eat. Then you can bring your horse up to the house."

"I'll get it," Buck offered. "It'll give me something to do."

"I'll ride with you," Evans offered.

Hannah ought to have felt a lessening of tension, but somehow it seemed worse than ever. She couldn't forget Buck's promise to see Gillett when the roundup began. Or Barraclough's promise to stop Buck if he tried. Somebody was going to get killed if she didn't do something.

But what could she do?

* * *

"You still planning to join Gillett for the roundup?" Evans asked. They rode side by side down a narrow trail between mesquite and prickly pear cactus. Zeke had described the draw. Evans had said he knew where to find it.

"Yes."

"Even knowing he's got that gunfighter working for him?"

"Yes."

"You keeping something from me?"

"Like what?"

"That you're a gunfighter or something."

Buck chuckled. "I'm no gunfighter. All I want to be is a cowboy."

"You're not afraid of Barraclough?"

"No, but I'm not fool enough to take him lightly."

"What are you going to do?"

"Talk to the other ranchers."

"Do you think Gillett will stick to his refusal to let us join him?"

"If all of us present a united front, I don't think he'll be able to refuse."

"Then what's bothering you?"

"I figure he's branding everything he can so when he does relent and let us join him, there won't be any Tumbling T stock left."

"Then let's talk to the others and start the roundup early. He won't be able to explain a lot of fresh brands."

"He will if he can phony up a bill of sale saying he just bought the stock."

"We can check on that."

"And by the time we got somebody in Austin to check it, he'd have those cows a hundred miles from here. No, we've got to take him by surprise."

"How?"

"I'm not sure, but I have an idea. It'll take me a few days to check it out. If I'm right, I just may have a way out without a fight."

They passed through a tiny meadow turned white with prickly poppies. Maybe he'd pick some on his way back for Hannah's mother.

Suddenly Evans laughed aloud. "I'll never forget the expression on Barraclough's face when Hannah knocked his gun out of his hand. I don't think anything like that ever happened to him before."

"I'm sure it didn't."

Buck remembered it all too well. He hadn't thought it a bit funny. He had tensed, fearful that Barraclough might hit Hannah. If he had, Buck knew he would have attacked the man despite his wounded shoulder. The impulse was backed by more than the natural desire of a strong man to protect a woman. It went beyond a feeling of responsibility. He had felt as though something that belong to him was being threatened and he must defend it because it was of value to him.

He couldn't explain where that feeling had sprung from. He'd disliked Hannah from the moment she turned her back on him years ago.

They detoured around a thicket of oak and cedar. A steer bounded out, dodged cactus and mesquite, and plunged into a bigger and more dense thicket.

But Hannah wasn't the same as he remembered. She wasn't even the same as he'd thought she was when he first came to the ranch. She was as touchy as a longhorn cow with a calf. She was changing so fast, he couldn't keep up.

She was bossy and pushy, and he was a fool for lusting after her. Some women weren't worth what it cost to put up with them. He was certain Hannah was one of them.

He shouldn't have been interested, but he was. He shouldn't have cared, but he did. He should have put all thoughts of her out of his mind, but he couldn't. Apparently his boyish liking for her had never died. What was more, he suspected it had begun to grow in the few days he'd been at the ranch. His brain might have been telling him he disliked Hannah because of the way she'd treated him. But another part of him had considered different evidence and reached an entirely different conclusion.

That startled him almost as much as Hannah's spirited defense of him. Facing Barraclough was much more dangerous than standing up to her father, but she'd never hesitated. Not for a moment would he have thought she'd take such a risk for him.

Did that mean her feelings for him had changed as well?

Evans broke the silence. "Sid Barraclough has a reputation as a fast draw who's not particular how he uses his gun."

Buck pulled his attention back to Evans. "From what I've seen, people don't judge a gunfighter by the quality of his opponents, just the number of fools who manage to get in the way of his bullets."

"I hope you mean to stay out of the way."

"If I can."

"Hannah won't like it if you get yourself killed."

"I know. She made me add a line to our contract negating my claim on the ranch if I got killed."

"She didn't mean it like that. She—"

"I don't intend to die at the hands of some hired gunfighter," Buck said, cutting him off before he could say something Buck didn't want to hear.

"Jake made sure all of his boys knew how to use a gun, but he taught us to use our brains first."

Why had he referred to himself as one of Jake's boys, as though he was his son? It was Hannah's fault.

He might not want to admit it, but Jake and Isabelle had treated all the boys like sons, taught them to respect and trust each other, to act like family, to feel like brothers. They might not have actually come to love one another, but their respect was much more than Buck had ever had before.

Buck had held back his feelings because his parents most likely were still alive. He appreciated what Jake and Isabelle had tried to do, but when he found his sister, he'd have his real family. He wouldn't need anybody else then.

"You seem to think a lot of that couple," Walter said.

"I do."

"I'd like to meet them someday."

"They're just ordinary people."

But they weren't. Buck was only now beginning to understand just how extraordinary they were. He was also beginning to wonder if he hadn't let something very precious slip through his fingers.

"There's Zeke's horse," Evans said. They didn't see any other hoofprints in the vicinity.

They reached a small canyon with a tiny stream flowing out of it. The area between the cedar and mesquite was choked with Indian paintbrush and bright yellow coreopsis. This would make a good hay meadow.

"See if you can get Zeke to lay low for a while," Walter said when they started back toward the ranch.

"You can't get Zeke to do anything except what he wants."

"That could cause trouble for Hannah and her mother."

"That's the second time you've said something like that. Why are you so interested in those women?" Buck felt a pang of jealousy, and a twinge of disgust as well. It wasn't unusual for young women to marry much older men, but not Hannah. The man was too old for her. Hell, he was practically old enough to be her father.

"Any gentleman should be watchful of the welfare of two unprotected women."

"They're not unprotected," Buck said, his tone a little harder than he wanted. "Zeke and I are there."

"Sometimes I wonder if you're protecting them or using them."

"If you don't trust me, why are you willing to help?"

"Gillett is a common enemy. We need to stand together against him. As for the women, they got a rough deal from Grossek. I'm going to see they get treated a lot better from now on."

"Then you'd better talk to Joseph Merrick. They're in more danger from him than from me."

"Merrick is your worry," Evans said. "Hannah's giving up half her ranch so you'll protect her from him. Just make sure somebody doesn't have to protect her from you."

"And if I don't?"

"You'll find somebody besides Barraclough on your trail."

Buck didn't know what Evans's interest was, but it didn't make any difference to him. He wasn't responsible for Hannah. She had a mother to look after her. And he wasn't responsible for Mrs. Grossek.

Buck hoped he had turned off Evans's questions without revealing how angry they made him. The rancher had no business thinking Buck was trying to cheat Hannah and her mother. He meant to take the ranch fair and square.

But what really made Buck angry was the lurking feeling of guilt. He hadn't felt the slightest twinge when he made his plans, hadn't felt that demanding half of a crippled ranch was too much to ask in return for four-hundred deeded acres and six months' work. He still didn't.

So why did this vague feeling of guilt persist? Because Walter Evans thought what he was planning to do was wrong. Whether he liked it or not, Buck respected Evans, even liked him.

Buck wondered what Jake would say. He knew Isabelle would say he ought to rescue the ranch and then give it back to Hannah and her mother. Isabelle had always been too idealistic for Buck, though he had every intention of being *fair*.

He wasn't going to cheat them, and he resented the implication. Evans probably wanted Hannah and the ranch and was afraid Buck might steal it out from under him.

Well, Evans wasn't going to get the ranch, and he wasn't going to get Hannah, either. Buck didn't know who she would marry, but her husband ought to be young enough to offer her companionship, not parental guidance.

"Do you have a horse and a plow?" Buck asked Evans. The request caught the older man by surprise.

"Yes."

"May I borrow it? I want Zeke to break up the garden."

"Sure."

"How about a wagon?"

"What would you want that for? You've got nothing to haul to market."

"I'm taking Hannah and her mother to town."

Chapter Eleven

"It's a good thing it's only ten miles to Utopia," Buck said as the first buildings of the town came into view. "This team would never have made it to Austin."

He had surprised Hannah the night before when he'd invited her and her mother to go with him to Utopia. Mrs. Grossek had declined. Hannah had, too, at first, but she changed her mind. The minute they finished supper, she announced, "I need you and Zeke to help me pack the wagon."

"What for?" Zeke asked. He hated doing anything for Hannah.

"I'm taking the pickled beef to Utopia to sell. Sauerkraut, too."

"Why?" Buck asked.

"You and Zeke won't eat it."

"You're damned right," Zeke said. He refused to adhere to Hannah's ban on profanity.

"I can use the money," Hannah said.

"What for?"

"I need so many things, I haven't decided yet. But it's my money. I don't have to account to you for it."

Buck didn't like that, but he didn't say anything. He had every intention of rounding up wild horses to sell and no intention of accounting to her for that money.

They'd packed the wagon with jars, jugs, and crocks full of things Buck doubted he could eat unless he was starving. He'd never realized how unappetizing pickled pig's feet looked. Hannah had used every quilt in the house to wrap the jars so they wouldn't break.

After that she stayed up writing a letter. Next morning she added a couple of dried apple pies to the load. The wagon groaned all the way to town, the various jars and jugs thumped and bumped, but nothing broke.

"Where do you want to go?" Despite his wounded shoulder, Buck had insisted upon driving.

"The mercantile. What will you do?"

"Talk to the sheriff. Then I'll see if they've got a cattle growers office here."

"Why?"

"I want to see who owns the star brand."

"What will you do then?"

"That depends on what I find out."

"Why won't you tell me? You're supposed to trust me."

"It works both ways."

She thought for a moment. "If I have enough money, I'd like to buy a horse."

"What for?"

"I want to learn how to run the ranch. I can't do that from the front porch."

He started to tell her she couldn't do it from horseback either, not if he had anything to say about it, but he changed his mind. She hadn't bought the horse. No need to fight that battle yet.

"I don't want to raise your hopes, but I'm looking for a way to get back the cows that have been re-branded."

"Can you prove they were my cows?"

"Not without slaughtering them and checking the hides."

"Then they're lost, aren't they?"

He could see some of the light go out of her eyes. He watched her struggle to keep up her spirits, to keep him from seeing how much her independence meant to her.

"No. I'll get them back. I just want to do it without bloodshed."

"Can you?"

"I don't know."

As far as he could see, he had one chance. If that didn't pan out, it would probably have to be an open confrontation.

"You take care of your business," she said. "I can handle the wagon."

"Are you sure?"

"Yes. I started driving almost as soon as I could walk. Papa didn't always have slave boys to work for him."

He climbed down from the wagon, being careful of his shoulder.

"We have to get back home tonight, so don't go to a saloon and get drunk. I can't leave mother alone."

Leigh Greenwood

"Not even with Walter Evans there to keep her company?"

"Not even then."

As she drove off, Buck wondered if she was anxious to get back home to see Walter. The familiar jab of jealousy struck again. Damn, he couldn't believe he was acting this way over a woman he'd spent years hating. He must be crazy. If he didn't get to Austin soon, he was going to do something desperate.

The town looked solid and prosperous. Homes and stores of stone lined the main street, solid structures that spoke of permanence and hard work. Windows of real glass, porches with rocking chairs, upper floors for family and servants. Gardens carefully laid out and maintained spoke of an orderly, methodical people starting families and putting down roots. Many of the sidewalks were paved with stone. Even the road in the main part of town had been lined with it. The people of Utopia wore their civic pride for all to see.

Only Buck knew of the violence and cruelty masked by this example of the ideal community. In his mind, the price was too high.

Buck was surprised at how easily he found Sheriff Yant's office, but he wasn't surprised that in such a small community the sheriff and the doctor should be brothers. Buck wanted to notify more than a dozen sheriffs and army officers where to find him in case they located his sister. He had already written the letters. He just wanted the sheriff to sign them. He knew from experience that an official endorsement would give more weight to his request.

"How'd you get that shoulder?" Sheriff Yant asked after he'd signed the letters.

"Somebody shot me," Buck said. "Why, I'm not sure."

"You a farmer?"

"No. I'm working on the Tumbling T."

Yant's expression didn't lighten. "Sarah Grossek ought to sell that place. It's not right for a woman to be out there without a man."

"She's got me."

Yant's expression turned stern. "I don't want you bringing your troubles to Utopia. We don't go in for violence."

Buck had to bite his tongue to keep from asking about the violence to women and slave boys, but he figured Yant would pretend he didn't know what he was talking about. He might not. A man who beat his wife and slaves wasn't likely to brag about it.

"Can you tell me where to find the office of the cattle growers association?" Buck asked.

After getting his directions, Buck thanked the sheriff and left his office. Outside, a crowd had gathered a short way up the street. Buck wondered what the attraction could be. He recognized Hannah's wagon and immediately felt certain something was wrong. He stepped off the sidewalk and headed across the street.

Hannah felt more out of place entering Bakker's mercantile than she had when she went to the post office to mail her letter. It had been nearly a year since she'd come to Utopia. She had been with her father then. She and her mother had followed behind him, silent, eyes downcast. Her father had done all the talking, all the looking, all the ordering. He would occasionally speak to her mother, never to Hannah.

For the people of Utopia, a woman had no identity of her own. She was some man's wife, daughter, or servant. Though Hannah was determined to be independent of any man, she was a little nervous about announcing it publicly. Telling Buck she intended to run her life without the help of a man was one thing. Telling the people of Utopia was quite another.

It was a close-knit community. Commerce had replaced religion as the primary enterprise of the sect, but their social life continued to be governed by a strict set of rules. Chief among these were that men made all decisions and women accepted them without murmur or protest. That, in itself, was enough reason for Hannah to refuse to marry.

She marshaled her courage and walked up to Mr. Bakker. His ill-tempered scowl had scared her as a child. It didn't inspire confidence in her now. It relieved her to see that the store was momentarily empty. She didn't want anyone knowing her business.

"Good morning," she said, smiling cheerfully as she greeted the rotund, florid-faced merchant.

"What can I do for you?" His question sounded more like a threat than an invitation.

"I'd like to sell some beef my mother and I pickled."

"I've got all the beef I need," Mr. Bakker said.

"You don't have any like this," Hannah said, handing him a jar. She would not be put off by his coldness. She didn't need him to be nice to her. She did need the money. "My mother makes the best in Utopia. What about sauerkraut? Somebody's always wanting more."

"How much have you got?" Mr. Bakker asked.

"A wagon full."

"Let me see."

Still looking at her with cold eyes, he moved quickly from behind his counter. Hannah followed him outside and stood silently while he inspected her wares.

"I'll sell it for three quarters of the proceeds."

"Three quarters!" Hannah exclaimed. "That wouldn't leave me enough to pay for the meat."

"That's my offer," Mr. Bakker said. "Take it or leave it."

"I'll leave it. You needn't think that just because I'm a woman, I'll let myself be robbed."

"You accuse me of robbery?" Mr. Bakker shouted, his face growing even more florid.

"You wouldn't have offered such a deal to my father. He'd have knocked you down."

"You're lucky I offered to do business at all with a woman like you."

Hannah froze in the act of climbing into the wagon. She turned deliberately to face Mr. Bakker. "What do you mean by *a woman like me?*"

"No decent woman lives out in the middle of nowhere with a man who doesn't belong."

"I'm not *living* with anybody, Mr. Bakker. Buck Hobson works for my mother."

"He's sleeping in your house."

Hannah had no idea how he knew that, but somehow everyone in Utopia seemed to know everybody's business.

"I don't see how our household arrangements could possibly concern you."

"We don't want your doings to reflect on our women," Mr. Bakker said.

Hannah was past being shocked. She was mad. Furious, in fact. "And just what *am* I doing, Mr. Bakker?"

"No telling, what with that man tomcatting around you every night."

No one had ever accused Hannah of improper behavior. They wouldn't have dared while her father was alive. As far as Mr. Bakker was concerned—and, she suspected, the rest of Utopia as well—she couldn't be chaste, virtuous, or honorable unless there was a husband or male relative present to keep her licentious inclinations in check.

Hannah was so angry, she felt the tears start. She stepped up and slapped Bakker so hard he swayed.

"If I had a pistol, I'd shoot you," she said. "If you say anything like that again, I will."

"You unrighteous bitch!" Bakker screamed, humiliated by the stinging slap. "I'll teach you to hit a man." He started toward her, his fist in a tight ball.

Bakker wasn't as tall as her father, but he was much bigger and stronger than Hannah. She couldn't stop him if he decided to hit her. From the look of fury on his face and his balled fists, that was exactly what he intended to do.

Hannah looked from one side to the other. A couple of women had halted at Bakker's shout, but she could see no help in sight. She tried to back away, but the wagon blocked her progress. She was trapped by the wagon and the hitching rail.

Hannah dived under the wagon. Just as she crawled out the other side, Bakker came around the corner.

"You won't get away from me that easily, you strumpet."

"I'm not a strumpet. If you lay a hand on me, you'll regret it."

Bakker didn't bother to answer such an impotent threat. She ducked back under the wagon and scrambled under the hitching rail, but Bakker reached the boardwalk at the same time. Behind her, Hannah's path was blocked by a crowd who had gathered to see what was going on.

"Let me through," Hannah begged.

"Stop the jezebel!" Bakker shouted. "I'm going to teach her never to slap me again."

The crowd, their faces cold and implacable, held her back when she tried to push through. Hannah turned to face Bakker. She wondered if he'd beat her worse than her father had.

"You touch that woman, and I'll kill you."

The words weren't very loud, but the click of a gun hammer stopped Hannibal Bakker in his tracks.

Bakker whirled as Buck stepped around the corner of the wagon, the gun in his hand pointed directly at the space between Bakker's protuberant eyes. To Hannah in that moment, Buck was the most handsome, most magnificent man in the world. Once more he'd protected her from a terrible beating.

"Who are you to interfere?" Bakker demanded.

"A more decent person than anyone in that crowd," Buck said, indicating the human wall behind Hannah. She noticed it didn't seem quite so solid now. "Only cowards stand watching while a bully beats a woman."

"You wouldn't say that without a gun in your hand," Bakker said.

Buck holstered his gun and then looked straight at Bakker. "You're a coward and a bully and a woman beater. You ought to be whipped in public. Now apologize to Miss Grossek."

"I'll do no such thing," he sputtered. "You don't know—"

"Do it, or I'll break this gun over your head." Buck actually smiled when he said it.

Bakker charged Buck, but the ponderous man had no chance of catching Buck, who moved nimbly out of his way. Buck's fist connected with Bakker's chin as the man turned around. "You've got five seconds."

For a moment, Bakker looked stunned, as if he couldn't figure out what had just happened. "She slapped me. A man can't expected to take that lying down."

"Three seconds."

"You've got no right to come in here, telling me what to do." Bakker charged again. "You don't even know—"

Buck jumped aside. As Bakker plunged past, Buck unholstered his gun, gripped it by the barrel, and then brought it down on Bakker's skull right behind his ear. The man dropped like he'd been shot in the heart.

"I guess you'll have to do without an apology this time," he said to Hannah. He turned to the people still gathered on the boardwalk. "Go home. You should be ashamed to show your faces on the street." In the face of his withering scorn, they pulled back. He turned to Hannah and headed her toward the wagon. "Where to now?" he asked.

She couldn't say a word. The events of the last few minutes had hurled her from one emotional extreme to another. Now Buck was asking her to act as though nothing had happened.

As she started to climb back into the wagon, she looked at Mr. Bakker lying on the boardwalk where he had fallen. She'd never liked him, but she'd never been afraid of him. She turned to stare at the remnants of the crowd that had blocked her escape. She didn't know all of these people, but she'd considered herself part of their community.

Now, like wild animals, they were forcing her out of the pack, compelling her to survive on her own. Hannah had never felt so alone in her life.

"Look them in the eye," Buck whispered. "Never let them know you're scared. That's what they're waiting for."

"How—"

"Don't turn around. Keep staring at them. Make them break eye contact." He settled on the seat beside her. "Where to next?"

"Home."

"No. You came here to do something."

Hannah tried to soothe her shattered nerves. She didn't want to sell her pickled beef. She didn't want to buy a horse. She just wanted to go home where she was safe.

"I've changed my mind."

"You can't, not unless you want these people to think you're a coward."

That brought Hannah up short, as she expected Buck knew it would. She was not a coward, and she defied anyone to say so. "Bechtler's Wholesale. It's two doors down."

They could have walked, but Hannah had to admit that riding was more effective. She could look down on everybody from the wagon.

"What happened?" Buck asked. "Keep smiling. Just talk."

"Bakker wanted three quarters of the proceeds."

"That's robbery."

"When I told him that, he said I was lucky he'd even consider helping a *woman like me*."

"I gather that refers to me."

"You're living at the ranch, sleeping inside the house."

"So they were going to watch you take your punishment for flaunting their rules."

"I suppose. I don't know. I never imagined anything like this could happen."

They stopped at the next store. Buck climbed down.

"Why did you make me keep staring at them?"

"People in crowds are a lot like animals. If you show weakness, they'll attack and destroy you. If you fight back, they usually get out of your way."

Hannah was still too upset, her emotions in too much upheaval, to be able to grapple with what he was saying. She was at the door of Bechtler's Wholesale. She braced herself.

The answer was the same at Bechtler's and the three other places she tried. They either refused her business or asked an inordinate percentage of the profits. As far as the merchants of Utopia were concerned, she was a fallen woman.

"I won't sell to any of them," Hannah said as she stalked out of the last store. "I'd rather throw in into the creek."

"It might be more useful if you ate it."

She turned on Buck. "How can you make jokes? No one wants anything to do with me."

"I was just being practical."

"I don't want to be practical. I want to hit somebody."

"You already did."

She laughed in spite of herself. "You must think I'm crazy. I haven't been in town an hour, and I've been in a fight and nearly started a riot."

"Actually you were rather magnificent. Now I

think it's about time we got something to eat. Are you hungry?"

She wasn't. How could she think of food when her stomach was doing such a crazy dance? Her wits weren't functioning too well, either. Had Buck said she was magnificent? He hated her. He couldn't have said that.

She looked up at him. She realized she wanted him to think well of her. His opinion was much more important than that of anyone in Utopia. "What did you say?"

"I asked if you wanted to eat."

"Before that. About my getting into a fight."

"I liked the way you stood up to Bakker. But next time I'll come with you."

Impulsively she reached out, took his hand, and gave it a firm squeeze. "I'd have been in a terrible fix if you hadn't showed up. I don't know how to thank you."

He seemed surprised that she would take his hand, but he didn't pull back. After a moment's hesitation, he squeezed her hand in return. "I had no choice. You haven't put a clause in the contract giving me your part of the ranch if you get trampled in a riot."

Hannah tried to get angry. Instead she felt herself grinning. She gave up and let the bubble of laughter escape. She very much wanted Buck to be her friend. She'd never had anyone to laugh with. It felt wonderful.

"Now, if you're not hungry, I am," Buck said. He released her hand and took up the reins. "You may remember we left without breakfast."

"Papa always ate at Sharmbeck's."

"Do they serve something besides pickled beef?"

"Papa said the hands preferred Grosswelt's."

"Let's go there."

Hannah was relieved when they entered the restaurant to discover that all the people were strangers to her. The smell of frying beef filled the air. Buck relaxed and smiled.

"It smells like Isabelle's kitchen."

Apparently it tasted like Isabelle's cooking. Buck ate enough for two men. Hannah decided he was well on his way to recovery.

Hannah drank coffee, consumed several pieces of dark rye bread covered with rich butter, and thought about what had just happened. Everything had changed between her and Buck.

She liked him. She enjoyed his company. She wanted to be his friend. It was pointless to deny it any longer. She'd never realized how lonely she felt. Even when her father was alive, her people had been a shield against outsiders rather than a comfort and support. She'd never felt they cared about her or would put themselves out for her.

Buck had—twice. She couldn't forget that.

But she wanted more than companionship, more than a squeezed hand. As hard as it was to believe, she wanted him to stay.

But did that mean she loved him? Her people didn't expect love between a man and his wife. A woman might love her children, but she respected her husband. If a man did his duty to his family, he considered that enough. Was it enough for her or did she need love? Did she know how to love? Before she could find any answers, Mrs. Grosswelt's arrival claimed her attention.

"I heard about the trouble you had this morning," she said. "Hannibal Bakker ought to be whipped for what he said. I told him as much, but no one listens to me. I'm too friendly with outsiders."

"Thank you," Hannah said. "It's a relief to know not everyone thinks I'm sunk in sin. Let me introduce you to Buck Hobson. He's the tomcat Mr. Bakker talked about."

"I'm always pleased to meet a man who can eat like you," Mrs. Grosswelt said, indicating Buck's empty plate. "There's no better compliment to the cook."

"Mighty fine," Buck said. "I'll come back again."

"I'll be glad to see you." She turned back to Hannah. "I heard you were trying to sell some pickled beef."

"Not anymore."

"You stop by Moffett's place on your way home. He's got a house full of boys and no woman to cook for them. He might be interested in buying your beef. And anything else you have."

"Thank you," Hannah said. She wanted to do something to express her appreciation, but Mrs. Grosswelt left as suddenly as she'd appeared.

"I guess we'd better get going if we want to reach home before dark," Buck said.

The door of the restaurant had barely closed behind them when a man came rushing up. Hannah turned to see the handsome face of Amos Merrick bearing down on her.

"I've just heard what happened this morning," he said, taking Hannah's hand and holding it possessively. "Marry me, and it'll never happen again."

Chapter Twelve

Buck felt himself tense. Amos Merrick was the answer to all of Hannah's troubles. If she said yes, she would have a rich husband, an unassailable position in Utopian society, and no need for Buck's help.

Buck would lose the best chance he'd ever have to own his own ranch. Even if she wanted to sell her ranch, he couldn't buy it now because he didn't have any money. If he had any sense at all, he'd do his best to ruin Hannah's chances at matrimony.

Buck wondered if Amos would treat Hannah well. After the way her father had treated her, she deserved a husband who would be kind to her, even love her. Buck was certain that if Hannah pledged herself to a man, she would do so with her whole heart. He wasn't sure Amos Merrick had a heart to pledge.

At least he was a better choice than Gillett. Amos

might be a self-important jerk, but he wasn't a crook. Buck didn't think he was evil, either, just convinced of his own superiority.

"Hello, Amos," Hannah said with a distinct lack of enthusiasm. "How are you?"

"You know how I am," Amos said. "Distracted, unable to concentrate on my work since you said you wouldn't marry me."

Amos didn't look distracted. He looked quite cheerful. Buck wondered if Hannah could see that.

"Don't be ridiculous," Hannah said. "You're far too pleased with yourself ever to become distracted over a female, especially me."

Amos laughed. Buck hated that sound. It had too much self-assurance in it, too much certainty that life would never deny Amos Merrick anything he wanted.

"You always were sharp-tongued," Amos said. "Mother says it's a bad trait, but I find it amusing."

"You wouldn't be amused for long. Listen to your mother, Amos. She knows the kind of wife who would please you."

Buck was relieved to see that Hannah wasn't overwhelmed by Utopia's most eligible bachelor.

"I know what pleases me," Amos insisted, "and it's you. It always has been."

"I'm quite satisfied to live on my ranch with my chickens and my garden," Hannah said.

"You can have all the chickens and gardens you want. Pigs and cows, too."

"I want to live on a ranch, Amos, not here in town."

Buck realized he'd miss Hannah if she left the ranch. Whether he wanted to or not, he liked her. A lot. He didn't want her to get married. At least not yet. Certainly not to anybody like Amos or Gillett.

What had gotten into him? Hannah wasn't his responsibility. He was quite willing to protect her, but Amos wasn't threatening her and she had a mother to give her advice. He had to be confusing his interest in the ranch with Hannah. That could be dangerous.

"I'll buy you a ranch," Amos was saying.

"I already have one."

"That old place will go under in six months."

"No, it won't. Buck will see to that."

Amos became aware of Buck for the first time. From the expression on his face, he wasn't impressed by what he saw.

"Do I know you?"

"We met in your father's office," Buck said.

"You'll never save that ranch. There's nothing out there but cedar and scrub oak. Rustlers ran off all the stock."

"I think I can save it," Buck said.

"You're nothing but a cowhand. What do you know about ranching?"

"Enough."

Buck didn't like being looked down on, and it was obvious Amos thought him ignorant, shiftless, and probably dishonest as well. Amos glared at him with a distinct lack of warm feelings. Buck stared right back.

"Why don't you go check on your horse or something," Amos said. "Miss Grossek and I have things to talk about."

"We have nothing to say we haven't said already," Hannah said. "I'm in a hurry. I've got to sell my pickled beef."

"Why?"

"Because I need the money," Hannah said.

"I knew it!" Amos exclaimed. "You're starving, and you're too proud to tell me."

Buck nearly laughed when Hannah grew pink with indignation.

"We are *not* starving, and don't you tell anyone we are."

"Then why—"

"I have more beef than I can use and less cash than I need. Does that satisfy you?"

"No." He took her by the arm and turned her in the direction of his father's bank. "I'm certain you're hiding something, and I'm going to find out what it is."

"Let me go, Amos."

But Amos didn't release Hannah. It was obvious he meant to escort her to his father's office whether she wanted to go or not.

"Get your hands off her," Buck growled. He tried to accompany his order with a non-threatening expression but doubted he'd succeeded. He wanted to do a great deal more than threaten Amos Merrick.

"This is none of your concern," Amos said. He did not release his hold on Hannah.

"It should be everyone's concern when a man tries to force a woman to do something against her will."

"It's not against her will."

"It certainly is," Hannah said, jerking her elbow out of Amos's grasp. "I told you I was in a hurry."

"But I want you to marry me."

"I don't want to get married, Amos. I've told you that over and over."

"You've got to marry somebody. You can't go on living by yourself."

"That's exactly what I intend to do. Now good-bye, Amos. Tell your father I shall pay the debt in full by the end of six months."

Hannah began walking away.

"You'll never do it," Amos called after her. "I can take care of you. That cowhand never will."

"Is he always like that?" Buck asked when they were out of hearing range.

"Amos can't understand why a woman with no prospects would refuse a man with so many. It entirely escapes his notice that the reason could be that he's part of the bargain."

"I get the impression he thinks he's the best part."

"Everybody agrees with him. Why should he believe me?"

"Has he wanted to marry you for a long time?"

"Over a year."

"Why haven't you accepted?"

"I have no desire to be under any man's control," Hannah said. "But even if I did want to marry, I wouldn't marry Amos. I don't love him. I don't think he really loves me."

"Is love that important to you?"

"It would be if I were getting married. Wouldn't it be to you?"

"I don't know."

Despite seeing how much Jake and Isabelle loved each other and all the boys, Buck had never really thought of anybody loving him. He hoped his sister would live with him if he ever found her, but he didn't put any dependence on love. If a mother and father couldn't love their own son, who else could?

"Didn't the people who adopted you love you?" Hannah asked.

"Isabelle said she loved all of us. But she'd have to say that to adopt us, wouldn't she?"

"I wouldn't tell a person I loved them if I didn't mean it."

"Have you told anybody you love them?"

"Mama loves me, and I love her," Hannah said. "We've never told each other, but we do."

"Then you should tell her. Jake says you should tell people how you feel."

Jake wasn't good with words, but the boys knew they were important to him, that he worried about them. Jake and Isabelle had been unhappy when Buck and Zeke left. Buck wondered if it could be because they loved him and Zeke. He couldn't be sure.

Yet he did know something of the feel of love. He remembered how much he enjoyed playing with Isabelle's baby, how good it felt when they were all around the table or working together as a group. He had held back from the feeling, thinking it didn't include him. Maybe he'd been wrong. Now he wished he'd tried to find out.

Was it okay to want love but not give it? He was afraid of what wanting love might do to him. It threatened his plan. He had this terrible feeling he was going soft on Hannah, and that scared him. It also confused him.

Buck wanted to get off the subject of love. It made him uncomfortable. "I need to go by the cattle growers association office before we go. I want to check on that brand."

"Can you find out who owns it?"

"If it's registered."

The registrations were kept in a lawyer's office. Buck's request to see the brand book didn't surprise the man.

"There's been a good deal of activity in the last year or so," he said as he brought the book out. "Mr.

184

Gillett has bought up several ranches along with their brands."

Buck's heart sank. If Gillett had bought the star brand, he had lost his one chance for a peaceful resolution.

"You wanting to register your brand?" the lawyer asked.

"Yes." Buck hadn't intended to, but it seemed like a good idea.

"Where's your place?"

"I'm looking to buy an interest in the Tumbling T. This is the owner, Miss Grossek."

The lawyer acted as though Buck hadn't mentioned Hannah.

"You'd be wasting your money," he said. "If Nathaniel Grossek couldn't make a go of the place, nobody can."

"I intend to try."

"Joseph Merrick said you were a determined man, but you'll need more than that. Merrick said the stock had been run off."

"It drifted over the winter, but that was to be expected with nobody to look after it."

Buck took the book the lawyer handed him and opened it. He flipped pages until he came to the last brands. He didn't see the six-pointed star on the last page. Nor the page before that. Hope returned. He looked through the entire list without finding the brand. He went through it again to make certain.

The brand wasn't there!

He told himself to remain calm. There were many possible explanations, one being that the brand was registered in a neighboring county.

"Let me look at it," Hannah said.

The lawyer didn't look as though he approved, but he made no objection when Buck handed the book to Hannah. "Any local brands not included in this book?" Buck asked.

"Not that I know of," the lawyer replied.

"How long would it take to get a new brand accepted?"

"A couple of weeks. As long as it takes to send it to Austin to make sure nobody else has it."

"I want to register two brands," Buck said. "The first is a six-pointed star."

Hannah looked up, surprised. When she opened her mouth to speak, he shook his head slightly. She gave him a worried look and then appeared to turn her attention back to the book. But she watched him out of the corner of her eye.

Buck drew the brand in the book, indicating how it was to be placed on the cow. "I want it registered in the names of Mrs. Sarah Grossek, Hannah Grossek, Buck Hobson, and Zeke Maxwell."

Hannah didn't react to that. Buck was relieved. He knew he'd have to explain later, but this wasn't the time. He didn't know what Zeke would think of being given Jake's last name, but Buck didn't think this lawyer would understand about Zeke's being a slave.

"That's a lot of people," the lawyer said.

"Zeke and I are partners. If we buy into the ranch, we'll all have an equal interest."

Buck watched while the lawyer wrote down all the necessary information. He wouldn't know if his plan was going to work until he heard from Austin.

"The second brand is a Z with an H attached," Buck said. "I want that registered in the names of Buck Hobson and Zeke Maxwell."

Hannah stared at him, her look angry.

"What do you need that brand for?" she asked.

"Zeke found some wild horses. We hope to catch

a few. They've got to be branded, just like cows."

Hannah watched while the lawyer wrote down all the information, distrust in her eyes. She looked as though she thought Buck was pulling a fast one.

"I want a brand as well," she told the lawyer.

"You're a woman," the man said. "You can't have one."

"Is there a law against women registering a brand?" Buck asked.

"No, but—"

"Then she can have one."

Buck knew he should keep his mouth shut, but it irked him that everyone seemed to think Hannah had no rights or feelings. Isabelle would have turned this town on its ear in less than an hour.

But by sticking up for Hannah, he was just causing himself trouble. She didn't need a brand. This lawyer would have done all the refusing for him. But no, he had to pipe up and insist she get her brand. He had no idea what she intended to do with it, but he could be certain it would cause him trouble.

"I don't know if they'll accept this in Austin," the lawyer said.

"You let us worry about that," Buck said. "Describe your brand or draw it in the book yourself," he told Hannah.

She eagerly took the pen and made an H attached to a squared-off G. She looked so pleased with herself, Buck didn't have the heart to point out that she had nothing to brand.

"I would like a dated letter outlining all we've done," Buck told the lawyer.

"You sure like documenting everything," the man said.

"My . . . father"—Buck hesitated over the word.

He'd never called Jake his father before; he didn't know why he should have done it now—"lost his ranch because he didn't have a proper title. I don't mean for that to happen to me."

"Nathaniel Grossek made sure of his ranch. I have all the documents in my safe."

Buck liked knowing none of the deeds were in Merrick's hands. He turned to Hannah. "We'd better be on our way."

He had expected she would attack him the moment they were out of the lawyer's office, but she didn't say a word. However, her silence was heavy with tension. He sensed that the good feeling growing between them since he faced down Mr. Bakker had dissipated. His registering a brand in his name had resurrected her doubts about whether she could trust him.

What Hannah thought of his actions shouldn't matter to him, but he was beginning to discover it did. He liked it much better when she smiled at him. It was easier to work with someone who liked you and whom you liked. It was certainly easier to work with someone you trusted, but neither of them trusted the other.

They found Moffett's farm without difficulty. It occupied two hundred acres of bottom land where three small streams came together to form a larger one. The farmer had been able to dam the streams to store water for his livestock and irrigate his crops.

Moffett was a member of the sect, but he was as cheerful as his fellow Utopians were sour.

"I was sorry to hear about your pa," he said when the wagon came to a stop. "You selling up?"

"Thank you, and no, I'm not. I'm trying to sell

188

pickled beef and sauerkraut. Mrs. Grosswelt said you might be interested."

Moffett's eyes grew wide with pleasure. "Bless the woman. I would be happy for some." He slapped his thigh. "I've got five strapping boys and no woman to do for us. It's nigh impossible to get enough food for them. At least, any that's good."

"You're welcome to have a taste," Hannah offered.

Moffett didn't give her a chance to change her mind. He opened a jar, took out a piece of beef, and bit off a mouthful. The look that spread over his countenance was pure joy.

"I'll take every jar you've got. I'll send one of the boys over to get any you left at home. I'll even send you a beef of my own if you'll pickle it for me."

Hannah smiled happily. "You can have the whole wagon load if you like."

Moffett whistled sharply, and two boys came at a trot. "Carry everything into the house," he ordered. "And if you break so much as one jar, I'll have the skin off your back. I'll take the pies myself," he told Hannah. "I don't trust them not to drop one."

Hannah tallied up the number of jars and they settled on a price. "You wouldn't take a cow in exchange, would you?" Moffett asked. "A man never likes to part with that much gold."

"I want a horse and a saddle," Hannah said before he could respond. "A cow pony. I intend to learn how to run my ranch."

Moffett studied her a moment. "You sure about this?"

"Quite positive."

"Then you'd better go see old man Hanson. He owes me for several loads of hay. You can have my wife's old sidesaddle. He'll never need one. Now let's see, I still owe you more money."

The youngest boy came out of the house. "Everything's put up, Papa. Heinrick wants you in the pasture. He wants to know what you want done about those calves."

"I want them out of my hair," Moffett said. "I was a fool to take them. I'm a farmer, not a rancher."

"What calves?" Hannah asked.

"A trail driver passed through here a few days ago. Traded me his newborn calves for milk and eggs. I thought I could raise the things. I forgot you have to feed the little cusses by hand. Now I can't get rid of them. Nobody wants them."

"I want them," Hannah said.

"What'll you do with them?" Buck asked.

"Raise them," she said, turning defiant eyes to him. "And put my brand on them. If you get any more, I'd like to have them as well."

"How will you get them home?" Moffett asked.

"Put them in the wagon."

"All six of them? What if they jump out?"

"Buck will catch them."

Buck started to tell her he needed two good arms to rope a calf but decided it wasn't worth it. Hannah was going to have those calves if she had to rope them together and lead them herself.

Moffett and his sons put the calves in the wagon. Buck was disgusted when every one of them obligingly lay down.

"See, I knew it wouldn't be a problem," Hannah said.

Buck bit his tongue.

"Keep your eye on Hanson," Moffett warned. "He's not one of us. He may try to cheat you."

Buck didn't tell Moffett that he'd trust Lyman Gillett and his whole crew before he'd trust one of the sect. At least with Gillett, he knew what kind of snake he was be dealing with.

The stop at old man Hanson's began smoothly. Hannah relayed Moffett's message, explained what she wanted, and they trooped out to the corral. The calves obligingly remained quiet in the wagon.

"Which horse do you think I ought to have?" Hannah asked Buck.

"Have you ever ridden a cow pony?"

"No."

"Then I'd say none of them."

"But I know how to ride."

"Riding a horse and working a cow pony are not the same, especially in a sidesaddle. You could get yourself killed."

"Which one do you think I ought to have?" she asked Mr. Hanson.

"I think you ought to listen to your husband."

Buck felt as shocked as Hannah looked. It had never occurred to him—or Hannah, either, from the look of it—that their appearing together would give the impression they were married.

"I'm not married," Hannah said. "Buck works for us."

It irritated Buck to see disapproval in Hanson's eyes. Did everybody assume he was so randy he couldn't keep his hands off Hannah? They'd feel a good deal different if they'd had to listen to Isabelle expound on the way men ought to treat women.

"There's nobody to run the place since Hannah's father died," Buck said. "Her mother hired me to do it for her."

It galled him to have to explain the situation to this man, but it would end up hurting Hannah if he didn't.

"I'm determined to learn how to do my own work," Hannah told Hanson. "I can't do that without a horse."

Buck hadn't meant to help her pick out a horse—he disapproved of what she was doing—but the rancher's attitude had put up his hackles. He refused to let anybody else treat her the way she'd been treated in Utopia. She'd have her horse. She'd have the best one in the corral.

"How about that pretty sorrel over there?" Hanson said.

"I'll pick out the horse," Buck said.

"What are you going to do?" Hannah asked when he crawled through the fence.

"Stir them up. I want to study their action."

For several minutes he hazed them back and forth across the corral. "Buy the hammerhead dun," he said when he walked back to the fence.

"He's the ugliest horse in the corral," Hanson said.

"Probably, but he's got the smoothest gait. He also has good legs and a deep chest. He doesn't throw up his head every time I approach. He's less likely to dump Hannah on her backside and leave her to walk home."

Hannah gave Buck a measuring look before studying the horse for several moments. "I'll take him."

"You sure you won't have the sorrel?" Hanson asked. "He's real pretty."

"He's also flighty and has bad fetlocks," Buck said.

"I'll take the dun," Hannah said.

Hanson's dissatisfaction pleased Buck. He was even more pleased that Hannah had accepted his advice even though she didn't understand it.

GET YOUR 4 FREE BOOKS
NOW—A $21.96 Value!

*Mail the Free Book
Certificate
Today!*

Get Four Books Totally FREE — A $21.96 Value!

▼ Tear Here and Mail Your FREE Book Card Today! ▼

PLEASE RUSH
MY FOUR FREE
BOOKS TO ME
RIGHT AWAY!

Leisure Romance Book Club
P.O. Box 6613
Edison, NJ 08818-6613

AFFIX
STAMP
HERE

"You want to ride him home?" Hanson asked.

"No. Tie him to the back of the wagon."

"He knew you'd picked out the best horse, didn't he?" Hannah asked when they were on their way home.

Buck nodded.

"I'd have bought the sorrel."

"I know."

"Why didn't you let me? You don't want me to have a horse."

"If you're going to learn to manage your own place, the first thing you've got to know is how to judge a horse."

"The first thing I've got to know is how to judge men," Hannah corrected. "They're much more dangerous than horses."

They were sitting next to each other on the seat, Buck handling the reins, the horse walking behind, the calves behaving like little angels.

"All men use women," Hannah said. "The only question is for what. Gillett wants me because he thinks I'm pretty. Amos wants someone who'll take care of his needs and never cause him a minute's trouble."

"And you're that woman?"

Hannah fixed him with a hard stare. "I'm not anybody's woman."

They rode for a few moments in silence.

"You, on the other hand, want my ranch."

Buck turned sharply.

"You've got scruples. You won't steal it—Amos would if he wanted it—but you mean to have it nonetheless. You know any money I make will go for debts. You plan to capture horses, maybe even round up stray cattle. I'll pay the debts, and you'll have the money. I won't have any choice but to sell out to you, or to give away more and more of my part of the ranch. You think I'll marry and settle down, leave you a ranch and a clear conscience."

Buck swallowed. She couldn't have outlined his plan more clearly if he'd explained it to her.

"But it's not going to work," she said. "I'm going to buy you out."

Buck didn't know how to respond to that. He felt guilty having his plan pulled into the open. It sounded underhanded when she explained it like that.

More unsettling, he wasn't sure he did want to see her married and settled down. He certainly didn't want her to marry Amos or Gillett. Everybody else was either too old or too young.

"Maybe it won't come to that," he said. "Maybe we can work out a real partnership."

The look Hannah gave him was not trusting. "Why should we do that?"

"We want the same thing."

"What are you trying to say?"

He didn't know. He didn't know why he was saying anything at all, certainly not that they could share the ranch on a long-term basis. That would mean . . . well, it would mean a whole lot of things he wasn't about to consider.

But he'd been thinking about it more and more. "Just something to think about," he said.

They drove into the ranch yard, and Buck was relieved of having to explain. Zeke and young Tom Gladdis walked out of the house, Gladdis picking his teeth, Zeke looking none too happy.

"What are you doing here?" Buck asked Gladdis.

"I don't like working for a rustler," the boy said. "I've come to ask you for a job."

Chapter Thirteen

"What do you mean?" Hannah asked, as she climbed down from the wagon.

"I hired on a week ago," Tom explained. "I didn't figure out what Gillett was doing until I ran across Buck and Zeke with those cows. Gillett has been running your stock off all winter. He plans to brand everything with that funny star and then drive them to Nebraska."

"Is the brand registered there?" Buck asked.

"I guess so."

Hannah turned back to Buck. "Then that means—"

"He intends to keep the stock here until after roundup," Buck said. He didn't want Hannah telling anyone they had registered Gillett's brand. Her look indicated that she didn't understand, but was willing to wait for his explanation.

"What the hell have you got here?" Zeke demanded on seeing the calves.

"Hannah decided to start her own herd," Buck said. "This is the beginning."

"I'm not babysitting calves," Zeke snapped.

"I'll take care of them," Hannah said, "if you and Tom would take them out of the wagon for me."

"Does that mean I'm hired?" Tom asked.

Buck grinned. "I guess so."

Zeke ignored the calves. "Nice horse," he said, giving the dun a good going-over. "Didn't know you were in the market for another one."

"That's Hannah's horse," Buck said.

"Don't tell me she picked him out." Zeke's disbelief was patent.

"Buck picked him out," Hannah said. "I'd have bought a flashy sorrel with an uncertain temperament and bad fetlocks."

"I'll bet you don't even know what a fetlock is."

Sometimes Buck wished Zeke would keep his mouth shut.

"I do, but I confess I can't tell good from bad."

"Where do you want these calves?" Tom asked.

"In the pen behind the barn," Hannah said.

Tom lifted a calf to the ground. No sooner had its feet touched the ground than it darted off like an antelope. The five in the wagon, rather than be left behind, jumped to their feet, tumbled out of the wagon, and tore off in different directions. Tom started laughing. Zeke's profanity brought a flush to Hannah's cheeks.

"Mount up," Buck said, unable to hide his grin. "I'll hold the gate for you."

"I ought to go after them," Hannah said. "They're my calves."

"You'd better see to dinner," Buck said and winked. "Everybody's going to be hungry before this is over."

"What's going on?" Zeke demanded even before Hannah was out of earshot.

"What do you mean?" Buck asked as he headed toward the barn.

"I saw you wink at Hannah."

"We've become friends. That's all."

"In one day?" Zeke's skepticism was patent.

"No, I guess it didn't happen in one day. We just didn't realize it until now."

Zeke's expression combined anger and disgust. "Why is it, no matter how smart a man is, he turns dumber than a basket full of rocks when you sit him next to a pretty woman?"

"There's nothing wrong with being friends."

"Ain't no woman alive that can be friends with a man. Either she wants him in her bed, or she wants him down the road."

"Don't be ridiculous. I have no intention of—"

"You didn't have any intention of being friends, either. You hated her when you came here, remember?"

"I shouldn't have. She never did anything to me."

"That's not the tale you used to tell. You said she—"

"I know what I said, but I was wrong."

Zeke subjected him to a hard stare. "I didn't come here to work for her. If you give her one cow, one horse, anything that doesn't belong to her, I'm leaving."

Zeke turned and left. Buck wanted to stop him, to explain, but he couldn't. He didn't know what was going on himself.

*   *   *

After giving her mother a heavily edited version of their day, Hannah went to her room to change her clothes. Instead she found herself sitting on the bed, trying to sort through the events of the day, trying to get her feelings in order.

But things had changed so quickly, she hadn't kept up. She kept saying she didn't want to get married. At the same time she was liking Buck more and more, wanting him to stay longer and longer. She kept saying she didn't trust men, but she'd never thought twice about trusting her property or herself to Buck's protection. She kept saying she wanted to run the ranch by herself, never wanted to depend on a man, even though she found it impossible to think of the ranch without thinking of Buck being there.

Nothing she did made any sense, and she couldn't blame it all on Buck. She had started to think things, feel things, want things . . . to act as she'd never acted before.

Strangest of all, she didn't care that she was making a bigger liar out of herself with every passing minute. She'd say one thing and feel another. She'd do one thing, then want to do something else. She didn't understand herself, but she couldn't get upset. She'd never felt better in her life.

She thought of telling her mother but changed her mind. This was her secret. It was all the sweeter for that.

Buck had expected dinner to be tense. After spending nearly half an hour rounding up Hannah's calves, Zeke was in a swearing mood. That always made Sarah Grossek nervous. Tom Gladdis treated her like a queen. That made her even more nervous.

"Can I carry anything to the table for you?" He asked that question a dozen times if he asked it once. "Watch out, you'll burn yourself. Here, let me."

They'd have been less likely to have an accident if he'd sat down and kept out of the way. They'd also have gotten the food on the table faster.

"Let me hold your chair, ma'am," he said when they were ready to eat. "Hold on there," he ordered Zeke. "Miss Hannah isn't seated yet."

Buck thought Zeke would bust a blood vessel, but he waited for Hannah to be seated while Buck held her chair. From the first bite he put in his mouth, Gladdis couldn't stop praising the food.

"This is better than my mom's cooking," he said, stuffing his mouth without any concern for the good manners he'd shown earlier. "I didn't think I'd ever taste anything that good again. Mr. Gillett's cook is French. He can ruin a fried egg. I don't want to tell you what strange things he does to good beef."

"We don't either," Zeke growled as he stuffed his own mouth.

"Maybe you always had good food," Gladdis said, "but I didn't. Sometimes it wasn't any better than pig slop."

"We know about pig slops," Zeke muttered.

The remark meant nothing to Gladdis.

"Sure is nice to be sitting at the table with two handsome females," he said to Sarah Grossek.

"Tom Gladdis," Hannah said with mock severity, "are you flirting with my mother?"

The boy turned a deep shade of crimson. "I didn't mean . . . I would never say anything . . . You don't think—"

"I don't mind if you do," Hannah said. "I just hope

199

someone thinks I'm pretty enough to flirt with when I'm as old as Mama."

"You're plenty pretty, Miss Hannah." He grinned, not the least bit embarrassed now. "But not as pretty as your mama."

"Remind me not to ask you when I want my vanity flattered."

Buck thought poor Sarah Grossek wouldn't be able to finish her meal after that. She got up to refill a bowl. Gladdis jumped to his feet.

"Keep your butt in that chair, or I'm gonna tie it down," Zeke growled.

"We appreciate your wanting to help," Hannah said, "but it would be easier if you didn't get up every time we did. You'll never finish your dinner."

"No worry about that." As proof, he wolfed down his food faster than Zeke.

"Now that you've hired yourself on here," Buck said, "what do you plan to do?" Maybe if he got Gladdis talking, he would act like a normal human being.

"I know all the places Gillett's got your cows hid," he said, his irrepressible grin broadening again. "While you're nursing that shoulder, I thought me and old Grumpy Gus could round up a few under cover of dark."

"Grumpy Gus" gave him a look that promised retribution. Buck figured the "nursing your shoulder" remark deserved at least one thump. When Hannah started fussing over him, Buck decided maybe several would be better.

"You'll get hurt," she said. "Buck and Zeke have been fired at."

"Shucks, Miss Grossek, I know just about every back trail on that place. We'll be in and out faster than an otter down a slippery creek bank. Grumpy Gus couldn't do it smoother."

"My name's Zeke," Zeke said.

"Sure. Is Zeke short for Ezekiel?"

Zeke reached over and took a handful of Tom's shirt. He practically lifted the boy out of his seat. "It's short for Zeke!"

"We'll hit Gillett on the far side of his range," Gladdis said, unfazed by Zeke's anger. "Maybe he'll think one of the ranchers west of him did it."

"I thought you said you were so smooth he'd never know what happened." Zeke's tone of voice reflected his complete lack of confidence in Tom's boast.

"He'll know he's missing cows," Gladdis said, "but not who took 'em."

"I wish you wouldn't go," Hannah said.

"He's going," Zeke declared. "I'm gonna find out if there's anything to him besides bluster."

Buck didn't find Hannah alone until nearly bedtime. He would rather have gone into his room, closed the door, and tried to forget she slept only a few feet away. He could take a ranch away from a stranger, especially one he didn't like. He didn't think he could take anything from a friend, even if everything he did was legal.

Buck reminded himself that he could only exorcise the cruelties of the past by possessing the land of the man who had brutalized him. But that didn't seem quite as important as it used to. He searched his mind for something that might have become more important, but he couldn't find anything.

"I want to speak with you a moment before you go to bed."

He'd stepped out into the hall as Hannah headed

toward her bedroom. He could see little more than her face illuminated by the light from the coal-oil lamp she carried.

"What about?"

She looked uncomfortable. She probably didn't want to be near him unless absolutely necessary. She didn't trust him, even looked a little afraid of him. He wondered whether that stemmed from years of being afraid of her father. He knew what that kind of fear could do to a person.

"I wanted to warn you not to tell anyone I registered that star brand. Not even your mother."

"Why?"

It bothered him to see the distrust in her eyes. Turning his back on Jake and Isabelle had bothered him. Now his conscience was telling him that he was going to use Hannah and turn his back on her.

He kept telling himself that he was doing nothing illegal, that he would actually leave Hannah and her mother better off than they were now, but that rationale didn't work anymore. The doubts, the questions, the feeling of guilt came back a little stronger each time.

"If Gillett suspects anything, he'll get the cattle out of the state and we'll never get them back."

"Mama won't tell anybody."

"It's not that. I haven't even told Zeke, and I trust him with my life. If nobody knows, they can't accidentally say anything to make anybody suspicious."

"Is that all you have to do, claim the cows at the roundup?"

"There'll probably be a blowup when Gillett discovers what I've done. I doubt he'll let all that work go for nothing."

"What will you do?"

"I won't know until I see what Gillett does."

"I don't see how you can talk as if this is no more serious than a barn dance." She looked worried. "I'm not sure I think those cows are worth getting shot over."

"They're not."

"Then why are you doing it?"

"It's a matter of principle. And of survival. If I let Gillett take my cows, he and men like him will strip me of everything I own. Somebody might even decide to take you. Or your mother," he added quickly when he realized what he'd said.

"They wouldn't do that."

"Your father kept me here as a virtual prisoner. No reason somebody couldn't do the same with you."

He hadn't meant to mention her father. It was unfair to make her feel guilty for something she didn't do. But it was hard to forget. Everything about this place reminded him of the months he'd stayed alive only because he'd sworn to get revenge.

"You're frightening me."

He took her hand, meaning only to give it a gentle squeeze of reassurance. Suddenly the hall, his body, even the air around him was charged with powerful currents. He nearly jerked his hand back. He'd never touched a woman in this way before, but he liked it. That scared him. It seemed to frighten Hannah even more. Her eyes grew big with surprise; her body stiffened.

"Nobody is going to do anything to you or your mother while I'm here." He meant to mention Zeke and Tom Gladdis, too, but somehow he didn't. He meant to release her hand, but he didn't do that either.

She squeezed his hand in return. It was a tiny,

nearly insignificant thing—she probably wasn't even aware she'd done it—but it electrified him. Only one woman had ever touched him like this. And it sure wasn't the same when Isabelle did it.

"I'm more worried about you, and Zeke and Tom," she added. "Mr. Evans, too."

"We'll be all right."

He squeezed her hand again. He just stood there, waiting, thinking how odd it was for the two of them to be standing in this narrow hall, holding hands. Yet he didn't think it odd when she turned her face up to his, nor when he bent and kissed her. It seemed the most natural thing in the world.

Her lips were soft, sweet. He'd been certain they would be. They quivered under his. She stood there, not backing away. Their lips touched in a series of tentative kisses, almost as if they were tasting each other. The warmth and softness of her kisses intoxicated him. He felt himself lean forward. Each kiss caused him to want more. He felt a need in him spring up full-grown.

The intensity of it rocked him; he feared it would frighten Hannah away. He didn't want her to flee. He might not have known it at the time, but he'd been wanting this from the moment he rode up and saw her sitting under that tree. A distant, analytical voice in his mind shouted at him that he was risking everything he'd come here to achieve, but Buck didn't care. His need had been held under control for too long.

He released Hannah's hand only to take her by the shoulders and pull her toward him. Their kiss deepened and became more intense. He could hear her breaths come more quickly, like tiny gasps of surprise. Each one served to ratchet his temperature another degree higher until he felt as if he was burning with a feverish desire to consume her.

Fearing he was on the verge of losing control, Buck drew back. As he let his hands drop to his sides, Hannah stared at him out of eyes big with surprise. Shock. Maybe even terror.

"I was proud of you today," he said. "It's not easy when your friends turn against you." He didn't know why he'd brought that up. She didn't need to be reminded.

"It doesn't matter," she said, her words even and uninflected, as if she were in a trance.

"It'll be easier next time."

She paused and then moved back a step. "I'd better get to bed. I imagine the calves are going to be hungry early."

"You sure you can handle them along with everything else you have to do?"

"Of course. I intend to make at least fifteen dollars apiece on them."

The spell broke, and they both blinked, bewildered and shocked by what had just passed between them. Everything had changed, yet everything was the same. Buck didn't know what to do next, although he did know he'd set out on a course that would change his life. But did he want such a change?

Hannah squirmed in the saddle. She knew she was going to be so sore that she would hardly be able to walk, but she refused to give Buck the satisfaction of admitting he was right. He hadn't wanted her to come with him while he spoke to the ranchers about joining together for the roundup. She didn't know whether he didn't trust her, thought it wasn't a woman's place, or just didn't want her to interfere. She did know he no longer disliked her.

Hannah had never been kissed. She had no girl-friends to exchange confidences with. She'd never seen her parents touch. The whole thing had come as a lovely surprise. She was bursting to know if they could repeat it.

All morning she hadn't been able to stop thinking of those few moments in the hall last night. Buck tried to act as if it had never happened. She could tell he wasn't unaffected, but she couldn't tell *how* he felt.

One minute she would be certain it was nothing more than a short burst of sexual energy between a man and a woman. The next minute she would be certain it had meant as much to him as to her, but he was too unsure of himself to let it show. It was difficult, however, to picture Buck as unsure of anything. He had set his goals, then focused his attention on achieving them. He wasn't about to let anybody stand in his way.

Since Buck's shoulder wasn't quite healed, Tom had helped her saddle her horse. Zeke had stomped off muttering about the stupidity of riding around a ranch in a sidesaddle.

Zeke and Tom's midnight foray onto Lyman Gillett's range had produced nearly thirty cows and calves.

"That boy is a born thief," Zeke had said. "If I could slide in and out of shadows like he can, those Indians would never have caught me."

"Not a lot more to find," Tom had told Buck. "Gillett has branded a lot already."

"Get what you can," Buck had said, "but don't take any unnecessary chances. Now get some sleep. We're off to see the ranchers."

Buck

* * *

The first ranch they came to was owned by Aldo Jenkins. The ranch house was no more than a crude cabin. A hen house, a lean-to, and two corrals were the only other structures. The garden was well cared for, but everything else looked a little run-down.

Jenkins was of medium height and stocky, with well-muscled shoulders. He had vivid black hair and eyes. He seemed to be about forty.

"Light and sit a spell," he said. "The wife has coffee on."

They dismounted and entered one of the two rooms in the cabin. The Jenkinses had three kids, two boys and a girl, all under ten and all barefooted. Mrs. Jenkins hadn't finished clearing away breakfast.

Hannah suddenly felt nervous. She'd met very few women since her father moved them to the ranch, none of them outside her own sect. The woman looked older than Hannah's mother, her face thin and pinched by worry, her hair streaked with gray. She wore a faded calico dress and heavy shoes. Hannah guessed she was under thirty. It frightened her to think she could look like that in ten years.

Buck looked almost boyish next to Mr. Jenkins, yet there was something about the way he carried himself that belied his youthful appearance. You might think of Buck as young, but you'd never think of him as a boy.

"What brings you over this way?" Mr. Jenkins asked.

"Miss Grossek and her mother own the Tumbling T," Buck said. "I work for them. We're here to talk to you about joining us and the other ranchers in this area in a common roundup."

Jenkins accepted a cup of steaming coffee from his wife. He poured some into a cracked, plain white saucer, blew on it, and eyed both of them while he sipped the hot liquid. Hannah declined Mrs. Jenkins's offer of coffee. Buck accepted. The three kids hovered in the doorway.

"You spoke to the other ranchers yet?" Jenkins asked.

"You're the first," Buck said.

"Why are you wanting to roundup together?"

"Mr. Grossek's stock wandered all over the county. I can't go looking on people's ranges without permission. Even then, I couldn't cover it all by myself."

"You don't trust me to return any of your cows I find?"

"When it's a question of lost stock, I find it's better to have all parties involved working together. That way there can be no misunderstanding."

"You expecting some kind of misunderstanding?"

"This was a particularly bad winter," Buck said, avoiding the question. "I thought maybe some of your stock might have wandered. Your neighbors, too. With enough people working, we could make a systematic sweep through the county. We'd miss fewer cows, have fewer mavericks to deal with in the fall."

Jenkins went back to sipping his coffee and staring at Buck over his saucer. Buck didn't seem bothered by Mr. Jenkins's long silence or the unnerving way he had of staring at him. Hannah wondered what could be going on in the man's head.

"What makes you think I'm missing stock?"

"Ranchers are always missing stock."

Hannah's attention was drawn to Jenkins's wife. The woman had remained at the stove, but now she faced them. She clearly wanted to say something.

"You never did answer my question about a misunderstanding," Jenkins said.

Buck put his coffee cup down. He looked from Jenkins to his wife and back to Jenkins. "There's no misunderstanding. Someone is rustling cattle, and I don't believe they're limiting themselves to Tumbling T stock."

"You have any proof?"

"No."

"Yet you want me and the other ranchers to help you get your stock back."

"Yes."

Hannah could almost feel the tension. As though he could feel his wife's gaze on his back, Mr. Jenkins turned around.

"Tell him, Aldo," she said. "You've got to tell somebody."

"It won't do no good now."

"He still ought to know."

"I can't prove nothing."

"Tell him." She turned to the kids. "Outside. You got chores waiting. They ain't going to do themselves."

Their hair was cut badly and their clothes needed patching, but they were bright-eyed children, alert and curious, unlike their parents, who looked tired and beaten down.

Mrs. Jenkins remained by the stove. Hannah imagined she'd never been invited to join in the decision making. Hannah didn't see any reason why she shouldn't. It was her life; the welfare of her children was at stake. Hannah pointed to an empty chair.

"Come join us."

Mrs. Jenkins hesitated.

"You might as well," Mr. Jenkins said. "You're the one wanting my shame broadcast all over the county."

"We shoulda told when it happened," Mrs. Jenkins said as she nervously took a seat in a home-made chair next to her husband. Much to Hannah's surprise, Mrs. Jenkins stretched out a dry, chapped hand to her husband. He didn't push it away. "Now tell him."

"It was last spring," Mr. Jenkins began. "I'd been laid up most of the winter with a broken leg. Don't keep riding hands on over the winter. Nothing for them to do, really."

"At least that's what we thought," Mrs. Jenkins said.

"Figured my oldest boy could handle what needed doing," Mr. Jenkins said. "He was going on nine. Come spring, when I hired hands for the roundup, I couldn't hardly find any cows or young stuff. It was like they'd disappeared. I went to all the ranches, but nobody had seen my cows. Some said they must have wandered clean out of the county."

"Did you talk to Lyman Gillett?" Buck asked.

"He sure did," Mrs. Jenkins said. "I went with him. Only we didn't get to talk to Mr. Gillett. We talked to that murdering gunfighter he's got working for him."

"Sid Barraclough?"

"That's him," Mr. Jenkins said.

"He told us Mr. Gillett didn't have time to worry about our cows. He said none of them had seen hide nor hair of them. Then he told us to get off the place."

"What did you do?" Hannah asked.

"What could he do?" Mrs. Jenkins said, speaking for her husband. "Aldo is no gunfighter. It was go or fight that man. Aldo has three children to think of."

"I didn't have any proof anybody did anything," Mr. Jenkins said. "None of the other ranchers lost stock."

"Or so they said," Mrs. Jenkins added.

"By the time I figured things out and started doing a little investigating on my own, it was too late. Whoever took those cows had taken them out of the county."

"But we know Mr. Lyman Gillett did it," Mrs. Jenkins said.

"I got enough stock to sell for this year and the next," Mr. Jenkins said, "but I don't know if I've got enough to keep this place going after that."

"Do you have any hands?" Buck asked.

"Can't afford to hire any. To be frank with you, I'm almost afraid to start roundup. If I've lost cows again this winter, I'll go under."

"Then how're we going to take care of our children?" Mrs. Jenkins asked.

"We lost even more of our stock," Buck said. "About two thirds. We found some of it, but we still probably lost half of our cows and young stuff."

"What do you think happened?"

"I *know* what happened."

Man and wife waited, their hands still clasped together.

"Gillett and his men ran off the cows and young stuff, barricaded them in canyons, then proceeded to put a new brand on them. When I asked him about it, he said there were none of my cows on his land. But we've found and brought back nearly a hundred head."

"How'd you do that?" Jenkins asked.

"I got shot the first time," Buck said. "The man who works with me nearly got shot the second time."

"So you want us ranchers to stick our necks out to help you?" Jenkins asked.

"I want us all to work together to stop this rustling. Gillett will hit somebody else next year, somebody else the year after that. If you and I survive, he'll hit us again."

"What about Barraclough?"

"Barraclough can't take on everybody."

Jenkins hesitated.

"It's your only hope. If you don't, you might as well sell up while you still have something left."

"You offering to buy me out?" Jenkins asked, suspicion in his eyes.

"I couldn't buy you out if you offered me the whole place for a hundred dollars," Buck said.

Relieved of his doubt, Jenkins made up his mind. "Talk to the others. If they go, I'll go."

"And if I have to go alone?"

Jenkins's expression was bleak. "I don't know. I don't know if I can start again, but my wife sure can't if I'm dead."

Buck and Hannah spent the following days visiting the other five ranchers in the area. The results were pretty much the same. When pressed, everyone admitted to losing cows and young stuff, but no one had lost very much. Most were small operations unable to hire a lot of hands. A joint roundup would benefit all of them.

But nobody wanted to risk a confrontation with Lyman Gillett and his hired gun.

"There won't be anything he can do if we all stand together."

Hannah heard Buck repeat that phrase time after time as he visited and revisited, reasoned and cajoled. After two weeks of negotiating, Buck forged a coalition. The ranchers would go if they all went together.

But Buck didn't have to tell Hannah the coalition was fragile. All the ranchers had wives and children. She had seen the worry in their eyes, the fear they tried hard to hide.

She'd also seen Buck quietly shoulder the role of leader. She'd been aware of his steely determination from the first, but she had supposed someone like Walter Evans would take over. The other men were older, more experienced.

But she had seen Buck's arguments make men listen; his forceful personality convinced them to consider doing what they had been afraid to do before. She saw them look to him for moral support when their own courage started to fail. It made her proud.

"Do you think their resolution will hold?" she asked as they rode home.

"I don't know," Buck said. "I'm sure Gillett has gotten wind of what I'm doing. My one fear is that he'll send Barraclough around threatening everybody one by one."

"You think that'll cause them to change their minds?"

"Don't you?"

Yes, she did. "What will you do?"

"Go ahead."

"You can't go alone."

"I won't be. Evans will be with us."

But Evans was only one rancher, not the six Buck

needed. She couldn't let him go virtually alone, but their situation was desperate. Without the missing cows, they would lose everything.

As they neared the ranch, Hannah's worry was replaced by curiosity. Two wagons stood in the lee of the barn. At least three dozen horses filled the corral to overflowing. The place seemed to be overrun with people.

Who were they? What were they doing on her ranch? A screech that Hannah was certain could only have come from a wild Indian rent the air. A moment later, two young boys came riding toward them at a breakneck speed. They brought their horses to a halt that was as reckless as it looked.

"Howdy, Buck," a blond boy with the looks of a cherub called out. "We've come to help you round up your cows."

"I'll shoot your rustlers," chirped a boy about the same age who was as dark as the first boy was fair, and even more handsome.

Buck's stunned surprise turned into a shout of laughter. "Hannah, I want you to meet the scourge of Texas, my adopted brother Will Haskins. And unless I'm badly mistaken, that's his equally dangerous friend, Zac Randolph. Apparently my family has come to make sure I don't get myself killed."

Chapter Fourteen

After a brief introduction to Jake and a heavily muscled redhead named Sean, Hannah hurried to the house before anyone could tell Buck *she* had written the letter that had brought his family. She found no sanctuary. The kitchen was full of strangers. She had never seen such a beehive of activity in her entire life.

"Hello, I'm Isabelle Maxwell, Buck's mother," said a pretty brunette who looked far too young, happy, and carefree to be responsible for this mob. She was cutting enough bacon to feed an army.

"His m-mother," Hannah stuttered.

"Adoptive mother," Isabelle said, her knife poised in midair. She must have noticed Hannah's wide-eyed stare. "I came prepared to do all our cooking outside, but your mother insisted that I use the kitchen. I'm afraid we've taken over."

That was an understatement. Three young men

were busy setting the table, bringing in wood and water, and peeling what seemed to be a mountain of potatoes.

"Be glad we didn't bring *all* the boys," Isabelle said. "We'd have eaten you out of house and home inside a week." She laughed at Hannah's stunned reaction. "Don't worry. We brought our own food."

"It's not that," Hannah said, finally gathering her wits and hoping Isabelle didn't take her for an idiot. "I'm not used to so many people. So much activity. Men helping in the kitchen."

Under these circumstances, Hannah expected her mother to be in a state of hysteria. Instead, she looked calmer and happier than Hannah could remember her ever being.

"My husband and I adopted eleven children," Isabelle said. "I made it clear from the start that they had to help or they wouldn't get fed. When I gave birth to a daughter four years ago, it became even more necessary."

"What can I do?" Hannah asked. She was too confused to think for herself.

"We have everything under control here. You probably have chores. Get the younger boys to help. Will is very good at milking if you can keep him on the stool long enough. I don't know about Zac Randolph. He's visiting. I understand he can do just about anything you can trick him into doing."

"If you can get around that brat, you're doing better than I can. He's worse than Will."

Hannah looked into the pale blue eyes of a blond man peeling potatoes. His sensual good looks nearly stunned her. He looked friendly, but there was a coldness in his eyes that chilled her.

"I'm Chet Attmore," he said. "That's my brother,

Luke, setting the table. We're getting our turn in the kitchen out of the way early."

"Don't want to miss any of the fun," Luke said. Blond and just as attractive as his brother, he set the table with practiced speed and precision. His eyes were even colder than Chet's. They made Hannah think of Sid Barraclough.

"I'm Matt Haskins," the third blond, blue-eyed man said. "I'm Will's brother."

For all his size, this young man seemed shy, as though he'd rather stay next to the woodbox. It was impossible not to know he was brother to the boy with the angel's face. They looked almost as much alike as Chet and Luke.

The introductions left Hannah feeling breathless. After years of seeing virtually no man but her father, she didn't know if she could stand this much male magnificence, all within touching distance. She would have given a week's butter-and-egg money for Amos Merrick to be here now. And he thought he was good-looking!

Hannah couldn't find the milk buckets or the egg basket.

"Ask Jake," Isabelle said without ceasing her work.

Hannah hurried back outside to find Buck and Zeke in close conference with Jake and Sean.

"Come join us," Jake invited.

"I've got to do the milking, pick up the eggs, feed—"

"Drew's taking care of that."

"Drew?" She hadn't met any man by that name. "He can't do it all by himself."

"She," Buck corrected.

"She's got Will and Zac helping her," Jake said.

"But I thought Isabelle said—"

217

"If anybody can get a lick of work out of those boys, it's Drew," Jake replied. "Now come listen to our plans and see if you approve."

Hannah found it hard to believe she'd truly been invited to be part of their deliberations. Even more difficult to accept was the possibility that Jake might actually alter his plans if she didn't approve of them.

"We've decided to start the roundup day after tomorrow," Buck told her. "Jake and I will go around with the news tonight."

"We can't stay more than a couple of weeks," Jake explained. "We left a neighbor and three of the boys to hold things together until we got back."

"We plan to go from west to east," Buck said, "starting with Aldo Jenkins and ending up with Walter Evans."

"Is that all right with you?" Jake asked.

"I guess so," Hannah said. She knew nothing about roundups. The talk stopped when Hannah saw a young woman she didn't recognize coming from the barn carrying a milk bucket. Will trailed behind carrying another milk bucket, Zac balancing the egg basket on one hand. Zeke followed, wearing a deep frown, and Tom brought up the rear, looking bedazzled and benumbed.

"The chores are done," the young woman announced. "Get this milk in the house before you spill it," she ordered Will, handing him his bucket. "And if you break another egg," she said to Zac, "you won't get any for breakfast. You can ask Zeke about the feeding," she told Jake. "I left that to him."

"I want you to meet Miss Hannah Grossek," Jake said.

"We already did," Will announced.

"Well then, Hannah, meet Drew, the only female in our brood."

"You don't have to announce it to the world," Drew said as she took Hannah's hand and gave it a very masculine shake. "I'm not putting up with any of that female nonsense." She gave Tom a severe look.

Hannah had no idea what to make of this young woman, if indeed she was a woman, which Hannah found hard to believe. Her clothes—jeans and a wool shirt which exposed a very feminine figure—would have caused a scandal in Utopia. Tom Gladdis looked at her with big eyes and a foolish grin.

"If you want that milk churned, let me know and I'll get the boys at it," Drew said.

The boys looked horrified. Hannah sensed rebellion. "Save it for dinner," she said. "What we don't drink, we'll feed to the calves."

"Can I do it?" Will asked, a spark of interest in his eyes.

"If you like," Hannah said. "They're greedy and not very polite."

"I know all about calves," Zac said, not about to be impressed by anything as insignificant as a pint-sized cow. "We got thousands of them."

"But you don't have to feed yours by hand," Drew said, not impressed by the calves or Zac. "Now get that stuff up to the house before you have an accident."

After the boys left, she turned to Jake. "When do we start? Can I do the roping?"

Hannah had never experienced a meal such as the one just completed. Sixteen people—Walter Evans had "dropped by" to see how things were going—had been fed in what seemed like one continual shift. As soon as one person finished, he got up and washed his dishes and refilled bowls while someone else took his place. This kept happening until everybody had eaten and everything was washed, dried, and put away. Even Tom Gladdis and Walter Evans helped. Hannah would have been willing to wager that Evans had never washed a plate before in his life.

But the most startling part of the evening had been the change in Buck. His affection for Jake and Isabelle was evident in the way he looked at them, in his happiness to have them there. His eyes even seemed younger, less cynical. But if he was happy to see his family, he was elated to be with Eden, Jake and Isabelle's four-year-old daughter.

"Buck's my bestest brother," Eden informed Hannah. The child ate her dinner seated in Buck's lap.

"She's spoiled rotten," Drew had informed Hannah with a disgusted look. "Isabelle tries, but you can't stop men from ruining a pretty girl."

Hannah, for whom dinner had been a riveting object lesson in what a strong-minded woman could train men to do, decided Isabelle couldn't disapprove as much as Drew said.

Eden was adorable. She had her father's dark blond hair and her mother's green eyes. She didn't like beans, so Buck made a game of it; he would eat one and then she had to eat one. She worked her way through all her vegetables that way. Buck cut her meat and fed it to her. He cleaned up her spilled milk when Will bumped her elbow.

"I don't usually let her sit in anyone's lap at the table, but she misses Buck," Isabelle said to Hannah. Then she added, a little sadly, Hannah thought, "We all do. He's the kindest boy."

Buck wouldn't have been judged the best-looking

man in the room, but he was to Hannah. Watching him with Eden made him even more appealing. Hannah had done without kindness or tenderness most of her life, but she saw plenty of both in Buck's attitude toward Eden. He adored the child. It wasn't just that he fed her or helped her with her milk. It was the way he did those things. He looked just as big and strong as ever, but he was as gentle as a lamb.

Even his tone of voice had changed. It was soft, with a slight drawl, alternately teasing and laughing. He was a big man used to working with horses and cows, but his touch was tender, his strength reassuring. His concentration on Eden was total. The child had every right to feel she was the center of Buck's world.

Hannah found herself wishing that could be her baby.

The thought was as disturbing as it was unexpected. She didn't want marriage and a family. She associated them with the submissiveness her sect expected of wives and daughters.

But seeing Buck with Eden changed her perception of him, knocked down some barrier, removed some unnamed fear. Maybe it was the amiable chaos that concealed a close-knit family unit so unlike the coldly efficient organization Hannah had grown up with. Maybe it was the obvious cheerfulness and good will in a group of young men who Buck said used to be angry and distant. Maybe it was the fact that the men of Buck's family obviously cherished Isabelle and Eden—even Drew when she'd let them—and they were perfectly willing to help with tasks no man she had ever known would consider doing.

None of this was familiar. She didn't understand

it, didn't know how to cope with it, wasn't certain she trusted it. Still, she found herself wanting to be part of this sprawling network of people and affections. She saw love showing itself in a dozen different ways—nurturing, giving, free, happy—all of which were new to her. She walked over to her mother, who was storing food in containers to put away.

"Have you ever seen anything like this?" she whispered.

"No," her mother replied, a half-sad, half-wistful expression on her face.

"Do you think people like us can ever be like that?"

Her mother suddenly gripped Hannah's hand so hard it hurt. "It's too late for me, but maybe not for you."

"What do you mean?"

But her mother said, "You'd better ask Mrs. Maxwell what she needs for breakfast."

Hannah wasn't interested in breakfast. She wanted to know what her mother meant.

"I hope we have enough coffee," her mother said.

It didn't matter. Isabelle had brought enough for the entire state of Texas.

As soon as they finished, Will and Zac escaped outside.

"I'll keep an eye on them," Drew announced as she followed them out.

"They'll know every inch of this place by morning," Isabelle told Hannah.

Jake and Walter Evans sat talking about ranching and the beef market. The three blond men and the big redhead sat with them, occasionally saying something but mostly listening. Zeke sat in a corner, his frown firmly in place. Tom Gladdis leaned against the wall near the door, taking in everything. Isabelle and Hannah's mother talked about the lace Sarah was making, comparing patterns, trading knowledge.

Hannah tended the coffee pot, replenishing cups despite Jake's assurances that they could take care of themselves. She was too keyed up to sit still.

She watched Buck as he read a book to Eden, pointed out things in the pictures, answered her questions, laughed with her. He was still doing it half an hour later when the group began to break up.

"He can do that by the hour." Hannah turned to find Isabelle standing next to her. "He's better with her than any of the other boys are."

"He's so different from how I've seen him," Hannah said, unable to keep her surprise to herself. "He growls and seems to be spoiling for a fight half the time."

"He's still very angry about what happened to him."

"I know. He doesn't let me forget it."

"He's most angry at his parents. His mother ran away, and his father sold him. He's been trying to find his sister for years. It's what he wants most in the world."

"I thought it was a ranch of his own."

"No. It's family."

"But aren't you his family?"

"We tried to be, but we couldn't give him something that's very important to him. Maybe you can."

"Me!"

Hannah's exclamation was so loud, every head in the room turned toward her. She felt herself blush. "We don't have any *tea*," she said. "But I'll be happy to make some if you like."

"That's all right," Isabelle said, struggling to hide a smile. "I've almost gotten used to the terrible coffee these men like. I've seen the way he looks at you," she said after the men went back to their conversation.

"How's that?" Hannah couldn't believe she'd asked such a question, but she had to know the answer.

"Men aren't very subtle creatures. If they want something, everybody knows it. The confusion comes because men usually don't know it themselves. But a woman can tell by watching their eyes."

"How?"

"Watch where he looks."

"He hasn't looked at anybody except Eden since she got up from her nap."

Isabelle laughed softly. "No four-year-old is going to take up all of a man's attention."

"Where has he looked?" Hannah asked, unable to wait for Isabelle's answer.

"At you."

"Probably because I can't run a household half as efficiently as you."

Isabelle laughed again. "I was brought up with servants and tea every afternoon at five o'clock. If I can learn, anybody can. Now I'd better put my child to bed, or she'll be out of sorts tomorrow."

"Do you need blankets or anything?" Hannah didn't know what to offer. Up until this minute she hadn't given a thought to where everyone would sleep.

"Everything we need is already there."

Hannah knew she must have looked blank.

"Buck gave us his room. Didn't he tell you?"

"No." He might refuse to say Isabelle and Jake

were his parents, but he treated them as though they were. Why couldn't he see how much he loved them?

"I think he's looking forward to the chance to be with the other boys. He probably means to make sure Chet knows he's on Buck's turf now. They squabble from time to time, but they've turned out to be great friends."

Just like real brothers, Hannah thought. "What about Zeke?" she added. He still sat in the corner frowning.

"I hardly know any more about him than I did that morning Buck brought him to our camp, a chain around his leg. But I do know that if anything threatened our family, Zeke would be the first to defend us."

"Buck said that. I just find it hard to believe."

"He and Buck have scars that will never heal. They find it very hard to trust anybody." She turned to Buck. "It's time for Eden to go to bed."

Eden didn't want to leave Buck's arms.

"We can read another story tomorrow," Buck assured her. "She likes me to read her stories," he explained to Hannah. "I'm the only one who gives the animals different voices."

Hannah didn't know what to say. Since Buck had come to her ranch, her life had been turned upside down. Even her mother didn't act like herself.

"I think it's nice," she said. "You'll be a good father."

Some of the animation left Buck's eyes. "I don't expect to get married."

"Why?" The question popped out before she could stop it. But it seemed Buck wasn't ready to explain his statement.

"I'd better claim my bedroll before I find myself bedding down in the hayloft."

"You'll get more sleep," Zeke said.

"Not if you snore again tonight," Tom said.

"I got a cold in my head," Zeke said, giving Tom a look that would have petrified Hannah. Tom just laughed.

"You're not as bad as Sid Barraclough. He snores like a freight train."

The mention of that name reminded everyone of the danger that lay ahead.

"I'll bed down with the boys," Buck said. "I've got to knock it into Chet's head that I'm running things this time."

Hannah could tell that Buck's sleeping arrangements had nothing to do with showing Chet who was boss. He just wanted to be with them. If Buck could like his brothers so much—love them, if she was any judge—why couldn't he love her?

Hannah refused to admit she'd asked herself that question. She forced herself to think of something else. "What time does everyone want breakfast?"

"We can get up late tomorrow," Jake said. "Six will be soon enough."

It was the first day of the roundup. Preparations for breakfast started at four o'clock. Buck said they had to be ready to move out at dawn.

Hannah didn't see why the men were so anxious to leave before they could see properly, but she'd learned that their acceptance of her opinion only went so far. They might ask her advice about policy, even strategy. But when it came to actually implementing the plan, it was men only.

"Why do we have to stay?" Will complained when he was told he and Zac would remain at the house.

"That's why I brought you," Jake said, impervious to Will's pleading. "Besides, George Randolph sent Zac to visit, not risk his neck in a roundup."

"He wanted me out of Rose's hair," Zac said, not the least abashed by the confession. "He says it's too much for any woman to have twin babies and me on her hands at the same time."

"You're old enough to help your brothers," Zeke said.

"I used to want to when I was little," Zac said, "but I got over that." He tried to stretch his thirteen-year-old frame taller than his five feet, ten inches. "I'm going to be a gambler and drink whiskey every night when I grow up."

Everybody laughed—except Hannah, who was horrified. She'd been taught that the only thing worse than gambling and whiskey was a woman who lost her virtue. And gambling halls were filled with just that kind of women.

"You boys are to help Isabelle in the kitchen and do all the chores," Jake said. "If you give her one minute's trouble, you'll answer to me."

Even after watching them for two days, Hannah couldn't get used to the way Jake treated Isabelle. The boys were helpful and respectful and showed their affection in many ways. But it was obvious from everything Jake did that Isabelle was the sun and the center of his universe.

He wasn't always hanging around her, trying to do everything for her. But several times a day Hannah would catch one of the many looks that passed between them, looks that reaffirmed the connection between them, looks that said quite plainly that he adored her. They touched often—a brush of fingertips, a pat on the arm, a stroke to straighten hair or a collar, a brief clasping of hands. Their

227

kisses, pecks on the cheek or on the back of Isabelle's neck, were brief, shared without self-consciousness. Isabelle had even kissed Will once and nobody had thought anything of it.

That opened up an entirely new world to Hannah. For the first time she realized that some men actually loved their wives, respected them, wanted them to be happy, and enjoyed their company. It was hard to believe, but she had seen the proof. And if these men would also wash dishes, set the table, and pick up eggs, what other things might they do for the woman they loved?

Hannah had never considered such things to be possible. But if they were . . . well, a woman would feel quite differently about marriage. After all, Hannah did like a few things about men. Having them around made her feel more secure and protected, less vulnerable. It was nice to have someone to do the heavy work.

When Buck had kissed her in the hall, she had known instinctively that there was more. But she didn't know what because she'd never seen it. Now she knew there was a whole different kind of relationship between a man and a woman that had nothing in common with what she'd seen between her mother and father.

She knew almost immediately that she wanted that for herself. She knew almost as quickly that she wanted it with Buck.

Preposterous. Outlandish. Ridiculous. But that didn't change the fact that she wanted it.

Buck got up from the table. "Time to saddle up. We'll be heading out in fifteen minutes."

Isabelle walked over to Jake and kissed him. "Be careful."

"You take care of yourself and Eden. Don't let

Will and Zac drive you crazy. Good-bye, ladies," he said to Hannah and her mother. "We'll see you in about ten days."

"You'll see me a lot sooner," Hannah said, making up her mind while she still barely understood what she was saying. "I'm going with you."

Chapter Fifteen

"You can't ride sidesaddle on roundup!" Buck exclaimed.

"I can ride astride," Hannah said. "I did it when I was a little girl." Once, and her father had beaten her when he found out.

"I still don't like it. You've never been on a roundup. You won't have the slightest idea what to do."

"I can learn."

"I won't let you."

"You can't stop me," Hannah fired back. "This time I have a horse. I can go anywhere I please."

"She's got you there," Jake said. He grinned as if he was enjoying seeing Buck get his horns tangled in a briar patch.

"No reason she can't go," Drew put in. "I don't think it's a good idea myself, but I'm going. And don't you even think of telling me *I* can't go."

"She'll probably get lost the first day," Buck protested.

"Don't worry," Drew announced. "I'll take care of her."

"Not on your life," Buck said. "You'll drag her through the deepest brush at a gallop and think nothing of it. If she's going, I'll see to her. I'd be grateful if you can find her some clothes by the time I get her horse saddled."

Hannah wanted to take issue with Buck for treating her like a package to be wrapped, but she settled for getting ready as quickly as possible. She had expected him to make more strenuous objections to her being anywhere near the roundup. Instead, he'd been concerned for her safety. This was a whole new attitude—one she didn't want to ruin before she could find out if it was somehow connected to the kiss.

"The first thing we have to do," Drew said, looking at Hannah with critical disapproval, "is get rid of that skirt. I'll lend you some pants. You're about my size."

"I can't," Hannah gasped. "I couldn't possibly—"

"It's either that or stay home. You'll get that blamed skirt tangled around your legs and fall in the fire the first day."

"I don't think things are that desperate," Isabelle said. "All you need is an old dress you're willing to sacrifice. You can wear it over Drew's pants."

Drew seemed to consider that a spiritless solution, but Hannah embraced it thankfully. It was as good an answer as she was going to find in the time she had.

Hannah blushed just from putting on Drew's pants. She couldn't get a good look at herself in her father's shaving mirror, but she could see enough to know she looked positively lewd.

"I can't wear these," she exclaimed. "I feel indecent."

Her mother looked horrified; Drew looked offended; Isabelle looked amused.

"You'll feel better once you put on the skirt," Isabelle said.

Hannah wasn't sure she had the nerve to wear pants, even under a dress with split seams, but she had to be ready to go when Buck brought her horse to the house, or he'd leave her.

"Okay."

While her mother packed some necessaries for her, Hannah put on the split skirt. She suspected her legs would be exposed far more than was proper, but she felt better. She expected everyone to stare the moment she walked out the door, but no one noticed. They were in the process of moving out.

Hannah needed moral support, but there was no one to give it to her. Drew had run off and was mounting her own horse. Isabelle had gone back inside. Her mother looked ready to faint. She had insisted upon forcing herself into a man's world, and she was going to have to do it on her own.

"We'd better hurry," Buck said. "Everybody's anxious to get started." He held out his hand. "I'll give you a leg up."

Because of Buck's shoulder, Tom had always helped her mount, but he was nowhere in sight.

"Grab hold of the pommel and put your left foot in my hands," Buck said when she continued to hesitate. "When I give you a lift, swing your right leg over."

"You got no business lifting anything with that arm. I'll throw her up."

Neither of them had noticed Zeke come striding up.

"I can—"

"You can't wear those boots," Zeke said. "You'll break your ankle."

"They're the only ones I have."

Zeke shrugged, linked his fingers, and held his hands out to Hannah. "Mount up if you're going to," he growled. "I ain't got all day."

He meant it. Taking her courage in her hands, Hannah gripped the pommel and stepped into Zeke's hand. The next thing she knew, she was flying through the air like a flung clod of dirt. She expected to find herself halfway across the yard. Much to her surprise, she landed in the saddle.

"Your stirrups are too long," Buck said. "Hold your leg up while I adjust them."

Buck adjusted her right stirrup. Zeke adjusted the left, muttering obscenities all the while.

"You're going to fall off before the day's out," Zeke predicted as he stomped off to mount his own horse.

"No, I won't!" she called after him. She should have said she hoped she wouldn't. But after the way Zeke had acted, she was too angry to be humble.

"Good. I wouldn't like you half as well with dirt on your nose and tears in your blouse."

Hannah was so surprised by Buck's comment, she nearly got left behind. When she did let her horse go, he jumped ahead, eager to catch up with the others. Caught off guard, she lurched drunkenly in the saddle. She was certain she was going to suffer the humiliation of being unseated in her own front yard.

Buck caught her horse's bridle and pulled him to a stop.

"You sure you don't want to stay here?" he asked.

"Quite sure," Hannah said. Settling herself squarely in the saddle, she gathered up the reins and slipped her feet back into the stirrups. "You can let go now. I've got him under control."

Buck didn't look as if he believed her. He released the bridle but stayed next to her. Hannah nudged her mount gently, and he sprang forward. She was prepared this time and quickly reined him down to a canter.

"How long do you plan to stay with the roundup?" Buck asked.

"Until the end. I told you I intend to learn everything there is to know about running a ranch. That means I have to know how to run a roundup."

"You wouldn't be allowed to. Your foreman or your husband would do it for you."

"I'm not getting married. I'll be my own foreman."

"No bunch of men is going to let a woman lead them. They'd be the laughing stock of Texas."

"You think a woman can't do the job?"

"I didn't say that. I said she wouldn't get the chance."

It didn't take them long to reach the first ranch. Hannah was relieved to see the rancher was ready, even though he didn't appear happy about it. But once he got a good look at Jake and the boys, his spirits rose. The story was the same at the second, third, and fourth ranches. Before long the men were full of high spirits. The boys started showing off for each other, roping rocks, bushes, then each other.

"Next they'll start racing," Buck told Hannah.

"Sean and Luke are each constantly trying to prove he's the best horseman at the ranch."

"Which one is?"

"Neither. Jake is. He rides like he grew up in a saddle. Next is Hawk. *Then* maybe Sean or Luke."

"You're awfully good, too." She didn't know why she had said that. She didn't know a thing about horsemanship. She certainly didn't know how he compared to his brothers, but she couldn't let him think everybody was better than he was. He looked wonderful in the saddle, tall and straight.

Buck looked nonplussed by her remark.

"Why do you say that?"

"Well, you are."

"How do you know?"

"Mr. Evans says you're good. I'm sure Zeke thinks so, too, or he wouldn't be seen with you."

"I haven't done anything. I couldn't with this arm."

"You organized this roundup. You've gotten these men to work together for the first time. You found out about that brand."

"Anybody could have done that."

"But *you* did. Without you, the rustlers could have gone on stealing forever."

Hannah hadn't realized all this until she said it. Buck had accomplished a lot. Gillespie County would never be the same after this roundup. Whatever the outcome, the ranchers now knew their strength came in acting together. That was how her father's sect had become so strong. That was why Buck's family had been so successful.

Hannah didn't want to be isolated anymore, either. She wanted Buck to stay. If that meant marrying him, she guessed she could do it.

Thoughts of marriage set her mind off in such a

different direction that she forgot to pay attention to her horse. Barely escaping being unseated when he unexpectedly jumped a fallen cedar, Hannah decided she'd better think about something that didn't have the power to disorient her mind and cause her muscles to go limp for absolutely no reason at all.

Jody Beamis had changed his mind. At least that was what his wife said.

"What happened?" Buck asked when he rode up to the porch of their modest dogtrot.

"Nothing," Mrs. Beamis said. "He just changed his mind."

But it was obvious something was wrong. The woman wouldn't look them in the eye, shifted her sparse weight from one foot to the next, twisted the end of her pristine apron string around her finger.

"Could I talk to him?" Buck asked.

She shook her head. "He ain't here. It wouldn't do no good no way. He won't change his mind."

"Everybody else is going," Buck said. "It's going to look strange, him not joining us."

"I can't help that."

Hannah noticed that her nervous gaze kept shifting to a window at the end of the porch.

"Some might even say he's turned coward."

"That's not true," Mrs. Beamis declared, a flush of anger rising above the collar of her faded calico dress. "It's not being a coward not to want to leave your wife a widow, your children without a father."

"We don't plan on letting anything like that happen," Buck said. "That's why it's important all of us go together. If he stands aside now, he can't expect us to stand up for him later."

"We'll get by," she said, her gaunt features as rigid as her posture.

"Sorry you feel that way, Mrs. Beamis. But before I leave, would you mind me asking a favor?"

"What?" She looked suspicious.

"When you get ready to sell up, would you let me know? I'd like to buy your place. With all your stock rustled, it won't cost much."

Mrs. Beamis turned red. When the door behind her opened and a tall, rope-thin man with shoulder-length straight black hair came out, she turned white. "No, Jody!" she cried. "You promised me. You know what that Barraclough said."

"He came here last night," Beamis said to Buck. "He said if we insisted on the joint roundup, there'd be trouble. He said Mr. Gillett hired him to settle his trouble."

"He meant he'd kill you if you didn't stay away," his wife cried.

"I can't do it, Margaret. If I back down now, I won't be able to look these men in the eye. We might as well pack up and leave. Let me get my horse," he said to Buck.

Hannah felt sorry for Mrs. Beamis. The woman's anguish was painful to see. Hannah didn't know what she thought she could do, but she had to do something. She slid from the saddle, walked up to Mrs. Beamis, and put her arms around her. A hound that had been lying on the porch yawned, got up, and ambled over to sniff Hannah's skirts.

"Your husband's not the only man with a family," she said. "That's really why he's going—to protect you, to provide for your future. If it were just him, he could pick up and go any old time."

"I told him I'd leave with him today," Mrs. Beamis said, her lips quivering. "I'll go anywhere. I don't care. I just don't want him dead."

"We'll take care of him." Hannah remembered

Buck's advice. *Smile when you face trouble. Never let them see you're worried.* "He'll be back. You've got to pretend you're not worried about him."

"I am worried sick." Crying had produced red blotches on her fair complexion.

"He knows that, but this is something he's got to do. He'll do it better if he thinks you're behind him."

"Is that why you're going, supporting your man?"

The question so surprised Hannah, she nearly couldn't answer. "I'm not married, ma'am. But if I were, I'd want to be here."

"What am I supposed to do?"

"I don't know. Maybe promise to have his favorite dinner waiting when he gets home."

Mrs. Beamis wiped her eyes with her apron and thought for a moment before she went inside. She was gone so long, Jody Beamis was back by the time she came out of the house carrying a long, heavy rifle. She walked down the steps and handed it to her husband.

"I hear tell people still sight a buffalo now and then. You'll have a better chance of getting one with Pa's old Sharps. We could use the meat."

They stood facing each other, a full-figured woman and a man so thin his clothes hung shapelessly on him. Their gazes held for a long moment. "Sure," Jody said. "I been thinking about a thick buffalo steak for some time now."

She stepped away from her husband's horse.

Hannah had followed Mrs. Beamis down the steps. Without thinking, she hugged her hard. "Buck won't let anything happen to him," she whispered.

"You put a lot of faith in that man. You sure he's up to it?"

"I'm certain he is."

Mrs. Beamis nodded without speaking.

Tom Gladdis helped Hannah mount, and everybody moved out. Each time Hannah looked back, she saw Margaret Beamis standing on the porch.

"How did you know what to say?" Buck asked when the Beamis ranch was finally out of sight.

"I didn't," Hannah said. "I guess I thought of how I'd feel if my husband were going off to face danger."

"You said you didn't want a husband."

"I know, but I can imagine what it would be like."

After a few minutes, he asked, "What would it be like?"

Hannah turned to him in surprise.

"Just curious," he said. But he kept looking at her, waiting for her answer.

"I wouldn't want him to get hurt. I'd be worried about him."

"Why? You don't like men. Why would you care one way or the other?"

"If I were married, I'd love him," Hannah said, irked that he thought she was so insensitive. "I wouldn't want anybody I loved to get hurt."

"You said you couldn't love a man."

"I said that when I thought all men were like my father. If my husband looked at me the way Jake looks at Isabelle . . ."

"How's that?"

"Like she's the most important person in the world." Hannah was immediately embarrassed. She knew she sounded dreamy, naive. "He obviously cares what she thinks, what she feels. And you and your brothers treat her just the way Jake does."

"I keep telling you, we're not brothers."

"A woman wouldn't mind working hard for a man like that. You probably wouldn't be able to stop her. And she wouldn't mind having a house full of sons."

"I keep telling you—"

"You can't see yourself, but I can. I've watched you. You love them, Buck Hobson. You may as well admit it."

Buck maintained a stubborn silence.

"Sometimes blood doesn't matter. They're your family because your *father* and *mother* and *brothers* and *sisters* all left what they were doing when they thought you needed help."

"Which reminds me," Buck said. "Zeke said he didn't write to Jake."

Hannah guarded her expression. She didn't know how Buck would react to learning she had written that letter. "Then why did he come?"

"He won't say, just that somebody told him I was in trouble."

She could tell he suspected her. "You never told me his address."

Buck had apparently forgotten telling her about Clyde Pruitt. He didn't look convinced of Hannah's innocence, but he had other things on his mind right now.

"Would you marry if you found a man like Jake?" Buck asked.

Hannah hadn't been prepared for that question. She thought they'd left the subject. Apparently Buck hadn't satisfied his curiosity yet.

"Just because I found him wouldn't mean he'd love me. Or that I'd love him."

"If he did. If you did, too."

"Why are you asking me all these questions?"

"Just curious."

"It sounds like more than curiosity to me." She

kept remembering the kiss, the way it had made her feel.

"Okay, maybe I'm nosy. It's just that you were so set against men, I wondered what it would take to change your mind."

"I'm sure I'll never marry," Hannah said, determined to put an end to his questions. "But I might consider marrying a man who loved me so much that no one else would ever be half as important."

Buck looked stunned.

"I guess I sound idealistic, even selfish, but that's the way I feel."

"Just unexpected," Buck said. "But then, just about everything you've done has been unexpected."

Buck knew he should have insisted that Hannah stay at the house. She didn't know enough to help. She'd just be a distraction. No matter how much she might try to be invisible, she was still an attractive female, someone men would naturally notice. From what Buck knew of Hannah, she would make no attempt to be invisible. It didn't matter that Drew was a female. She walked, talked, and acted like a man. It was easy to forget she was a woman.

Hannah couldn't be unfeminine if she tried. She might talk about avoiding men, never marrying, but everything about her was calculated to draw men to her.

She wasn't the most beautiful woman in the world, but there were times when Buck thought she might be close. Each part of her seemed to work closely with every other part to get the most out of what nature had given her. A rounded figure, gentle grace, and piquant features made it hard to put her out of his mind. Impossible, actually.

Now she was going to be underfoot for two weeks. He didn't mind her presence as much as he minded his inability to ignore it. He needed to keep his mind on business. But how could he when he saw her every time he turned his head?

Buck cursed himself for his lack of control, for holding her hand, for kissing her. He cursed his wound, which had kept him from being out on the plain, rounding up wild horses, looking for stray cows. He cursed Lyman Gillett for stealing the cows that were supposed to pay off the ranch's debt. He cursed himself for developing a conscience that whispered it wasn't right to take her ranch, even though it might be legal.

He cursed himself for asking about the conditions under which she would marry. As long as he'd thought she was dead set against husbands and marriage, he could keep his thoughts from wandering in that direction. He cursed his body for confusing his mind. He was certain he didn't love Hannah, that he just lusted after her.

Her demands were too great. What man could feel that way about a woman, even his wife? Wives left their husbands and children and never came back, never wrote.

Buck knew Isabelle and Jake would never leave each other, but they weren't like other people. Most people were like his own parents, like Hannah's father. Jake and Isabelle loved each other.

He'd never been curious enough to examine the meaning of their relationship. He had only cared that it provided him with a home. But now he wanted to know, needed to know, what made it work. Maybe he could better understand his own feelings if he could understand theirs.

He didn't dislike women, but he didn't want to get married, either. It was crazy even to think about it. The only family he wanted was his sister. His adoptive family had been a good substitute, but it wasn't the real thing.

Hannah was becoming a serious threat to everything he wanted. He liked her more and more. He was certain his feelings were based entirely on his physical need. But even in his erotic dreams, he thought as much of her eyes or her unflagging spirit as he did of her breasts of her provocative hips. This was a clear danger sign. No matter how much trouble it caused, he should have forbidden her to come on the roundup.

Hannah hated roundup. And that didn't change when Zeke found her father's missing horses running with a herd of mustangs. She promised herself, if she managed to gain sole ownership of her ranch, she would never go on roundup again. She had to agree with Isabelle's opinion that a roundup was no place for a woman who enjoyed being treated as a lady. Everything was loud, dirty, and brutal.

The day began before dawn when Matt Haskins pounded on a skillet to announce that breakfast was ready. The food was basic, the coffee viscous, the cold biting. Sitting on the ground, she was too miserable to have an appetite. Before she had her eyes open properly, Buck was tossing her into the saddle.

Hannah was fast coming to the conclusion she didn't care for horses, either, especially when she had to ride them. They were bigger than she was, stronger, had a will of their own, and were very uncomfortable after the first fifteen minutes. Whenever she had a disagreement with hers, Buck always sided with the horse. She was tired of being told by every man present that she had the best mount in the roundup. He was a cantankerous brute who enjoyed pitting his strength against hers.

She was glad somebody had gelded him.

Even though they were female, she liked cows even less. They insisted upon hiding in the most inaccessible places, weren't cooperative when you wanted them to come out, and were positively belligerent if they had a calf. They all seemed to be under the foolish misapprehension that she was going to try to take their babies away from them. As far as she was concerned, the companionship of cabbages and turnips was preferable to that of calves any day.

Fortunately, the men ignored the steers. They were even bigger and more frightening. Buck said they would round up the steers in the fall. She was determined to come down with some convenient illness before then.

Once the foul-tempered cows had been gathered near camp, they all insisted on bawling at once, even before the riders tried to separate them from their calves, who bawled even worse. They raced this way and that, trying to avoid being caught. A waste of time. It would have been much easier on everybody if the cows had just lined up, let their precious brats be branded, and then run back to the briars they seemed to think made such dandy homes.

Instead they milled about and bellowed incessantly. The noise was deafening. It gave her a headache. The dust was worse. Her hair felt gritty. Her clothes and skin were covered with the stuff. She was certain her lungs were as well, despite the handkerchief Buck gave her to wear over her face. She imagined she must look like some cheap bandit preparing to hold up a wagon train.

She couldn't take a bath. She had no privacy. Even if she had, she couldn't bring herself to wash in a stream the way Drew did. Hannah had never thought of herself as prissy, but there were certain things she just couldn't do.

And they wouldn't let her do anything. Buck agreed to take her with him when he searched for cows, but he made her stay back when he found one. When they started branding, he told her to stay with the chuck wagon. When she disobeyed him, he picked her up and carried her back. That mortified her so much—angered her just as much—that she swore she wouldn't touch his old cows.

But that meant she had nothing to do except help Matt with the cooking. She tried helping Drew heat the branding irons, but Drew made it painfully clear that if she couldn't maintain the fire at exactly the right temperature, she ought to go back to the ranch.

That was exactly what Hannah longed to do, but her pride wouldn't let her. The men made it crystal clear that roundup was the most important operation on a ranch. She had sworn she'd learn everything there was to know about a roundup. She had to stay.

Chapter Sixteen

"Had enough of horses, dust, and cows?"

Hannah jumped. She hadn't heard Buck come up behind her. She'd left the group around the fire to avoid another evening of roundup stories. How could intelligent men spend so much time talking about cows?

"I was feeling guilty about leaving Mother to do the garden by herself." Well, she *had* thought of her mother that morning.

"Don't worry. Isabelle will get Will to do all the heavy work."

"He's such a handsome boy."

"He trades on it."

She had walked to an outcropping of rocks that allowed her to look across land falling away to a stream, then to hills rising on the other side. Most of the spring flowers had faded, to be replaced by new grass and the blooms of early prickly-pear cactus. The new growth took on a darker hue in shadows cast by the setting sun.

"You aren't enjoying this, are you?"

She postponed answering Buck's question while she settled herself on the rock. Despite the presence of so many men, there was a wildness about this land that sometimes frightened her. It was so big and empty, she felt small and helpless. She couldn't imagine what it must feel like to be the first man in a place like this. The *only* man.

"No, I'm not," she answered truthfully, "but that's not why I came."

"I know. You came to learn how to do a man's job." He settled down next to her. He didn't have to be so careful of his shoulder now.

"Will it make you feel better if I admit I can't do this by myself?"

"It would make me feel better to know you were safe back at the ranch."

"My mother and I survived nearly eight months alone. I can survive two weeks in the middle of twenty men."

She no longer walked around stiff-legged. Her bottom wasn't as raw as rare meat. The muscles in her back and shoulders didn't ache or cramp so badly she could hardly lie down. She wasn't so afraid of falling off her horse. Only half of each day was she so miserable she wanted to die. The rest of the time she only counted the minutes until she could return to a civilized way of life.

"You still don't belong here."

"Do you think I'm such a poor excuse for a female?"

Buck grinned. "I don't think you're much of a cowboy, but I think you're a prime example of a female."

That was fine with Hannah. She'd take being a prime female over a cowboy any day. "You don't like women, remember. You don't trust them." She didn't know why she had to remind him. If she'd shut up, maybe he'd forget long enough to kiss her. Those few magic moments were never far from her mind. Being alone with Buck brought them galloping to the forefront.

"I don't hate females."

"You sure act like it. If you so much as brush against me, you jump away. I won't give you a fever."

"I'm not so sure," Buck said. "I think I've come down with something already."

"Don't be absurd." She knew he wasn't talking about a disease. "Your shoulder's healing fine. You never seem to get tired. You're as healthy as a horse. You—"

Buck grabbed her by the shoulders and kissed her. There was no preparation, no lead-up. He just grabbed her shoulders in a tight grip and pressed his mouth on hers.

Hannah didn't mind in the least. She kissed him back just as hard. She'd waited for this, dreamed about it, feared it might never happen again.

But it had, and a great tension inside her eased.

Buck was breathing heavily when he broke the embrace. "See what I mean? I can't stop thinking about you. I've been wanting to do this for days."

"But that's not being sick."

"It feels like it."

She wasn't sure she appreciated that, but she had to admit she hadn't been feeling exactly wonderful herself lately. In fact, some of the time she'd felt acutely miserable. It surprised her that Buck had felt the same way.

"But I feel a lot better when I kiss you," Buck said.

Apparently his need to feel better was urgent. The deed followed hard on the words. Hannah wasn't certain it made her feel better, but it did make her feel happier. She knew that didn't make a lot of sense, but she couldn't stop to figure it out just then. She couldn't concentrate on anything except that Buck was kissing her and she hoped it would never end.

"I shouldn't be doing this," Buck murmured without separating his lips from Hannah's.

"Why not?"

"I'm doing exactly what I said you'd cause other men to want to do."

"But I don't want anybody to kiss me but you."

That startled Buck so much that he backed away until he could look her in the face.

"But you don't want to get married. You don't like men. You don't trust them."

"I trust you. I must like you to want you to kiss me."

Hannah was willing to let that thought settle for a few seconds, but Buck apparently thought time spent settling thoughts was wasted. He put his arm around Hannah, drew her to him, and kissed her quite enthusiastically. Apparently he didn't disapprove of what he was doing so very much after all.

Hannah had never kissed anyone other than Buck. She didn't even know how to kiss, though it seemed to come naturally enough now that she was doing it. But a couple of things did surprise her.

She hadn't expected Buck to hold her so close. Finding her breasts pushed hard against his chest almost made her forget what she was doing. Holding hands was intimate. Kissing was several steps beyond that. But practically pushing herself inside

Buck's clothes . . . well, that was something altogether different.

Hannah hadn't been prepared for the myriad sensations that attacked her body. She actually felt an
impulse to unbutton his shirt, put her hand inside
to feel his flesh. The thought so shocked her, she
gasped for breath.

Buck broke their kiss. "What's wrong?"

"N-nothing. I'm just not used to being held so
close." She wasn't used to any of this. She was petrified, but she wouldn't have pulled out of Buck's
arms for all the ranches in Texas.

"Has anybody ever held you?"

"No."

"Kissed you?"

"No."

He backed off immediately. "I've frightened you."

"No, you didn't," she hastened to assure him. "It's
just that I didn't know what to expect. I liked it.
Really I did."

She didn't know how she had the nerve to make
such an admission—it made her seem immoral—
but she didn't want him to stop kissing her.

It did confuse her; it did frighten her, but she'd
never felt so *alive* in her whole life. Every nerve in
her body, every sensory perception, was a dozen
times more acute.

"I feel like I'm taking advantage of your innocence."

"You're not. I'll tell you if I want you to stop."

Hannah couldn't imagine Amos Merrick holding
back for fear of wounding her sensibilities. As for
not taking advantage of her innocence, that was exactly what Gillett had tried to do.

"I like being kissed," Hannah confessed. "I
thought I wouldn't, but I do."

There, she'd been about as brazen as she could be. Surely he couldn't think he was taking advantage of her now.

She never got a chance to find out. Zeke stormed up, mad as a bull with a bee sting on the end of his nose. "What the hell do you think you're doing?"

Buck jumped to his feet between Hannah and Zeke. "None of your business."

"Looks like you forgot what you came here for."

"I haven't forgotten anything."

Zeke glared at Hannah. She felt an urge to hide behind Buck.

"Then it looks like you changed your mind about what you want. You shoulda told me. I ain't helping you catch no female."

"I haven't changed my mind.

"Then you'd better get your tail back to camp and act like you're running this show."

"We've already talked everything out. It's all under control."

"You musta forgot to tell that fool Olie Speers. He's trying to convince everybody they ought to sneak up on Gillett and burn him out."

"Damn the man! I told him I didn't want any fighting."

"Speers doesn't, either. He wants to shoot Gillett's men as they run out of the burning bunkhouse."

Buck swore again. "I've got to talk to him," he said to Hannah. "You'd better come back with me."

"I'll stay a little while longer." The mood had been shattered, but traces of it lingered. She wanted to savor each one. "Go on," she said when Buck hesitated. "I'll be all right."

"Zeke can wait for you."

"No," she said before Zeke could refuse.

Hannah needed some time to herself to try to sort through all the feelings, sensations, and emotions that whirled about inside her like debris in a cyclone. She'd never felt so confused, excited, and worried all at the same time. She hadn't thought it was possible to feel so many emotions at once, conflicting or not.

Buck liked her. She could no longer doubt that. Even more clear was the fact that she liked him. More than she thought possible. More than she thought safe. The way she was feeling now, she'd do anything he wanted. As long as Buck was the man to ask her, she'd changed her mind about marriage. She didn't even compare him to Amos. One was a paragon. The other was a snake.

But getting Buck to let down his defenses enough to kiss her was one thing. Getting him to ask her to marry him was quite another. She didn't know how to go about doing that, but she expected Isabelle might. She had five months. That ought to be enough time for a man who liked to kiss as much as Buck did.

"What the hell do you think you were doing?" Zeke demanded as they walked back to camp. "That's a woman back there. Do you remember what you've always said about women?"

"Hannah's different," Buck said.

"I imagine your pa thought your ma was different."

Buck spun, caught Zeke by the shoulder. "Don't you ever compare Hannah to my mother."

Zeke shrugged off Buck's grasp. "She's a woman. They're all alike."

"Not Hannah."

"You thinking about marrying her?"

"Good God, Zeke, I just kissed her. I'm not thinking about marrying anybody."

"Didn't look like your head was what was doing the thinking."

Buck stopped again and jerked Zeke around to face him. "Just what are you trying to say?"

"If you don't start thinking with your head instead of what's in your britches, you're going to find yourself stuck marrying that woman because her belly's big with your baby. I'm not working my butt off for that."

"I'm not getting married, and I'm not planting any babies," Buck growled. "I like Hannah. I think she's pretty. I just kissed her twice. That's all."

Now it was Zeke's turn to pull Buck around to face him. "You mean this wasn't the first time?"

"No, it wasn't," Buck snapped. "It may not be the last, either, but it's none of your business. If it'll make you sleep any better, my sister is the only female I want in my house. None of the others are worth the trouble."

But while that statement seemed to satisfy Zeke, it left Buck feeling as if he'd insulted half the women he knew. Naturally, Isabelle was exempt from his statement. And Eden. Drew would drive him crazy, but she'd never be dishonest.

And though he didn't want to marry her—or anybody—it didn't apply to Hannah. Mrs. Grossek would knock herself out for any man who was kind to her. He suspected Hannah would do the same. If he did want to get married, he couldn't ask for a better wife.

"Who's Jonathan Ridgely?" Hannah had asked the moment Buck had ended their whispered conversation. "What's he doing here? What were you talking about?"

Ridgely had ridden into camp the previous evening to give Walter Evans the news that his daughter had taken ill. Buck had done everything he could to convince Hannah to go back with Walter, but she refused.

"I'll tell you when the right time comes," Buck had said.

He had known that answer would make her mad, but he had no intention of telling her Ridgely was a lawyer for the cattleman's association. Buck expected an explosion today. He didn't know what form it would take, but if he could make Hannah angry enough to stay away from him, she'd be safe. If she knew he expected a showdown, she'd dog his heels no matter how mad she was.

Lyman Gillett had been the only rancher not to join the roundup. Today they would ride onto his range. Hannah was on pins and needles, worrying what would happen. The other ranchers appeared nervous, but last night Jake and the boys had kept everybody entertained with stories of what Will had done on past roundups.

This morning, however, even Jake and Sean appeared anxious. Chet and Luke acted as if they were looking forward to the expected confrontation.

Buck rode at the head of the group as they approached Gillett's range

"Do you think Gillett will try to stop us?" Hannah asked for the dozenth time.

"I don't know."

"But there are nearly three times as many of us."

"I expect he'll notice that."

"What will you do if he refuses to let you on his range?"

"He won't have a choice," Zeke said. "We can push him all the way to Oklahoma if we want."

"What about Sid Barraclough?"

"We'll soon find out," Tom said. He was riding on the other side of Buck. "Gillett's brought his whole crew to meet us."

They were lined up across the trail, seven men wearing guns. All the ranchers wore guns today as well.

"That's Sid riding next to Gillett," Tom said for the benefit of Jake and his boys.

"Don't make any difference where he sits," Zeke said. "We got him covered."

Everybody had fanned out—Buck at the center, Chet and Luke on opposite sides, Jake and Sean opposite Buck and Zeke. The ranchers rode in between. A line of twenty men faced Gillett.

"Welcome to the Rafter D," Gillett said, a broad smile on his face. "Just don't sit there," he said when nobody moved. "Let's round up some cows."

Hannah sighed with relief.

But Buck wasn't deceived by Gillett's smiling invitation. He knew Gillett thought he had them fooled. He wasn't going to be pleased when he discovered he was the one who'd been caught unaware.

Buck had been certain Gillett would want to keep his men in a tight group. He was therefore surprised that Gillett didn't object when Buck scattered them among the group for the first sweep through Rafter D range. Buck looked to his left. Gillett was barely in sight. Barraclough rode in the middle, visible to everybody.

Hannah rode on his right. "What's going to happen about the rebranded calves?" she asked.

"If I've planned this right, there'll be nothing he

can do. A fight will only make his position worse.
If there are other new brands, as I suspect there are,
he may even try to leave the state. There'll be no
reason for shooting, and everything will end peace-
fully."

"But you don't think it will turn out that way."

"I hope it will. He's outnumbered and outmaneuvered. He has no choice."

Hannah had left it at that. Buck believed it would
happen that way *as long as Gillett was a sensible
man.* Even a thief knew to run when the cards were
stacked against him.

Nobody commented on the unfamiliar brands
that kept turning up on Gillett's range. No one remarked on the surprisingly large percentage of
cows and calves. Buck had insisted that he do all
the talking. A couple of ranchers had argued, but
with Barraclough in the middle of everything, they
seemed more than willing to let Buck take all the
risks.

Following more of Buck's instructions, the
ranchers volunteered to do all the roping. That left
Gillett's men to do the branding. They finished all
the unquestioned brands by late afternoon. Of the
cows left, about a dozen had unfamiliar brands.
The rest were newly branded with the six-pointed
star.

Nobody claimed ownership of the unfamiliar
brands. Gillett said he'd never seen them, didn't
know where they had come from. He thought
they'd probably wandered in from some place farther east, and offered to take charge of them. Buck
suggested they wait to see whether they came up
with any more strange brands. If they did, it might
be better to consult someone from the cattle growers association office in Austin.

Gillett didn't like that suggestion, but it was too sensible to ignore.

"What about this other brand?" one of Gillett's men asked, pointing at the six-pointed star. "We got a whole bunch of them."

The man had been primed. He looked at his boss when he asked the question. But this was the moment Buck had been anticipating for weeks. He spoke before Gillett could open his mouth.

"That's the brand for my new partnership with Miss Grossek," Buck said.

The announcement stunned everyone. Feet shuffled; gazes shifted nervously between Buck and Gillett. Buck had planned what he would say very carefully. Before Gillett could open his mouth, Buck wanted him hedged about so tightly, he wouldn't be able to say a word without convicting himself of rustling.

"I registered it in Utopia a few weeks ago," Buck said. "I just got confirmation from Austin yesterday that there's no other brand like it in the state. As you can see, I made it so it would fit over the old Tumbling T brand."

Buck's last few sentences fell into a pool of absolute silence. It was as though some wizard had waved his magic wand and frozen them all into a tableau.

"If you'll look closely, you can see they're all new."

Buck looked at Gillett. The man was white with rage. Whatever he might have suspected, this had caught him by surprise.

When Gillett finally found his voice, he didn't scream or rage or make threats. "You couldn't do any branding, not with that shoulder," he said, his veneer of calm at variance with the cold rage in his eyes. "Besides, you've been riding all over the county talking up this roundup."

Zeke spoke up. "He had me working for him."

"Me, too," Tom Gladdis said.

"He's got a mighty big family," Jake said, "all of us experienced with cattle."

"You just got here."

"So everybody thinks," Jake said.

Gillett was stymied and angry, but he could find no reason to call their collective word into doubt. "Then how did these cows get on my range?" Gillett demanded.

"I can't say," Buck said. "Maybe they resented being branded twice and ran as far as they could, fearing I'd change my mind and do it a third time."

Gillett didn't find any humor in Buck's answer. "I don't believe that's your brand. I never saw it before. I don't believe it's registered."

"It is." Jonathan Ridgely spoke for the first time. Buck had asked him to keep out of sight before, but he stepped forward now. "He and Miss Grossek registered the brand in Utopia three weeks ago. I have a letter from the lawyer stating the particulars. I came out yesterday with the official confirmation from Austin that the brand was theirs."

"I don't believe they're his cows," Gillett insisted. "It's somebody else's brand. He's just trying to claim it."

"Whose could it be?" Buck asked.

"I don't know, but it damned well isn't yours."

"We can settle that," Buck said. "Anybody up for steaks tonight?"

"What do you mean?" Gillett demanded, his skin going a shade whiter. Buck knew Gillett understood exactly what he intended to do.

"We'll butcher a cow. The old brand will show up when we skin it."

It took only minutes to choose a cow and shoot it. Buck had the hide off in even less time. The old Tumbling T brand was clear on the underside.

"I guess that settles any question," Mr. Ridgely said. "You can go ahead and brand the calves. I brought the new branding irons you ordered," he said to Buck. "It'll be a lot easier than using a running iron. After I have one of those steaks, I'll head back to town."

They branded the calves, but all of the easygoing camaraderie that had developed in a week of working together had disappeared, leaving the ranchers with strained faces and taut nerves. Everyone knew Gillett had branded those cattle for himself. And Gillett *knew* everyone knew it. The question on all the men's minds was whether he'd accept that he'd been outmaneuvered and let the cattle go.

Buck was certain he would for the time being, but Gillett might attempt to seek revenge later. Buck would have to stay alert.

"Why didn't you tell me?" Hannah asked. "I could have kept your secret."

"I know that, but you can also betray knowledge by being confident when you shouldn't be."

He could tell she wasn't pleased he hadn't trusted her. He'd wanted to tell her, but he'd gotten used to keeping his own counsel. He hadn't even told Zeke. He'd told Jake only after Mr. Ridgely arrived.

She looked hurt. That bothered him, but the look of resignation, of acceptance, bothered him more. It was as though he'd lived down to her low expectations, as though he'd fallen into the category of men like Amos Merrick.

Buck wondered if Jake, had he been in Buck's

place, would have told Isabelle. He suspected he would. But Isabelle was experienced. She'd survived being an orphan, a governess, a school teacher, all before she ever met Jake. Hannah had been kept locked away in that house. She didn't know how to carry off a bluff.

"You think you've pulled a fast one, don't you?"

Buck turned to find himself facing Sid Barraclough. "I don't know what you're talking about, Sid."

"Claiming those cows as yours, that you branded them."

"Are you saying they belong to someone else? You saw the brand on the underside of that hide."

"You're not fooling me."

Barraclough had his hand on his gun handle. Buck wondered if he was trying to make him angry enough to do something stupid.

"I wasn't trying to," Buck said. "I wasn't even thinking of you. Now if you'll move aside, I'm taking Hannah over to pick out her steak. Since it's her beef, I think she ought to get the best cut."

"Our business isn't over yet," Barraclough said.

"I never had any business with you, Sid. I don't deal with errand boys. If I have anything to say, I say it to the boss."

Sid's hand flew to his gun. He stopped, the gun halfway out of its holster.

"I've got no fight with you," Buck said. "If you draw on me, I'll kill you. If by some chance I miss, you'll be dangling from a tree inside five minutes."

Barraclough looked around him. Nearly every man in the camp was staring at him—poised, alert, ready. Chet, Luke, and Jake had their guns drawn. Barraclough eased his gun back into its holster and turned back to Buck.

"There'll be another time," Barraclough said.

"I hope so. I'd hate to think you were the kind of man who built his reputation by drawing on wounded men."

Buck knew he risked pushing Barraclough into doing something foolish, but he refused to let him think he was afraid of him just because the rotten little gunslinger had a reputation with a gun.

"Come on, Buck," Hannah said, pulling at his sleeve. "I'm getting hungry." Linking her arm with his, she led him toward the food. "Were you trying to get yourself killed?" she hissed as soon as they were out of earshot.

"Sid was just trying to push me. I thought he might enjoy it more if I pushed back as well."

"You think Gillett sent him?"

"I don't know. Gillett hired Sid to protect his rustling. Sid failed. Maybe he's trying to salvage his reputation."

"Well, I don't intend for him to do it by shooting you."

"Why not? You'd have your cows and your ranch back."

He didn't know why he'd said that, but he regretted it the moment the words were out of his mouth.

Chapter Seventeen

Hannah made him pay for it, too. "Do you think I'd kiss a man and then want him shot for a few cows?" she asked.

"Of course not." But he might as well not have answered. He had put his foot in his mouth, albeit unintentionally, and she was going to keep it there until she was good and ready to let him pull it out. She didn't ignore him or go eat with Drew. No, she let him sit next to her, but she projected such an icy demeanor, he decided a snowstorm would have been warmer.

"I can't believe you would say such a thing, even in jest."

"I wasn't thinking. I've been worried about Gillett."

That wasn't the right thing to say either. It reminded her that he hadn't been willing to share his plans with her.

Leigh Greenwood

"You'll have to excuse me for forgetting," she said. "Since I, a mere woman, couldn't be trusted to know your plans, I haven't given them much thought."

Buck figured he was firmly in the doghouse—only he couldn't figure how he'd gotten there. All he'd done was kiss her. A little thing like that shouldn't tie him up for life. But those had been no ordinary kisses. He hadn't kissed a lot of women, but he'd kissed enough to know something unusual had happened between them.

Jake came over and made some small talk. Then suddenly dropping his voice, he said, "I think your rustler is up to something."

"Why?" Buck asked.

"He's kept his men tightly about him ever since you skinned that cow. Now they're spread out. I'll alert the boys."

"I'll keep my eyes open," Buck said as Jake walked over to Luke who was sitting near the fire.

But Buck didn't want to have to think about Gillett just now. He wanted to thaw Hannah out before they finished eating. He'd been thinking about those kisses ever since last night. No woman had ever affected him the way Hannah did. He was anxious to see if the effect was the same two nights in a row.

But even as he turned back to Hannah, he positioned himself so he could keep an eye on Gillett. "I'm sorry I hurt your feelings."

She didn't even look at him.

"Aren't you going to accept my apology?"

"Yes."

Still she didn't look at him. She didn't seem to be eating her food either.

"At least look at me when you say that."

"Why?" she asked, turning to glare at him. "Do you think your handsome face is going to make me forget what you said?"

For a moment Buck was too stunned to reply. No one had ever called him handsome. With the blond Attmore and Haskins brothers around, nobody ever noticed the rest of Jake's boys.

"Do you really think I'm handsome?"

"I don't know about the other women you kiss, but I wouldn't kiss a man I thought was ugly."

Despite the scalding quality of her tone, Buck felt himself swell with pride. Hannah thought he was handsome.

"As handsome as Chet?"

"No."

Oh. Well, he'd always known that. But he figured, if Hannah was blind enough to think he was handsome, she might be blind enough to think he was better looking than Chet.

"I think you're pretty, too," he said, "the prettiest girl I've ever seen."

"I don't believe you."

But he could tell she wanted to. She was listening.

"I thought so when I was working for your father."

"You hated me then. You told me so."

"I still dreamed about you."

"I don't believe you."

"I did."

A flash of anger arced through Buck. Why was he turning his soul inside out when she was ignoring him, just as she had so many years ago? Where was his pride? Had he forgotten he'd sworn never to love any woman for fear she'd leave him?

No, but he couldn't let Hannah stay angry with

him. He might be mixed up about other things, but he was very clear about that.

"When I first got here, I tried to hold the things your father did against you. It didn't take me long to find out I couldn't."

"Why?"

That was a very good question. He didn't know why. He just knew he'd kissed Hannah, and now everything was different.

"I guess I was too busy worrying about Gillett and the missing cows to know my feelings for you were changing. When I finally did notice, it had already happened."

Her posture ceased to be so rigid. She stopped stabbing at her food. She turned her head to look at him.

"It happened like that for me, too."

"What?"

"Deciding you weren't like all the other men I'd known, that I could trust you. At first I was afraid of you. I thought all you wanted was my ranch."

He still did, but the ranch was all tangled up in his mind with Hannah. He'd been getting crazy notions lately, thinking maybe he could have both.

"I think we have a lot of things to get straight between us," Buck said. "Suppose we see if we can find a quiet spot."

Hannah turned. It was hard to tell in the twilight, but he thought she blushed ever so slightly.

"Is that all you want to do?"

"That will depend on you."

Hannah stood up to take her plate over to the pot of hot, soapy water Matt Haskins kept on the fire. Buck jumped to his feet so quickly, he nearly tripped himself. He got his feet under him and started after Hannah. She turned back to him and opened her mouth to speak. At that moment she caught sight of something behind him. Suddenly her expression changed to terror.

"Luke, watch out for the fire!" she cried.

Buck spun on his heel in time to see Luke wrench his body to one side in a frantic effort to avoid the red-hot coals of the campfire. He rolled forward a split second after he hit the coals. Buck grabbed up a blanket and slapped it against Luke's shoulder to extinguish the tiny tongues of flame that ate away at his shirt. A moment later Matt doused him with a bucket of cold water.

"What happened?" Buck asked.

"I don't know," Luke said. "One minute I was walking, and the next I was falling."

"Barraclough tripped him," Hannah said. "I saw him. He stuck a stick between Luke's legs."

Buck turned to find Barraclough standing just behind him, his feet spread, his hand suspended above his gun. He had intentionally tripped Luke to force a confrontation.

"That was a coward's trick," Buck heard himself say, his voice surprisingly calm for all the anger that resonated in it.

"No man calls me a coward."

Buck looked down. Hannah was on her knees, ripping away the charred shirt to expose Luke's burns. The angry red marks on his shoulder and down the side of his arm were nothing compared to the disfiguring burns Luke would have suffered if he had fallen directly into the fire.

"I'm calling you a coward," Buck said, his voice clear, his words unequivocal. "Any man who hides in the dark to trip another man is a low-down, yellow-bellied snake."

"Let me up," Luke growled through gritted teeth. "I'll kill him."

"You're not going anywhere," Aldo Jenkins said. "You're staying right where you are until Miss Hannah can see to those burns."

"You just signed your death warrant," Barraclough said to Buck.

"I didn't know your kind could read," Buck answered.

Luke struggled to sit up, but Jody Beamis and Jonathan Ridgely added their strength to Aldo's.

"You can't do anything," Aldo said. "Buck's made his play. Now he's got to back it up."

A smile of satisfaction settled on Barraclough's face. "You should let the kid fight his own battles."

"If I did, you'd be dead. He's faster than both of us together."

It would have been common sense to let Luke fight him. The boy had a lightning draw with either hand. But Barraclough had only used Luke to get at Buck. Buck wasn't about to let Luke risk his life in a battle that was rightfully his.

For six years he and Luke had lived and worked together. They'd laughed over some things, fought over others, but they'd always done it together, Luke and all the rest of Jake's boys. Now, even though he and Zeke had left the Broken Circle, they had come to help him. Never once had Buck shown these men what they meant to him; never once had he called even one of them brother.

"Let me have him," Chet demanded. "Luke's my brother."

Buck didn't take his eyes off Barraclough to look at Chet. "This is my quarrel."

"But I'm faster. He could kill you."

"Lend me your guns."

"Buck, this is crazy. You know—"

"This is my territory, Chet, and it's my fight. Now are you going to lend me your guns, or do I have to ask Jake?"

"You always were a hard-headed know-it-all," Chet grumbled as he unbuckled his gun belt and handed it to Buck. "I didn't travel all this way to watch you get killed."

"Have a little faith. After all, you helped teach me how to shoot. Now go see how your brother's doing."

Buck and Barraclough were barely six feet apart. At that range, neither could miss. As they started to back away from each other, the men moved back to give them room. That was when Buck saw Jake. He was standing next to Gillett. Gillett's hand was poised above his gun. But that was where it stayed. Jake held a gun against Gillett's temple. A quick scanning of the group showed him that each of Gillett's men was covered. One very surprised cowhand found himself staring at a pistol Drew held squarely between his eyes.

"Don't back up too far," Buck called to Barraclough. "I don't want you disappearing into the dark."

Buck wanted to goad Barraclough, insult him, make him so furious that he would draw in anger. It might not throw off his aim by much, but it might be just enough to keep him alive. Buck was under no illusions. He was not a gunfighter. Barraclough was probably faster. It was up to Buck to think of some way to even up the odds.

"Say your prayers, boy," Barraclough taunted.

"I already have," Luke called back. "I asked the Devil to come for you personally. He could hardly wait. He said he hadn't had such a big piece of carrion come his way in a long time. He's here already. Just over there. If you turn around you can—"

With a shout of fury, Barraclough went for his gun.

Jake always said, *Watch the eyes. They'll always tell you when a man is ready to draw.*

Barraclough's eyes widened ever so slightly before his hand dropped to his gun. In the same moment Buck drew; as he did, he threw himself to the ground and to one side. Barraclough's first bullet buried itself in the ground next to Buck. Buck fired one quick shot, brought his other arm up as he rolled over and fired a second shot.

Barraclough was still on his feet, his gun leveled at Buck, but he didn't fire. The vast emptiness around them swallowed up the last echo of their shots. A cow bellowed, and a couple of horses whinnied nervously. Barraclough looked down in surprise at a small red spot on his shirt. Then he sank to his knees, his gun going off into the ground in front of him before he keeled over.

Chet walked up to the body and checked the wound. "Two shots to the heart with less than an inch separating them. Either you're a damned good shot, or I'm a better teacher than I thought."

"Just lucky," Buck said. "Very, very lucky."

The rest of the roundup went quickly. Gillett offered no further resistance to Buck and Hannah's ownership of the cattle branded with the six-pointed star. It was decided that one cow representing each of the unclaimed brands would be slaughtered. Their hides proved they had all been rustled. The others carrying those brands were returned to their rightful owners.

Buck was certain most of the cattle Gillett had

rustled had already been sent to Nebraska. That was where Hannah's cows would have gone before the end of the summer.

When they reached Walter Evans's ranch, they found Sarah Grossek there tending his sick daughter. Walter helped them with the rest of the roundup.

"I must say I'm a little sorry to be going home," Jody Beamis said to Buck when it was time for the crew to break up. "This is the first time since I've been in Texas that I feel like I'm among friends."

"I'm sure your wife will be glad to know that," Hannah said. "But she won't be truly happy until you're home again. You'll have to bring her over. It's time all the women got to know each other, too."

There were no good-byes from Gillett or his men. They had pulled out of the roundup as soon as it left Gillett's range.

Mrs. Grossek decided to stay with Walter Evans's daughter another day or two. "You won't need me as long as Mrs. Maxwell's there," she said.

The ride back to the ranch turned into a loud, joyous trip for most of the boys. Even Zeke joined in some of their hijinks.

But Buck couldn't get over a heavy feeling in his heart. He'd thanked Jake for coming. He would thank them all again before they left, but he knew that wouldn't be enough. There was so much he wanted to say. He felt as though he had a huge bubble inside him, growing bigger and bigger, as though he couldn't find the words to let out everything trapped inside him.

"What is it?" Hannah asked, sensing his troubled mood.

"It's them," he admitted a little reluctantly, "my *brothers* as you would say, my *family.*"

"When did you admit that?"

"When I faced Barraclough while the others made sure Gillett and his men didn't interfere."

"Not before then?"

"Probably, but I couldn't deny it after that."

"Are you going to tell them how you feel?"

"It's too late. I should have said these things years ago, but I didn't know how."

"Maybe you can do something for them."

"The only thing Jake wants is for me to go back home."

Hannah grinned at him.

"I know," Buck said. "I guess I do feel the Broken Circle is home. Jake offered me land before I left, but I can't accept a ranch from Jake. I've got to earn it for myself."

"I don't know what to say. I never had any brothers, sisters, or friends. I envy you that."

Will and Zac met them at a gallop. Isabelle and Eden weren't far behind. By the time they reached the ranch, everything around them was pandemonium. They spent the rest of the day heating water for baths to wash away the accumulated grime of a two-week roundup.

By the time they had eaten and cleared away after dinner, everybody was too tired to do anything but burrow into their bedrolls and fall into an exhausted sleep. Despite their exhaustion, there was a camaradarie among them that Buck remembered from the days when they'd all been Jake's boys bedding down in the bunkhouse together. Even Zeke pulled his mattress out of the barn to be with them tonight.

Buck didn't get much sleep. When morning came, he found it difficult to match everyone's high spirits. Will and Zac were delighted to give Hannah's chores back to her. Buck thought Isabelle would be relieved to get back to her own house, to have her brood safely around her once more. Jake and the boys would be happy wherever Isabelle was.

Buck had been anxious to leave the Broken Circle, to strike out on his own. But now that he'd been given a second chance to appreciate what he had left behind, he didn't want to let go. As they all gathered outside in preparation for departure, he held out his arms to Eden. She ran into them.

"Bye, little sister," he whispered into her filmy hair as he picked her up. "I'm going to miss you."

"Me miss you, too," Eden said and hugged him hard around the neck and kissed him on the middle of his mouth.

Buck hugged her back. At least he could express his feelings for Eden without feeling self-conscious.

"You're squeezing me."

He hadn't realized he was holding her so tightly. "Sorry. I don't want to let you go."

"You won't have to if you come back."

"Buck has a new home now. Maybe he'll come visit us during the winter."

Buck looked up to see Isabelle watching them.

"You'd better go tell Zeke good-bye," she told her daughter. "Don't forget to thank Hannah for letting us stay at her house."

Together they watched Eden run off. "She misses you a lot," Isabelle said. "I do hope you can come home for Christmas."

Buck thought of their Christmases together, the first two spent in a hotel, the last four on their own ranch, and knew that was where he wanted to be this year, too.

"I'll be there."

"Promise?"

The doubt in Isabelle's eyes hurt him. He leaned over to kiss her cheek, something he'd never done. She seemed surprised, but happiness quickly warmed her eyes. When he started to straighten up, she put out her hand to stop him.

"Don't tease me about Christmas."

"I'll be there," he said. "Zeke, too."

Isabelle put her arms around his neck and hugged him. "Thank you," she whispered. "It wouldn't be the same without both of you."

Buck suddenly felt awkward, as if his arms were foreign parts that had no function. So he hugged Isabelle back. She was shorter than he was, surprisingly slender and fragile. He'd always thought of her as strong, virtually indestructible.

Knowing she wasn't made him feel protective.

"Turn my back one minute, and you're trying to steal my woman."

Buck jerked back, embarrassed. Jake's broad grin didn't prevent heat from scorching the back of Buck's neck. But he didn't back away. This was a chance to say something he should have said years ago.

"Just saying good-bye. Since Isabelle's the closest to a ma I'm ever going to have, a handshake didn't seem enough."

"Since I'm the closest thing to a pa you've got, you going to hug me?"

Buck thought Jake was kidding, but he couldn't be sure. Hell, the worst Jake could do would be to knock him down. That wouldn't kill him.

"Sure."

Buck wasn't sure which of them was more surprised. Or more awkward and stiff. He'd never do it again, but he was glad he'd done it once. He hoped the gesture thanked Jake in a way his words never could have.

"Jake's promised to come home for Christmas and bring Zeke with him," Isabelle said, wiping her eyes.

"Is that a reason to cry?" Jake asked, taking longer to recover his composure than Buck would have expected.

"Don't pay any attention to me," she said. "Ever since I had Eden, I cry at everything. Now you take care," she told Buck. "I let you out of my sight for a little more than a month, and you got shot and got in a gunfight."

"Run while you can," Jake said. "She'll have you wrapped in cotton in a minute."

"I've come to say good-bye," Drew said gruffly. "Don't think of hugging me, or I'll slug you."

Buck felt a huge bubble of happiness swell up inside of him. "Threaten me, will you?"

He pounced on Drew, forced her hands behind her back, kissed her soundly on each cheek, then hugged her struggling body tightly against his chest. The feel of her young breasts against his chest startled him so much, he nearly dropped her. He'd always thought of Drew as practically sexless. He wouldn't do that any longer.

"You big lummox!" Drew said, pushing him away and wiping each cheek with the back of her hand. "I ought to shoot you in the other shoulder." She spun around to find the two mischief-makers right behind her. Will stared wide-eyed at her; Zac's eyes sparkled with laughter. "Either one of you mentions this to a soul, and you're dead meat."

She stalked off.

"I don't mind if you hug me," Will said.

Buck knew he couldn't back out now. Of all the

boys, Will had always been the one who needed the strongest demonstration of affection. Buck felt awkward; Will acted as if it was nothing out of the ordinary. Buck wished he could feel that natural.

"I don't want you hugging me," Zac said. "I ain't your brother."

"Nobody could pay me to hug you," Buck said. "I don't want to get cooties."

"If I'd known I had to hug you, I'd have stayed home," Luke said.

Buck looked up. They were all there—Chet, Matt, and Sean.

"If I'd known I had to hug *you*, I'd have sent you back," Buck shot back.

There was a moment of hesitation. If he hugged one, he had to hug them all. What had started as an impulse had suddenly assumed enormous proportions. But a hug couldn't even begin to express what he felt for these people, for their coming to his aid without his asking. Neither could it thank them for the feeling of belonging that they provided, of being part of something warm and wonderful.

He'd never hear the end of it from Zeke, but he'd lived through worse.

"Don't stay away forever," Luke said when he returned Buck's embrace. "Eden doesn't like anybody's stories as much as yours."

After that it was easy to hug Sean. He had grown so big and heavily muscled it was like trying to get his arms around two people. "I don't know why you bother roping steers," Buck said to Jake. "Just let him wrestle them to the ground."

Sean grinned, full of pride in his magnificent body.

"You sure you don't want us to stay?" Chet asked.

He and Buck had always competed with each other to be Jake's foreman. They'd shared most of the duties for the last six years, Jake rarely putting one over the other.

"I had everything under control," Buck said. "But after you came all this way, I figured I might as well let you help."

Chet punched him playfully in the shoulder.

"Hurry up, you two," Jake said. "Drew has already ridden out with Will and Zac hard on her heels."

"Thanks," Buck said as he hugged Chet. "I hope I can return the favor."

"Just don't get yourself killed. Isabelle and Eden couldn't stand it."

As Buck watched them ride away, he felt a part of him go with them. It hurt a little. He almost wished he could be going, too, that things could be the way they used to be when they were first adopted.

"That was disgusting."

Buck turned to Zeke, but his irritation disappeared the moment he got a look at his friend's face. He saw there the loneliness, the sense of separation, that he himself had felt until just now. He realized he'd made a journey Zeke had yet to make.

"It made me feel good," Buck said. "I wish I'd done it sooner."

"I think it was sweet," Hannah said. "If I had brothers and sisters, I'd hug them all the time." She'd hugged everybody along with Buck.

"Females are always hugging," Zeke said. His tone was scornful.

"I can't say as I'd do it," Tom said, "but I guess it's all right when it's family."

"They aren't," Zeke said.

"Yes, they are," Buck contradicted. "They're a better family than either you or I deserve."

The tension had been growing all afternoon. Buck's letting down the barriers with his family had served to eliminate some of his resistance to his growing attachment to Hannah. It was funny how a person could want something and not even know it. Well, now that he'd admitted he had a family, that he loved them despite his best efforts to remain emotionally uninvolved, he found he didn't mind admitting he liked Hannah.

He wanted a family of his own. He had a very strong notion he wanted to have that family with Hannah.

Hannah seemed to know something had changed between them. She didn't behave differently, but the look in her eyes had changed. She glanced his way more often. Sometimes Buck thought she was eager. At other times she seemed thoughtful. Still other times she seemed almost frightened. He guessed their new relationship was as much of a change for her as it was for him.

Zeke also knew something had changed. He hadn't said anything, but a dozen times during the afternoon, Buck could feel Zeke's gaze boring into his back. During dinner he'd been his usual morose self. But rather than ignore everyone and growl when anybody dared speak to him, he kept shifting his gaze from Buck to Hannah. From his expression, he didn't like what he saw.

Only Tom Gladdis seemed unaffected. Once he'd been assured that Buck wanted him to stay on through the summer, he chattered on about jobs that would keep him busy until fall roundup.

"I think we ought to build a few dams in some of

these canyons," he said. "We get plenty of water in spring and early summer, but it won't stay around without something to hold it back."

"The creek runs dry in late summer," Hannah said. "I imagine the other streams around here do, too."

"I suppose you know all about building dams," Zeke grumbled. He wasn't happy about having Tom around all summer.

"I've seen a few built," Gladdis said.

"The cows can go down to the river," Zeke said. "I don't suppose you're going to tell me it runs dry."

"I don't want the stock walking that far in hot weather," Buck said. "They'll walk off too much weight. You can look round the next few days, see how many places you think would hold a dam."

"What'll I be doing while he's playing with rocks and mud?" Zeke asked.

"Doctoring for screw worms. That ought to keep you busy all summer."

"What about you?" Zeke asked. "You planning to work in the garden?" He eyed Hannah in a very unfriendly fashion.

"I've got to see about turning this ranch into a successful operation. I want to locate some hay meadows, or places where we might start them. I need to find the best pasture for each season. I have to know if the range can carry more cattle or if we should scale back to prevent overgrazing. When I get a chance, I'm going to look over our bulls and see if we need to upgrade."

"That ought to keep you in the saddle for three months," Zeke said, looking a little more friendly. He pushed back his chair. "You'd better get your mattress and come along. You need all the rest you can get."

279

"Get my mattress?" Buck echoed. "What are you talking about?"

Zeke looked at Hannah and back at Buck. "You're not sleeping in the house," Zeke said.

"Why not?"

"Because Mrs. Grossek isn't here."

Buck didn't have to look in Hannah's direction to know she'd already thought of that. "Would it upset you?" he asked her.

"I can't see any reason why it should." She got up and carried her plate to the sink. Without thinking, Buck did the same thing.

"You ought to sleep in the barn," Zeke said.

"There are only two bunks," Buck said.

"I can sleep outside," Tom offered. He brought his plate and coffee cup to the sink.

"We've got five beds and four people," Buck said. "I don't see any sense in anybody sleeping outside."

"Maybe I ought to stay here and keep an eye on you," Zeke said.

Buck didn't know what had gotten into Zeke, but his telling him what to do was getting annoying. "You want to sleep at the foot of my bed, or is outside the door close enough for you?"

Zeke brought his fist down on the table so hard that a knife clattered to the floor. "No place is close enough with you two acting like you're starved for each other."

Chapter Eighteen

"You really don't mind if I stay in the house?" Buck asked Hannah. Zeke had stormed out earlier. Tom had stayed behind, still talking about what he planned to do, while Hannah and Buck did the dishes and put things away. After helping Isabelle, Buck felt it would be churlish not to help Hannah as well.

"No, I don't mind," Hannah said.

"You sure?"

"Of course she doesn't mind," Tom said. "No woman likes staying by herself. I started to tell Zeke, but he didn't look like he wanted to hear anything from me."

"Me, either," Buck said.

Tom got up and rinsed out his cup. "Guess I'd better turn in. I got a lot of riding to do tomorrow."

"You and Zeke keep your eyes open for Gillett or his men," Buck cautioned.

"You don't expect him to cause any more trouble, do you?"

"I don't know," Buck said, "but he doesn't seem the kind to let things drop."

"What can he do?" Tom asked.

"Not knowing the answer to that question is what worries me," Buck said.

"Not me," Tom said, grinning. "That's one good thing about not being the owner."

After Tom left the kitchen, the silence grew too deep to be comfortable.

"When did your mother say she was coming back?"

"In a day or two, depending on how Mr. Evans's daughter is doing."

"That leaves a lot of work for you."

"I'll manage."

He started to offer to help but changed his mind. He'd lost too much time already, and he didn't want to hear what Zeke would have to say. Besides, he'd have a difficult time keeping his mind on his work and his hands to himself. Ever since Zeke had interrupted them that night during the roundup, he couldn't stop thinking about kissing Hannah again. And again. And again.

"Are you sure you don't mind me staying in the house?"

"I told you already."

He took her by the hands and turned her to face him. "I know what you said, but you've been fussing around this kitchen ever since you got up from the table. Everything has been washed and put away. You're just moving things around. What are you trying to avoid?"

She looked up at him. "You. And me, too."

That felt like a dipper of cold water in the face. "Then I ought to sleep in the barn."

"That's not what I meant."

She tried to pull her hands away, but he wouldn't let her.

"I like you, but I don't know what it means," she said. "I've tried to figure it out, but I can't."

"Does it have to mean anything? Can't it be just that?"

"I don't know."

"Can't we try?"

"I guess so."

"You don't sound very enthusiastic."

"I'm confused."

"What about?"

"Everything. I didn't like men. I didn't like you. I planned to learn all there was to know about ranching and then get rid of you. Now I don't like cows, I hate roundup, and I don't want to think of you ever leaving."

"Then don't think about it," Buck said. He turned her face up to his so he could kiss her. "Just think about me holding you, kissing you."

"I can't think when you do that."

"Then don't."

Buck wasn't doing a very good job of thinking himself. He ought to be in bed rather than getting himself more deeply involved with Hannah. But once the walls he'd built around himself had come tumbling down, he discovered he had no resistance.

He kissed her gently. She was so trusting. She might say she'd never trusted him, but they'd both trusted each other from the beginning. It must have come from something they'd learned about each other six years ago, something he couldn't see then for the anger and the hate.

He didn't hate her. He never had. He'd probably been in love with her from the beginning. He was just picking up where he'd left off in his dreams.

Well, not exactly where he'd left off.

She felt good in his arms. Warm and soft and supple. She fitted against him nicely, right in the crook of his arm. She felt too small and fragile to do all the work he'd seen her do in the garden.

Their kiss deepened and lengthened.

"I think this is what Zeke was afraid you'd do," she murmured.

"Forget Zeke."

He had. He couldn't think of anything except the woman in his arms, the woman who gave him back kisses as ardent as his own. He wondered if his nearness excited her as much as hers excited him. The feel of her breasts pressed tightly against his chest had produced a nearly instant change in his groin. He feared that if she noticed, it would scare her.

He hoped his kisses would distract her.

He kissed her on the nose, then the eyelids. That surprised her. It pleased her as well. She smiled.

"We ought to get some sleep," she said. "I'm sure you're still tired after the roundup."

"I'll hold up a little longer."

He kissed her again, pressing his tongue between her lips. She parted them in surprise. He took advantage, plunging his tongue into her mouth. She responded with a gasp of shock and a stiffened body, which pushed her into intimate contact with his groin.

She recoiled, her eyes wide with astonishment, but Buck didn't let her break their kiss. His arms continued to hold her close to him; his tongue continued to explore her mouth. Tentatively at first, then with more confidence, her tongue joined his in a sinuous dance. In a twinkling she became the more aggressive of them. She was also the one to break the kiss.

She turned her head when he tried to kiss her again.

"We've got to stop."

"In a little bit." He didn't mind kissing her ear or the side of her neck. It was nearly as much fun as kissing her lips.

"Now," Hannah said, putting her hands against his chest and pushing him away.

"What's wrong? You didn't stop me before."

"That was different."

"How?"

"It was new. It was just about kissing. Now it's about what comes next, and I don't know what I want that to be."

"Why do you have to think about that? Why can't we just enjoy kissing each other?"

"I can't do that. Nothing is an isolated event. Everything is related to everything else."

Buck didn't understand why women had to make things so complicated. Hannah had probably made it all the way to marriage and at least a half-dozen children. He shivered at the prospect. There was no reason a kiss had to be anything more than a kiss.

He relaxed his hold on her, and she slipped out of the circle of his arms. She headed straight for the door. "Good night. I'll see you in the morning."

She stopped just before she stepped through the door. "I did like kissing you. I liked it very much."

He stood there a few moments after she had gone. He could hear the sound of her bedroom door closing. He imagined her inside, letting down her hair, brushing it. He imagined her slipping out of her clothes, her naked innocence bared for a short moment before she pulled on her nightgown and got into bed.

He roused himself out of his reverie. This was no good. It only made his need more urgent, his body harder. He considered going to the barn, after all, but that would be admitting defeat.

Hannah closed the bedroom door behind her and leaned against it for support. She loved him. She wasn't quite sure when it happened, but she had fallen in love with Buck.

The thought thrilled her. It also terrified her. What if he didn't love her? What if he did love her but was so frightened of marriage that he left?

But what if he did want to get married? Was she ready to take such a step?

Part of her said yes without hesitation. Another part of her wasn't so sure. She'd always concentrated on what she didn't want. She was quite positive about that. But what *did* she want? She wasn't sure anymore.

Did she want to be a wife? Did she want to take care of a man, bear his children, satisfy his body?

From somewhere deep inside her, a clarion call came ringing forth. Yes, she wanted to do all that and more. While her mind still grappled with this stunning about-face, her body and heart had already cast their enthusiastic votes.

She straightened away from the door and walked over to the tiny table that served as her dresser. She lighted her lamp, sat down, and began to take the pins out of her hair. With long, steady strokes, she brushed out the waves and knots.

It was already difficult to think of the future without Buck. Maybe that should have been her first warning of change, when he suddenly become part of her plans.

She got up and walked to the window, her nerves taut, her muscles tight.

When did she start to trust him? She wasn't certain she trusted him entirely yet. Buck might love her, but he had loyalties established long before he'd met her. One of the strongest was his desire to have a ranch of his own. She doubted love for anybody could cause him to give up that dream.

She stopped brushing long enough to stare at her hazy reflection in the window pane. She wished she had a mirror. She wanted to study her face. She didn't know if she was pretty enough to hold Buck's attention. He must have seen many women far prettier. She knew her drab, faded clothes were a severe handicap, but she didn't own anything alluring. Her father wouldn't have allowed it.

Returning to her chair, Hannah laid her brush down. With practiced quickness she plaited her hair into a single braid. Then she stood up and removed her dress and chemise. She pulled a thick, cotton nightgown over her head, blew out the light, and got into bed. The hard mattress was cold. She pulled her legs up close to her body while she waited for the bed to warm up.

She could feel Buck's arms around her. More than that, she wished they were around her right now, keeping her warm, safe, and secure. She felt her body flush with heat at what that thought implied, but Hannah didn't back away from it. She knew she wanted him. She also knew he wanted her. She'd felt the heat and hardness of his arousal. She had felt her own body's response.

She had pulled away because the intensity of it had frightened her. After having been repelled by men all her life, desire had taken her unawares. She recognized it now and knew what it meant, but it was only one of many new feelings. Some were of the heart. Others of the mind. Still others of the body. But all three were part of her. If she was to be happy, they couldn't be in conflict. She had to study them, find a way to make them fit together.

Only then would she know what she wanted of Buck Hobson, and what she had to give in return.

Her mother didn't come home the next day. Or the third day. Hannah was finding it very difficult to act even close to normal around Buck. If he hadn't spent most of his time away from the ranch, she might not have succeeded. Mealtime was agony. Nighttime was even worse.

"I probably won't have time to build more than two dams this summer," Tom Gladdis said the third night over dinner, "but I found the perfect places for 'em. Would it be okay if Grumpy Gus stopped chasing blow flies for a couple of days and gave me a hand?"

"You keep forgetting my name, and you may find yourself buried under one of those dams," Zeke growled back from across the table.

"Maybe I'll ask Gillett to lend me a hand," Tom said. "He'd be just about as friendly."

"You seen him about?" Buck asked.

"Just once, coming back from town."

The Rafter D cook still came by for his usual order of butter and eggs, but he didn't relay any more messages from Gillett. Hannah figured Gillett's liking for her had evaporated when she and Buck claimed the cows.

Later, while Hannah washed the dishes and put away the food, the men talked about ranch business. As he had each day, Buck asked if she needed help in the garden. As usual, she said no. Since Zeke had used Walter Evans's team to break up the garden, there was nothing Hannah couldn't do herself. She preferred it. Only when she was alone could she feel even partly at peace with herself.

Each night, after Zeke and Tom left to go to bed, Buck had kept up his assault on her resistance. She told herself she ought to retreat to her room before the others left, but she couldn't. All day long she dreaded being alone with him. But when the time came, nothing could have kept her away.

"Come on, Sour Puss," Tom said, getting to his feet with a big yawn. "You'll need lots of sleep if you're gonna tote rocks all day."

"If you're not careful what you call me, I'm going to break your head open with one of your precious rocks."

"You know, I think Zeke actually likes Tom," Hannah said after the door closed behind them.

"As close as he can come to liking anybody."

"Can we afford to keep Tom on?"

"As long as you can feed him. He's not asking for wages until we sell the steers."

"Why?"

"He says he likes it here."

"Why?"

"Why not? He's got Zeke to fight with, me to handle the worries, and you to feed him."

"Is that all men want?"

"Pretty much."

"What do you want?"

"You."

"What else?"

"Just you."

She knew that wasn't true, but she liked hearing it. She was feeling particularly vulnerable tonight. As much as Buck appeared to want her, as much as he liked being with her, he'd never mentioned anything more. Hannah knew she wanted more, but she didn't know if Buck did. And she was afraid to mention anything that extended beyond the moment, afraid it might drive him away.

Yet he might be considering marriage. He might be expecting it. Nice girls didn't stand around kissing a man night after night unless they were hoping—planning—to get married. Did he still consider her a nice girl? She wished her mother would come home. She needed someone to talk to.

Buck tried to put his arms around her, but she moved away from him. His surprise showed plainly.

"Since you're helping Tom with that dam, hadn't you better get to bed, too?"

"A few extra minutes won't make any difference."

He reached for her again. She took hold of his hands to keep them from encircling her waist. "We always end up spending more than that."

His surprise turned to confusion. Hannah wondered if she saw a little irritation as well.

"Are you trying to say you don't want me to kiss you?" he asked.

No. She definitely wasn't saying that. She wanted him to hold her and kiss her more than anything else. But first she needed clarification of his intentions, of whether he had any intentions at all.

"Maybe it would be better if we didn't."

"Why? You haven't objected before."

"I know, but it might be better if we stop before things go too far."

"What do you mean by *too far?*"

Now she'd made him angry, but she couldn't go on not knowing what he wanted from their relationship.

"I don't know how things are done elsewhere, but with my people, a woman doesn't let a man kiss her unless they're married, or at least promised in marriage."

She could tell from the shocked look on his face that he hadn't been thinking about marriage. She felt something inside her wither.

"I'm not saying you and I have to be married, but we can't go on kissing every night just because we like it."

"Why not?"

Why indeed? She groped for the words to explain the feeling that was growing stronger and stronger.

"For a woman, a kiss is not something you do just for fun. A kiss says I like you. A second kiss says I like you a lot more. Each kiss adds something to the deepening attachment until the relationship has to go forward. Or it has to stop."

"You mean I can kiss you twice, and we can stay friends. But if I want to kiss you after that, I have to want to marry you."

She shook her head. "You don't understand. I didn't let you kiss me—or kiss you back—just for fun. A kiss is the beginning of a promise. If you don't want to make the promise, you don't take the kiss."

"You should have made the rules clear from the start," Buck snapped. "Is this how women trap men into marriage?"

That hurt, but maybe she had led him on without intending to. "I don't know about other women, and I don't know about any rules. I just know about me, and for me kissing means you care. Caring means you want to be with each other for more than a few nights, a week, or even a month. We haven't talked, Buck. I don't even know if you like me."

"Of course I like you. I wouldn't have kissed you if I didn't."

"You never told me."

"You should have known it."

"I can't read your mind."

"Why not? You expected me to know all your rules."

"You don't understand."

"You mean you aren't saying I have to promise to marry you if I want to kiss you again?"

"No."

"Then let me kiss you."

"Not before we talk."

"About marriage?"

"About something.

"You mean marriage. My mother talked about marriage. She promised to love my father, stay with him, bear his children, take care of him. Well, she had his children all right, but then she got tired, or bored—hell, I don't know what she got! But I do know she walked out. We never heard from her again."

Hannah realized she'd stumbled onto a pocket of deep anger that had nothing to do with her. But in Buck's eyes, it had everything to do with women.

"I'm sorry."

"My father made promises, too. But when he needed money to pay a gambling debt, he sold me so I could end up being a slave for men like your father. Don't talk to me of promises. They can all be broken."

"I never meant—"

"I like you a lot, Hannah, more than I thought I could like any woman. I'll take what you give me, I'll give what I can in return, but I'm not making any promises. I'll never be sold out again."

Hannah couldn't stand it. She'd never meant to hurt Buck. She'd never meant to make him mad at her. She'd done both. It was all over. There was nothing left between them. It would be better if she never had to see him again. She ran from the kitchen. She reached her room, slammed the door behind her, and threw herself on the bed.

The expected tears didn't come because she kept thinking of Buck rather than herself. She couldn't picture her mother leaving her, never wanting to see her again. She couldn't imagine how terrifying, how devastating that must have been to a little boy.

But to have his father sell him to pay a gambling debt? Hannah couldn't conceive of anything more horrible. She hated to think what terrible loneliness, what feelings of worthlessness, must have come from knowing his parents didn't want him. She didn't know how he'd had the courage to keep on living. She didn't think she could have.

No wonder he'd had trouble believing anybody could love him. No wonder he avoided making promises. He wasn't avoiding them as much as refusing to give anybody the power to hurt him the way his parents had. She couldn't blame him.

She ought to go back to the kitchen, find some way to apologize, but she didn't know what to say. How did you begin to rebuild a person's loss of faith in humanity, loss of belief in his own self-worth?

A knock at the door startled her.

"Hannah, are you all right?"

She sat up on the far side of the bed. "Yes."

He paused. "Are you sure?"

"Yes."

Another pause. "May I come in?"

"No."

He came in anyway. She couldn't see his face in the shadows. She could tell from his step that his anger had gone. But she was certain his soul remained firmly encased in the bitter hurt he had suffered so many years before.

"I didn't mean to make it sound like I blamed you for what happened to me." His voice came out of the shadows, firm and reassuring.

"I didn't think you did."

He came closer and sat down on the side of the bed across from her. "When I came here, all I wanted was to pay off the debt and buy you out. I tried to ignore you, but I couldn't. Next thing you know, I couldn't stop kissing you. Tonight I realized I liked you so much, I didn't want to stop."

Hannah felt her breath still a moment. Then her heart started beating much too rapidly. Buck didn't know it yet, but he loved her. As long as that was true, she wouldn't worry about the rest.

"But I can't make any promises," Buck said. "Maybe, after a while, but I don't know." He reached across the bed to take her hand. "I don't expect you to tell me you love me just because I—"

"But I do," Hannah said, horrified that she'd asked him for promises before she'd made one herself. She grasped his hand with both of hers and pulled him into the pool of light that fell across her bed. "None of this would have happened if I didn't love you."

He leaned forward, put his hand behind her head, pulled her to him, and kissed her. "I still can't make any promises."

"I understand. As long as I know you care for me, that's enough."

They lay down on the bed on their sides, facing each other, fingers linked between them.

"You shouldn't have that much faith in me. I've done nothing to deserve it."

"You haven't done anything not to deserve it."

Buck rolled up on his elbow. The moonlight illuminated one side of his face as he stared down at her. He looked like a ghostly lover come to claim his prize. A shiver zigzagged through Hannah. Before the questions could form in her mind, Buck leaned down and kissed her, a long, languorous kiss.

But this was nothing like the kisses they'd shared in the kitchen. The feel of his body lying next to her own sent much more powerful tremors racing through her. She was in the arms of the man she loved, the man she was certain loved her. In her bedroom. On her bed. Alone!

But the fear that washed over her, the strictures her mind threw at her, were swamped by the excitement of knowing that Buck cared for her, of wanting to be with him, of hoping to convince him what they felt for each other was worth a promise that would last a lifetime.

Despite the nectar of his kisses, the sweetness of his presence, she couldn't throw aside all caution. As she yielded to the power of his caresses, relied more on her passion than her reason, she found her physical need moving into conflict with her fear of men. Could she love him enough to trust him with her body? Did she need him enough to try?

Yes. She would never be a whole person as long as she rejected him out of fear. That was what Buck was doing to her. She couldn't show him he was wrong if she couldn't do it herself.

She put her arms around him and pulled him down to her. Despite the inadequate light from the moon, she saw the question in his eyes. She kissed him.

Released from any remaining restraint, Buck's need for her leapt forth like banked flames breaking through. It enveloped Hannah, whipping up the hot embers of her own need until it became a raging blaze. It burned through the shackles of her reason, the fetters of her dread, until she was left free and willing.

She didn't pull away when she felt her breasts crushed against his chest. Neither did she stiffen when she felt the hardness of his desire press against her. A heat began to burn deep within her loins. It spread until it engulfed her entire body. It drove her to move against him, to press the vee of her thighs against his heat.

"Why do you have to wear a dress with so damned many buttons?" Buck muttered.

Hannah wondered herself as she struggled to help him undo the dozen or more buttons from her throat to her waist. The moment she undid the last one, Hannah's fingers moved to the buttons on Buck's shirt. Ever since she'd taken care of his wounds, she'd been wanting to run her fingers over his chest.

His skin was soft and warm against her hands. She nearly lost track of what she was doing when he opened her chemise and took her breast in his mouth. She had only the most rudimentary idea of what passed between a man and a woman. This hadn't been part of it.

The delicious feeling of aching pleasure added to

the heat in her loins, making her feel as if she was about to go up in flames. When he took her nipple between his teeth and sucked it gently, she was certain she would expire in a wild burst of fireworks.

She offered no objection when Buck wanted to remove her clothes. "Yours, too," she murmured when he slid her chemise under her hips and dropped it on the floor.

It took Buck less time to shed his clothes. She held out her arms to him when he rejoined her on the bed. She put her arms around him, felt the scars that covered his back.

The heat that had inflamed her body turned to ice.

"Don't think about it," he whispered as he kissed her neck and shoulders.

"I can't help it. When I think of who—"

"Don't. It has nothing to do with us."

She took his face and held it where the moonlight shone on it. "Are you sure?"

"Yes. I never blamed you."

But she would always blame herself. Buck seemed to understand that she needed to be held close. They lay still for a few magical moments, Buck holding her close, she resting safe and warm in his arms.

But the fire they had kindled in their bodies would not be held at bay. Within minutes they began to move against each other, driven by a primal need that could not be satisfied by anything less than the merging of their bodies.

Buck's gentle caressing of her nipple engulfed her body in a conflagration of desire. Their kisses, hot and hungry, turned frenzied when his hand trailed down her hip, over her thigh, and to the soft flesh between her legs. She knew it would happen, but it still seemed shockingly intimate. A part of her screamed for him to wait, give her time to adjust to the invasion—the downright seizure—of a body that, up until now, she had allowed no one to see, much less touch.

But a much stronger part of her sensed that what lay ahead was so wonderful, it was beyond imagination. She didn't dare hesitate for fear it might vanish before she could find it.

Still, she stiffened when Buck gently parted her flesh. Her breath caught in her throat when his fingers invaded her. But both sensations paled into insignificance when he began to rub a small incredibly sensitive nub. Flames of sweet agony shot through her body like sparks from an exploding firecracker. Within moments, her breath started to come in desperate, tortured gasps. She writhed beneath his touch, craving escape, longing for the torture to become even more exquisite.

Suddenly she reached the peak, and the tension flowed from her like hot liquid. Hannah sank into the mattress, her body damp with perspiration, her breath still too rapid for coherent speech, even if she'd wanted to talk, even if she'd been able to think of anything to say.

She felt Buck push against her.

"Open for me," he whispered.

Instinctively opening her body to receive him, she was startled by a tiny, sharp, stabbing pain.

"It's over," he said. "I won't ever hurt you again."

Tiny though it was, the pain so startled Hannah, she was hardly aware that Buck had moved deep within her until she felt the liquid fire begin to spread through her body once more. She held her breath, hardly daring to hope that the same feelings would once again erupt within her.

Buck's mouth claimed hers in a series of deep, searching kisses that would have left her breathless if she had not already been nearly deprived of breath. Slowly her attention narrowed until it focused only on the flame that threatened to consume her, inch by tortured inch, the spiral of sweet agony that threatened to deprive her of reason.

"Please." Her voice was a ragged whimper, her need relentless. Buck held to his steady rhythm. Hannah thought she would go crazy. She couldn't stand it. He had to reach the need buried deep within her right away, or she would lose her mind.

She threw herself against him, trying to force him to penetrate deeper. When he would not, she sank her teeth into the side of his neck.

At that Buck seemed to catch fire, tormented by the same flames that scorched her entire being. Their bodies slick with moisture, their breathing harsh from the force of their desire, they drove each other onward until the raging storm within them burst.

Hannah was sure she was dying. She seemed to fly apart, to fragment. Her entire body shuddered so hard, she thought it would never stop, but gradually her shaking weakened until she felt she might survive.

Buck collapsed at her side, his body heaving, his breath hot and heavy on the side of her cheek. She reached over and caressed his cheek. Whether he knew it or not, he was hers now. She would allow him time to learn to trust love, to believe in her, if not in all women, but he belonged to her.

Forever and for always.

Chapter Nineteen

Hannah could hardly wait for Zeke and Tom to finish breakfast. She wanted to talk to Buck. He had said he couldn't make any promises, but he'd also said he cared for her. She wanted to believe that meant he would someday grow to love her, would want to marry her, but she knew men didn't think making love automatically meant marriage. She might be naive, but she knew that much.

She should have remembered it last night. Not that she expected it would have made much difference. She had wanted him as much as he wanted her. She just feared they wanted each other for different reasons.

She thought Zeke looked at her more closely this morning, but that might have been her own self consciousness. Did Buck look different? She couldn't tell. Did he act different? She didn't think so. But men didn't invest the same emotion in making love that women did. She should have remembered that, too.

She was so nervous, she couldn't eat. It was all she could do not to scream when Zeke asked for a third cup of coffee. She waited, nerves on edge, lips pressed tightly together, hands behind her apron to hide the fact that they were clenched.

Finally, Zeke pushed his chair back. "I guess we'd better get going if we're going." He subjected Hannah to a searching look. "Maybe you'd better take it easy today. You're looking a little peaked."

Before Hannah could recover from the shock of having Zeke show some concern for her, the kitchen door opened and her mother entered, followed by Walter Evans. A smile wreathing her face, her mother ran across the room and threw her arms around her startled daughter's neck.

"I'm getting married," she said. "Walter has asked me to be his wife."

Hannah was stunned. Speechless. She forgot about Buck and herself. While everyone stood around congratulating Walter and her mother, she could only stare in disbelief. After all that had happened to her, her mother was committing her life into the keeping of another man.

Hannah could hardly wait until everyone left. Even watching Walter kiss her mother good-bye had a quality of unreality about it. Her mother had never kissed her father.

"Are you sure about this, Mama?" Hannah asked the minute the kitchen door closed behind the men.

"Absolutely," her mother said. "I never thought I'd find a man who would love me like Walter does."

"But it happened so quickly."

"He said he fell in love with me that day I invited him to have a cup of coffee."

"But what about you? Before Buck came, you were afraid to speak to anybody."

"I'll never be able to thank Buck enough for bringing me out of my shell."

Hannah couldn't take it all in. It was too unbelievable. It was contrary to everything her mother had ever said, everything she expected her mother to do.

"What's Walter's daughter like?" Hannah asked.

"Ten years old and scared of her own shadow."

"Do you want to raise another daughter?"

"I'd raise ten daughters to be with a man like Walter."

Hannah had always liked Walter, but she'd never thought of him as a paragon.

"What's so wonderful about him?"

Her mother pulled up a chair to the table and motioned for Hannah to sit next to her. "He cares about me—what I think, what I feel, what makes me happy."

"How do you know he won't change once you're married?"

"I refused him when he first asked. I think I was too surprised to believe him. I told him I would never marry again and why. Then he asked what it would take for me to change my mind." Her mother took Hannah's hands in hers. "I'm afraid I wasn't very honest. I told him things that weren't true. I even said I wouldn't live on a ranch. He said he'd sell out and move to Utopia. I said Austin. He agreed."

"Do you believe him?"

"I wasn't sure at first. But after I saw the way he treated his daughter, what she told me of the way he'd treated her mother before she died, I decided he was telling the truth. So I decided to tell him the truth. I'd live anywhere he wanted. All I wanted was to be loved and cared for. Never beaten, never taken for granted."

"And?"

"He said he wanted a partner and a companion, not a slave."

A smile brightened her mother's face. For the first time, Hannah realized that her mother was pretty. She didn't look old, tired, or frightened. She looked pretty. And why shouldn't she? She was just forty-two.

"He said he wanted a lover as well. I'm afraid I stammered worse than a young girl talking to her first young man. He said I was beautiful, that thoughts of making love to me had ruined his sleep for more than a year. Imagine, Hannah, anybody thinking me beautiful! Never once did Nathaniel say he thought I was even a little bit pretty. I nearly asked Walter if a horse had kicked him in the head."

Hannah put her arms around her mother and hugged her. Before last night, she wouldn't have understood why this was so important to her. Now she did.

"I think you're beautiful, Mama. I always have."

Her mother hugged her back. "Thank you, darling, but it's not the same as when a man says it."

Sarah clasped her hands together and held them under her chin. "I can't believe this is happening to me. I keep thinking I'll wake up and discover I've only dreamed it. I keep wishing Nathaniel were here so I could spit in his face." She looked guilty. "I know that's a terrible thing to say, but I hated that man. He took pleasure in being cruel. After twenty years with him, it's hard to believe Walter wants to make me happy."

"Have you talked about a date?"

"The end of the week."

Hannah wasn't certain she actually believed the marriage would take place. That it would happen in five days stunned her. Suddenly the reality of the situation hit her.

"Where will you live?"

"At his ranch."

"What about me?"

"You'll stay here. You always wanted your own ranch. I'll come over to help you, but you won't need so much of a garden now that I'm not here."

Hannah decided not to point out that any one of the three men ate several times more than her mother.

"I didn't mean that. How can I stay here by myself?"

"Marry Buck. I told you to do that weeks ago."

"Buck hasn't been falling in love with me for months. Besides, I've always said—"

"I know what you've said," her mother interrupted. "But we both said what we did because of your father. Walter's not like that. Neither is Buck. It's time we both changed our minds about a lot of things."

The days that followed weren't nearly as frantic as Hannah had expected. "Walter has promised to buy me all new clothes," her mother had announced. "His house is already fully furnished. I won't need anything from here."

She didn't even want her bed.

"I want to forget the years I spent with your father. That bed would only remind me of them."

"You will come visit me," Hannah said.

"Of course."

But Hannah could tell her mother was already

putting the last twenty years of her life behind her. Hannah understood, but it still made her feel sad and alone. Not even Buck's support could do much to ease the loss of the woman who'd been her only friend and companion for her entire life.

Walter had insisted that the wedding take place in Utopia. "I don't want any of those people to be able to say we didn't do everything properly," he said.

"I don't care what they think," Hannah's mother had said.

"I do. I want everybody in that town to think as much of you as I do."

They arrived in Utopia a day before the wedding was to take place. They'd no sooner settled into their rooms than Walter sent Hannah and her mother off to buy a wedding dress.

"Walter doesn't realize you can't just walk into the mercantile and find a dress ready made," her mother said.

"What are you going to do?"

"There must be someone with a dress packed away that they'll let me buy, or at least use."

"Mama, I don't think—"

"I know what you're going to say," her mother said. "They'll be rude to me. Maybe they will. Maybe they'll even refuse to let me in the door. I don't care. I want a dress. Walter need never know what I had to do to get it."

But Hannah wasn't about to have her mother subjected to the same treatment she'd suffered when she tried to sell her pickled beef. "Amos and his father are always saying they'll do anything they can to help me," she said. "Well, this is their chance."

Joseph Merrick didn't look happy when Hannah

informed him he had to find someone who would lend her mother a wedding dress.

"People haven't forgotten what you said when you were last here," he said.

"Neither have I," Hannah snapped. "I hope they've all found time to read their Bibles since then, especially the part about casting the first stone."

Hannah knew Merrick didn't want to get involved in this social tug-of-war, but she suspected times weren't going well enough for him to lose the business of a successful rancher like Walter Evans.

"I'll ask my wife. Meanwhile, why don't you let Amos squire you around."

Hannah put up with Amos only as long as it took her mother to come to an arrangement with Mrs. Merrick for the use of her wedding dress. "You'd better run along," Hannah told Amos when they left the Merrick home.

"Father said I was to see you back to the hotel."

He never had lost that half possessive, half condescending attitude Hannah found so irritating. No woman could ever be happy with Amos so long as he considered marriage to himself the greatest favor he could bestow on any female.

"Mother and I will be busy fitting the dress. There won't be anything for you to do but hold the pin cushion."

"It fits perfectly," Mrs. Grossek said as Amos walked off.

"I know that, but Amos doesn't."

Much to Hannah's surprise, her mother insisted that their next stop be the lawyer's office. She was even more surprised when she discovered her mother's purpose.

"I wish to sign over my interest in the ranch to

my daughter," she informed the lawyer the moment they were seated. "I don't wish to retain anything that once belonged to my husband."

She wouldn't listen to Hannah's protests or the lawyer's warnings. She kept insisting until the papers were written up and signed. She sighed deeply when they stepped out of the office.

"Now I feel like I can go to Walter free of the curse of that man."

Indeed her mother did seem to be a different woman. She passed strangers without cringing. She spent much of the evening trying to make Walter's daughter as comfortable as possible. Celestine Evans was a pretty child, but she seemed frightened of everyone. She clung to Hannah's mother as if she were her own. Already Hannah could see her mother being absorbed into the circle of Walter's life.

"Do you think they'll be happy?" Buck asked when Walter and Sarah had their attention directed toward Celestine.

"Yes, I do," Hannah replied. "I was worried at first. I was a little jealous, too, but I know it is the best thing that could have happened to her. She's like a different person. I feel I hardly know her."

"This will be our last night together," her mother said when she and Hannah were alone in their room. Celestine had decided she wanted to stay with her father. "My future is settled. Let's talk about yours. You're in love with Buck, aren't you?"

Hannah looked up, surprised. "How did you know?"

"I would have known even if I weren't your mother. You look at him as if there's no one else in the room. Even when you're arguing with him, he's all you see. Any woman would know you were in love with him."

"Then I guess I don't have to answer your question."

"Is he in love with you?"

"I think so."

"Are you going to marry him?"

"He hasn't asked me."

"Do you want to?"

"Yes."

"What's stopping you?"

"Buck's mother left him when he was little. His father sold him to pay a gambling debt. He doesn't have much faith in promises."

"My God."

"He doesn't think love makes any difference."

"Do you think he can learn?"

"I don't know."

"What will you do?"

"Keep on loving him. I can't do anything else."

"He's been scarred deep and often, but Buck's a good man. I think he's worth the wait."

"I do, too."

"You want to come stay with Walter and me?"

Hannah knew her mother needed to be alone with her new husband and daughter. "There's no point. Everybody in Utopia already thinks I'm ruined."

"I'm not talking about them. I'm talking about you."

"No, I want to be close to Buck. Something could happen to change his mind. I want to be there when it does."

The wedding was a small affair. Farmer Moffett and his sons were present, along with Joseph and

Amos Merrick. Mrs. Merrick had come down with a sudden indisposition and regretted she couldn't attend. Apparently the indisposition had struck all the ladies of Utopia except Mrs. Grosswelt.

"I wouldn't have cared if no one came," Sarah told Hannah during the brief reception. "I married Walter for myself, not for anyone else."

It was obvious that Walter and his daughter felt Sarah already belonged to them. Frightened by the noise and the presence of so many strangers, Celestine clung to her stepmother. Walter watched her with so much pride that no one could question his happiness.

"There's no reason we can't get married now."

Hannah whirled to see Amos Merrick at her elbow.

"I could understand why you didn't want to leave your mother alone, but now that she's married, there's no reason for us to put off marrying any longer."

"There's only the same reason I've given you from the beginning," Hannah said, amazed that Amos hadn't given up by now. "I don't love you. I wouldn't make you a good wife."

"But you must marry for your reputation."

"Look around you, Amos. Do you see your mother here? Any of the other ladies of Utopia?"

"Mother is ill. Father told you—"

"Your mother and the other ladies didn't come for the same reason no one wanted to buy my pickled beef. I'm already ruined in their eyes. Marrying you would only hurt your reputation."

Hannah nearly laughed at the series of emotions that flashed across Amos's face—shock that anyone could believe anything bad about him or any woman he chose to honor as his wife; fear such a thing might happen; indignation that it could.

"That's absurd. Nobody would—"

"Forget me, Amos. I would make you miserable. I'm stubborn, I insist upon living on my ranch, and I ride astride."

That last shocked him most of all.

"Find some woman who thinks you're marvelous and would like nothing better than to yield to your every wish."

"But you're the woman I want."

Somehow he didn't sound quite as convinced as before.

"No, I'm not. Some day you'll thank me for refusing you. Now I must go say good-bye to my mother."

Hannah immediately forgot Amos. She was doing something she'd never thought she'd have to do—saying good-bye to her mother. As happy as she was for her mother, she was sad for herself. Already she could feel the loneliness of the days ahead, but she was determined she wouldn't cry.

Sarah cried for them both.

"I feel like I'm deserting you."

"I'm a grown woman." Hannah hugged her mother. "I can take care of myself. You've got others to worry about now."

She watched while her mother hugged Buck and Tom. It surprised her when Zeke actually put his arms around her. Maybe even Zeke was not immune to the emotion of weddings. They left town right behind Walter and his new bride. Zeke and Tom rode. Buck drove Hannah in the wagon. He said he wasn't going to give anybody reason to gossip about her riding astride. Hannah didn't tell him that riding out of town with him was all the reason they needed.

Tom and Zeke rode alongside the wagon for a short while, but they soon cantered off. Buck tried to make conversation, but Hannah already missed her mother so much, it was all she could do not to cry.

"Maybe it wouldn't be so bad to be married."

The words came out of the blue. It took Hannah a moment to beat back the fog of her own depression. "What did you say?" she asked, certain she must have misunderstood him.

Buck kept his eyes on the road. "Marriage might not be so bad. Not right now, but sometime in the future."

Hannah told herself to be calm. The word "future" didn't sound too promising to her ears. As far as she was concerned, people put off to the future things they never intended to do.

"How far in the future?"

"I'm not sure. The idea still makes me nervous."

"It makes every man nervous. He knows he'll be stuck with one woman for the rest of his life."

"That's not the reason. I'm afraid you won't want to stick with me."

"I'm not a fickle female."

"I know."

"Then why wouldn't I stay?"

He turned toward her. "What have I got to offer a woman? I'm not handsome like Chet or strong like Sean. I'm not rich like Amos, and I don't own a ranch like Walter. Hell, I don't own anything. Even the horses I ride came from Jake."

"I wouldn't care if you came naked."

He didn't smile as she hoped he would.

"With my parents, what kind of kids would we have?"

"Buck, you're nothing like your parents. You

might as well be Jake and Isabelle's son for all the similarity you bear your real parents. You take your responsibilities seriously or you wouldn't feel so guilty about everything Jake has given you. You believe very strongly in people, or you wouldn't have risked your life to go back to rescue Zeke from Rupert Relson. Whether you believe it or not, you love your family."

Buck hunched his shoulders.

"And for what it's worth, I think you're more handsome than Chet or Matt."

"You said I wasn't."

"I changed my mind."

"You can't mean it," he said, obviously hoping she would contradict him.

"Actually, I've lost my heart to Zac Randolph. If he has a big brother that handsome, I could—"

Hannah suddenly found herself in a crushing embrace. She doubted Buck was paying any attention to the horses.

"Don't trifle with me, woman," he said. "Do you really think I'm better looking than Chet and Matt?"

"Of course I do, you big idiot. It never occurred to me to want either of them to pay me any attention. But that isn't why I gave myself to you."

"Why did you?"

"Because I fell in love with you. I couldn't do anything else."

"But why me?"

"You may not be rich or own your own ranch, but you're handsome, big, and strong. I can trust what you do and say. I know you'll do everything you can to take care of me. But most important of all, I love you. I don't want to be with anybody else. I'm happy only when I'm with you."

"Only with me?"

"Only you."

"You promise?"

"Buck, what do I have to do to make you believe I love you enough to spend the rest of my life with you?"

"I don't know. It's just—"

"Do you think Isabelle is going to leave Jake for some rich banker or merchant?"

Buck looked at her as though she'd lost her mind. "Isabelle wouldn't leave Jake if you gave her her pick of every man in Texas. She'd sooner—"

He broke off.

"Do you think Isabelle is the only woman in the world who can be faithful?"

"It's not that."

"Then what is it?"

"I couldn't stand it if you ever left me. I'd want to kill you."

"Then you don't have to give it a thought. I can't imagine not being in love with you. I think I was half in love with you six years ago. I just didn't know it. Now kiss me and stop worrying about things that are never going to happen."

They managed to occupy the remainder of the journey quite pleasurably. Except for Walter's mules trying to take them to Walter's ranch instead of the Tumbling T, nothing happened to distract their attention from each other.

"Are you convinced now?" Hannah asked, as she emerged from his embrace. The house was in view. She wasn't ashamed of loving Buck, but she wasn't ready for Zeke to see them kissing like a couple of adolescents.

"Yes," Buck said, not wanting to let her go.

"Now let's get back to your statement that you might consider getting married sometime in the future. Just how far in the future do you mean?"

"How far do you think would be far enough?"

"Well, I don't think we ought to get married next week."

The mention of such a short length of time startled Buck, but he covered it up rather well. "It can't be that soon. Isabelle would behead me if I got married without her, and I would kinda like Jake to be my best man."

Hannah decided Buck really was on the way to accepting the Maxwell tribe as his family. All he needed was a little more time and nothing to upset things.

Hannah looked up as they turned into the lane leading up to the house. A woman who had been sitting in a chair under the trees got up and walked toward them.

"Who's that?" Buck asked.

"I don't know," Hannah replied. "I've never seen her before."

Nor was she likely to see anybody like her in Utopia. A black-haired beauty dressed in that style would have caused a crowd to gather. The woman waited, quiet and self-possessed, until Buck stopped the wagon and helped Hannah down. Then she stepped forward, addressing herself to Buck.

"Hello. I'm your sister, Melissa."

Chapter Twenty

Hannah decided she must not be a nice person. She didn't like Melissa Hobson. Part of her antipathy stemmed from the fact that Buck had hardly been aware of her existence since his sister had announced her identity. But the main reason was that Buck acted as though the appearance of his sister was the most wonderful thing that had ever happened to him. He kept turning to Hannah, wanting her to be as ecstatic as he was. After half an hour, Hannah found the pretense too exhausting and went inside to fix dinner while Buck and Melissa tried to catch up on the past fourteen years.

"Who would have thought Buck had such a stunner for a sister," Tom remarked when he and Zeke entered the kitchen. Hannah was surprised he could talk at all with his tongue hanging out so far.

"When did she show up?" Zeke asked.

"You didn't see her when you got back?" Hannah

asked, hurrying to get food on the table. Zeke must have been as upset as she was. He was helping her in the kitchen.

"We didn't come up to the house," Tom said. "You can't see the front of the house from the barn."

"She was waiting when we drove up," Hannah said. "They haven't stopped talking since."

"Did you see that pile of luggage in the hall?" Tom asked.

"Is she planning to stay the rest of her life?" Zeke wanted to know.

"I can't say. She hasn't bothered to talk to me yet."

She sounded petulant, but she couldn't help it. She would try to behave better, but it would have helped if Buck hadn't forgotten her existence.

"You can call them in now," Hannah said.

Zeke opened the window, stuck his head out, and shouted, "Come eat."

Hannah had never heard Zeke shout at Buck. Obviously he wasn't thrilled with Melissa's appearance either.

It would probably be hard for any woman to like Melissa Hobson. Outside of the fact that she was beautiful in a dark, sultry way that every blond woman in the world envied, she drew every man's attention as easily as flowers draw bees. She flashed brilliant smiles at Zeke and Tom. Zeke didn't appear to be affected, but Tom stared at her like an adoring puppy. Hannah itched to smack some sense into his head.

"Everything looks so good," Melissa said. "Are you sure I'm not putting you out?"

"Of course not," Buck said. "One more doesn't make any difference." That was true, but Hannah would have been less irritated if Melissa had spoken to her rather than Buck. It would also have been nice if she'd offered to help, even if she couldn't boil water.

"I'd have offered to help, but I'm hopeless in a kitchen," Melissa said.

With her looks, Hannah figured Melissa probably had men fighting for the chance to buy her more food than she could eat.

But Hannah's reservations went deeper. She didn't approve of Melissa's dress. It was too tight, the bodice cut too low, the color too bright. Neither did she approve of the way Melissa had blackened her eyes and lashes. She doubted it spoke well of a woman's character to paint her lips a brighter red than that of spring poppies.

She certainly didn't approve of the way Melissa flirted with Tom. Hannah didn't know much about the world, but she did know that a woman like Melissa had no use for a common cowhand.

Melissa dominated the conversation with stories centered around herself. Hannah didn't find them very amusing. Maybe she was prudish, but she didn't think they showed Melissa in a flattering light. The story she was telling now was a good example.

"They both insisted upon taking me to dinner. I didn't know what to do. I couldn't let them fight over me right there in the hotel lobby."

Hannah got the impression that Melissa would have enjoyed such a spectacle.

"I told them to toss a coin. I would have dinner that night with the winner, the next night with the loser. Connor dropped the coin, and it rolled under a sofa occupied by two bird-faced old women. You should have heard the squawk when he dropped to the floor and started pushing their dresses aside.

319

You'd have thought he was attacking them."

Her laughter filled the room. Hannah was certain Melissa had been pleased to be the cause of such a scene.

"Connor ordered the manager to remove the ladies and lift the sofa off the gold piece. He threatened to shoot anyone who touched the coin. You never heard such an uproar—Connor shouting at everybody, those old biddies threatening to faint any moment. Not that anyone would have noticed. When they removed the sofa, poor Connor found he'd lost. He demanded the table next to DeWitt and me, then spent the whole evening staring at me and growling at the waiters. Every time DeWitt proposed, Connor proposed, too. It quite ruined DeWitt's dinner."

"Which one are you going to marry?" Tom asked, hanging on Melissa's every word as if it were gospel.

"Neither. Men don't fight over their wives or take them to dinner. They get them pregnant and leave them home. I don't intend for that to happen to me."

Hannah realized she'd like nothing more than to have Buck's babies. She was certain he'd never leave her at home to go chasing women like his sister.

When they finished eating, Hannah rose to start cleaning up. Tom and Zeke cleared the table while Buck put on a second pot of coffee. Melissa kept talking. The more food Hannah put away, the more dishes she washed, the angrier she became.

"I know I should offer to help," Melissa said just about the time Hannah was ready to explode, "but I've lived in hotels and rooming houses all my life.

I can't remember being in a kitchen. I know I've never eaten dinner in one."

That might have been a harmless remark, but Hannah took it as a slight. "There were only three people in my family," she said. "My father didn't see any need for a separate dining room."

"Now that Buck owns the ranch, I'm sure he'll—"

"Buck doesn't own this ranch," Hannah said. "I do." She tried not to sound as if she was gloating. She wasn't sure she succeeded.

That news obviously came as an unexpected and unpleasant surprise to Melissa. "But I thought—"

"We have six months to pay off a debt," Buck explained. "If I can do that, I get half of everything. Until then, I'm just a cowhand."

"You mean you don't have any money?"

"He's as broke as a busted saddle," Zeke said. "The only cash around here comes from Hannah's butter and eggs."

Melissa looked dumbfounded. "Where do you get money to buy food?"

"I grow it," Hannah said. "I have a garden, chickens, cows, and pigs."

"It sounds like a lot of work," Melissa said.

"It's too much, especially since Hannah's mother got married again and moved out," Buck said. "I'm glad you'll be here to help her."

.That obviously shocked Melissa almost as much as finding out Buck didn't own the ranch and had no money.

"I don't know a thing about gardens. And I've never even seen a pig."

"It won't be hard to learn," Zeke said. "I bet Hannah'll be glad to teach you."

Melissa looked hard-hit. She gave Hannah a measuring look, as if she was sizing up the situation anew.

Buck stood up. "We'd better get to bed. Dawn comes early."

"Where's she going to sleep?" Zeke asked.

"In Mrs. Grossek's room," Buck said.

Hannah had already decided that was the most logical arrangement, but she was furious with Buck for giving away her mother's room without asking her. "I'm not sure it's in condition to be occupied right now," she said. "I wasn't expecting it to be used right away."

"I'll clear everything out for you," Buck offered.

Hannah started to object but then thought better of it. "I'll do it."

She knew it was irrational, but she felt embarrassed at the plainness of her mother's clothes and their worn condition. The furnishings had been chosen for function rather than appearance. It took only a few minutes to remove the few possessions her mother had left behind. It was impossible to remove the bare-bones condition of the room.

Melissa's opinion of the room was written on her face, but Buck salvaged Hannah's pride.

"You got the best room in this house," he said, "and the biggest bed."

"Where will I put all my clothes?" Melissa asked, frowning at the single wardrobe.

"Leave them packed," Zeke said. "You won't need anything like that when you work in the garden."

"That" was a blue silk dress decorated with enough ribbon and rosettes for a dozen dresses. The off-the-shoulder neckline was cut so deep, Hannah wondered if Melissa had confused it with night wear. In her opinion, such a dress wouldn't be proper at any time of day outside a woman's bedroom.

"I don't have anything plainer than this," Melissa said.

"Hannah can lend you something," Buck said.

Hannah was much smaller than Melissa in height and build. Melissa couldn't possibly wear any of her clothes, and Melissa would know it.

"You'll find bed linens in the wardrobe," she told Melissa, "blankets in the chest. Buck can bring your trunks in. I'll leave you to get settled. I can't imagine how you got so much out here," she said as she left the room.

Buck was so happy to have found his sister, he wouldn't have minded hauling a hundred trunks into the room. He couldn't stop smiling, telling Melissa how happy he was she'd found him, that he would finally have a family at last.

"I didn't even know you were alive until a few days ago," Melissa said. "I heard this army colonel talking about a letter he'd received from a man looking for his sister and knew right away it had to be you. I packed up and came straight here."

"I hope you'll stay," Buck said. "You can have this room as long as you want."

"I imagine that'll be for Hannah to decide," Hannah heard Melissa say.

"She'll be delighted to have you," Buck assured his sister. "You'll be wonderful company for her."

Hannah wondered what defect in men made them incapable of understanding that certain women would never be *wonderful company* to each other.

But when he finally told his sister good night, entered Hannah's room, and took her in his arms, he was so happy, Hannah hadn't the heart to say anything that might ruin his pleasure.

"I can't believe she's here!" he said for the dozenth time. "Isn't she beautiful? And so sophisticated. I feel like a dirt-behind-the-ears cowboy, but she doesn't put on airs or try to show off. Did you see Tom's eyes?"

Hannah decided it wasn't so wonderful being held in a man's arms while he talked about another woman, even his sister.

"You've got to help me talk her into staying."

"I'm not sure she'll like it here. She doesn't look like the ranch type to me."

"She hasn't had a chance to find out what it's like. You heard her say she's only lived in boarding houses. I bet my old man dragged her to every gambling hall this side of the Rockies."

"Did you ask her about your father?"

"No. If I knew where he was, I'd have to kill him."

Hannah hoped Melissa would keep his father's whereabouts a secret. She didn't want Buck hanged for shooting anybody, even a gambler so despicable he'd sell his own son.

"I know you two will be friends in no time. She can tell you all about the places she's been, and you can teach her how to get along on a place like this."

Hannah doubted Melissa would enjoy learning how to milk cows and gather eggs, but she was determined she wasn't going to let her jealousy make up her mind before she gave Melissa a chance. She didn't like the woman, probably never would. But for Buck's sake, she had to be fair.

"I'll do what I can, but she may not want to be stuck on a ranch."

"She told me she's delighted to be here. She said she's not sure she ever wants to leave."

"She might not feel that way when we get married."

Hannah felt Buck stiffen.

"Why not?"

Hannah didn't know whether Buck had reacted to the idea of marriage or of Melissa's leaving.

"She might feel we need privacy."

"That's absurd. I'll never need to be private from my sister. I wouldn't have expected your mother to leave."

Fairness forced Hannah to admit she would never have considered asking her mother to leave. "We'll have to wait and see what she thinks."

"There's plenty of time."

Buck stopped talking about his sister and turned his attention to kissing Hannah. As satisfying as that was, her uneasiness returned after he'd left without making love to her. She had the feeling Melissa had already come between them. Hannah told herself she had to give the situation time, but she couldn't rid herself of the fear that Buck had already taken at least one step back from loving her and wanting to marry her, a very serious situation with a man as skittish about marriage as Buck.

Melissa cursed bitterly as she got ready for bed. Damn! Buck didn't have any money. He didn't even own this stink hole. She'd come all this distance, made DeWitt furious by running out on him, only to find herself stuck at the end of the earth with no way to get back to Galveston. Even San Antonio or Austin seemed out of reach now.

She had no intention of staying here—she'd go crazy—but she couldn't leave until she had put together a stake. She had to find some money, and Buck was her only option.

She laughed when she thought of that washed-out little *hausfrau* who thought she was going to marry Buck. She cringed at the thought of a brother of hers marrying such a dreary little creature.

Not that Buck had turned out to be anything to brag about. Melissa had missed Buck at first, but now she realized her father was right when he'd said Buck was useless. Buck was happy on this rocky dirt patch. The fool even thought she was going to work in the garden. Feed chickens!

Melissa Alexandra Hobson would cut her throat before she would be caught doing any such thing.

Well, there was no point in stewing about it. She'd better get this paint off her face and see if she could get some rest. She'd discovered a new wrinkle. Twenty-five wasn't old, but each year it became a little harder to compete with the younger girls. So far her brain had kept her ahead.

She could kill DeWitt for taking her last dollar. He thought she'd have to give in and become his wife if he stripped her of everything she owned.

Well, she wasn't going to belong to any man. She'd been careless before. She'd thought he was too besotted to defeat her. She was paying for a mistake she wouldn't make again.

Melissa decided to sleep in her silk robe. She couldn't stand the feel of coarse cotton sheets against her skin.

She found the bed much more comfortable than she'd expected. Maybe she would stay for a little while. She could use some rest. But not for long. She had to get back to Galveston. She had a date with DeWitt.

If she worked things right, maybe he'd take her to New Orleans. She was tired of this damned state.

She should have ignored her father and left it years ago.

Melissa didn't get up for breakfast.

"She's probably worn out," Buck said. "It's a long trip from Galveston."

"How did she get here?"

"She said she rode with a freighter taking a load of furniture over to Gillett's place."

"With all her trunks, I'm surprised he had any room for the furniture," Zeke said.

"She sure is a knockout," Tom said to Buck. "What happened to you?"

"I think Buck's very nice looking," Hannah said.

"Maybe," Tom said, dubious, "but he's not in a class with his sister."

Hannah didn't like having Buck's looks disparaged, but he didn't seem to care.

Tom spent the rest of breakfast rattling on about the women he'd seen, which left Hannah with the impression that he'd hardly seen any woman other than Melissa.

Melissa still hadn't gotten up when the men left. Nor by the time Hannah finished the milking, set it aside to let the cream rise, and went out to the garden. Melissa made her appearance just before noon. She wandered out of the house in a dark green dress very much like the one she'd worn the day before. She had made herself up just as fully.

"It's too hot to be working in the garden," Melissa said as she settled into one of the chairs in the shade.

Hannah stood up and wiped perspiration from her forehead. She didn't bother to shake the dirt from the hem of her dress. "We have to eat regardless of the heat," Hannah said. She went back to

327

weeding the potatoes. It always amazed her that the weeds managed to grow twice as fast as the vegetables.

"You ought to make Buck's hands do all that. I tried to grow some flowers once. I gave it up after I broke my second fingernail."

"This is my ranch," Hannah said. "The men take care of the cows. I take care of everything around here."

"Suit yourself," Melissa said.

Hannah was glad she'd picked the peas earlier. It was okay to jerk at the weeds. Melissa didn't sit still for long. She was soon up and pacing about under the trees. She would fling herself down in the chair only to get up a few minutes later.

"How do you stand it?" she said finally.

"Stand what?"

"The boredom."

"I'm too busy to be bored."

"You can't tell me pulling weeds is interesting."

"I have other responsibilities."

"Just things you do over and over again. That's boring."

Hannah stood up and glared at Melissa. "Don't you do the same things over and over again?"

"Yes, but they're interesting."

"So's running this place."

"I don't see how."

"I imagine I'd find what you do boring."

Melissa's look was contemptuous. "I have to know the rules for dozens of card games, be able to remember every card played, calculate odds in my head, know the character of every man I play with, whether he cheats and his favorite tricks. You'd never even begin to do what I do."

"Then I guess it's a good thing I don't want to. If

it requires you to dress like that, I wouldn't like it."

Melissa took umbrage immediately. "What's wrong with my appearance?"

Clearly Hannah had hit a sensitive spot. "You can't work in those clothes. You'd get a terrible sunburn."

"I have no intention of working in the dirt, in or out of the sun." She threw herself down in the chair. "I'm hungry," she announced a few minutes later. "When are you going to fix something to eat?"

Hannah put a handful of carrots in her basket. "I fixed breakfast at six o'clock."

"I never get up that early."

"We'll eat dinner sometime after six tonight."

"I'll starve before then."

"You're perfectly free to fix something yourself."

Melissa flounced into the house. For the rest of the day, she followed Hannah about, complaining about the heat, the boredom, the fact she'd found only bread and milk for lunch. Hannah didn't slow down in her work. At mid-afternoon, Melissa went inside for a nap, but she was back outside within an hour. She was so desperate for company, she even held the basket while Hannah collected the eggs.

She didn't follow Hannah to the barn when she went to feed the animals or do the evening milking.

"I'm going to need some help with dinner," Hannah said, determined to squeeze some work out of Melissa.

She wasn't entirely successful. Melissa managed to set the table. But what with worrying about messing up her clothes, her hands, or her makeup, she wasn't much good at anything else. Hannah was relieved when Buck walked in the door an hour earlier than expected. Instantly Melissa was trans-

Leigh Greenwood

formed from a petulant beauty into a smiling enchantress.

"I'm so glad you're back," she said before Hannah had a chance to open her mouth. "Let's go for a walk until supper. I still have so much to tell you."

She took him by the arm and marched him outside before he could do more than nod a perfunctory greeting to Hannah. Hannah next saw them walking through the trees along the edge of the creek. She told herself not to feel angry or left out. She'd never expected to fall in love or find a man she wanted to marry.

But the moment she did, Melissa showed up and spoiled everything.

Buck had spent most of his day trying to think of ways to convince Melissa not to go back to Galveston. He'd been so pleased that she wanted to be with him, he let her carry him off for a walk. He was sure Hannah wouldn't mind. They'd have their time together later.

"Did you have a nice day?" he asked. "Did you sleep well? Is the bed comfortable?" He wanted Melissa to be happy at the ranch.

"I slept fine, better than I have in weeks, but I'm not really used to living on a ranch. I feel out of place."

"You'll soon feel more at home. If you have any questions, ask Hannah. She'll be happy to help you."

It was hard for Buck to believe he was walking and talking with his sister as though they hadn't been separated for most of their lives. He hadn't admitted it, but he'd almost given up hope of finding her.

"I don't think Hannah likes me very much," Melissa said.

Buck felt a stab of panic. "You've got to be mistaken. Hannah's a wonderful woman. If she can like somebody as difficult as Zeke, she'll love you."

"I'm not so sure she can like another woman."

"I'm sure it's all a misunderstanding. I'll speak to her." He would. He'd speak to her that very night. He didn't want anything to happen that might cause Melissa to leave. He paused a moment and then finally decided to add, "I think I'm in love with her."

Melissa's fingers dug into his arm. "Sorry, I stumbled on a tree root. Have you settled on a date for the wedding?" she asked a few moments later.

"We haven't gotten that far yet."

They walked a few more moments in silence.

"I don't think a woman like Hannah would settle for anything else," Melissa said. "Maybe I ought to leave."

The panic squeezed tighter inside Buck's chest. She couldn't leave—not now, not after he'd looked for her for so long. "You can't leave. You're the only family I have."

Melissa stopped, turned, and looked up at him. He'd never realized just how beautiful she was. It made him proud to be her brother. There must have been many more exciting places she could have gone—many men anxious to do anything for her—but she'd chosen to come to him the minute she found he was looking for her. He didn't need to think about his parents abandoning him ever again. His sister loved him. They had each other. That was all they needed.

"I may not be able to stay," she said, looking at him with eyes glistening with moisture. "I owe a lot of money. If I can't pay it back, I will have to find a job."

"I'll help you," Buck said, not sure whether he was more upset for himself or Melissa. "I'll give you all the money you need."

"I need a lot."

"It doesn't matter. I'll find it." How could money compare to having a family once again?

"Can you find ten thousand dollars?"

She might as well have asked him for a million. It was an impossible sum.

"How could you owe so much money?" He couldn't imagine how one person could spend so much money. It didn't take that much to support Jake's whole family for a year.

"It's very expensive to live in Galveston. I have to buy clothes, eat, have a place to stay."

"You can stay here. You have plenty of clothes, and we have more than enough food."

"They will come after me."

"Why?"

She seemed reluctant to tell him.

"I have to know if I'm going to try to help you."

"It's really Papa's debt," she said. "He had me co-sign a note. He swore it was only for a hundred dollars. Then he got drunk and fell off a boat into Galveston Bay. I didn't know anything about the rest of his debts until they came after me. I had to escape in the middle of the night or they would have taken my clothes. I barely had enough money to get here."

Buck felt the surging hatred he'd felt every time he thought of his father. The bastard was dead, and he was still ruining Buck's life.

"I'd offer to sell my clothes, but they won't be enough. Besides, the only place I can earn that much money would be in one of the fancy gambling halls. I'll need all my clothes for that."

"Nobody's going to make you to work in a gambling hall. The bastard dragged us through enough of them before he sold me. I don't have any money now, but I will when we sell the herd in the fall. We've got to pay the debt on this place. But if I sell every steer I can get my hands on, I ought to have enough left over to give you ten thousand."

"I need some money to give them now—you know, a good-faith payment to make them wait until fall."

"How much?"

"A few hundred dollars."

"I'm sure Hannah has that much."

"Will she let you have it?"

She didn't sound very hopeful. It was the first time in his life he'd ever had a family to ask something of him, and he didn't mean to let her down.

"I'm sure she will. I'll ask her tonight."

Chapter Twenty-one

Hannah was certain Melissa didn't love Buck and was only there to get what she could from him. She had decided to talk to him about it when he came to her room, but she never got the chance. He started by kissing her thoroughly. Before she could collect her thoughts and decide how best to say what she wanted, Buck spoke.

"Melissa's thinking about leaving. You've got to help me talk her into staying."

"Why should she want to leave?" What Hannah really wanted to know was why a woman like Melissa would ever consider staying.

"She thinks you don't like her."

Hannah didn't. She considered Melissa a lazy, manipulative woman, but she knew she couldn't say that to Buck.

Buck had cherished the memory of his sister all these years. He wanted that memory so badly, he couldn't see his sister as she really was. He believed she would give him the love he'd failed to get from his mother and father, the love he couldn't see he was already getting from his adopted family.

Even if Melissa had been everything Buck hoped for, it would have been an impossible dream. She couldn't make up for all he'd lost, but he couldn't see that. He had chased this dream for too long, placed too many hopes on it.

Hannah couldn't tell him the truth. He wouldn't believe her. Worse still, he might hate her for destroying his dream. She wasn't willing to take that chance. She'd have to wait and let him discover the truth for himself.

"She probably feels that way because I had too much work to do today to spend time with her. I'm sure she's lonely, that she misses her friends and the life she's used to."

"She doesn't miss either one. She wants to stay here."

"Did she say that?" Hannah hoped she didn't sound as horrified as she felt.

"She didn't have to. It was in everything she said. I want her to stay. I want her to make her home with us."

"Buck, she knows nothing about living on a ranch, and I don't think she wants to learn. Our worlds are so far apart, we can't even talk to each other. I can't imagine she'd feel any more comfortable with the other ranchers' wives."

"Are you telling me you don't want her to stay?"

He had gotten his back up, just as she'd feared.

"I wouldn't dream of saying that. But you have to realize she may not like it here."

"She does like it, and she'll soon learn to fit in. I

had the same upbringing she did, and Jake had no trouble turning me into a cowboy."

"But you were seventeen and desperate, not twenty-five and beautiful with trunks full of clothes that will be ruined here."

"You can lend her some of yours until she can make something of her own."

Buck didn't seem to realize that Melissa would probably rather die than be caught in any dress she had to make or borrow from Hannah.

But it wasn't the issue of clothes or helping in the garden or being bored that bothered Hannah the most. She couldn't get it out of her mind that she had slipped into second place in Buck's affections. She had the terrible feeling that if he had to choose between them, he'd choose his sister.

Hannah hoped she was imagining things, that her lifelong fear of being controlled by a man was manifesting itself in another form. But no matter what she told herself, the fear wouldn't go away. That was a terrible thing for a woman who only one day before had been thinking about getting married.

"You and Melissa are the two most important people in the world to me," Buck said. "I want you to love each other as much as I love you. I want us to be a family."

Hannah's heart beat wildly. Buck had said he loved her. He probably wasn't aware of it, but he'd said it. Still, Buck's love seemed conditional on her loving Melissa. And Hannah wasn't willing to accept any conditions.

"Are you forgetting Jake and Isabelle and the boys?" she asked.

"Of course not, but Melissa is my *real* family."

Hannah gave up. Buck couldn't see that it took

more than blood to make a family. "Okay, Buck, I'll do what I can to make her feel more wanted and less out of place. But it would be helpful if you were around more. There's a lot she has to learn, and I suspect most of it will come better from you."

"I don't know why you say that. Women always get along better with other women."

"Not a woman who's been around men most of her life. Besides, she probably doesn't want to share you with me any more than I want to give you up to her."

He looked at her as though she'd said something completely beyond his understanding.

"But I want you to love each other."

"You'll have to give us time. We just met yesterday."

"I know." He took her in his arms and held her tightly. "It's just that I've waited so long. Now that she's here, I want everything to happen immediately."

Hannah settled herself on his lap. Maybe things weren't as bad as she had feared. Maybe Buck was afraid Hannah wouldn't like Melissa, not the other way around.

"Why did she come?" Hannah asked. "I mean, why didn't she write first or ask you to meet her in Austin or someplace like that?"

At this he sat up ramrod straight. "She's being dunned for my father's debts. The son-of-a-bitch died owing ten thousand dollars."

To Hannah, who'd never been allowed any money until her father's death, ten thousand dollars was an enormous sum.

"I told her I'd help her," Buck said.

Hannah sat forward and turned so she could see him. "How?"

"By giving her some money to satisfy her creditors until we can sell the steers."

An icy feeling flowed through Hannah's veins with the speed of a flash flood. All her fears and doubts coalesced into a ball of cold panic in the pit of her stomach. Buck had promised money from *her* ranch to his sister! He was jeopardizing their future for a woman he hadn't seen in thirteen years, a woman whose love and loyalty Hannah very much doubted.

She wanted to scream at him, to shake him, to tell him to take a good look at his sister before he started giving her everything she wanted. But she forced herself to be calm. Losing her temper would only hurt her position.

"I didn't think you had any money." She didn't care about his money. It was the fact that he would pledge their future without even talking to her that upset her most.

"I don't. I was talking about the money you get from selling butter and eggs."

Panic turned to anger. She got up off his lap. She tried to keep control of her temper, but she was so upset, her lower lip quivered.

"You told her you'd give her *my* money?"

"I don't have any myself."

She determined to keep her voice down, but she could feel the anger rising in her throat. "You promised her my money without even asking me?"

"I was sure you would—"

"How would you feel if I promised your money to Amos Merrick?"

"He doesn't need it."

"That's not the point. But since the right of ownership doesn't seem to mean anything to you, I might point out that it's my money, earned by my work even before you came here. I use it to buy food to feed you and Zeke and Tom. You might not have noticed, but any one of you eats more than mother and I together. How do you think Zeke and Tom will feel when they learn they won't have any coffee, sugar, salt, flour for biscuits, canned fruit, apples for pies, raisins for—"

"I'm just asking for a few hundred dollars to hold the creditors off."

"Then let her sell some of her clothes. She won't need them if she stays here."

"You *don't* like her, do you?"

She could feel the ground slipping away from under her, but she couldn't stop.

"It has nothing to do with liking. She's not my sister. I don't owe her anything."

"But she's my sister."

"Fine. *You* pay her debts. As for the money from our steers, how could you even consider that? What about the money we owe to the bank?"

"We'll pay off the debts first. But the rest of the money—"

"The rest of the money belongs to us, you and me. We need it for the future of the ranch. I heard you talking to Zeke about buying better bulls, even buying more land. Where did all those plans go, Buck? Are you willing to jeopardize your future to pay off a debt that's not yours?"

"It's my father's debt. It's as much mine as hers."

"No, it's not. If it's your father's debt alone, if she had no part in it, then neither of you is responsible. I don't know much about the law, but I've learned that much from Amos."

"That's not the point," Buck said. "The point is, you won't give her any money, either now or later."

"If she has debts, she ought to pay them herself.

In the meantime, I'll be happy to give her a place to stay until she can get back on her feet."

Hannah knew she was drawing a line in the sand, but she couldn't help it. If she allowed Melissa to rob them of this money now, there'd be no reason for her not to do it again. A woman like Melissa could never have enough money.

"I don't understand," Buck said. "You know how important this is to me. Melissa is the only family I have."

By blindly holding on to an impossible dream, Buck was pushing the rest of the world away and clinging to Melissa. Only now was Hannah beginning to realize the depth and seriousness of the wound Buck had suffered when his parents deserted him. The scars were far deeper and more disfiguring than those on his back. She wanted to put her arms around him and hold him close, assure him that she and Jake's family loved him as much as any blood relative could.

But he wouldn't believe it. He pulled away from her in anger. In rejecting Melissa, he felt she had rejected him as well. She had to reach out to him, to make him understand.

"A sense of family is not built on money," she said. "It's built on love, trust, loyalty, on years of shared experience."

"But she needs help."

"Then let her start by helping herself. She can get a job."

"I won't let her work in a gambling hall."

"There must be other places, other jobs. Let her look."

"She'll need money."

"I can spare enough money to get her to Austin."

"And the rest?"

"We have to eat. And as long as she stays here, so does she."

Buck looked at her as if she was a traitor. "I can't believe you'd turn on me. After everything we said—"

"I haven't turned on you, Buck. I love you just as much as ever, but this has nothing to do with us."

"It has everything to do with us."

He turned and left her room. She wanted to run after him, to tell him the money didn't matter, but she couldn't. She wanted Buck to love his sister. She wanted him to want to help her. But if she was to marry Buck, she had to know she wouldn't come second in his heart. He couldn't sacrifice her, their future together, even their children's future, for anyone else. Not even his sister.

This was one decision Hannah couldn't help him make.

"Zeke and I are leaving for several days," Buck announced after breakfast. Zeke and Tom had already left the kitchen. Melissa was sleeping late, as usual. "We're going after some wild horses we saw a month ago."

The announcement came as a shock to Hannah. Buck hadn't mentioned this plan. It was just one more sign of the distance that had developed between them since Melissa arrived. She looked into his eyes, trying to see what lay behind the blank expression. But he'd closed the door to his inner self. Even his kisses had become less ardent.

Neither did he try to make love to her. She wouldn't have let him, but she grew worried when he didn't try. She didn't know much about men, but she'd always heard that their sexual appetites were insatiable. Could Buck still love her if he didn't want to make love to her?

"When did you decide to do that?"

"I always meant to go."

"But your sister's here."

"That's why I'm going."

He was going to earn the money she wouldn't give Melissa. In other words, it was her fault he was leaving.

"How long will you be gone?"

"At least a week. I'll leave Tom here to look after things. Maybe your mother can come over."

"You will take care of yourself, won't you?"

"Horses aren't as dangerous as steers."

They stood looking at each other, the tension palpable, so much between them unsaid. She searched his face for a sign that the love he professed for her still existed. She saw instead the taut, blank expression of a man caught between two loves and feeling unable to embrace one without rejecting the other.

She couldn't stand to see him so miserable. He might feel torn apart, but she had no doubts in her mind. She loved him. She always would. Nothing he did could change it. It was as simple as that.

She crossed the room toward him, her arms held out. "Don't stay too long. I miss you already."

His kisses seemed to have been made more fierce by his uncertainty. She could feel the intensity of the battle going on within him in the fierce pressure of his lips against hers, in the way he nearly crushed her in his arms. He still loved her, of that she was sure, but she wasn't sure he would realize it before it was too late.

She returned his kiss with equal fervor. She couldn't get the fear out of her mind that every kiss might be the last. She didn't have that many kisses to remember. They had to be memorable ones if they were to last a lifetime.

She felt the evidence of his physical desire for her burning hot against her abdomen. An answering response flared from deep within her. No matter what had happened, regardless of the strain between them, she wanted him as badly as he wanted her.

She could feel her nipples harden and become achingly sensitive to the pressure of being pushed hard against his chest. Buck's tongue drove deep into her mouth, waking the need that had simmered below the surface since that unforgettable night more than a week ago. She no longer had any desire to refuse him, to require him to make up his mind before he could claim her. She was his, and he could have her this very moment.

"Oh, God, I can't stand it," he muttered.

"Neither can I."

It was all the encouragement he needed. In seconds he had led her to his bedroom. Hannah hadn't realized how much tension had accumulated in her body during these last days. Only Buck could release the pressure that made her feel she was about to explode. In no time at all they had shed their clothes and were clasped in a tight embrace.

Buck made love to her body with his mouth and tongue until she thought she would die of pleasure. She gasped with shock when he moved between her thighs. She hadn't known it could be done this way. The pleasure was heightened by the newness, the unexpectedness of it. She was certain this was a sin; she was certain she would suffer some terrible punishment for the exquisite pleasure that consumed her entire body. She yielded, all resistance gone.

For this she didn't mind punishment. Moments later she shuddered from the force of her release.

Even before the tension had subsided, she felt Buck enter her, fill her with his need. Within moments she was soaring once more, her sounds of pleasure swallowed by his kisses. It didn't seem possible that any man could give her such pleasure. Yet every moment, every movement of Buck's body, increased her sensitivity until she thought she would scream.

Only when she was certain she could stand it no longer—when she pounded on his back with her fists, begging for release—did he drive them over the edge.

Buck walked toward the barn with his arm around Hannah. He was feeling a little guilty about being so late, but he was glad he and Hannah had made love. It removed much of the tension that had grown up between them. He still didn't understand her attitude toward Melissa, but he felt reassured that she still loved him. The specter of being abandoned again had been lurking in the back of his mind. He was glad to be able to banish it—this time, he hoped, forever.

He expected to find Zeke frowning. He did. That frown deepened when Zeke saw his arm around Hannah. "If I'd known you had women on your mind, I wouldn't have hurried myself to get the horses ready," he grumbled.

"Not women, Zeke, Hannah."

"Same thing."

But Zeke didn't sound nearly so angry as he would have a month before. Buck wasn't sure Zeke would ever like his being in love with Hannah, but he seemed willing to accept it.

"I don't know how long we'll be gone," Buck told Hannah. "It could be a week, it could be two. I've got to get enough horses for Melissa. Tom, you watch after Hannah and—"

"What do you mean, you've got to get enough horses for Melissa?" Zeke demanded. "You didn't say anything about Melissa before."

Buck didn't like having to explain Melissa's problems. It embarrassed him, but he figured Zeke had a right to know.

"Melissa's responsible for some big debts. She needs money right away to keep her creditors from selling her clothes."

"Let 'em. She don't need all those ridiculous dresses out here."

Buck decided it was better to ignore Zeke. "We'll get the rest when we sell the steers." But Zeke didn't like being ignored.

"How much money you talking about?"

"Five hundred dollars for now."

Zeke's black eyes seemed to turn all white.

"How much altogether?"

"Ten thousand dollars."

Tom whistled. Zeke seemed to swell up until he was about to bust.

"You mean you let that greedy little bitch talk you into promising her ten thousand dollars?"

"She's my sister, Zeke. Watch what you say, or I'll knock your words back down your throat. It's my father's debt. She's stuck paying it."

"There's no fool like a white fool," Zeke shouted. "Can't you see nothing? That gal come here out of nowhere. We don't even know for sure she's your sister. She sets herself down like a queen bee, making Hannah wear herself out waiting on her while she won't lift a finger. A baby could see she's no good."

It was all Buck could do to keep from knocking Zeke to the ground. He didn't understand why the two people he loved most disliked Melissa. She didn't fit in yet, but she would if they gave her time.

"Zeke, we've been friends for a long time. But if you say any more, I'm going to knock you down."

"Knocking me down won't change nothing. I don't believe your daddy left those debts. She's just trying to squeeze money outta you, and you're dumb enough to believe anything she says."

"Zeke, I'm warning you—"

"I'm not breaking my neck chasing wild horses so you can give the money to some painted tart. You want 'em, you—"

A fury had been building inside Buck ever since Melissa arrived. No one had given her a fair chance. She was his sister, by damn, the only family he had. Nobody was going to talk about her as long as he was around.

He launched himself at Zeke. He didn't think. He just did it.

It felt good to feel his fist smash into Zeke's jaw. It felt even better to hear the breath whoosh out of Zeke's lungs as he hit the ground. Maybe Zeke would think next time before he opened his mouth about Melissa. They wrestled on the ground, too close for either one to deliver a disabling blow. Buck didn't even feel the blows Zeke rained on his body.

Buck pounded Zeke's head into the ground. "Take back every word, or I'll beat your brains out."

Zeke wasn't willing to give up. Buck heard something tear as Zeke threw him off and lunged at him. Buck dodged, then threw himself at Zeke again.

They rolled in a heap again, fists flailing. Buck connected with Zeke's jaw. Zeke landed a blow to Buck's face.

Buck felt hands pulling at him before he heard Hannah's voice screaming at them to stop trying to kill each other. He tried to pull away. Zeke landed a blow to his jaw that made him dizzy.

"Stop it, both of you!" Hannah screamed as she hit Zeke with all her might.

Somehow she'd gotten between them. Tom was wrestling with Zeke, but he was no match for him. Buck tried to attack Zeke again, but Hannah wouldn't get out of the way.

"She doesn't care two cents about you!" Zeke shouted at Buck. "She's no more family than that milk cow. She just wants money, and I ain't helping you get it for her."

"I don't need you!" Buck shouted. "I can catch all the horses I need by myself."

"You can't do nothing but make a fool of yourself over that fancy woman."

"If you say one more word against my sister, Zeke, so help me God, I'll—"

"Don't bust a blood vessel!" Zeke shouted back. "I'm leaving. I used to think you were a real smart man. After you stole those cows from under Gillett's nose, I was ready to do things your way. But you ain't smart enough to see through one little ole fancy piece of white trash." Zeke swung into the saddle. "She's not good enough to take out Isabelle's slops." He jerked his horse toward the trail. "Hannah's either."

The oppressive silence made Buck certain that Zeke had voiced Hannah and Tom's unspoken thoughts.

"Come up to the house," Hannah said. "I'll take care of those cuts."

"You're going to have a shiner," Tom added.

"I can take care of myself," Buck said. He walked to where his horse was ground hitched. He gathered up the reins. "I may be longer than I planned."

"You can't leave now," Hannah protested. "You've got blood on your face."

"I left here before with blood all over my back. At least I have a horse and food this time."

Buck regretted his words the moment he saw the stricken look on Hannah's face. But he didn't turn back. Melissa couldn't be all those things they thought. They didn't understand what it was like to have your mother desert you, to have a father who used you to make money and ignored you the rest of the time.

It made you hard. It made you scared to trust anyone ever again. He couldn't blame Melissa for turning out the way she had, dressing like that, acting like that. It was what she'd had to do to survive. Things would be different when she got the money to pay off her debts. She'd be a different person then. They'd see.

Chapter Twenty-two

The last three days had been the most miserable of Hannah's life. She missed Buck more than she had thought possible. Dozens of times a day she found herself stopping her work to stare into the distance, hoping to see him ride up, hoping at least for a dust cloud to announce his arrival.

His fight with Zeke still upset her. They were best friends—inseparable, she had thought. Yet Melissa had come between them.

No matter how many times Hannah stopped her work to stare out the window or over the rise, she saw nothing. Even as the hours of Buck's absence rolled by, quickly increasing in number, her remembrance of the hour spent in his arms burned more deeply into her memory. She couldn't give him up. No matter what she had to do.

Hannah had done her best to be friendly and helpful, but Melissa had made it clear there would be no developing friendship between them. Neither did Melissa have any desire to learn to work. She was bored, restless, and irritable.

Until the cowboys started coming.

It seemed the grapevine had carried the message. Cooks Hannah had never seen came by to ask about buying her eggs and butter. Cowboys dropped by to place their own orders for vegetables and jam. It was a funny thing, though—they nearly always ended up talking to Melissa.

Melissa was sitting in the shade, entertaining two cowboys from the Rafter D, when Hannah's mother drove up in a wagon. Hannah instantly forgot Melissa in her delight at seeing her mother.

"Is that Buck's sister?" Sarah Evans asked as soon as they were inside.

"Yes," said Hannah as she put on water for coffee. Her mother started to grind some beans. It felt almost like the time before Buck arrived. "She was waiting for us when we got back from Utopia."

"I heard about her."

Hannah pointed to where Melissa could be viewed through the kitchen window. "Everybody's heard about her. This ranch now seems to be on the road to everywhere. I sometimes think not a cowhand stirs off his range but what he finds his way here."

"How is Buck taking all of this?"

"Sometimes I think he's hardly aware anybody else exists."

"Even you?"

"Especially me."

Hannah hadn't had a chance to tell her mother that Buck had said he loved her. It hardly mattered. Buck hadn't mentioned marriage since Melissa arrived.

"What happened?" Her mother dropped the ground coffee into the water and sat down to wait for the pot to boil. Hannah sat down across from her.

"Melissa has huge debts. Buck wants to pay them off when we sell the steers this fall. He wanted me to give her my butter and egg money to hold off her creditors."

"And you refused?"

"Any money left when we pay off the debt ought to be used for the ranch. What kind of future will we have if we don't invest to make the place better?"

"You still love him, don't you?"

"Yes."

"You want to marry him?"

Hannah nodded. She might as well confess to what her mother knew already.

"You can't see your way to giving her that money?"

Hannah looked up, shocked. "You think I should?"

"What I think doesn't matter. I'm asking you."

"No, I can't," Hannah said, emphatically. "I might consider giving her something if I thought she really loved Buck, but I don't think she does. I'd even consider it if I thought it would get rid of her. Maybe I'm being unfair—I can't like a woman who dresses as she does, flirts with every man she meets, and refuses to do a lick of work—but I think she only came here to see what she could get out of Buck."

"What does Buck think?"

Hannah hadn't noticed the coffee had boiled. Her mother got up and poured out two cups.

"All he can see is that the only remaining member of his family has returned. I think Melissa could ask

353

for the clothes off his back and he would gladly give them to her."

Her mother set the two cups on the table and sat down. She poured some coffee into her saucer, blew over it to cool it, and sipped it. "Does Buck love you?"

"He says he does."

"Does he want to get married?"

"A week ago I thought he did, eventually. Now I'm not sure. It looks like it's coming down to a choice between me or Melissa."

"Drink your coffee," her mother said as she drank some more of her own. "Men are very odd creatures. It's difficult for a woman to understand them. I'm not sure they understand themselves. They talk about being strong and rational and fearless, yet they're incapable of handling their own feelings. They're scared to death of commitment. They lose all pretense of rational behavior when it comes to women."

Hannah couldn't help laughing. "For a newly married woman, you have a very jaundiced view of men."

"Walter is the rare man who knows what he wants in a woman and is not afraid to ask for love. As for the rest of it, he's pretty much like other men."

"What are you trying to say, mother?"

"Men want what they want, whether it's good for them or not. It doesn't do any good to try to reason with them. If Buck wanted to find this sister more than anything else, it's going to take him a while to realize she doesn't measure up to his dream. If you want to marry him, you can't be the one to destroy his illusions."

"I'm not sure I can stand it much longer."

"Sure you can. There's one thing women can do that men can't. That's wait."

"I shouldn't have to wait."

"I imagine he's trying to put you both first in his heart. In a little while, he'll figure out he can't do that. Then he'll make up his mind."

Hannah looked out the window. The cowboys had left. Melissa sat under the trees fanning herself. It was almost impossible to contain the anger Hannah felt for this woman. Did Melissa know she was destroying Buck's dreams? Hannah was certain she wouldn't care if she did.

"Be patient," her mother said. "I waited twenty years for Walter. I doubt you'll have to wait more than a month for Buck. He's an intelligent man."

Hannah couldn't believe her eyes when she saw Lyman Gillett ride up to the ranch. She brushed her hands on her skirt and walked toward the fence that enclosed the garden. What with having to plant late crops, weed and water those already up, and continue to harvest the last of the late spring crops, she seemed to spend half her time in her garden. She'd become so used to male visitors seeing her at her worst, she didn't think anything of it any more.

"Good afternoon, Miss Grossek," Gillett said in his most courtly manner. "My cook tells me you have a guest. I thought I'd drop by and make her acquaintance."

At least he didn't waste her time by pretending he wanted to see her. Melissa remained seated, waiting for Gillett to come to her. Hannah thought it was easy to have confidence when you knew you were the most beautiful woman within a week's ride.

Hannah went back to her work. She could hear

the buzz of voices, the occasional sound of laughter, but she didn't understand what was said. She was glad. She didn't want to know. She hated to think what Buck would say when Melissa told him about her new acquaintance.

Hannah finished in the garden, pulled some parsnips, and went inside to prepare them for supper. Melissa entered the kitchen a few minutes later.

"Why didn't you tell me you had such a charming and delightful neighbor?" she said. "I haven't been so well entertained since I got here."

She positively sparkled. Every trace of listless irritation had vanished. She looked radiant and beautiful. She responded to a rich, handsome man like morning glories to a summer shower. Melissa sat down without offering to help.

"I doubt Buck will be pleased to hear that," Hannah said, not looking up from her work. "Lyman Gillett tried to steal my cattle. Only Buck's cleverness enabled us to get them back without a gun battle."

"Why should a rich man bother to steal cows?" Melissa asked.

"Maybe that's how he got to be rich."

"I don't care. He's the first person I've met who has any idea how to treat a woman."

"How about all those cowhands?"

"Just boys. They don't have the slightest idea what they're doing. Lyman invited me for a ride. He's coming by tomorrow with his buggy."

"I'd wait till Buck gets back and speak to him about that if I were you."

"I don't have to ask Buck or anybody else what I can and can't do," Melissa snapped, bright sparks of anger in her eyes. "Though I'm sure you'll tell him the minute he walks in the door."

"What you do is none of my business." Hannah kept her hands out of sight so Melissa couldn't see that they were shaking. "I just thought you might like the benefit of your brother's advice."

Melissa bounced to her feet. "I know more about men than Buck will if he lives to be a thousand. You, too, honey. You think you're going to marry my dear brother. He probably deserves a faded mouse like you, but I don't like you any more than you like me. I know you refused to lend me money. I also know you want to get rid of me. I'm going, but before I do, I'm going to make certain Buck walks out that door with me. You'll die an old maid if you sit here waiting for him to come back."

Hannah hadn't expected the attack, but she was determined not to let Melissa see her vulnerability. This woman would exercise her power just for the fun of it.

"I have no feeling for you at all except as it affects Buck. I don't care whether you ride with Gillett or go back to Galveston this minute. I do care that Buck has spent years looking for you, even longer wanting a family. Do you have any idea what your arrival meant to him? He thinks you can do no wrong. He would give you the earth if he could. He has no idea you're only using him."

"Have you told him?"

"I don't snitch on people."

"Don't give me that holier-than-thou stuff. What did you tell him?"

"Nothing." Because he wouldn't believe her if she did.

"Make sure you don't."

"I don't need to. You'll give yourself away soon enough."

Melissa looked at her as if she were crazy. "You're

a fool." Then she started laughing. Hannah could hear her laugh all the way to her room.

Hannah sagged against the sink. Was she being a fool? Was she losing all chance of keeping Buck's love? She hoped not.

Melissa wasn't about to let Buck's disapproval keep her from riding with Gillett. If he did disapprove. She didn't trust that sniveling little bitch. She didn't care where Gillett got his money as long as he had it, and no one was better than Melissa at recognizing the presence of money. She wasn't about to stay buried in this rock and thorn-infested desert for six months waiting for Buck's handouts. This might be her chance to get out of here sooner, and she meant to take it.

Buck had said he was riding west to capture horses to sell so he could give her money, but she'd seen too many men ride off with promises to return, never to be seen again. Her father was the perfect example. No, she much preferred a bird in the hand to any number in the bush. Besides, this bird had wonderful plumage. Buck had been plucked bare.

Melissa could sense that Gillett wanted something he thought she could help him obtain. That was fine with her. If he wanted it badly enough, he'd be willing to pay. If he paid well enough, she could be out of here long before fall.

She'd ridden with him four times now. Lyman seemed pleased Buck was away. That made her even more optimistic that what he wanted was worth enough money to enable her to leave this hellhole.

"You know," Melissa said when Lyman pulled the buggy to a stop in the shade of some oaks and maples along the riverbank, "I can't get rid of the feeling you have something you want to ask me."

His slightly startled look caused her to laugh merrily.

"Not that. You're no more the marrying kind than I am. No, it's something else, something you're not quite sure I'll do."

Lyman leaned back, regarding her with admiration. "I didn't know reading minds was among your talents."

"Let's just say I have a wide experience of men. Tell me, what do you want?"

"Hannah Grossek."

That was coming to the point with a vengeance. "What on earth could you want with that pale-faced, mealy-mouthed, sanctimonious wren?"

"Not everyone is up to handling the reins of a high-bred filly like you," Lyman said. "Some of us prefer a quieter ride."

"You mean boring."

"It all depends on how you look at it. I suspect that behind her quiet front is a very passionate woman."

"So does my brother. I can't understand why so many men are gullible fools."

"But what a mess things would be in if we all wanted the same woman."

"True," Melissa said, but she thought the man was an idiot to be infatuated with Hannah. Five consecutive minutes in her company ought to cure him of that. "Okay, you want Hannah. How am I supposed to help you get her? I take it she won't come running if you call."

"She's let your brother convince her that I tried to rustle her cattle."

"Did you?"

"It doesn't matter whether I did or didn't. She certainly won't come to my ranch."

"Kidnap her, carry her off over your saddle."

Lyman's smile was amused. "You've obviously never tried carrying an unwilling female across your saddle. I have. Besides, it would be virtually impossible to reach my ranch without running into at least one cowhand."

"Do it in the middle of the night."

"There's Tom to be thought of. And those very long ten miles with a furious female kicking, screaming, biting, and scratching every foot of the way. Finally, there's my own men. They might be willing to rustle a cow here and there if I ask them, but not one of them would sit still while I kidnapped a lady. Cowhands are very touchy about the way women are treated."

Melissa made a face. "I wish cotton barons were equally touchy. You sure you want Hannah?"

"I have ever since I set eyes on her."

"Okay, what do you want me to do?"

"Lure her to my ranch."

"What will you give me if I get her there?"

"What do you want?"

Melissa smiled. Men never seemed to learn. When you ask a woman what she wants, you're at her mercy. "A rather large sum of money would come in handy right about now."

"I'll give you five hundred dollars."

Melissa had been leaning back against the seating, enjoying their bargaining. At the mention of such a paltry sum, she sat bolt upright. "I wouldn't enter your house myself for five hundred dollars. My business is gambling, and I'm momentarily out of funds. I was thinking of ten thousand."

The only sign of surprise Lyman showed was a

slight widening of his eyes. "That's rather a lot of money."

"I only play with serious gamblers. Besides, if you get Hannah, you'll get her ranch as well."

"How do you figure that?"

"My brother thinks he's in love with her. If he thinks she's thrown him over, he'll ride out. There are three thousand cattle on the place, not counting this year's calves. At a conservative ten dollars a head, that's more than thirty thousand dollars. You couldn't buy that place for ten thousand."

"Five thousand."

"Ten, or no deal. Buck will give me the money when he sells his steers, but I think I'll go crazy if I have to wait that long."

"You don't like the country?"

"I hate it. I don't know how you stand it."

"It has its attractions."

"Cows that don't have the good sense to know they're being rustled?"

"Some people might find that an attraction."

Melissa laughed. "You're not going to admit to anything, are you?"

"Would you?"

"Never. Do I get my ten thousand?"

"Yes, if you can get Hannah to my house without anyone coming with her."

"That's easy enough. Come for me tomorrow morning around ten o'clock. When we get to your house, you'll send one of your men to Hannah with a message saying I've been hurt and she's to come immediately. Tom never gets back until late, so she won't be able to send anybody else."

"Does she like you enough to do that?"

"She hates me, but she'll come because she's in love with my brother."

"Are you sure?"

"Yes. Now take me back. It's unbearably hot out here. I don't know how you stand it."

The summons was no surprise to Hannah when it came. She had expected Melissa to get into difficulty sooner or later. She just wished it hadn't happened at Lyman Gillett's ranch. Buck would be furious when he found out she'd been forced to go there.

She considered contacting her mother but changed her mind. She couldn't expect her mother to leave her new family to help a stranger. Melissa was Buck's sister and Hannah's responsibility.

"Can you tell me how she's been hurt?" she asked the nervous cowhand who'd brought the message.

"No, ma'am."

"Have you any idea?"

"I think it's something to do with her leg."

Clearly the boy didn't know. She'd have to take her father's medical kit as well and hope Gillett's cook had anything else she might need. If not, she could send someone for Dr. Yant. He wouldn't like it, but she imagined he'd come for Gillett.

Hannah had forgotten how far ten miles could feel on the back of a horse. She was actually glad when they reached Gillett's ranch.

Gillett met her at the door when she dismounted.

"How is Melissa?" Hannah asked.

"She'll be better now that you're here," he said. "Go on in. I'll be with you as soon as I speak to Frank."

Evidently Gillett's instructions were brief. She'd barely shed her cloak before he was at her side.

"I put Melissa in the bedroom upstairs," Gillett said. "I thought she'd be more comfortable."

"What's wrong with her?" Hannah said, following him up the narrow stairs.

"It's her leg. Or maybe her foot. I can't tell. She won't let me touch her."

That sounded decidedly odd to Hannah, but then maybe Melissa felt differently about things when she was hurt and in pain.

"How did she get hurt? Did she fall or stumble?"

"She caught her foot and fell getting out of the buggy. I asked her to wait, but she was sure she could manage it on her own."

That did sound like Melissa.

"It's the room at the end of the hall," Gillett said, stepping back and allowing Hannah to precede him.

A runner on the stairs. Carpet in the halls. Hannah wondered where Gillett got his money, why he had spent so much of it on this house.

Hannah opened the door to the bedroom and came to an abrupt stop. Melissa stood at the window, a glass of wine in her hand. Hannah could see nothing wrong with her foot or her leg.

"Come in. Make yourself comfortable."

Hannah thought her smile particularly unpleasant. "I thought you were hurt. Why did you tell Mr. Gillett—"

She stopped. She'd been pushed into the room and the door closed behind her. "What's going on? Why did you bring me here?"

"Lyman knew you wouldn't come here on your own, so we sent you a note saying I'd been hurt," Melissa said, her smile getting uglier all the time.

"Why?"

"Because, you little simpleton, Lyman is so enamored of you, he can't stand the thought of living without you any longer. You have twenty-four hours in which to agree to marry him. But whether you do or not, before that time is over, he will have taken you to his bed."

Chapter Twenty-three

Buck was glad to be getting home. He'd been lucky to capture so many horses so quickly. After building his chute and corral, he'd expected to have to ride as far as fifty miles to find the horses. But one group after another had drifted in his direction. At first he suspected a prairie fire might have driven them toward him, but he never caught the smell of smoke.

He'd only been gone eight days, but it seemed much longer. Even though Melissa was the reason he was out here, he hadn't thought of her very much. He'd missed Hannah something awful.

Without Zeke to talk to, he'd had plenty of time to think. He hadn't found his thoughts very comforting. The first and most important was that he'd been a fool to let Melissa cause a rift between him and Hannah. He'd been so happy to find Melissa, so desperate to keep her at the ranch, to create the family relationship he'd never had, that he hadn't seen reality.

As much as he loved his sister and wanted her to stay, she wasn't suited for life on a ranch. She was a child of the city and would never be happy anywhere else. They didn't share the same values. Even knowing her clothes were designed to be worn under different circumstances, Buck didn't approve of her style of dress or the amount of paint she used. It made her look cheap, and Buck wanted his sister to be perfect.

Then there was the problem of sleeping late and refusing to help around the house. Buck was used to people pitching in and doing their share of the work. And he'd had no right to ask Hannah to give her money to Melissa.

It hurt Buck to admit it, but Melissa was selfish. He'd have to talk to her. He couldn't allow her to take advantage of Hannah's kindness or be rude to her. He loved Hannah. He wanted to marry her. He wanted the three of them to be happy together. Hannah had done her part. Now it was up to Melissa.

All Buck wanted now was to get home to Hannah, hold her in his arms, try to make her forget all the times he'd doubted her love, doubted his own love for her. He couldn't understand how he could have been such a fool. She'd refused richer and more handsome men; yet she had given herself to him willingly.

He recollected the sweetness of her body, every moment of their time together, in agonizing detail. Just thinking about it inflamed his body. He'd spent several miserable nights thinking of what he wanted to say to her—what he wanted to do. Now, nearing the ranch, his body stiffened in anticipation.

He longed to go straight to the house, but it wasn't easy to get the horses into the big corral by himself. For a while, the job occupied his mind to the exclusion of all else. But even as he slipped the corral poles into place, he felt that something wasn't quite right. Tom was probably out on the range, but Hannah couldn't have missed all the noise. She would know he was back.

Why hadn't she come to meet him? He'd left in a huff, but she had to know he was angry at Zeke rather than her. Deciding he could unsaddle his horse later, he walked up to the house. He rubbed his shoulder. It still hurt occasionally.

He felt better when he didn't see Hannah in the garden. It would soon be time for dinner. She was probably in the kitchen. But he found Melissa by herself. Even more disturbing, she was cooking.

"Where's Hannah?" he asked.

"I don't know."

Melissa didn't look at him. She was stirring something on the stove, but he got the distinct impression that she didn't want to look at him.

"Didn't she tell you where she was going?"

"No."

"Why not?"

"I don't know."

Buck was certain she knew something she wasn't telling him.

"When did she leave? Did she ride or walk? How was she dressed?"

"I don't know."

Melissa still wouldn't look at him. Buck stomped over to the stove, took the spoon out of Melissa's hand, threw it into the pot, and turned her toward him.

"Now look what you've done," Melissa said.

"I don't give a damn what you're cooking," Buck said. "Where's Hannah?"

"I don't know."

This time she looked him straight in the eye. She was lying. She had the same look their father had had when he lied. "You know something. What is it?"

"It's not good news."

"Has something happened to her mother? Or Walter?"

"No."

"Then what is it?" He shook Melissa so hard that one of her curls came unpinned. "Tell me!"

"She left a note."

"Where is it?"

"I burned it."

"What did it say?"

"It said she was leaving, that she was going to marry Amos Merrick."

Melissa might as well have been speaking in a foreign language for all Buck understood of what she said. Hannah wouldn't go off to marry Amos. She had refused him when she was in trouble and didn't see any way out. Even if she weren't in love with Buck, she wouldn't consider marrying Amos.

"That's impossible. Hannah wouldn't do that."

"I don't know her as well as you do," Melissa said, stung by his words. "I only read the note."

Buck knew there was something wrong here, but he wouldn't figure it out by shouting at Melissa. "What did it say?"

Melissa looked slightly mollified that he finally appeared to believe her.

"She said she hated the ranch, was tired of being poor and working herself to death in that garden. She said Amos came out this morning and asked her again. She said she finally realized she was a fool to refuse him."

"That's nonsense. Hannah loves this place."

"She also said she hated me," Melissa said, a spot of anger on each cheek. "She said she couldn't stand the thought of sharing a house with me for the rest of her life."

This was the first thing Buck was tempted to believe. Hannah had tried to get along with Melissa, but it was obvious neither of them could live with the other.

"Did she say anything else?"

"She said you were a fool to think she loved you. You were just a way to save her ranch. She said Amos was going to pay off the debt, and she was going to get Tom to run the ranch for her."

The bitter taste of rejection filled Buck's mouth. He'd spent his entire life being afraid this would happen. He'd held back his feelings for Jake's family. He hadn't let himself respond fully to Zeke's devotion. He had never let himself get close to a woman. Now when he had finally let go, had come to believe someone could love him enough to stay with him forever, his worst fears had materialized. Hannah had deserted him.

But even as his life-long fears threatened to consume him, a part of him refused to give in to despair. Standing out more clearly than all the rest of what whirled in his mind was a conviction that Hannah wouldn't do this. She might have decided she didn't love him, but she would never have been such a coward as to write a note and run off when he was away. His Hannah was honest and straightforward. If she had anything to tell him, she'd say it to his face.

"She'll have the ranch *and* a rich husband," Melissa said. "She's left you, Buck. I'm sorry, but there it is."

"No, she didn't," Buck said.

"What do you mean?"

"I don't believe she ran off to marry Amos Merrick, and I know she wouldn't just leave a note."

"Do you think I made all this up?"

"I don't know. Why did you burn the note?"

"I was angry she would do this to you."

"What was the handwriting like?"

"I don't remember. Ordinary looking, I guess. Why?"

"Hannah writes in a beautiful, large flowing script. You couldn't fail to notice."

"I—

"I don't think she wrote that note. I think somebody kidnapped her and left that note to throw me off the trail."

"That's impossible. I couldn't have slept through somebody carrying off a screaming woman."

"Hannah wouldn't scream. She'd bite, kick, and scratch, but she wouldn't scream."

"How can you say things like this when she's left you?"

"Because I don't believe she has."

Melissa laid her hand on his arm. "Buck, I know how hard it is to accept this kind of truth about someone you love, but—"

Buck threw off Melissa's hand and stalked out of the room. With Melissa on his heels, he checked Hannah's bedroom, then every room in the house. Everything seemed the same, nothing out of place.

"Well, at least I know she didn't run off," Buck said. "She didn't take any clothes with her."

"Why should she want these rags?" Melissa asked. "If I were marrying a rich man, I'd make him buy me everything new."

"Hannah doesn't care about clothes."

"Every woman cares how she looks."

Buck went outside and starting looking at the ground. Melissa followed him.

"What are you doing?" she demanded.

"Somebody came here in a buggy," Buck said, showing Melissa the wheel marks. "Three times. If it wasn't for that note, I'd be certain it was her mother. Are you sure you're telling me the truth?"

Melissa looked furious. "Why should I lie about something like this?"

"Because you don't like Hannah."

"No, I don't," Melissa snapped. "I tried to. I'm not lying. If you go looking for her at her mother's, you'll find that out."

Something about the tone of Melissa's voice nagged at him. She knew something else she wasn't telling.

"How do you know she's not there?"

"Because the note said she went to Utopia." Melissa was almost screaming now.

Buck stopped. Maybe Amos had dreamed up some story that had caused Hannah to go to Utopia with him, most likely saying something had happened to her mother and she was at Dr. Yant's. Then somehow he'd left the note Melissa found. It didn't sound very plausible, but Buck couldn't think of anything else.

"I'm going to Utopia," Buck announced.

"What for?"

"I don't know why Hannah went there, but I

know she didn't go to marry Amos. I'm going to bring her back."

"Buck, I know this is hard for you—"

"Not hard, impossible. Don't look for me tonight. I'm going to break Amos's neck. They'll probably put me in jail."

"You can't. What will happen to me? What about the money you promised?"

"Tom will be back soon. Tell him I said to take you over to Hannah's mother. She'll take care of you until I get back."

"I won't go there," Melissa shouted. "She hates me, too."

"Then you'd better hope your dinner hasn't burned."

Buck walked toward the barn, ignoring the things Melissa shouted at him. Before he was half-way there, he heard the sound of a galloping horse. Zeke. He felt a surge of happiness at seeing his old friend again, but he knew something must be wrong for him to have come back. Buck stopped and waited.

"What's Hannah doing at Gillett's place?" Zeke shouted before his horse came to a stop.

Buck's vague fears and swirling uneasiness congealed into a ball of cold, hard fear. "What are you talking about?" Buck asked.

"I saw one of Gillett's men riding out," Zeke said. "He asked about Tom. He said Gillett was getting married, that he was going to town to fetch the preacher. I thought it might be your sister latching on to the only rich man in the area. The cowhand said he hadn't set eyes on the bride, so I rode by to see if I could get a look." He glared angrily at Melissa. "I figured if your sister married Gillett, I could come back to work at the ranch. I saw Hannah at an upstairs window. I knew something was wrong, so I came to get you."

"How did you know I was home?"

Zeke smiled. It was such a rare occurrence, it took Buck by surprise. Zeke would be a nice-looking man if he'd stop looking like he wanted to kill somebody all the time.

"I followed you when you went to get those horses," Zeke said. "I watched you work your ass off building that chute and corral. I knew it'd take you a month to get enough horses by yourself, so I rounded up a few and chased them in your direction."

"Why you sneaky son-of-a-gun."

Zeke's grin turned serious. "I told you I wouldn't leave as long as you needed me. Now stop standing there with your mouth open and mount up."

Buck turned back to his sister. "What's Hannah doing at Gillett's?"

"I have no idea." She met his gaze without faltering, but he knew she lied.

"Yes, you do."

Zeke dismounted and walked toward Melissa. "Tell him before I cut your throat." She backed away from the hatred she saw in his eyes.

"The note didn't say she wanted to marry Amos. It was Gillett. I didn't tell you because I thought it would hurt too much."

"That's a lie," Zeke said. "You never thought of anybody's feelings in your whole life but your own."

Melissa was careful to keep Buck between her and Zeke. "Gillett's been in love with Hannah ever since he came here," she said. "He's been courting her ever since you left. She finally gave in and accepted him." •

"That's a lie," Buck said. "Hannah would never marry Gillett."

Melissa's eyes flashed with anger. "You believe her instead of me?"

"Anybody would," Zeke said. "You're nothing but a lying white whore."

Melissa charged around Buck and slapped Zeke. He knocked her to the ground.

"Are you going to let him get away with that?" she demanded of Buck, hatred blazing in her eyes.

"Why did Hannah go to Gillett's?" Buck demanded. He made no move to help his sister off the ground.

Rage flamed in Melissa's eyes. "She got tired of you," she spat at him. "She said she wanted a lover who wasn't so clumsy, it was pitiful. She said she wanted a man who was rich and nice to look at, not some penniless scarecrow on a horse."

Zeke started for Melissa. She scooted away, dragging her clothes through the dirt.

"Leave her alone," Buck said. "I know she's lying."

He looked at Melissa lying in the dirt, her dress dirty, her hair coming down, and he saw a different woman from the sister who'd cried when his father pulled them apart, a different woman from the beautiful sister who said she'd come to him the moment she knew where to find him.

She was beautiful, but she was as selfish as his parents. She'd lie to anyone, including her own brother, if it would get her what she wanted. She might have loved him thirteen years ago, but she didn't any longer. He was just another nameless male to be fleeced and discarded when he was no longer useful.

He felt nothing but disgust for her and for himself for being such a fool. He'd held back from loving so many wonderful people because of his stupid notion that blood made a family. Hadn't he already seen that blood couldn't make his mother and father love him?

Jake and Isabelle loved him. No reason. They just did. Hannah loved him even though he'd wanted to take her ranch. Zeke loved him even though they'd had a fight. Melissa didn't love him, and he would have given her everything he owned.

He looked at Melissa and wondered how he'd ever thought she could compare to Hannah, Isabelle, or the boys. She was just like his father.

"Get up," he ordered. "I want you gone by the time I get back. You can always be sure of finding a home with me, but you'll have to treat Hannah with respect."

"What about the money you promised me?" Melissa asked.

"I won't give you a cent. I spent five years looking all over Texas for you. I was so glad to find what I thought was my *real* family, I would have given you everything I had. But I wasn't family to you, just someone to prey on. You tried to drive Hannah and me apart for pure spite."

"I don't care enough about you to bother," Melissa spat. She saw the dirt ground into her dress when she got to her feet. "Look what you've done, you ignorant fool," she shouted at Zeke. "This dress is worth more than the lot of you."

"Come on, Zeke," Buck said as Tom rode up. "Don't bother to dismount," he told the boy.

"No need to rush," Melissa said with malicious pleasure. "It'll be too late, no matter when you get there."

Buck turned back. "What do you mean?"

"Lyman thought she might be more willing to

375

stand before the preacher if they got the honeymoon over first." Her laugh was liked a slap in his face. "I imagine your dull little Dora is well broken in by now."

Something snapped inside Buck. Suddenly Melissa's laughing face was an embodiment of all the evil in the world. He was so angry, he thought he might hit her.

"Get out of my sight. If you're here when I get back, I won't be responsible for what I do. If you leave your clothes, or anything else of yours, I'll burn them. If you want to change your life, I'll try to forget what you've done, at least enough to help. But I'll never again risk losing Hannah for you."

Buck turned his back on Melissa. "Let's ride," he said to Zeke and Tom.

Despite being locked up in Gillett's house for the last six hours, Hannah found it difficult to believe anything this absurd was happening to her. No sane man locked a woman in a room with an ultimatum to marry him or face ruin. It was too ridiculous, too absurd, too impossible.

Yet, unless she was having a very bad dream, that was exactly what was happening. And now she was on her way downstairs with her captor to have dinner.

"I'm sorry you can't dress for dinner, but I couldn't very well tell you to bring your best gown," Gillett said when he unlocked her door.

"I don't have a best gown," Hannah said.

"What a shame. I should have asked Melissa to lend you one."

"She wouldn't have."

Hannah glanced around when she reached the bottom of the stairs.

"Don't think of dashing for the door or throwing yourself through a window," Gillett said. "The doors are locked and the windows shuttered. As soon as you agree to become my wife, you can go anywhere you wish."

"I'll never agree to that."

"Then I suggest we go into the dining room. Maybe you'll feel better once you've eaten."

Hannah didn't think she could eat a bite. As much as she disliked Buck's sister, she wished Melissa had stayed. She felt safer with someone else around. But Melissa had gone back to the ranch. Hannah didn't know what story she planned to tell Buck, but she imagined it would be too late. No man wanted a ruined female.

Any hope Hannah harbored that Tom would come after her had disappeared hours earlier. All Melissa had to do was smile, and the poor boy would believe anything she said.

"After you," Gillett said when they reached the dining room.

Hannah continued to be amazed by Gillett's house. The dining room was lit by two candelabra, each holding three candles. The table was set with silver, linen, and fine china. Even Mrs. Merrick couldn't set a table like this.

Hannah allowed Gillett to seat her. "Do you always eat like this?"

"The candles are special."

As soon as he was seated, the cook served the food. He refused to meet Hannah's gaze.

"Is that wine?" Hannah asked when she saw the red liquid in her glass.

"Yes."

The people of Utopia reserved wine for very special occasions. It tasted good to her inexperienced palate. The soup was hot and delicious. Even more so because she hadn't had to prepare it herself.

They ate mostly in silence. She tasted some of everything, but didn't eat much. Gillett ate with a hearty appetite. He drank as if he had an even greater thirst. As they neared the end of the meal, Hannah could tell by the flush in his cheeks that he'd had more than was good for him. She didn't know if this would work to her advantage or not, but she hoped so.

"You're not an ordinary rancher," she said when she'd taken two bites of the chocolate torte served for dessert and decided she'd had enough. "How can you afford to live like this? Is this why you rustle cows?"

Gillett smiled in amusement, but it wasn't a smile that made Hannah feel better. She'd always had a feeling he could be a dangerous man. Now she knew it.

"My family has a great deal of money," Gillett said, "more than is good for them. It gives them much too great a sense of their own importance."

The last words were bitter.

"They don't care for the way I choose to conduct myself. They said if I'd go far, far away, they'd send me all the money I needed."

"Why didn't you go to New Orleans or someplace like that?"

"They're full of people worse than my family. I like it here. So many boring people with absolutely no imagination. They can't believe I would steal their cows. I do it just to prove I can."

"Did you steal me just to prove you could?"

"I want you. I have ever since I laid eyes on you."

"Why? You're handsome and rich. You could have virtually any woman you want."

"I want you."

"But I'm boring, dull. I want to be a rancher's wife. I want to keep chickens and pigs, milk my own cows, make my own butter. I'm not even pretty."

"I think you're the most beautiful woman I know."

Hannah decided that any man who thought she was beautiful after seeing Melissa had something seriously wrong with him.

"Are you really going to keep me here?"

"Yes."

"I'll never agree to marry you."

"You will after you've spent the night with me."

"No, I won't."

Gillett didn't look startled or surprised.

"You'll be ruined. Your cowboy won't marry you. Neither will the banker's cub."

"I know that, but I still won't marry you."

She would like to think Buck would still love her, still want to marry her, but she knew better. Men held women to a different standard than they used for themselves. A man who knew many women was experienced. A woman who slipped even once was . . . she wasn't prepared to put the thought into words.

"You'd be ruined if you didn't marry me. You'd have to leave the area."

"No, I'd stay at my place."

"None of the women from Utopia would speak to you."

"I'd stay nevertheless. I fail to see why a woman should be the one shamed when a man forces himself upon her."

"You can't change the way people think."

"I'd be wasting my time if I tried to run away. Gossip would find me wherever I went."

Leigh Greenwood

Gillett smiled at her, but it wasn't the same easy, confident smile she'd seen when he came to take her down to supper. "There's no point in worrying about any of this. Marry me, and you can have anything you want. I'll even move to New Orleans if you wish."

"No."

His eyes hardened. "Then you leave me no alternative."

"You can't salve your conscience—if you've got one—with that lie," Hannah said. "You have many alternatives. You simply choose not to take any of them."

He sat watching her, studying her, as though he was trying to figure her out.

"You seem awfully calm. Don't you believe I'll do what I say?"

"I believe you can. I hope you won't. As for being calm, would you change your mind if I screamed or cried or begged for mercy?"

"No."

"Then I would have humiliated myself for nothing."

"I don't understand you. I tell you I'm going to make love to you, that I'm going to—"

"Love has nothing to do with what you have in mind. It's rape."

"That's a hard word."

"What you're planning to do is a hard thing."

"But you can endure it?"

"For twenty years my mother was wife to a man she hated and despised. I can survive one night."

"Do you hate and despise me?"

"I will if you do what you've threatened."

Hannah almost smiled at his confusion. Obviously she wasn't acting the way he'd expected. Buck wouldn't rescue her. He might not be back for weeks. Zeke wouldn't. He had left. Tom wouldn't. He didn't know where to find her. Walter and her mother wouldn't because they would know nothing about it. She had only herself. But she wasn't helpless.

Gillett rose to his feet. "It's time to go up."

Hannah continued to face him squarely.

"I said it was time to go up."

"I heard you."

"Then why haven't you moved?"

"You can't seriously expect me to walk willingly into the bedroom where you plan to take my virtue." She could tell from the look on his face that he'd expected just that. "If you want me there, you'll have to take me by force."

"But you said you wouldn't scream or cry out."

"I didn't say I wouldn't fight you."

Gillett smiled. "I'm much stronger than you."

"Probably."

"I'll have my way in the end."

"Possibly."

"Aren't you afraid of me? Aren't you going to jump up and try to run away? Are you going to just sit there saying *possibly* and *probably*?"

"Most likely."

He pushed his chair aside and came around the table. He held out his hand to her. "I really do want you. I will marry you. I might even be able to stand my family long enough to take you back to Philadelphia."

Hannah felt a twinge of pity for him. He probably did like her, or had convinced himself he did. He might even turn out to be a decent person if he could find somebody to love him. But as much as she might feel sorry for him, she had no intention of allowing herself to be sacrificed to save him.

"You may want me, but you don't love me. I won't insult your intelligence by telling you what love is, but I can assure you it's not forcing yourself on a woman who loves another man."

"Stop this foolish resistance. Come with me. I promise to make you forget your cowboy."

"Can you forget him? Isn't my being here more to get revenge on him than for love of me?"

She could tell instantly she'd scored a hit.

"It might have been, but I forgot about him hours ago."

"I'm very sorry for you."

"Why?"

"Because you can't take my virtue. I've already given it to my cowboy."

For a moment Hannah questioned whether she'd been wise to tell Gillett she'd already made love with Buck. She had seen inflexible purpose in his eyes, but she'd also seen a kind of warmth that encouraged her to believe he really did care for her, at least as far as he understood caring. Now that disappeared, replaced by a hard anger. Ironically, he seemed to be reacting as if she'd cheated on him.

"Just how far have you been spreading yourself around?" he asked, his tone harsh. "You haven't been servicing the banker's cub, too, have you?"

Hannah struggled to keep a firm grip on her temper. No matter how much right she had to be angry, losing her temper wasn't going to help her come out of this in one piece.

"I made love with Buck because he loves me. We plan to get married. I have never let anyone else touch me."

She wasn't sure that made things any better. In a way he looked almost pleased.

"Then I can't be accused of spoiling you. Knowing Buck considers you his private property will make taking you all the sweeter. Come, now, let's make an end of this."

Hannah reached for the pistol that had been lying in her lap all during dinner. She pointed it directly at Gillett's shocked face.

"Where did you get that?" he demanded. "I had every gun in the house locked up."

"I snatched up my father's medicine kit when I left," Hannah explained. "He kept a pistol in it for dispatching animals that couldn't be saved."

"What do you propose to do?"

"Lock you in your miserable bedroom while I leave."

"Don't be absurd. Even if I let you go, you'd get lost in the dark."

"I'll take my chances."

"I won't let you."

"You can't stop me."

"Yes, I can. You wouldn't use that pistol on me."

"I don't want to, but I will."

Gillett jumped at her. Hannah flinched. He laughed.

"See, I knew you wouldn't shoot me. Now give me that pistol, or I'll have to take it from you."

"I don't want to shoot you, but I will. Now go upstairs. I'll be right behind you."

Gillett dropped his hands. "And if I don't?"

"I'll be forced to shoot you."

"You don't give me any choice."

For a moment Hannah thought he was going to charge her, but he turned and walked quickly out of the dining room. She got up and ran to the door to keep from losing sight of him, but he had disappeared around a corner. She stopped immediately. She knew he meant to wait until she turned the corner and then grab the pistol from her. She also knew that if she made a run for the door, he would be on her before she could get it unlocked.

She looked up and down the hall. He could come at her from two directions. She couldn't watch both at once. She backed into the doorway to the dining room. It gave her some protection.

She waited.

She listened intently, hoping for the sound of a creaking board to give her some idea where Gillett was hiding. She heard nothing. Perspiration popped out on her forehead. Her hands got clammy, making it hard to grip the smooth handle of the pistol. She felt her nerves start to unravel.

This is stupid she told herself. Your father was hard and cruel enough to beat Buck until he nearly died. You can at least have the courage to outwit a man who intends to rape you.

The squeak of a board caused her to jump and turn to her right. Almost at once she knew she'd made a mistake. Gillett was coming at her from the left. Hannah spun around, closed her eyes, and pulled the trigger.

Chapter Twenty-four

All during the ride to Gillett's ranch, Zeke and Tom discussed and discarded one rescue plan after another.

"You can't go busting into that place," Tom said. "It's built like a fort—stone walls and shutters an inch thick. You gotta smoke him out."

"He's not coming out when he's got what he wants inside," Zeke said. "He knows his men will come running at the first sign of trouble."

Buck couldn't concentrate. He kept worrying about Hannah, what she'd do if Gillett raped her. He had no question in his mind about what *he'd* do. If Gillett so much as touched Hannah, Buck would kill him.

But he knew Hannah would feel humiliated, contaminated. She might try to send him away. It made him sick to think of Gillett even touching her, but it made him feel empty inside to think of losing her.

Nothing could happen that was so bad he wouldn't want her.

He hoped she would believe him. He would tell her over and over, but he knew that no matter what he said, she'd still feel defiled and degraded. It would be far worse than the beatings her father had given him. His scars were on the outside where they couldn't hurt him. Hers would be on the inside where they would never stop hurting. Shooting would be too good for Gillett.

As it turned out, they didn't use any of their plans. They arrived to find Gillett's men gathered at the house, the foreman pounding on the door, trying to get inside.

"What happened?" Buck asked as he dismounted.

The foreman eyed him suspiciously. "The boss told us to keep away from the house until the preacher got here, but we heard a shot a few minutes ago. I'm worried somebody's hurt, but we can't get in to see."

Buck pushed his way past the foreman and pounded on the door with his fist. "Hannah, it's me, Buck. Let me in."

"How do you know who's in there?" the foreman demanded, his suspicions fully aroused now.

"Because his worthless sister told us," Zeke said. "Now get out of the way. The less Hannah sees of your ugly face, the more likely she is to open that door."

"We wouldn't hurt her," the foreman said.

"How's she to know that?" Zeke said. "You were quick enough to steal her cows."

Buck would have liked to see the expression on the foreman's face, but at that moment the door opened and Hannah catapulted into his arms, sending him staggering back. If Zeke and the foreman hadn't caught him, he and Hannah would have tumbled right off the porch.

"I knew you'd come," she said, laughing and crying at the same time. "I knew you would."

"Did he touch you?" Buck asked, primed to murder Gillett the moment he got his balance back.

"No."

"Then what was the shooting about?"

"He was going to make me go upstairs with him, so I shot him."

That stopped everybody in their tracks.

"You shot him?"

"Yes."

"With what?"

"A gun."

"Where did you get it?" the foreman asked. "I locked up every gun in the house myself."

"He told me Melissa had hurt herself, that I had to come take care of her," Hannah explained, not looking at anybody but Buck, not once loosening her hold on him. "So I brought my father's medical kit. He kept a pistol in it. Gillett never thought to search it."

"Did you kill him?" the foreman asked.

"No, but he's got a hole in his shoulder to match the one he gave Buck."

"He shot me?"

"Yes."

"How did you get him to confess?"

"I threatened to let him bleed to death."

Buck felt like laughing aloud. He couldn't imagine why he hadn't fallen desperately in love with Hannah the moment he saw her. He had no idea how he could have doubted her love, questioned her loyalty, considered believing Melissa. He was a fool and a blockhead. He'd be a worse fool and blockhead if he ever doubted her again.

"Does he need a doctor?" Buck asked.

"No. The cook's taking care of him."

"Then let's go home."

The joy fled from Hannah's face; her body tensed. She pulled away from Buck. "I don't want to go back to the ranch. I want to go to my mother."

Buck gripped her hands. "Is it because of Melissa?"

"I . . . You don't . . ."

"I know what she did," Buck said. "And I know what she is. I told her to be gone before I got back."

The stiffness in Hannah's demeanor didn't go away. "But you've been looking for her for years."

"I was looking for something Melissa can't give me, something I doubt she'll ever be able to give anyone. Worse than that, I couldn't see I had it already."

"What was that?" She wasn't pulling away from him anymore.

"Love and a family to belong to."

"Are you sure about Melissa?" Hannah asked. "After all, she is your sister."

"Drew and Eden are my sisters. Melissa is a stranger."

Hannah relaxed and returned the pressure of Buck's grasp. "Let's go home."

As they started down the porch steps, Zeke said, "You got to ask her something first."

"What?" Buck asked.

Zeke followed them down the steps. "If you can't figure that out, maybe she should marry this Gillett fella after all."

His arm still around Hannah, Buck turned back to Zeke when he reached the ground. "I can't believe you're doing this."

Zeke flashed one of his rare smiles. "Me either, but it's the right thing to do."

"Later."

"Right now. I'm not letting Hannah go one step with you until you ask her."

Buck glanced down at Hannah and felt himself flush. She knew what Zeke was talking about, but surely she couldn't expect him to talk about something this private in front of so many people.

Tom and Zeke stared at him expectantly. Each one of Gillett's men was watching him with equal curiosity. He felt the heat of embarrassment rising above his collar. He couldn't do it, not now, not in front of all these people.

But as he looked into Hannah's eyes, the words of postponement died on his lips. She looked up at him, her heart in her eyes, and he felt as if he would burst with all the love bundled up inside of him. He couldn't imagine waiting a moment longer.

He drew her close.

"I had hoped to say this in private, but maybe now really is the best time. I love you. I have almost since the moment I first saw you. I want everybody to know I love you with all my heart. And if you can stand being married to such a blockhead, I'd very much like you to be my wife."

"Are you sure?"

She hadn't let herself go, let herself fully believe him.

"I've never been more certain of anything in my life. I know what a family is now. I know mine can only start with you."

Buck could see Hannah's last doubt disappear and happiness bloom in her eyes.

"In that case, I would very much like to marry you."

Buck pulled Hannah to him and enfolded her in his embrace. Loud cheers from the onlookers startled him for a second, but nothing could destroy the magic of that moment. After a life of wandering, he'd come home at last.

Epilogue

The grounds around the ranch house echoed with the noise of dozens of young people. Jake's whole family had come for the wedding. Even Ward had brought his wife and three sons, the youngest barely a month old. All of the neighboring ranchers were there as well. Celestine Evans, watching in wide-eyed amazement, had allowed Drew to draw her into the center of the hubbub. Hannah privately believed it was a devastatingly handsome Zac Randolph who had really done the trick.

"She'll be overwhelmed," Jake told Hannah. "Maybe you'd better rescue her."

"Nonsense," Hannah said. "If anybody can bring her out of herself, it's Drew."

They were sitting under the trees, Buck with his arm around Hannah's waist. She had turned the wedding preparations over to Isabelle and her mother. "I chose the groom," she had informed them. "I don't care about anything else."

"What are your plans?" Jake asked Buck.

"We'll stay here until we sell the steers and pay off the debt. We haven't decided where to go after that."

"Why go anywhere?" Jake asked. "You've got a decent ranch and the makings of a good herd."

"Walter Evans is looking to expand," Hannah said. "He's offered to buy it."

"But why sell? You could be doing very well in five or six years."

"We have our eye on another place," Buck said.

"Where?" Jake asked.

"In a little valley about ten miles north of a ranch called the Broken circle."

Jake's face suddenly became intense. "Do you mean it?"

Buck hugged Hannah and smiled. "I want to go home, Jake. Besides, there are a lot of memories here we'd both like to leave behind."

"I'll buy the land and get things ready for you," Jake said, his eyes bright with enthusiasm. "I'll have no trouble finding you a herd. I know—"

"You'll do nothing of the kind," Buck said. "Hannah and I will buy our own ranch and bring our own herd."

"But I could—"

"No."

Jake gave in. He looked disappointed, but not a whole lot. "When are you planning to move?"

"I promised Isabelle I'd be home for Christmas."

"Does she know—I mean, about the ranch?"

"Not yet."

"I've got to tell her."

"Before you do, there's one more thing I'd like to ask."

Jake looked a little suspicious. "What now?"

It had seemed like such an easy thing to ask. When Jake had adopted the boys, he'd said they could do it. But now that the time had come, Buck found it hard to get the words out. He guessed it was because, even though the words were simple, the need behind them was urgent and deep.

"I don't want Hannah or our children to bear the name Hobson," Buck said. "There's no one by that name I want them to remember. Would you mind if I changed my name to Maxwell?"

Buck realized that Jake was just as close to losing control of his emotions as he was.

"People will think you're my son," Jake said.

"I won't mind if you don't."

"I won't mind at all," Jake said, his voice thick with emotion. "Now I've got to tell Isabelle right away. If I don't, she'll never forgive me."

"You didn't tell me you wanted to change your name," Hannah said after Jake had gone.

"Do you mind?"

"I don't care what name I'm called as long as it's the same as yours. But are you sure?"

"Isabelle was right when she said I'd never be happy until I had a family. Taking Jake's name means I've found it."

"You realize Jake will be looking over your shoulder all the time, don't you?"

Buck laughed. "And I'll be looking over his. I figure I can give as good as I get."

Buck settled back with Hannah comfortably tucked into the crook of his arm. He had to make sure he built his house near at least one tree big enough for a bench just like this one. He couldn't think of a better way to spend the next fifty years than sitting next to Hannah, looking out over his land, surrounded by his family.

At home.

LEIGH GREENWOOD'S
SEVEN BRIDES
Laurel

Although Hen Randolph is the perfect choice for a sheriff in the Arizona Territory, he is no one's idea of a model husband. After the trail-weary cowboy breaks free from his six rough-and-ready brothers, he isn't about to start a family of his own. Then a beauty with a tarnished reputation catches his eye and the thought of taking a wife arouses him as never before.

But Laurel Blackthorne has been hurt too often to trust any man—least of all one she considers a ruthless, coldhearted gunslinger. Not until Hen proves that drawing quickly and shooting true aren't his only assets will she give him her heart and take her place as the newest bride to tame a Randolph's heart.

_3744-0 $5.99 US/$6.99 CAN

SEVEN BRIDES
VIOLET

LEIGH GREENWOOD

"Leigh Greenwood is a dynamo of a storyteller!"
—Los Angeles Times

Jefferson Randolph has never forgotten all he lost in the War Between The States—or forgiven those he has fought. Long after most of his six brothers find wedded bliss, the former Rebel soldier keeps himself buried in work, only dreaming of one day marrying a true daughter of the South. Then a run-in with a Yankee schoolteacher teaches him that he has a lot to learn about passion.

Violet Goodwin is too refined and genteel for an ornery bachelor like Jeff. Yet before he knows it, his disdain for Violet is blossoming into desire. But Jeff fears that love alone isn't enough to help him put his past behind him—or to convince a proper lady that she can find happiness as the newest bride in the rowdy Randolph clan.

_3995-8 $5.99 US/$7.99 CAN

Dorchester Publishing Co., Inc.
P.O. Box 6640
Wayne, PA 19087-8640

Please add $1.75 for shipping and handling for the first book and $.50 for each book thereafter. NY, NYC, and PA residents, please add appropriate sales tax. No cash, stamps, or C.O.D.s. All orders shipped within 6 weeks via postal service book rate. Canadian orders require $2.00 extra postage and must be paid in U.S. dollars through a U.S. banking facility.

Name_____
Address_____
City_____ State_____ Zip_____
I have enclosed $_____ in payment for the checked book(s).
Payment <u>must</u> accompany all orders. ☐ Please send a free catalog.

Jade — **NORAH HESS**

BESTSELLING AUTHOR OF
BLAZE

Kane Roemer heads up into the Wyoming mountains hell-bent on fulfilling his heart's desire. There the rugged horseman falls in love with a white stallion that has no equal anywhere in the West. But Kane has to use his considerable charms to gentle a beautiful spitfire who claims the animal as her own. Jade Farrow will be damned if she'll give up her beloved horse without a fight. But then a sudden blizzard traps Jade with her sworn enemy, and she discovers that the only way to true bliss is to rope, corral, and brand Kane with her unbridled passion.

___4310-6 $5.99 US/$6.99 CAN

NOBLE AND IVY
CAROLE HOWEY
Bestselling Author of *Sheik's Glory*

Ivy is comfortable being a schoolteacher in the town of Pleasant, Wyoming. She has long since given up dreams of marrying her childhood beau, and bravely bore the secret sorrow that haunted her past. But then Stephen, her cocksure brother, ran off with his youthful sweetheart—and a fortune in gold—and Ivy has to make sure that he doesn't wind up gutshot by gunmen or strung up by his beloved's angry brother.

Noble—just speaking his name still makes her tremble. Years before, his strong arms stoked her fires hotter than a summer day—before the tragedy that left a season of silence in its wake. Now, as the two reunite in a quest to save their siblings, Ivy burns to coax the embers to life and melt in the passion she swears they once shared. But before that can happen, Noble and Ivy will have to reconcile their past and learn that noble intentions mean nothing without everlasting love.

_4118-9 $5.50 US/$6.50 CAN

Dorchester Publishing Co., Inc.
P.O. Box 6640
Wayne, PA 19087-8640

Bestselling Author Of *Blind Fortune*

Wealthy and handsome, Reese Ashburn is the most eligible bachelor in Mobile, Alabama. And although every young debutante dreams of becoming the lady of Bonne Chance—Reese's elegant bayside plantation—none believes that its master will ever finish sowing his wild oats. Then one night Reese's carousing ends in tragedy and shame: His gambling partner, James Bentley, is brutally murdered while Reese is too drunk to save him.

Entrusted with the care of James's daughter, Reese knows that he is hardly the model guardian. And fiery Patience Bentley's stubborn pride and irresistible beauty are sure to make her a difficult ward. Still, driven by guilt, Reese is bound and determined to honor Bentley's dying wish—as well as exact revenge on his friend's killers. But can he resist Patience's enticing advances long enough to win back his pride and his reputation?

_3943-5 $4.99 US/$6.99 CAN